Dedicated to the girls who took that jump when everyone said you would fall, but there was one person who said you would soar.

Take the jump.

Made For You

Sunny Brook Farms, Book Three

USA TODAY bestselling author

RENEE HARLESS

All rights reserved.

ISBN: 978-1-962459-02-0

Copyright ©2024 Renee Harless

This work is one of fiction. Any resemblance of characters to persons, living or deceased, is purely coincidental. Names, places, and characters are figments of the author's imagination. All trademarked items included in this novel have been recognized as so by the author. The author holds exclusive rights to this work. Unauthorized duplication is prohibited and this includes the use of artificial programs to mimic and reproduce like works.

All rights reserved

Cover design by Porcelain Paper Designs

Editor: Kayla Robichaux

Proofreader: Crystal Clear Author Services

Sensitivity Reader: Encompass Press, LLC and Author Daryl Banner

Paperback edition

Made For You

Sunny Brook Farms, Book Three

USA TODAY bestselling author

RENEE HARLESS

Heading to a teachers' conference hundreds of miles away from my small town should have been a nice break. Until I was propositioned by a stranger to be his wife for the next six months. And for whatever reason, I said yes.

Talon Beckett was a domineering billionaire with a steely-blue gaze that made me forget my own name. It was my excuse for agreeing to his terms…that and he agreed to play up our recent vows when we attended my ex's wedding.

We both decided that we'd go our separate ways when our six months were up. He'd get full control of his bank account and the hotel chain that bore his mother's maiden name, and I'd get whatever I needed in return.

When our time was coming to an end, I realized the one thing I wanted was something he had no desire to give. It was the affectionate side he'd kept hidden from everyone despite his need to say, "My Wife" when we were out in public. And as I crossed the days off the calendar, it was harder to remember that our marriage wasn't real. Especially when we needed to sign those termination papers.

I feared I'd lose not only my new last name and job, but my heart along the way.

Prologue

Aurora

"You can let me out here," I said to the rideshare driver as he inched forward in the early-evening Miami traffic. The hotel I was staying at was roughly three blocks down the road—at least, according to the GPS app I pulled up on my phone. The driver remained stoic, his hands clenching the steering wheel as we pulled forward another inch.

Wondering if he didn't hear me over his radio, I repeated a little louder, "Sir, can I please go ahead and get out here?" I watched in the rearview mirror as his eyebrows pinched together and his lips pursed.

After what felt like an agonizing amount of time, he pressed the button to unlock my door, which had automatically locked earlier when he put the car in Drive.

"Thanks. I'll pay for the full ride, of course, leave a tip, *and* give you five stars," I shouted hurriedly as I jumped free from the confines of the car and looped my weekend bag over my shoulder. He popped the trunk, and I grabbed my small rolling suitcase, grunting under its weight as I heaved it at hip-height and placed it on the ground. Despite my mood, I gently closed the trunk and dashed over to the sidewalk to get out of the crazy line of traffic.

In the app, I went ahead and paid the driver, rated him as promised, then joined the rest of the crowd shuffling down the busy sidewalk as I made my way to the hotel.

The noise of the street vendors and honks of cars melded together in an orchestra that was solely *Miami*. I couldn't explain it, but this was one of my favorite parts of the city. The tourists and city-goers meshed as they went about their day. A woman in a neon-pink and yellow, skin-tight jumpsuit zoomed past me on rollerblades as a man in a three-piece business suit talked loudly on his Bluetooth next to me.

Apparently, he had forgotten his anniversary and was trying to snag a last-minute reservation at a restaurant downtown. I chuckled to myself, thinking about the world-famous television star, Roland McEntire, having a restaurant in my small town of Ashfield. And how my family had a standing reservation at said restaurant. A man who had the entire world in the palm of his hands with bestselling cookbooks and a top-rated cooking show.

Sweat started beading along my hairline and neck from the humidity and heat as I trekked on. I wish I'd thought of pulling my long, thick hair up into a ponytail before hightailing it out of the car. It was likely going to be a frizzy mess by the time I made it to the hotel's reservations desk. I didn't want to think about the small amount of makeup I wore. A drowned rat was going to look like a supermodel compared to me.

I apologized when my suitcase tripped up a few people as I hurried past them. Registration for the teachers' conference began two hours ago and would close in thirty minutes. Traffic had been an issue, and that was after my flight was delayed. Before all that, my best friend, Franny, caught a nasty stomach bug last night. I spent most of the evening by her bedside, almost sleeping through my alarm in the process.

Now, as I approached the main entrance of the hotel, I was irritable, frustrated, and embarrassed. The valets eyed me warily as I lugged my suitcase through the rotating doors with a huff. My free hand pushed my hair back from my face, and as I glanced at a mirror across from me, I winced at the nest I was sporting at the top of my head.

"Great," I mumbled as I took in the lobby, trying to find a sign that would point me in the right direction. I needed to check in for the conference before I did the same for the hotel, since time was of the essence. Luckily, I found the sign easily enough and made my way in that direction, noting how outdated the lobby appeared.

The marble columns were a garish pink marble with bronze accents. And mirrors hung on every available erect surface. It reminded me of something I'd seen in a movie from the '80s, and I couldn't help but wonder when the place had been renovated last.

Down the carpeted hall toward the room designated for the teachers' conference registration I scurried, and then I grabbed my name badge and packet after receiving a snarling onceover by the woman in charge. I wasn't sure what her deal was, but I pretended like I didn't care. Unfortunately, I wasn't the best liar. My expressions always gave me away, and I was so far out of my element in this big city that I was afraid everyone could tell.

But I reminded myself *they* had invited *me* to the conference based on some of my research and professional essays, and that gave me the confidence to continue the task at hand.

Dragging my suitcase behind me, I made my way back toward the main lobby to check in and relax before the ice-breaker session that evening. Reading over my laminated badge, noting they spelled my first name wrong, I turned the corner that would lead me to the desk, only to find myself whipped around in the direction I'd come from. Losing the grip on my suitcase, I fell flat on the floor, my arms and legs sprawled out on either side of my body. I somehow kept my head from knocking against the marble floor and giving myself one hell of a headache.

"What the—?" I cried out as I pushed up onto my elbows at the same time a deep voice growled, "Watch it."

"Excuse me?" My voice was snide as I got off the floor with very little grace. As I stood, I pushed the heavy mass of waves away from my face and narrowed my gaze at the heavily bearded man holding an ancient flip phone to his ear. His hair was almost as long and scraggly as his beard, and his attire of ripped shorts and a threadbare shirt made him appear like a man who hadn't showered or changed his clothes in months. I'd think he was exactly that… if I hadn't caught a whiff of the most intoxicating scent coming from his direction.

Too bad he was a grade-A dick and was already poised to scurry away as if *I'd* been the inconvenience.

"I mean, would it hurt you to at least *try* to help me?" I asked as I reached for my suitcase now lying flat on the floor. Just as I reached for the extendable handle, it popped off in my hand with a snap. "Are you kidding me?"

"Look, I don't have time for this," the man said, his steely gray-blue eyes focused on me.

"Seriously? *You* don't have time for this? Well, *I* don't have time for this either. The least you could do is make sure I'm not hurt from the way you rammed into me."

"Are you done?" he growled, and when I didn't respond, he continued whatever conversation he was having on the phone and stomped his way down the hall.

"Hey! Wait! Hey!" I shouted, but he didn't even bother turning back around. "Jackass," I mumbled as I grabbed the single strap on the top of my suitcase and wheeled it alongside me. I was thankful it had quad wheels.

Luckily, there was no line at the check-in counter, and I knew my day could only get better.

Or so I thought.

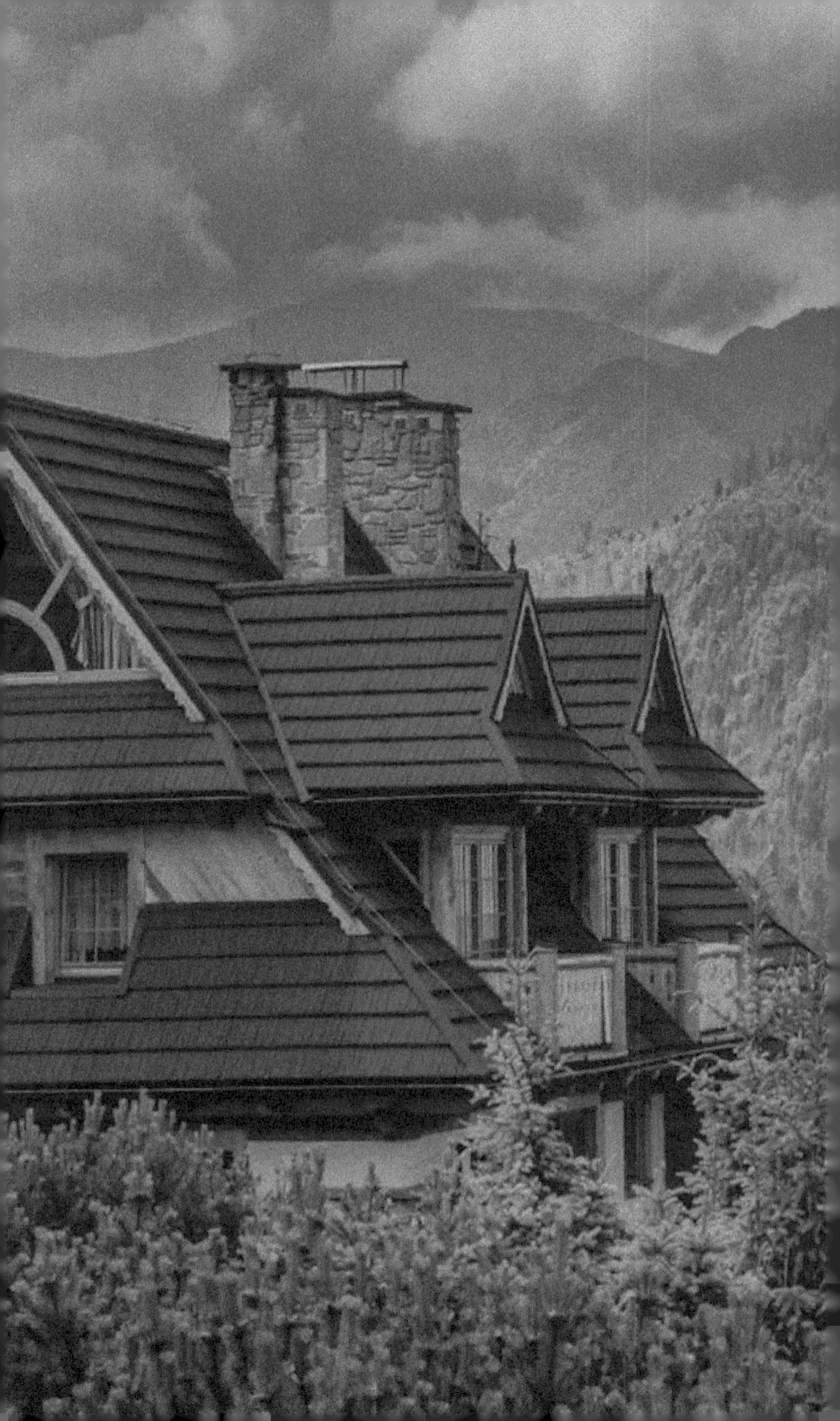

Chapter One

Aurora

One year later...

"No cucumbers today?" Mrs. Hensen asked as she steered toward my family booth at the Ashfield farmers market. While Sunny Brook Farms, my family's livelihood, grew various crops in rotation, the primary source of income was corn.

My great-great-grandmother started a small veggie garden on the farm and began selling them at the local market. My sisters and I carried on the tradition

"Not today, Mrs. Hensen," I replied, taking in her pinched frown. "But I do have some fresh eggplants and peaches. Let me show you." I directed her toward the purple and orange display.

Beside me, my best friend, Franny, started giggling as the customer picked up and stroked the largest of the eggplants, inspecting it from all angles. Unsatisfied, Mrs. Hensen reached for another that was stockier and not so long.

"Hmm…," she murmured, and I had to nudge Franny in the belly with my elbow to keep her from snickering further. Seeming happy with her new choice, Mrs. Hensen set down the first eggplant and moved on to the peaches.

Her wrinkled fingers slid across the velvety skin of the fruit as she raised it close to her face.

"How juicy are these?" she asked, and I had to bump Franny with my foot when she cackled again. Luckily, she covered it with a cough. "I really enjoy making peach pie, so I need them to have just the right amount of moistness."

"Well, how about we cut one open and find out?" I suggested as I tugged my pocketknife from the back of my pants. A Girl Scout never forgot to carry one.

Prying a fresh peach from the batch, I carved into the skin and exposed the inside. With a quick twist of my wrist, I removed the pit, sliced off a small sliver of the fruit, and held it out for Mrs. Hensen. She eagerly accepted the offering, then asked to hold the peach.

Franny turned her back to the customer and covered her face with her hands as her shoulders shook. I immediately bit my lip to hold back my own laughter as Mrs. Hensen moaned while she savored the juicy bite. What was worse was she held the eggplant and peach up at eye level. I felt like I was sitting in middle school Sex Education again.

"Yes, this will do fine. Just fine indeed."

Trying my hardest to keep a straight face, I packaged up the six peaches and the single eggplant she selected. I had zero desire to know what she planned to do with that vegetable. She'd been widowed for years, and I always imagined fruit play was something people made up. But I guessed people had to get their kicks where they could.

Holding out the plastic bag, I exchanged it for her cash and thanked her for the purchase. "You have a *great* day, Mrs. Hensen."

"You as well, dear."

I waited until she was out of earshot before turning back to Franny. "Oh my gosh, why did you have to do that? I could barely hold it together."

My best friend since kindergarten had the decency to look chastised. "I'm sorry. She just always does the most innocent things... provocatively. Without fail."

"I know."

"Seriously. It's been years. And month after month, I expect a normal conversation with Mrs. Hensen, but it never comes. I swear she gets naughtier every time I come to help."

"I guess it's one way to keep her mind sharp. She always did love those romance novels. Remember when we saw her reading one in church?"

"Yes! I thought Father Santos was going to have a heart attack."

Shrugging, I said, "It *was* a good book. I couldn't put it down either," then went back to restocking the display.

"You read it?"

"You seem surprised. I enjoy reading romance novels, but no one in the book club wants to vote for them."

"I've known you forever, and I had no idea you enjoyed reading those kinds of books."

"Well, it's better to fall in love with a fictional boyfriend than with the jerks I've dated."

"Too true."

Our conversation died when another regular customer showed up at the booth. Instead of payment, we bartered with a lot of the farmers in town. An exchange of jam for some fruit. Flour for vegetables. It worked well for us, since the stand itself wasn't our livelihood. My parents had their corn, wheat, and soybean fields, and my siblings had their own endeavors, all of them doing well for themselves.

My eldest sister, Autumn, ran a successful bed-and-breakfast with her husband, Colton Crawford. He was a retired hockey player who was now a television host for a cooking show and sometimes made appearances on sports shows. Alex was next in line, and she met the love of her life, Nate Sullivan, on a one-night stand two years ago. He showed up at the bed-and-breakfast last summer while she was helping there, and the rest was history. He had these two perfect little girls, Molly and Eloise, who had all of us Easterlys wrapped around their fingers.

Together, most of the siblings helped run The Easterly Event Venue—a pet project of Autumn's. We were mostly silent partners, but the venue did excellent. It was booked solid for the next two years, except for a few dates here and there. I helped when I could in the summer, but during the school year, I was devoted to my students. Even more so now that I changed from teaching first grade to eleventh.

"So, when do you fly out?" Franny asked after the marketplace began to die down. It was closing in on noon, and the stands started packing up.

"Andrew is taking me to the airport in Nashville tomorrow at nine. My flight leaves at noon."

"I can't believe I can't go with you to the conference *again*. Last year, it was a stomach bug. This time—"

"I know. I'll miss having you there, but your grandma needs you. Plus, I need someone to watch Draco." Draco was my black cat with green eyes and was named after my favorite fictional character.

"Your cat only likes *you*, Rory. He only tolerates the rest of us."

We used Alex's vintage truck when we worked the farm stand. It helped draw in the customers. Hefting one of the crates of traded-for goodies into the back, I added, "He'll like you when you feed him."

"Right. Then he'll claw my face off."

Shaking my head, I continued to load the empty crates until the stand was bare, then I rallied Franny to help me take down the extra canopy cover. Summer in Ashfield, Tennessee was no joking matter, and the sun made sure it stuck with you for weeks later if you didn't stay covered. Franny darted off once I stored everything into the truck bed, with plans for me to call her when I landed in Miami, Florida tomorrow.

A haze settled over the marketplace as it emptied out. I'd been coming here since I was in diapers, and I always loved the thought of the community coming together. The farmers market had gotten so popular it was slowly becoming a tourist attraction of its own. Not to mention the dozens of people who flocked to our small town in the hopes of catching a glimpse of our local celebrities, Colton and Nate.

Just beyond the market stood the Smoky Mountains. They were a towering force that cradled our town and had a knack for making me feel so much smaller in the world.

"Everything okay, Miss Rory?" Mr. Gravely, the grocery store owner, asked as he finished packing up his booth of homemade soaps he helped his granddaughter sell.

"Yep. Just fine," I lied. Nothing in my life was fine, and I felt like the world was weighing me down. There seemed to be a curse set on me, and I had no way of ridding it. Ever since that day in Miami a year ago....

Waving in his direction, I hopped into the truck and started the ignition. It wasn't long before I was headed down Main Street toward my family's farm. I had a small bungalow a bit closer to the downtown area, but I needed to drop off Alex's truck and the crates. This was one of the lucky weeks where we offloaded all the produce. Otherwise, I would've been making a detour at the church.

The truck swept down the road, taking the winding curves with ease as we crested one particular turn that separated the townies from the tourists.

High on the hill sat Autumn and Colton's bed-and-breakfast. The house was once a rundown, centuries-old farmhouse that belonged to our Easterly ancestors, then Colton splurged on it as an investment property. It was a devastating blow to my sister, but luckily it all worked out in the end, as she and Colton were now happily married, and I hoped they'd consider adding to their family soon. I couldn't wait to be an aunt again.

Alex and Nate's home with Molly and Eloise was out of view of the road, but it wasn't far from the bed-and-breakfast. Nate built a beautiful house that mixed both craftsman style with that of a rustic cabin. It was gorgeous. I may have been a little envious, but I did love my little bungalow. It was just me and Draco, after all.

After one last tickle bump, as I liked to call the short, steep hills in the road that took your stomach, the metal and stone sign for Sunny Brook Farms came into view. I always marveled at the structure as a kid, and as an adult, I had the same reaction. The stonework gave way beautifully to the wooden fencing around the wheat fields that swayed in the breeze. It wasn't until you drove down the dirt-and-gravel road a good ways that the corn and soybean fields came into view.

A tractor driven by one of the ranch hands lumbered through the path in the corn, as my father was prepping for harvest next month. September was always a little chaotic at the farm, and it was all hands on deck for our family. My older sisters missed a few harvests over the years—especially Autumn, when she went out of state for college. But my younger sister, Aspen, and I always made it a point to make ourselves available, even when I had college classes of my own.

The large farmhouse finally came into view, starting as a small dot in the distance and growing with every yard I crossed.

My excitement quickly dwindled when I saw my mother wasn't alone on the front porch. Mrs. Mitchell, my ex-boyfriend's mom and wife of the town's previous mayor, joined her. It had been a handful of months since Jeremy and I ended our relationship, but it wasn't on the best of terms. His entire family moved to Nashville, Tennessee when Jeremy's father decided to make larger political aspirations. Even though she had been good friends with my mom, it was surprising to find her on my family's doorstep. Especially after the falling out with her son.

Any chance I had of sneaking into the house was squashed when the old truck backfired as I got closer.

"Shit," I murmured as both sets of eyes turned toward me.

My morning started off so well, but it seemed to head downhill fast as my trio of sisters and my older half-brother joined my mother on the porch. Thankfully, Mrs. Mitchell was heading down the steps and toward a very-expensive-looking car. One I definitely didn't remember them having when they lived here. I supposed she had to keep up with the Joneses now.

Luckily, by the time I parked the truck in front of the garage, Mrs. Mitchell was already settled inside her flashy car. As I stepped free of the confines of the truck, I noted the weary faces of my siblings. It was strange enough that all of them were at our parents' house on a Saturday, but with Mrs. Mitchell's visit, I knew it couldn't have been good. She was a few hours away from her new residence. And they obviously excluded me for a reason, and not just because I had market duty that morning.

As a teacher, most people thought I was the soft-spoken one in the family, and most of the time, I was. But I didn't care for lies nor secrets, and I made sure everyone knew how I felt about any given matter. My mom used to say I had no filter.

I didn't bother grabbing the empty crates out of the bed of the truck. Instead, I dusted off my denim shorts, grabbed the only one loaded with trades, and made my way to the front porch. The keys made a jingling sound as they swung on my finger, then smacked against the wood of the crate with each step.

I gazed at my family with a mix of trepidation and irritation.

"So, who wants to tell me why my ex's mom was just leaving the farm?" There was no point in asking my mom, knowing she used to be close with the woman currently leaving a trail of dust down the driveway. She'd simply brush it off as a friend visiting a friend, despite the three-hour driving distance.

I felt like I was shooting laser beams as I focused my gaze on each of my siblings. My younger sister, Aspen, mimicked my stare as Autumn cowered slightly. She was the one I expected would cave first. Unfortunately, she was saved as our dad pulled up on his UTV.

He joined me in front of the porch and wrapped me in his powerful arms. I'd always been a daddy's girl. "Well, now. To what do I owe the pleasure of having my entire family here this afternoon?"

"That's a great question, Dad," I replied dramatically.

"Marisol, do we have the fixings for some sandwiches?"

In her delicate voice that held just a hint of twang, Mom said, "You know we do."

"Great. Let's everyone head inside for some lunch." Speaking to Autumn and Alex, he suggested they call their men over to join. Eloise and Molly would be a bonus for us all. "Autumn, have Colton bring his sister. Isn't Sadie staying with y'all this weekend?"

Before my sister could respond, Andrew inserted a brusque, "No."

My dad's leathery face scrunched as he looked at Andrew in confusion.

"Yes. Absolutely have her come as well. It wasn't up for discussion," Dad said after a moment, and using his arm around my shoulders, he guided us up the steps until he was face-to-face with Mom. She couldn't fight the blush as he leaned down and kissed her gently, just as we'd seen them do all our lives. They were always affectionate toward each other.

When he stood back up, he demanded, "Now, as we wait for everyone else to arrive, someone tell me why *that* woman was leaving our farm."

Mom had laid out an impressive spread of sandwich makings. We stacked loaves of French bread next to an array of deli meats and sliced vegetables. She'd rallied all the ranch hands to join us for lunch, so we converted our dining room into a buffet, and the ten or so workers were out on the back deck, enjoying the break. The rest of my family sat around the breakfast table we normally ate at when we were dining together, but unlike those nights, no one was speaking. Not since Mom dropped the bombshell about Mrs. Mitchell's visit.

Across from the buffet, from my perch on a chair in the dining room's corner, I heard my siblings murmuring in the kitchen. I felt betrayed by everyone, and if I hadn't been so hungry, I'd have left an hour ago. Molly and Eloise were also nearby, keeping watchful guard over me. Even at the newly turned age of six, those girls acted more like adults than some of my soon-to-be students at the high school.

"Are you sure we don't want to get out of it?" I heard Mom ask Autumn.

"We would not only face a breach of contract, but the aftermath of her wrath in political society could do some actual damage."

"Gah. How did this all happen?" Alex questioned.

I could guarantee there were two reasons they wanted to host the wedding at my family's venue. First, The Easterly Event Venue had a waitlist a mile long, since Colton had spread word on television, and we'd hosted a few hockey and football player events. So, it was now the *it* place to host an event, especially an exclusive exchanging of vows. Second, they wanted to rub it in my face. Well, Jeremy did, most likely. He was one of the most vindictive people if you got on his bad side. And it seemed, as his ex, that included me, even if I hadn't been the reason for our breakup—*just a few months ago*.

Begrudgingly, I stood and made my way back into the kitchen, dumping my paper plate in the trash along the way.

"I'm going to head to my place. I need to get ready for my flight."

As if realizing I rejoined the room, everyone spun in their chairs to face me.

"Sweetie, we're so sorry. When she came here today with the signed contract and a scheduled look-around with Autumn, I didn't know what to do. We had the dates open from a few cancellations." I knew she was feeling terrible. We usually didn't advertise when any cancellations happened, giving our crew a few days of respite. But if someone asked, we tried to make it work. "When she called, she didn't mention it was for a wedding. I thought maybe it was something for her husband. And then I couldn't turn down a personal invite for the family to the event. We all used to be so close."

Walking around the table, I leaned down and wrapped my arms around my mother's neck in an embrace. Her skin was splotchy, as if she'd been on the verge of tears. "It's okay, Mom. I know you two used to be good friends."

"What are you going to do? I have a feeling it's going to cause more of a scandal if you *don't* show up. Jeremy was always one to instigate a scene," Alex said.

"I guess I'm showing up. I'll bring Franny or someone from school to diffuse the situation."

"Or it could just make it worse."

"I can't really control what he does. It's clear he's doing this, knowing it's going to affect me. He probably planned it all this way. The wedding is in… what, two or three months? His goal is to probably drive y'all crazy with his fiancée's demands."

"Seems like something he would do," Mom added as I pulled away and started toward the door. "I'm sorry about all this, Aurora. Maybe we can read over the contract again and try to get out of it."

"It's okay, Mom. You don't have to worry about me. I'll be fine. It's just a wedding, right? How bad could it be?"

Chapter Two

Talon

Cracking an eye open, I reached toward my nightstand, even though I knew without a doubt it was somewhere close to 4:00 a.m. My body had chosen that ridiculous hour to awaken since I was ten. No matter what time I went to bed, I never slept past the ungodly hour. Though it gave me a leg up on starting my workday.

Grasping my phone and pressing the power button, the light from the screen illuminated the room. I winced at the startling brightness. Beside me, there was a groan, and I jerked to attention.

Who the fuck was in my bed?

Quickly, I started recalling the night before. I didn't remember bringing anyone home with me last night. Of course, I was exhausted after attending another charity event in lieu of my uncle. That was my third one this week while he was spending his days gallivanting around the world with his fourth girlfriend. Maybe it was his fifth? Once he was given the CEO title of Wilder Hotels, he and my aunt went their separate ways. A divorce was never finalized, but the two lived entirely apart. My cousins were the same. Delilah spent her time flitting from party to party. And her brother, Charles, hadn't had his nose… or veins… clean in years. To my uncle, they were a complete disappointment.

Just as I was.

Phone in hand, I launched out of the bed and stomped toward the adjacent bathroom. Once I flicked on the light, it cast its yellow glow across the threshold and over to the edge of the bed.

"Talon?" the scratchy voice questioned. I didn't need her to turn over to know it was Allison, my neighbor and sometimes bed partner. Except I hadn't slept with her, or anyone, in over a year, despite what the rumor mill and magazines claimed about me.

With a quick glance down the path from my bed to the bathroom, I noticed there weren't any discarded condoms, and I was *never* out of it enough to go bareback.

An exhale of relief left my lungs as I gathered her clothes strewn across my bedroom floor.

"Out," I said brusquely as I dropped the pile of material on top of her.

"What?" she shrieked as she bolted upright in the bed, as if she'd been faking sleep all along.

"You heard me. Or do I need to call security and have you escorted out?"

She mumbled under her breath as she jumped down from my bed and began tugging on her discarded clothes. While I'd always appreciated her body, seeing her clad in her lacy undergarments was doing nothing for me.

Stomps followed me as I made my way toward the foyer area of my penthouse. I could feel her eyes on my boxer-brief-covered ass as I walked. The motion-sensor lights in the penthouse flicked on with every few steps I traveled. Beyond the floor-to-ceiling windows, the lights of Miami shown below.

Just as I approached the circular table of dark walnut that served as a catchall for most of my things, despite my maid's disdain, I turned to face Allison.

Her long, red nails scratched down my bare chest. I immediately thought of her drawing blood with each inch she descended.

"Allison," I began as I gripped her wrist. Her eyes dilated as I touched her skin. She stumbled as I dragged her behind me toward the door a few steps away. "Out," I commanded as I yanked her outside.

"But," she began, and I immediately cut her off with a seething glare. The same kind that evoked fear in my employees.

"I suggest you start looking for a new place to live."

"What?" she shrieked.

"Once I tell security what you've done, they will evict you immediately."

"I didn't do anything!"

"You broke in without my knowledge, and I was so out of it I didn't even know you were hiding in here."

"Well, I thought I would surprise you." She pouted, pursing those overly injected lips of hers. It left me wondering why I let our arrangement go on as long as it did.

As I started to shut the door behind her, Allison wailed at the top of her lungs. I was thankful this was the only residence on this floor.

The deadbolt clicked as I locked it behind me. I made my way to the expansive kitchen and used the complex-issued phone to dial the security team on duty. As an heir to the Wilder Hotel chain, my safety was paramount.

"Mr. Beckett, what can I do for you? Do you need a car called?"

"Leon, Allison St. Clair broke into my apartment, and my guess is she manufactured a copy of the key card for my door."

"Mr. Beckett, I sincerely apologize. We'll have this addressed right away, and I will personally install a new kind of lock for you today."

"Biometric. I'll have the company bring you the prototype."

Biometric security was something my best friend, Dean, invested and dabbled in. Another kid from old-school wealth who had the money to burn. He worked with a company to create a biometric scanner that utilized thermography.

"Yes. Apologies again, Mr. Beckett."

"And I'll need a car in an hour."

"Yes, sir."

Without another word, I ended the call and moved toward my walk-in pantry. Grabbing a yellow-and-black container, I twisted the top and measured out some pre-workout powder. My maid stacked my shaker cups on the small counter, and I poured the powder into the top one, then gently tugged it free from the cups below it. At the fridge back in the main kitchen, I filled the cup with water, twisted on the top, shook the contents, then chugged it all in one go. It wasn't my favorite flavor, and the powder had an odd texture despite how many times I shook the cup with its stainless wire ball inside. It always made me feel like I was swallowing chalk. But I had a routine and was already behind, due to the Allison debacle, so I choked it down and tossed the empty cup into the sink.

Back in my bedroom, I tugged on a pair of sweatpants and bypassed my running shoes for a pair of old Chuck Taylors. Mondays, Wednesdays, and Fridays I worked out in my home gym, while for the rest of the week I ran for an hour outdoors. As much as I'd appreciate hitting the pavement, I was a creature of habit, and rarely did I deviate from my routine.

I started with the dumbbells, following the sequence that my personal trainer created for me. After sixty minutes, my arms and thighs burned, and my heart raced, but I never felt better. I loved the rush after a good workout. Not only did I feel refreshed all over, but it was one of the few times during the day where my mind was at ease.

An hour and a half later, I was nestled into the backseat of a town car, scrolling through my phone with one hand as my other tugged at the collar of my dress shirt. The clothing was something I was still getting used to. I'd worn sweaters and polos while attending boarding school and swore I'd never have a collar wrapped around my neck again once I turned eighteen. Yet, here I was, filling in for my absentee uncle and acting as CEO. It was all a ruse though. Without my grandfather's permission, I could never take control of the hotels my mother should have inherited. And he was the reason I was about to do something crazy.

A year ago, I was spending my time on my houseboat, working on the financials and books, and now here I was, long hair slicked back away from my face and a suit incasing my body. I hated it, but I played the part as I needed. I saw the prize waiting at the end for me and my late mother.

My driver darted through the early-morning traffic, something that never seemed to ease in the city, as we approached our most popular hotel. I kept an office onsite, never wanting to step foot in the administrative buildings that I believed were a waste of money, since most of our employees worked remotely. But it was a futile argument with my relatives who believed they could only accomplish productive work in an office building surrounded by their peers.

The car jerked to a stop, and I exited before the driver could put it in park. He was on contract with the apartment complex and didn't work for tips, yet I always leaned forward and slipped a couple of twenties between the front two seats to leave on the center console. I'd learned through his many one-sided conversations he was a single dad of four children and continued to work past retirement age to send his youngest to college. I probably could do more for him, but he seemed the kind who wouldn't accept any handouts. So, my few hundred bucks extra a week would have to suffice.

I didn't toss out a farewell as I slammed the door and hurried up the steps, my phone already pressed to my ear as I dialed my one and only friend, Dean. He didn't answer, of course, not that I expected him to at 5:30 in the morning.

When his voicemail clicked on, I said, "I need an update and a plan this morning. My office at nine. Bring everything. Time is of the essence."

There was no eye contact as I brushed past the doorman when I ended the call.

As always, I took the time to appreciate the renovations in the lobby. The first project I headed when I took over for my uncle was a complete overhaul of the outdated space. I replaced the washed-out pinks and creams with white and black. It made it feel like the high-end resort we should have been marketing all along. My grandfather had been hesitant to spend the dollars on the renovation, but our reservation numbers had tripled since the completion of the remodel.

I had my eye on the first Wilder Hotel, which had been left to deteriorate over the decades. It's the one that had always been my mother's favorite. But I had to wait it out before making that proposal, because there was a reason my family avoided the association with the old building. And a reason they held on to the building all these years.

Employees shuffled out of my way as I walked across the marble and down the hall toward my office. They knew I'd never return a greeting nor respond if they asked a question. They had managers for that kind of nonsense. I was here to get the Wilder Hotel chain back on the map, not to make friends with the employees. Though I attempted to smirk at one of the front desk clerks as she stood behind it. A look of fear flickered across her face, and I immediately schooled my expression.

My grandmother always fussed at me for not smiling more. Clearly, she didn't realize how terrifying my smiles came across.

The small office corridor was empty as I stepped inside. There were four more offices that belonged to the direct hotel staff and a desk just outside my corner suite for my assistant, Olive. She tended to leave me alone most of the time and was efficient in her work, but I never missed the flirty eyes she made toward me. Unfortunately for her, I never slept with my employees, nor someone fresh out of college. And there was no way in hell I was *dating* anyone—ever. At least not for real.

As I sat behind my desk, flicking on the lamp with a quick pull of the chain, the thought of what I was going to have to do for the next few months or even year left a nasty burn in my stomach. I was going to have to make a commitment of epic proportions, but it was worth it to rectify what my family had done to my mom.

She died before I could ever get to know her, but I had one solid memory of her from my third birthday. Our small house was filled with balloons, and there was a bright-red bow on the Power Wheels truck she bought me. My dad was by her side as they watched my reaction, and I remembered it being the happiest I'd ever seen my mom. Her smile was the best memory she could have left me.

Twenty-seven years later, I was determined to put that smile back on her face up in heaven.

"Here," a familiar voice startled me from across my desk. A large coffee in a familiar white-and-green travel mug was gripped in the hand of his outstretched arm.

"Thanks. You're here early," I said to Dean as I accepted his offering. I knew without a doubt that it would be a black coffee with two sugars. After knowing me for the last twenty years, there was no doubt he knew how I took my early-morning beverage, in addition to my go-to drink order at a bar. Just like I knew both of his.

I glanced down at the corner of my computer screen and confirmed it was still well before the normal start of his day. My office space was still barren.

"Well, when I got your message, I assumed it was more urgent than not."

Dean folded his large body onto one of my stiff office chairs. The wood frame creaked under the weight of his muscular form. I stood at six foot two, and he towered over me. Many times when we were out, people would mistake him as my bodyguard. The comical part was that he was a one of the kindest people I knew. I liked to think our friendship softened me a bit. Without him, I'd have grown hard years ago.

"You assumed right," I replied as I sipped the hot liquid. Dean was smart enough to know we had very little time to get my plan into action, and we needed to start without the prying ears and eyes of my employees lurking about.

As he tugged a leather bag from around his chest and set it at his feet, he leveled his eyes on me. "Are you sure you want to do this?"

"I don't have any other choice. You saw the document just as I did."

He sighed heavily as if it were him having to tie himself down with a ball and chain for the next few months. "I read it, and I even had my own lawyers look over the living will. It's ironclad. You have to be married to take ownership of the business."

That was only part of the stipulation. I also had to be married to take full control of my trust fund left by my mother. After six months of "wedded bliss," everything would be handed over to me, the rightful heir to Wilder Hotels.

The contract in question was why my mother had excommunicated herself from her family. They'd called her a disgrace when she wound up pregnant with me out of wedlock, despite the promise from my dad to marry her before I was born, and he'd stayed true to that. It was that only a male could be promised the business. An old, misogynistic rule I planned to rectify when it became mine.

"It's a burden I'm willing to bear. The business should have gone to my mom. *He* knows that, and I have no doubt, even from his deathbed, he's going to try to weasel it away from me. That's why our plan is perfect."

"But… no offense… you're not really husband material. Your idea of a commitment is using the same driver every day and your weekly calls with your grandmother. I've never known you to be in a relationship of any sort. You can't even commit to someone in your bed more than a handful of times."

Though he wasn't wrong in his assessment, his words still burned me with shame. But I needed to do this. Not just for me or for my mother, but for my family as a whole. My grandma was never the same when my mom left their family, and she held it against my grandfather since that day. She told me all the time that she would have divorced him if she could have survived on her own.

Survival. That's all this is, I told myself.

Ignoring his comments, I tapped on my desk, letting my fingertips mash against the hard walnut wood. "So, did you bring what I asked for?"

With a not-so-subtle roll of his eyes, he replied, "You know I did. It was easy enough. You're lucky the group hosting the organization didn't even password-protect the file with the list of attendees. After that, it was just using a simple background check to get everything you needed."

His large hand dove into the leather bag and pulled out a stack of papers. Binder clips separated each person in question. The papers landed with a thud on top of my desk, triggering my laptop to come awake. I quickly folded the screen down and looked over at the person on top.

Reflexively, I grimaced as I took in the three-by-three image clipped in the corner.

"Gertrude Powers," I said as I read her name. "Teacher of Biology at Sunset Hill High School."

Glancing up at my friend, I asked, "People still name their kid Gertrude?"

"Well, she is fifty-two."

"Fifty-two? Is there anyone remotely close to my age?"

Not that I had a problem with dating older women. Some of my favorite pastimes involved a woman knowing what she wanted in bed, and their age was key to that knowledge.

"There are a few. Not many though. You know, if you waited two weeks, there is that bridal fashion show hosted in the main ballroom. I'm sure one of those models would be a much better fit."

"No. The teachers' convention is perfect."

Dean sighed as he leaned back. "Explain to me why again."

"It's simple," I began, before there was a knock on my door, and Olive, my assistant, popped her head in.

"Good morning, Mr. Beckett. I'm clocked in if you need anything."

"Thanks," I responded, and then as she started to shut the door, I called out, "Olive, I need you to gather a list of all the check-ins for the teachers' convention today and tomorrow."

She hesitated, and I noted the confusion in her gaze before she agreed.

"We had some issues during the check-in last year. Multiple double bookings, and we were lucky they even wanted to return this year. I want to make sure all the attendees are personally taken care of."

"Understood," she replied as she closed my door. Through the transparent wall of glass, I could see her return to her desk and sit.

"You think she really bought that?"

"It's the truth… well, mostly. We did have a ton of overbookings, which was why I changed out the ancient computer system the day I came on board. And a teacher will take what I am offering. The salaries are low, and time spent high. They are the ideal candidate to jump at the chance to gain one million dollars for a six-month commitment."

Dean returned to sipping his coffee as I shuffled through the stacks of attendees. Each one grew more boring and duller than the last, and quickly my hope to get this deception underway fizzled out.

Ten minutes later, I'd only made it through a quarter of the stack, wondering if I was going to have to suck it up for the next six months until I could find someone my grandfather would believe could actually knock me off my feet. I was picky about my women, after all, and I had a clear type.

Did she need to match exactly? No, but she needed to have a spark about her. And none of the potential wives had anything that was jumping out at me. Except the one who was also a skydiving instructor. I always enjoyed an adrenaline rush. But she was already engaged and, though not a deal-breaker, I preferred not to start something messy, like a scorned fiancé.

"Dean, be real with me right now," I said with a heavy exhale. I leaned forward, my elbows on the desk and my hands sliding back along my hair. It was moments like this I wished my strands were free so I could tug at them in frustration. "Is there any potential in here? I know you're smart enough to skim through these before handing them over."

"There are a few." He nodded as he sat back against the chair, resting one of his feet on the knee of his other leg. Dean looked more at home in my office than I did.

"Tell me which one you would choose."

He cocked one of his jet-black eyebrows as if he'd heard the most outlandish thing ever.

"I trust you, Dean. And I don't have time to scour through this stack."

"Fine," he resigned as he stood from the chair and walked toward the console table against the other wall. It housed an antique whisky decanter and two glasses that hadn't been filled in years. Turning toward me, he perched his frame against the console, large hands gripping the edge. "Third from the bottom. The clip is about a quarter of an inch offset."

"Good," I replied as I pulled it free from the others. "You should have just led with this one."

"But where is the fun in that, my friend?"

"Fun for you," I mumbled, and I shoved the rest of the stack aside and plopped the chosen one in the middle of my desk.

Her picture caught me off guard at first. She was pretty, with long, wavy blonde hair, a nose that looked to be slightly upturned, and a wide smile that did nothing to hide her plump lips. But with a second glance, I could see the kind eyes. The dark-brown irises shaded by long lashes looked vaguely familiar, but she was definitely someone I would remember.

"Aurora Grace Easterly. Just turned twenty-four. Recently began teaching grade eleven at Ashfield High School." I tried not to let my excitement show as I skimmed over the front page. Settling back in my chair, the wheels squeaked as I turned it to face my friend. "She'll do."

"Don't you want to know more about her? I ran an extensive background check on everyone."

"Is she a serial killer? Have a restraining order against her? Any major red flags I should know about?"

"No, but there are a few things you should know—"

"Look, she'll do. She's pretty enough to convince my grandfather I'm attracted to her, and I'm sure the mil will sweeten the deal."

"Okay, what do I need to do?"

"Help me make sure she shows up at the hotel bar tonight after she checks in."

He chuckled as he stepped over to my desk and began gathering all the documents. He knew this was all hush-hush and absolutely no one could know what I was up to, except for maybe Aurora. And the ironclad NDA she was going to sign would make sure she didn't share the information with anyone.

"Welp, I'll be sure to stay close by in case she's a runner. I'll see you at seven?"

"Sounds good."

The room fell silent as he situated the bag across his chest again, his coffee cup from earlier disregarded on the small table next to the chair.

I was flipping open my laptop to review a couple of reports when I heard Dean's restrained cough.

"Hey, Talon. This is a big step. Are you sure this is what you want to do? It's not just going to affect you and your life; it's going to affect hers too."

We'd argued this point back and forth when I learned of the stipulation a month ago. But I was the kind of guy who jumped in feet-first and rarely ever second-guessed myself.

Ignoring my friend, I turned my attention back to my computer. "I'll see you at seven, Dean."

Out the corner of my eye, I watched him duck his head as he left my office and gave a wave to Olive before he was out of my line of sight. Quickly, I began drafting an email to the guest services manager, informing him to give everyone checking in for the teachers' conference a ten-dollar bar voucher.

Once sent, I placed a call to the front desk, where a nasally voice answered.

"Please let me know when Aurora Easterly checks in. And make sure we place her in one of the suites."

"Sir?"

"That is all," I said gruffly as I ended the call.

If I was going to ask her to be my wife, I was going to need to show her what I could provide. One of the best rooms in our hotel was a good place to start.

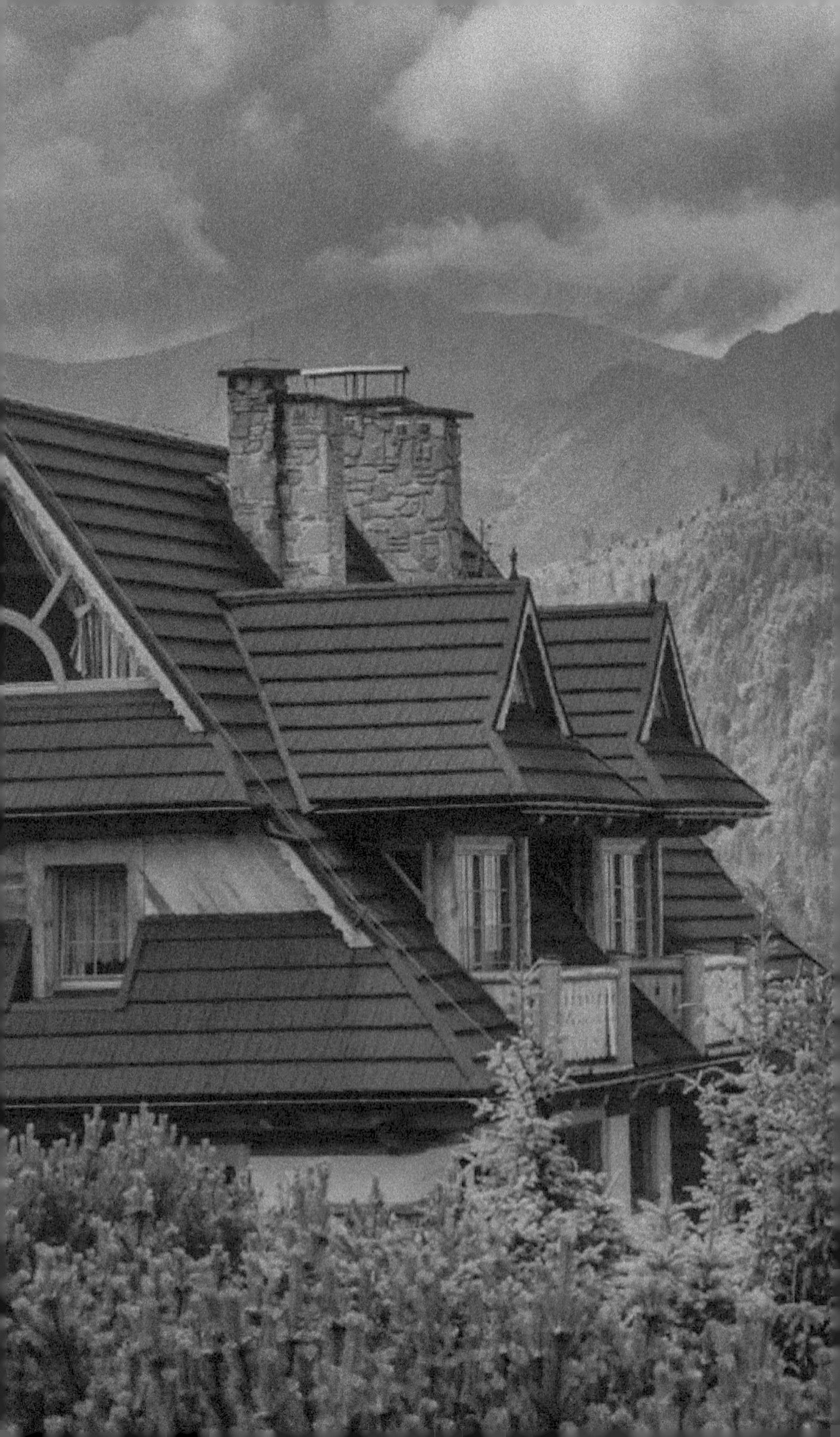

Chapter Three

Aurora

Andrew's truck hit a pothole on the highway, and my entire face scrunched in horror as my carry-on luggage slammed against the side of the truck bed. I couldn't see it, but I sincerely hoped the new suitcase was unscathed.

"Um… thanks for driving me to the airport. I know you'd rather be helping Dad today." The harvesting of corn at our family farm was about to go full-force in the next month, so I knew they needed Andrew at Sunny Brook. But here he was, carting his little sister to Nashville. I tried not to linger on the memories of the last time my brother had to *pick me up* from the airport.

He continued to stare forward, eyes on the road, not showing any recognition that he heard me.

As the silence grew, it began to crawl over me like fearsome spiders and scorpions, until it was too much to handle. Finally, the lack of noise became overwhelming, and I needed to break it.

"I'm so glad I'm able to go back this year… after the fiasco from last year, you know?"

Andrew answered with a grunt, so I continued.

"I mean, after the hotel double-booked my room, they were more than willing to set me up for this year, and the conference comped my fee and airfare. That was about the only bright side to the trip last year."

In his naturally deep, gruff voice, Andrew said, "It's the least they could've done, when they left you stranded in Miami with no way home."

My half-brother couldn't see, but my eyes rolled at his response. I wasn't left stranded, despite what he and our family thought. I'd been saving money since I took my first babysitting job at thirteen, and my savings account was nicely padded. My grades and essays earned me scholarships to a local college that covered all my tuition to earn my degree in education.

No one would listen to me when I relayed everything that happened last year and that I didn't need any immediate help. I could have easily booked a new hotel in the area and taken a much-needed vacation, but I made the mistake of calling my sister, Autumn, and not ten minutes later, I found myself in the back of a taxi with a chartered flight home, courtesy of Autumn's husband, Colton.

I was helpless, little Rory, and no one thought I could stand on my own two feet. They let me shape the young minds of our students, yet nobody believed I could survive on my own.

But I wasn't nearly as naïve as they believed.

"I had a way home. Y'all just chose to ignore me."

Turning his attention toward me briefly, Andrew snarled, "And what would you have done, Rory? You, a single female, were in one of the busiest cities in the country."

"Oh, but our sister living in *New York* was better off?"

Andrew jerked his face back toward the windshield, eyes on the road. The leather on the steering wheel squeaked as he twisted his palms against it, fingers outstretched as he repositioned them, then squeezed tightly once more.

"You're... different."

"I'm not a little kid anymore."

"You'll always be a little kid to me, Rory."

"Why am I not surprised?"

Finally, we took the exit off the highway that led to the airport a few miles south of Knoxville, Tennessee. I peered out the window at the passing buildings until the landscape gave way to runways and the departure area. Before the truck came to a complete stop, I flung the door open and jumped down.

"Fuck, Rory! Wait."

The truck lurched as he hit the brakes while I hopped on the running board, gripping the edge of the truck bed to hold on. "Don't worry, big brother. I can do this myself."

I reached down for the strap of my suitcase and hefted it upward. It was heavier than I remembered, and my arms struggled to lift it over the side. I felt a strange sense of satisfaction when a wheel on my carry-on ran down the side of the vehicle. Unfortunately, it didn't leave a scratch. I probably would have felt bad though. But only a little bit.

My suitcase landed with a thud, and I jumped down.

"I could have done that for you," Andrew exclaimed as he clicked the button on the luggage handle that rose it up.

"Yes, but then little ol' helpless me would never learn how to do anything." Reaching out, I grabbed the handle and held it in my grip as I turned and closed the passenger side door. My neck pinched as I looked up at my brother. "I'll be back in a week. I'll text you my flight info. If you can't be here, I'll call Franny."

Crossing his arms, Andrew frowned. "I'll be there."

"Okay." I shrugged.

"Rory," he said, his voice laced with regret. "We love you." He held his arms out, and I released my suitcase to nuzzle into his embrace. My cheek rested on his sternum as I squeezed my arms around his waist. "Travel safely," he whispered into my hair.

"I love you too. I'll call when I get there."

After a minute, I watched him pull away as I stood inside the terminal—since he waited until I got fully inside—ready to give Miami a second chance. I was very nervous about returning, but there was a discussion happening during the conference that I was extremely interested in. It could directly affect the students and the schools in Ashfield in an exciting way, but I needed to learn more before I started allowing my excitement to cultivate.

I'd booked a first-class flight this time, and I enjoyed the extra space and amenities during the flight. It disappointed me that our time in the air was only a couple of hours.

After exiting the plane, I made my way down the terminal thoroughfare toward the pick-up area. I'd hesitantly booked a ride share again, but this time I was prepared for the Miami traffic.

My hair swished with each step I took as I navigated the crowd. Another thing I remembered about the heat and humidity, my hair was going to take a while to adjust, so I'd thrown it up in a high ponytail, letting the wavy ends brush against my shoulders.

Finally, I made it to my waiting car and allowed him to place my bag in the trunk. As I settled into the back seat, I slipped my sunglasses free from my purse and slid them on over my eyes.

This time, I was prepared, and I was going to enjoy myself regardless of the outcome. And I knew better than to call my family if anything went awry.

The drive lasted forty-five minutes before we made it to the hotel, even though the map estimated it would take twenty. After paying and exiting the car, I took my luggage that the driver insisted on grabbing from the trunk and started toward the hotel's lobby.

I knew the place had undergone renovations over the past year, but I was taken aback when I stepped through the glass doors. They replaced the retro aesthetic with a modern overlay that immediately felt luxurious.

"Good afternoon," a man said with a tip of his hat as I took in my surroundings.

"Oh. Good afternoon," I replied as I moved out of the way of the entrance, my eyes flicking toward the top of the three-story lobby and taking in the Miami sun pouring through the glass panels.

"Wow," I murmured, following a group of people to the main desk for check-in. I learned my lesson last time, and I planned to secure my room before registering for the conference.

The line was long, and I considered stepping out and grabbing my seminar packet and name badge, but I knew I'd be waiting just as long later. Instead, I scrolled on my phone while I waited, posting a picture on my social media from when I arrived in Miami. I'd taken it at the airport in front of a window when the sun was making everything glisten.

Collectively, we all shuffled forward as they helped each person until finally it was my turn.

"Next," the young man standing behind the desk hollered without looking up from his computer screen. Reaching down, I gripped the handle of my suitcase, then began shuffling toward the clerk just as a harried woman darted in front of the line and cut me off. I stumbled back into the man standing behind me, and I quickly apologized. The group in the line behind me all groaned in unison as the lady began to reprimand the man at the front desk.

I didn't normally like to cause a confrontation or draw attention to myself, but my instincts went on high alert as the man behind the desk turned a sickly ashen-gray. The woman who continued to berate the clerk took another step closer to the desk so that her body practically hovered over the top.

At that point, I'd had enough and released my bag, then carried myself over to the desk as if pushed.

"Excuse me, is there a problem here?" I asked the woman as I sidled up next to her. I had to tilt my head back to make eye contact with her, but my lack of height had never deterred me from commanding attention when I sought it. I quickly glanced at her name tag, one that signified she was one of the teachers here for the conference.

"No," she said, ignoring me with a flip of her frizzy red hair.

"Actually, I think there is, Gertrude. We've all been waiting patiently in this line, and you thought it right to jump in front of us. You're causing a ruckus, when all we want to do is get checked in to our rooms. As a teacher, I think you'd know how to speak with others. Instead, you're berating this man, who is just trying to help you."

"Well… I…," she replied, her mouth flapping open and closed like a fish.

Turning toward the clerk, I asked him what caused the confrontation, and he explained Gertrude wasn't satisfied with the view outside from her room. He added that she made a standard reservation, not an upgraded view of the pool or gardens.

"So, you're giving this young man a hard time because of your view? Aren't you here for a conference that runs the majority of the day? You will barely be in your room for it to matter what you'll see when you happen to glance out your window."

"Yes… I…." She seemed to lose all her steam as I continued to stand there, eyeing her.

"First, please apologize to this man. He's only trying to do his job. Second, remember you could have waited in line like everyone else. Third, please move so the rest of us can get checked in."

"I've never," she mumbled as she stomped away, her frizzy mane bouncing with each of her steps. No apology given for her outburst.

Once it was clear she wasn't coming back, the group waiting in line broke into applause, and my cheeks felt like I'd been sitting out in the sun for too long. Apparently, I had not only drawn the attention of the crowd close by, but people who were in the lobby had gathered. Thankfully, I didn't notice any phones out to film the interaction. Our school superintendent in Ashfield was very old school, and it didn't take much for him to find a reason to write you up. Our teachers were already in short supply, but he fired one of the high-school teachers for a social media post he didn't care for. It wasn't even bad, if you asked me, but it wasn't my decision.

That firing was also why I had been moved from teaching first grade to eleventh, or whatever high-school level they needed me at. I almost regretted getting a license in all levels of teaching.

Reaching up, I tried to tuck a piece of hair behind my ear, my nervous habit, then remembered the strands were pulled back in a ponytail. Instead, I twisted the small pearl earring in my lobe as I stepped to retrieve my suitcase and then went back to the man whose face had finally returned to its natural hue.

"Hi," I said as calmly as I could. My heart was still racing at the confrontation I willingly put myself in.

"Hello," he squawked, then immediately cleared his throat and repeated the greeting. "Welcome to The Wilder Hotel and Spa. Are you checking in?"

"Yes. The name is Aurora Easterly."

"Of course." A tapping noise came from behind the ledge of the desk as he typed on the keyboard. Without lifting his head, the man's eyes darted up to mine as he said quietly, "And thank you."

"Oh. Well, it was nothing," I replied with a smile. By his tone, I could tell the interaction embarrassed him.

"It's only my second week on the job," he declared.

"You're doing a fine job. I promise most people aren't like that."

A few beats of silence passed as he continued to type away on his computer. "Mrs. Easterly."

"Ms.," I clarified and let him continue.

"Yes. Sorry. Ms. Easterly, the payment for the room was declined. Do you have another form of payment you'd like to use?"

Of course, it was. Leave it to the school to book the room for me after the fiasco last year and the card being maxed out.

"Oh, sure. The school booked this for me," I explained as I reached inside my purse for my wallet and hesitantly handed my card over to the desk attendant. "You can use mine, and I'll get reimbursed."

It would be a cold day in hell before I ever saw the money. The school system was tight on their budget for a reason.

"I'm sorry about that. It's not the first time it's happened this afternoon."

It did not surprise me to learn that.

"Okay, Ms. Easterly. I have you set up in our Junior Deluxe Suite. Your room overlooks the gardens and has a view of the ocean as well. With this room, you also have access to our rooftop bar and complimentary happy hour."

"Um, they didn't book that sort of room—" I glanced at his nametag. "—Davey. They booked a standard room without a view specification." As much as I wanted a room with a view of the ocean, I knew my boss wasn't going to approve it.

"This is on the house, ma'am."

I wanted to be angry that he called me *ma'am*, because I probably wasn't much older than him, but I held back my retort, because it was most likely part of his training and considered good manners. I also had a sneaking suspicion he was upgrading my room for coming to his defense.

Leaning closer to him, I whispered, "You don't need to do that because I said something to that woman. I'm happy with a standard room."

The man's cheeks reminded me of ripe tomatoes. "I wish I could say this was my doing… ma'am." His cheeks flushed deeper. "But there is a note here saying this is courtesy of the hotel after the… um… issues last year. They want to make sure you enjoy your stay."

"Oh." I never expected the hotel to remember the double booking or the fact that they couldn't switch me over to one of their sister hotels. The entire strip had been booked solid.

"Well, I appreciate it, though it wasn't necessary."

"There is also a voucher for dinner and ten dollars toward drinks at our lobby bar."

The offer was tempting, since two of the sessions I wanted to attend were hosted that evening. I would not get a chance to explore the city and find a place to eat until much later.

He handed me a room key, even though I already had a notification that the digital key was available on my hotel app.

"Thank you."

As I gathered the key and pamphlets, I used my free hand to grab my suitcase.

"Have a nice stay, Ms. Easterly, and please let me know if there is anything I can do for you."

With a quick nod, I made my way back to the center of the lobby, ignoring some looks from people who witnessed the earlier conflict. I sought the sign for the conference registration, and despite wanting to get to my room and relax before the first session, I trekked over to the room and grabbed my information.

The same woman who manned the table last year was there again, and she quickly apologized for everything. Apparently, she led the conference and was embarrassed the hotel double-booked me and several other teachers, causing us all to miss the convention. It was hard to be angry at the woman who resembled Mrs. Claus, and I knew none of it was her fault.

While I checked in, I asked her about the grant sessions being hosted that evening and told her I was very interested in learning more about some specifically for rural areas. This was one way I could help my students and the community. She explained new grants were being offered every year, and the money was just sitting on the table. The session was going to focus on some of the lesser-known funds and how to get them.

I had no plans to miss it.

But as I arrived at my room, all thoughts about the seminar fell to the wayside as a glimmer of the bay peeked through my window. I was on one of the upper floors, and the room was huge, but all I could focus on was the view. Living in Tennessee, I didn't get a lot of chances to see the ocean. Sure, we vacationed a few times at Coral Bell Cove, a small country town in the bay of Virginia, but there was something different in seeing the span of blue sea outside my window.

I don't know how anyone expected me to leave this room, especially when I explored the space. The bathroom was bigger than my bedroom and bathroom at my house combined. And there was a full kitchen attached to the living area.

I wasn't sure what I anticipated when I was assigned the room, but that wasn't it. It felt like a luxury apartment, not a hotel room.

The fixtures all looked up to date—something I wouldn't have imagined, knowing how the hotel lobby looked last year, but with the renovations downstairs, they must have made some small improvements to the rooms as well.

Before leaving the bathroom, I promised the standalone tub that I'd be revisiting it later with a bottle of wine I was definitely ordering from room service.

I unpacked the clothes I brought, excited to know I'd be spending the week at the resort. This was going to be one of the best vacations I'd ever had. As I shut the last dresser drawer, I peered over my shoulder, where the bed was calling my name.

As much as I wanted to explore the hotel, the flight and ride and the argument with my brother—plus the confrontation with the other teacher—left me drained.

Quickly stripping off my clothes, I donned a pair of silk shorts and matching cami and crawled under the sheets. The smell of bleach and a hint of lavender was almost comforting as I snuggled deeper beneath the down comforter.

My phone rested on the nightstand, where I plugged it in before emptying my suitcase, and I set the alarm so I wouldn't miss the keynote speaker and first session tonight. It would also leave me time for a shower and to find a snack.

"Just an hour," I said out loud as I closed my eyes. Even with the sun glaring outside the window, I plunged into a deep sleep. Exhaustion from the weekday and the nonsense my ex was trying to pull left my body in need of relaxation.

That's why, when the alarm blared, I sleepily pressed the snooze button.

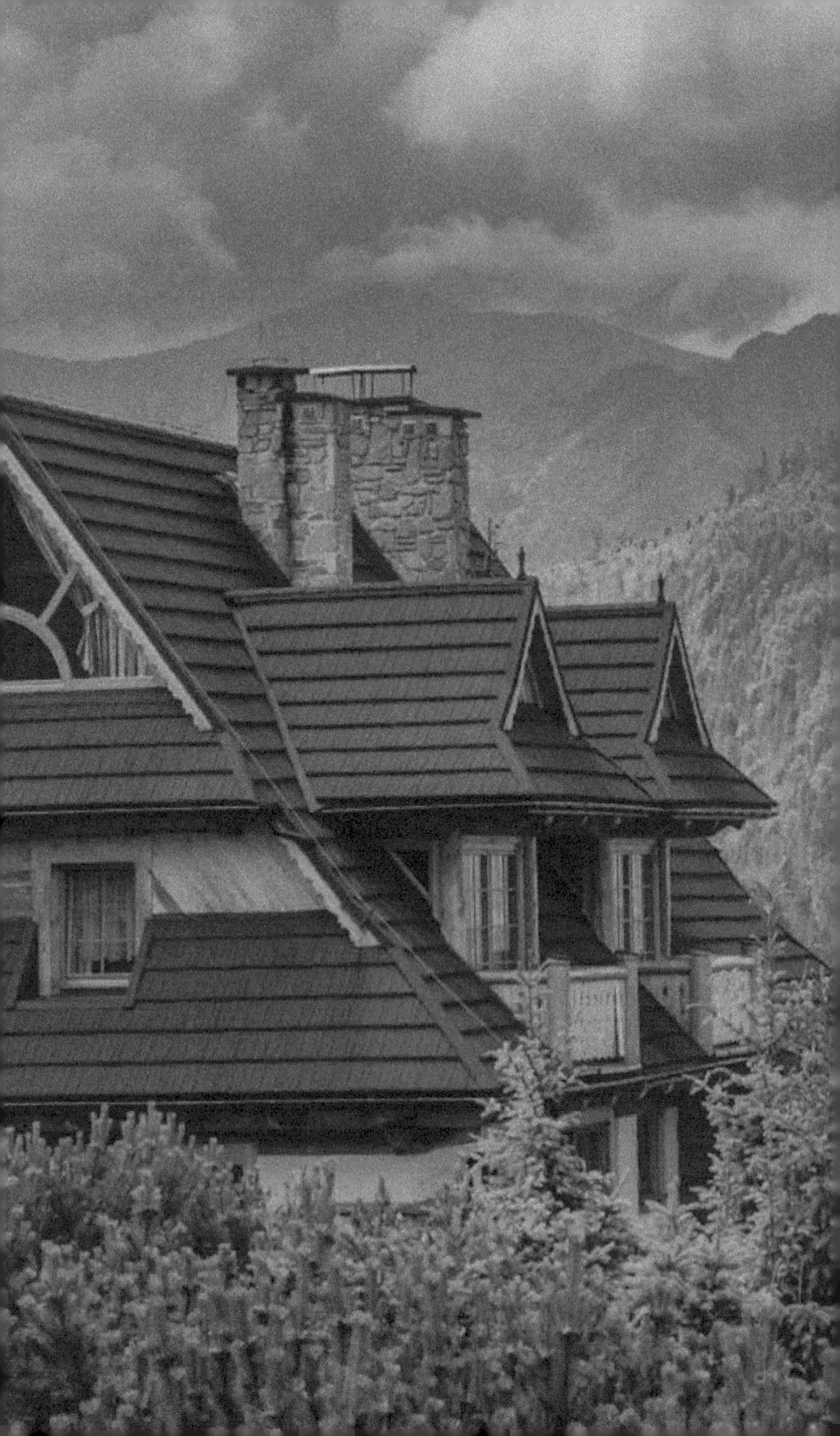

Chapter Four

Aurora

Memories of my first day of freshman year of college assaulted me as I rushed through my shower. I remembered oversleeping, for the first time in my life, and was about to miss my first class of the day. An 8:00 a.m. course on entry-level childhood development. Growing up on the farm, I'd become accustomed to waking up on my own at five in the morning or earlier. Whether it be an alarm, the animals, or my own internal clock, it was a rarity that I ever slept past the sunrise. But it seemed living in the dorms knocked my body off kilter, and I left myself just enough time to toss on some clothes, brush my teeth, and sprint to the class across campus.

As I turned off the shower, I reminded myself that no one would be watching me. These were teachers, after all, and it was just the keynote speech. I would not miss anything that was critical.

It didn't matter what I continued to repeat to myself; the moment the elevator dropped me off in the lobby, I dashed down the hall. I waved to Davey at the front desk as I made my way down the corridor toward the ballroom where the keynote was going to be held.

A quick glance at my watch told me I had two minutes before it was about to start. I looked up just in time to knock shoulders with a man who walked briskly in the other direction. He continued walking as if nothing happened, but I was certain a bruise on my shoulder was going to remain in the aftermath. I peered back to find him already a great distance away. His hair was cropped short on his head, and his black suit was almost too tight for his body, as his limbs strained against the material. He was also double the size of some patrons as he walked past. He looked like someone in security.

"Sorry!" I shouted but the man never acknowledged my apology.

"Hmm," I mumbled as I stepped through the auditorium doors. A gaggle of people followed behind me, searching for a seat, but my eyes were drawn to a small snack table in the back corner. I contemplated at first, but then my stomach was the deciding factor as she rumbled like a monster truck starting its engine.

"We'll let you all get settled and start the keynote in five minutes," an announcer said as I grabbed a croissant and a cup of water and leaned against the wall.

The buttery, flaky dough was exactly what I needed to hold me over through the evening. Heck, if they were serving these throughout the convention, I was going to fill up on them and wouldn't need to splurge on dinner.

I did hate that I was going to miss the complimentary happy hour in the concierge area offered by the hotel for my newly appointed room. I enjoyed a good dirty martini every now and then, but I didn't want to miss the start of the conference.

Scarfing down the final bits of the baked good, I tossed my empty water cup in the trash and found a seat in the third row... directly behind Gertrude. Thankfully, she was too engrossed in the trio of women when the keynote started, but when the speaker finished up, she turned to leave, narrowing her eyes in my direction.

I stayed back, letting the room empty before making my exit and heading toward the session I was most interested in. Fortunately, I didn't run into Gertrude again at the session, and I almost made it scot-free until I headed toward the lounge area just off the lobby. She was seated with her friends, drinking something green that reminded me of the kale smoothies my brother drank when he was on the football team.

I'd tried it once, and it tasted like the grass Dad mowed in the summer. That was the only time, and I vowed to never try it again.

Her friends all turned in my direction as I passed, each one looking like a different version of Gertrude. All with frizzy manes in various colors, glasses a bit too large for their faces, and an earthy bohemian look. I'd admire their carefree, natural look if Gertrude's didn't mask an ugly inside.

I smiled sweetly at them as I walked by their table, not letting them know they made me uncomfortable. At first, I looked around the room to see if there was anyone I recognized, but I knew it was futile. Everyone was lost in their own conversations with fellow teachers from their school. As independent as I was, I really wished Franny had been able to make the journey with me.

Taking a steady breath, I told the host I was going to sit at the bar and sidled onto a stool with a view of a pre-season football game. I wasn't much into sports, but it was something to keep my attention for a little while.

Under the bar, there was a hook where I hung my purse and the tote I brought to hold all the packets handed out during the sessions. I planned to look over the grant information in my room later, but now seemed as good a time as any.

It didn't take long before the stools beside me filled up with other guests, many I didn't recognize from the keynote speech earlier, so I assumed they were here on vacation or for business. That's when I noticed the man from earlier, my shoulder immediately aching as I recalled the way he bumped into me. Without a second thought, I reached up to rub the area.

He was giving his phone all his attention, even as the bartender moved in front of him. She had to crane her neck as he answered her question with a quick headshake. She lingered, and I watched as he nodded once before his eyes met mine. Immediately, I ducked my head and pulled out all the papers I received just an hour ago. Something about him made me uncomfortable, but not in a scary way. It was like he was assessing me, waiting on my next move in a game of kings. And I was a terrible chess player.

The bartender made her way over to me, and I asked for a dirty martini with three blue-cheese olives and a copy of the dinner menu. She quickly handed me the laminated paper and went to make my drink as I scanned it over. Everything looked delicious, and I had a hard time settling on one thing. When she set the drink in front of me, I asked for her recommendation, and I ended up ordering the filet mignon with bearnaise sauce. We chatted for a bit, her asking what I was in town for, as the guests around the bar vied for her attention. I didn't care, though; it was nice to have someone to talk to, even if the man to my right started getting mouthy in her direction.

With a roll of her eyes, she left me and took all their orders, quickly making their cocktails and not-so-nicely setting them on the bar.

As I sipped the best martini I'd ever had, I skimmed over the grant listings, searching for one in particular.

"Here you go, babe," the bartender said as she set out my dinner, and I saw a sneer fester on the face of the man beside me.

"Thank you."

I cut a slice of the meat, the perfect amount of pink on the inside, and took a bite. There was nothing I could do to mask the moan that escaped from my lips. The steak was heavenly. Right up there with Rolan McEntire's.

"I'd love to hear you make that sound later."

"Excuse me?" I asked, covering my mouth with my hand as I chewed and faced the man beside me.

"Yeah, I bet you'd make that sound with my dick in your mouth."

As I finished my chewing and swallowed, I couldn't help but bark out a laugh. This man beside me really thought he had done something extraordinary as he gazed at me with a cocky grin.

"I'm sorry. I don't mean to laugh, but does that line usually work?"

His eyes widened in surprise at my retort. I couldn't believe there were men out here who thought something like that would make a woman want to fall into bed with him.

"Look here, bi—" he started, but the bartender quickly stepped up to us.

"Finish that sentence, and I'll have you kicked out of this hotel. Now, as she clearly made it known, she's not interested, so I suggest you leave this bar with what little dignity you have left."

His gaze darted back and forth between me and the bartender before he grumbled, "Must be a cat chaser," as he slunk off the barstool.

"I wish," the bartender said as he slammed a twenty-dollar bill on the bar and pushed through the crowd to the exit.

"Sorry about that," I apologized as she cleared away his half-empty beer and the cocktail glass with only ice left in the bottom.

"Not your fault. I witness it more times than I can count. You just sit there and enjoy your dinner. I'll check on you in a bit."

Checking the time on my watch, I noted it was closing in on seven at night. I texted my family while I was waiting to check in to the hotel to let them know I arrived safely, and they replied in the group chat that they were all going to the ice-skating rink in town as a treat for my soon-to-be official nieces, Eloise and Molly. Even though I was on vacation, I felt the tiniest ounce of homesickness.

I bet my mother would have loved this hotel. People in town always talked about how classically beautiful she was. It had been mentioned to her numerous times how she looked like the late Grace Kelly when she arrived in the town of Ashfield with my father. I could see her now, floating into the lobby with an air of classic Hollywood, commanding the attention of everyone in the room. My sisters, Autumn and Alex, took after her in that regard. Eyes always followed their every step. It would have been easy to hate them for it, if they hadn't been completely oblivious. Men were just happy to be in their presence.

My younger sister, Aspen, and I took after our father. Our faces weren't as soft, and our bodies were less graceful. If it weren't for our mother's blonde hair, we wouldn't look related to our siblings at all. I laughed to myself as I remembered how similar Aspen and I looked to our half-brother, Andrew, who was our mother's son from her first marriage. Though we looked more like our dad, we could've been triplets with our brother. Genetics was a funny thing.

The bartender—Fiona, I learned was her name—set another martini in front of me as I finished my meal and ordered dessert. There was a chocolate lava cake on the menu that I absolutely couldn't say no to. I almost ordered the sorbet but briefly recalled Alex divulging what she and Nate had done with the chilled treat, and I knew I'd never be able to eat it again.

Fiona cleared away my plate and my empty glass as I went back to looking at the list of grants. There were a few I starred with my pen to look back over, but there was one in particular mentioned in the seminar that I wanted to learn more about.

"Ah! There it is," I said gleefully just as Fiona set the dessert in front of me, the ice cream already melting atop the warmth of the decadent cake.

"That excited about dessert?" she asked with a smile, and I giggled.

"I am, but no. I was looking for an education grant specifically for agriculture and education in this huge packet, and I finally found it."

"Well, I don't know anything about that, but I do know you'll enjoy this lava cake. It's my favorite. Let me know if you need anything."

"Thanks." I watched as she took a few other orders and then scurried over to the large man in the corner who had yet to leave his post. I began to wonder if he worked security for the hotel. With the large crowd in the lounge, it made complete sense to me. She was nodding at whatever he said, and I knew with his furrowed brows and the wrinkles in his forehead that it was important.

"Mind if I sit here?" a voice that sounded smoother than the chocolate ganache in the center of the cake asked from my right.

"Um… no… I mean…." The man had robbed me of conscious thought. It felt like I was sinking into the depths of the ocean, and the only sound was my heartbeat. The entire lounge drifted away as I turned toward him. After a deep breath, I replied, "Sorry. No one is sitting there. Help yourself."

"Thanks." He smiled as he settled his body on the stool and all the noises in the lounge rushed back in to overwhelm me.

This man stared forward, waiting for Fiona to amble over for his order, but kept his attention on the game playing on the television screen. I first noticed his hair was slicked back and tied at the base of his neck. It was dark, with just the lightest hints of warm tones throughout the strands. I bet it was gorgeous when it was loose.

The dark hair complemented his tanned skin, looking like he spent just the right amount of time in the sun. He didn't appear to be a beachgoer, nor someone who used a tanning bed. He probably had a boat. With the perfect fit of his suit, I imagined it was custom-tailored for him. So, he probably had a yacht.

The suit would be out-of-place in my hometown, but not in this lounge. The bar was filled with suit-clad men.

His nose had a slight bump, and his jawline was sharp, which only accentuated the domineering vibe he gave off. I noticed the man on the stool next to him scooted closer to the woman he was with, as if to keep her from this man's gravitational pull.

There was a slight scruff on his face, which was in stark contrast to the put-together nature of his appearance. It reminded me of the days my father would spend on the farm. He'd shave before dawn, and by dusk, he'd grow a scratchy shadow on his chin.

I wondered how this stranger's stubble would feel between my legs.

I chirped in alarm at where my thoughts had veered and turned back on my stool to face forward. With a shaking hand, I reached for my martini and lifted it to my lips, only to spill a little on the packet as I set it back on the bar.

"Shit," I mumbled as I reached for the napkins in the holder in front of the newcomer. As I reached across him, I whispered an apology.

"Everything all right?" he asked.

"Yeah, everything is fine. I just spilled some of my drink." I dabbed at the paper with the napkin, groaning when the ink was smeared.

"I hope that wasn't anything important."

"Only the main reason I was here today. No biggie."

I kept dabbing at the packet, hoping with each pass the words would magically reappear, but it was futile. The spill ruined the entire section I had been hoping to read. If I'd been alone in my room, I would have popped a bottle of pinot and cried into the glass.

I was so lost in the damage that I didn't hear him place his order, but Fiona set a small glass filled with amber liquid in front of him before hurrying off.

"I'm sorry," he said sincerely, and I truly believed him.

I turned to tell him it was fine and not his fault, but when our eyes locked, I forgot exactly what he was apologizing for. His eyes glimmered from the lights in the bar, and they reminded me of the night sky—dark and mysterious with only the light of the moon to illuminate the surroundings. They mesmerized me.

He cocked his head subtly, as if he were one of my students trying to figure out how to pronounce the next word in a sentence.

"Everything okay over here?" Fiona asked, suddenly reappearing once again, breaking whatever spell this man had put me under, and I was thankful for the disturbance. "How's the cake?"

"It's delicious, just like you said it would be. I had to borrow a few napkins for a spill I made."

"No problem. It happens all the time. Those martini glasses are the worst. Let me get you a new one."

"Oh, that's okay. I think I used up my voucher for tonight as it is. I should probably head back to my room."

"Another drink for her, if she'd like, please. You can put it on my tab."

I'd only had the two martinis, and they really were delicious. I knew I was coherent enough to have another and make it back to my room, but I felt I should decline the offer. Expectations tended to come along with drinks bought by strangers, and I didn't want him to anticipate something from me in return.

"Why?" I asked him. There was no point in beating around the bush, and I'd be able to tell if he was lying.

"Because I've had a shitty couple of days." He chuckled. "Honestly? I've had a really shitty couple of years. And doing a kindness for someone who just ruined the whole reason she's here might make me feel a little better."

I nodded because I certainly understood having a rough go of it for a while. Heck, one of the appeals of being here in Miami was that I got to escape Ashfield for a short time. Plus, it *did* make *me* feel better to do nice things for others as well.

"And also," he began as he leaned in, "it's always nice to have a drink and conversation with a beautiful woman."

It was clear when my cheeks flamed that he enjoyed my response. I didn't know how anyone could keep from blushing in his presence. He may have been throwing me a line, but I was an inquisitive little fish ensnared by his hook.

"Okay. One more. Thank you."

"You're welcome."

Holding out my hand, I tried to mask the nervous tremble. "I'm Rory, by the way."

His large hand reached for mine and wrapped around it with a strength I'd never experienced, but it wasn't physical. It was a sensual connection between us I'd only ever read about in romance novels.

"Talon. It's nice to meet you, Rory."

Something about him felt familiar, and I couldn't help asking, "Have we met before?"

Chapter Five

Talon

"You just seem familiar; that's all." She quickly pulled her hand away, and I yearned to reach out and grab it back. I wasn't sure what possessed that reaction, but I knew I wanted to feel the warmth of her skin again.

Her question alarmed me at first, and I feared that somehow she was aware of my ruse to convince her to be my temporary wife. But then I remembered she would have absolutely no way of knowing that information.

"I don't believe so," I told her as I took a sip of my top-shelf bourbon, thankful I reminded Dean to have Fiona play it like I was a regular guest at the bar. It was something we'd done before when I took over to gain some information about our guests. Get them a few drinks, and they'd tell you about their stay, the hotel, and their entire family background.

"Hmm…," she hummed, as Fiona placed Rory's fresh drink in front of her, and I watched my bartender flush when Rory thanked her. It was a surprising reaction from Fiona. Not because she swung for her own team, but because she rarely let her attraction to a woman show. She kept her emotions as close to the vest as I did. Apparently, Aurora had that kind of effect on everyone.

The front desk manager had made me aware of how she came to Davey's rescue this afternoon when an irate guest cut in line and talked down to my newest staff member. I didn't believe him at first, because Aurora came across as a sweet Southern girl who held her tongue and only spoke when spoken to. But as I rewatched the security footage, I was almost proud of the way she stood up to the guest.

Gertrude Powers, of all people. Dean got a good laugh out of that one.

I spared a glance at my friend, who was keeping watch over the bar. He reminded me of a silverback gorilla hiding in the bushes, waiting for his prey. It was almost comical the way he stood out in the crowd.

"This is so good, Fiona. Give my compliments to the pastry chef or get me the name of the shop you guys order it from."

Fiona explained we had an in-house pastry chef who made these each day, and I noted the downward turn of Aurora's mouth at the news before she took another healthy bite of the treat. My cock jumped behind the zipper of my pants as her lips closed around the fork. I watched as Fiona scurried away quickly, probably experiencing a similar reaction to what I was.

"Wow, this is so good. Have you had it before?" she turned to ask me with another forkful poised at her mouth.

Biting back a groan, I replied, "Can't say that I have."

"You should really order one. It's probably the best I've ever had. Just don't tell my sister that."

I couldn't tell her that the simple dessert was made by one of the top pastry chefs out of France. The man was a genius but hated that this dish was his most popular.

"Why shouldn't I?" I questioned as I turned to face her fully, leaning my arm on the bar with the glass of bourbon in my hand.

"Shouldn't you what?"

"Tell your sister."

"Oh!" she exclaimed before those plump lips opened to welcome the morsel of chocolate into her mouth. Her eyes closed with the bite, and I was seconds away from having Fiona take the dessert off the bar top before I came in my pants like a juvenile. "Sorry. I can't stop eating this. Anyway, my sister owns a cake shop in our small town, but she gets orders in from all over the world."

"Really? What's it called?" I asked curiously. I didn't care to read the background check on Aurora. It felt like an invasion of her privacy, and even though I wouldn't be her real husband, I knew she'd be hurt if she ever found out.

"Show-Stopping Sweets."

I sputtered after the announcement. "Really?"

"Yep. She opened it last year all on her own, though her now fiancée invested in the business."

"I've had her cakes. They're delicious."

"They really are. She's a great baker."

"What about you?" I asked. "What is it you do?"

"I'm a teacher. I usually teach first grade, but this year they're moving me up to high school." Her body slumped as she said it, and I wasn't sure if it was because of the change in grade level or that she just finished her last bite of cake.

"You don't sound too thrilled about that."

"I love to teach. I've always been good with kids. I just have a hard time commanding attention from kids who aren't much younger than I am. Hell, I get mistaken for a teenager all the time."

Thinking back to my boarding school, I know I would have walked all over a teacher like Aurora. Most of the kids there would have seen her as weak and beaten her down until she caved. But remembering the way she spoke up for Davey, maybe she had an inner commanding strength she had yet to fully tap into.

"I don't think you'll have anything to worry about. After the way you—" I began, then halted my words, since there would have been no way for me to know what happened earlier.

"Oh, you saw what happened at check-in today?" she asked, and I realized there would have been people in the lobby at the time to witness the act.

"Yeah." It wasn't exactly a lie, though I felt a little guilty.

"I just don't enjoy seeing someone talked down to, especially when he had done nothing wrong. Plus, I hate line cutters."

"Don't we all?" We chuckled as I took another sip of my drink, and she peered down at her ruined papers.

"Was that *really* something important?"

She sighed as she gathered the papers and placed them in a tote hanging from a hook under the bar.

"It was just something I was interested in during the conference today. I teach in a rural area, so I wanted to learn more ways I could bring money to the school through grants and possible scholarships for the students. Most of the kids are from farming families. And while some are still very profitable, many are going under."

"Tell me more," I prompted, genuinely interested as she spoke about her family and their farm. It surprised me when she mentioned helping out and running the large tractors and combines. I had a hard time imagining it.

"Wow. I feel like I talked your ear off."

"I enjoyed learning more about you. Would you like another drink?" I asked as I reached for her empty glass.

"I probably shouldn't."

Her gaze darted around the room, and while her attention wasn't on me, I used the moment to take her in. Her picture didn't do her justice. She really was quite beautiful. Aurora was petite—I guessed no more than five feet and an inch or two at most. Her hair was tied back at the top of her head, but the waves looked soft, and I yearned to run my fingers through them. And my cock jumped every time I focused on her lips.

I watched as they pursed as her stare focused on something across the room.

That's when I noticed Gertrude standing.

"Ah. Enemy Number One."

"Not my enemy, but I have to be around her all week. I should probably apologize for earlier."

"No," I said more forcefully than I expected. Something about watching her cower to a bully didn't sit right with me. "She deserved more than the stern talking-to you gave her. I should have her kicked out of the hotel."

Laughing, Rory looked over her shoulder at me with a grin. Fuck, her smile was gorgeous.

"And how would you do that?" she asked, and I remembered I hadn't told her a thing about me. She'd find out soon enough though.

"By leaving a note in the suggestion box."

"Smart," she replied with another chuckle and turned her attention back to the women standing with Gertrude. "I just don't want them to ruin this conference for me, you know? Some people can be so vindictive."

Didn't I know it? She was sitting next to someone like that and would be marrying him if I got my way.

"So, that drink?" I asked, trying to take her mind off the group.

"I'm going to have to decline. My day starts early." She hopped off her stool and began gathering her things, pulling some cash from her wallet.

"Well, Talon, it was nice to meet you, and I enjoyed our chat. Enjoy your stay."

As she went to place the money and a piece of cardstock I recognized on the bar, I set my hand on top of hers. "I'll take care of it. Keep your money."

"What? No. I can pay for my stuff. Especially since I had a voucher for dinner."

"I know you can, but I'd feel better if you let me. You gave me your time tonight, so let me take care of your meal. Save your coupon for another night."

Her eyes searched mine, and it felt like I was under a bright-white light, being interrogated.

"If you're sure."

"Positive. Tonight is my treat."

"Well, thank you," she said hesitantly as she placed her wallet back in her bag.

"You're welcome. Maybe I'll see you again?"

Instead of answering, she shrugged but left me with a smile as she sauntered out of the lounge. Every man, even those who were there with someone, turned to watch her leave.

"I like that one," Fiona said from behind me.

Yeah, me too. And that was going to be a big problem.

The next morning, I arrived at my office before sunrise, just as I had every morning since moving to Miami. Only this time, I spent the night before tossing and turning and felt like a tractor trailer had hit me by the time I settled into my office chair.

I'd been thinking about Aurora as I went to bed and reminded myself I could not catch feelings for her. Absolutely none, or the entire plan would go to shit. I was not made to be a husband. All my examples in life had been shit to their wives. I would never want to put her through that. The marriage was temporary, with one goal in mind.

But during the night, I kept having visions of my mother and Aurora together. It was the memories of my mom as I remembered her. Young, full of life, and happy. Aurora had mimicked her in the dreams.

It felt so real that at one point I'd woken in a state of shock, not believing I'd been asleep. I was terrified of falling back to sleep and losing my mom all over again. That had been the hardest part—thinking she was alive and then waking to her being gone.

A knock on my door sounded, and I sat up in alarm, checking the time. It was only seven in the morning, and dawn was washing the sky in peaches, oranges, and pinks.

"Olive?"

My assistant peeked her head through the door.

"What are you doing here this early?"

"I couldn't sleep, so I figured I'd get started on that report you requested."

"Oh. Okay. Please make sure you leave early today then."

"Yes, sir. Also, Mr. Rossi called and will be here shortly."

Weren't we all just a lovely bunch of insomniacs?

"Thanks."

Something about Olive being in the office early didn't sit right with me, and I'd have to make a note for myself about it. She was usually the one who showed up late but got her work done, so I never questioned it.

While I waited on Dean, I pulled up an internet browser and searched for Show-Stopping Sweets. The page filled with a professionally done website that showcased the retro-style cake shop. It impressed me, to say the least. I clicked on the About Me section and was directed to a page where there was a picture of a smiling woman and a detailed paragraph next to it. I could see the resemblance between the woman named Alex and Aurora. It was clear they were related.

From what I read, it seemed Alex traded in her dancing career for cakes and desserts.

As I closed the browser, it left me wondering if being a teacher was what Aurora wanted in life. Was she one of those little girls who played school with her siblings, always wanting to be the teacher? Did she ask Santa for a desk and chalkboard? Or did she have bigger aspirations?

I needed to remember those were things I had no right knowing about her. Those were her secrets, and even as her husband, I would have no right to ask about them. It was all going to be temporary.

I had no idea why I had to keep reminding myself of that, and I hadn't even convinced her to be my wife yet.

There was a flash of movement outside my office door, and I glanced up to see Olive leaning over her desk while she spoke with Dean. I couldn't make out his expression, but from all appearances, she was trying to flirt, and he wasn't receptive to her advances.

"Dean!" I shouted, and Olive's back went rigid. Dean stepped past her and into my office.

After he crossed the threshold, he closed the door and flipped the switch to turn my office windows opaque. "Yo?"

"Stop letting my assistant flirt with you."

He guffawed as he sat in the chair across from me. We both knew he wasn't doing anything to lead her on.

"So," he began, "what did you think of our little bookworm?"

"Bookworm?"

"Yes. Aurora. She likes to read romance novels. Did you read any of the information I gathered for you?"

"No, just the demographics page in the front. It felt invasive." My collar felt tight against my neck as I thought about the extra information Dean had pulled on everyone. I only cared about what Aurora would think about it though.

"Aw. Maybe Talon Beckett has a heart after all."

No, just a dick that wanted a piece of my hopefully soon-to-be bride.

"Can it, Dean. I'm just as heartless as I was yesterday."

"Sure. I saw the way you were chatting her up last night. I've never seen you hold a conversation longer than a few grunts with a stranger. I thought Fiona was going to have you analyzed at the end of the night. The grumpy asshole we all love had been flirting with the blonde beauty like a love-sick teenager." Dean laughed like he was watching a chimp throw his own feces at a crowd.

"Are you done?" I asked, exasperated.

He held up his finger as he let out another moment of laughter, then calmed down.

"Finally. I do have a job for you."

"What am I? Your minion?"

Rolling my eyes, I explained how I needed his help this evening when I went to meet with Aurora and explain my plan. Something about her left me thinking she would not give me the time of day. I was going to need Dean to keep her from leaving. And possibly slapping me.

"You know I have a life."

"I do, but you also want to help me."

"And why is that again?"

"Because if you don't, then my family risks losing the hotels, or even worse, it goes to my cousin, who will probably turn them into brothels. And there is a good chance if I don't get full access to the trust fund that's rightfully mine, then I'll be sleeping on your couch."

Dean hummed as if considering my reasoning and found it lacking.

"And you want to do it for my mom." I knew mentioning my mom would seal the deal. Dean had lost his mother when he was ten to cancer. That had been another thing that further cemented our friendship. So, if anyone knew what it was like to want to do something for their deceased parent, then it was Dean.

"You're right. Plus, your family sucks. I can't believe they're sticking to all this old shit. I mean, who requires someone to get married to run a business or get full control of their bank account?"

"Apparently, my grandfather."

"And your grandmother has no say? Wasn't the hotel from *her* side of the family?"

"None of the men in this family listen to the women, which is a fucking joke. Grandma could run this place after a bottle of wine and her hands tied behind her back."

As if I conjured her, my cell phone rang with a video call from the person in question. I answered the call, smiling at the video of my eighty-five-year-old grandmother in her yoga room. She was more athletic now than I remembered her being when I was a child. Once my grandfather fell sick a decade ago, she began focusing on her own health.

"Oh man, Gigi!" Dean shouted from his seat. "Call a doctor. Talon's smiled twice in the last twenty-four hours."

"What? My sweet Talon smiled? Why?"

I sneered over the phone toward my friend and tried to silently mouth to keep his trap shut. But Dean snickered as he replied, "His girl is visiting."

"Girl!" Gigi, the name I gave my grandmother, shrieked. She moved from her yoga pose with arms extended in a lunge form, to standing with her hands resting at her heart. Not even excitement over a girl could break her from her yoga time. It always made me wonder why she usually chose this time to call me. I much preferred when she was in her sunroom that was decked out in psychedelic paintings, which matched her personality.

"Since when do you have a girl?"

Sighing, I explained, "A while." I hated lying to my grandmother, and seeing the excitement in her eyes left me feeling like a nasty piece of gum stuck to the bottom of a shoe.

Dean coughed at my lie.

"When do I get to meet her?"

"Um… soon… maybe."

"Maybe? What? Are you embarrassed of your Gigi?"

"No."

"Well, tell me about her. What's her name? Where is she from? Does she want a big family?"

"Oh, look. I have a meeting to get to. I'll call you later, Gigi."

"Fine. I know when you're being elusive. You don't have to tell me about your lady friend."

"Gigi…."

"I love you, Talon."

I sighed as I told her I loved her as well, then hung up the phone just as the video ended with her bending in a way I'd never witnessed any human bend.

Dean stood from his chair, winding his body around my small office like a snake. "I always did love your grandma. I like to think our moms would have been like that in their old age," he said wistfully.

I agreed with him, minus the craziness my grandmother exemplified. "Stop ganging up on me with her."

"I do what I want."

Boy, did I know that. I also tried my hardest not to let their antics get to me. Those two were the only ones who knew I wasn't a complete asshole, and I planned to keep it that way, especially with Aurora. If I ever let her past my barbed-wire fences, I was afraid I'd never let her out again. And that would cause even more problems than the fact that I was going to be lawfully hers.

"So, are you in?" I grunted, reminding Dean why he was here with me to begin with. He'd always had my back, even when I was a scrawny kid in boarding school. That didn't change as we became adults. He wanted to give my family a big fuck-you too, after the way they treated me when my mom and dad died.

"You know I am."

Leaning back in my chair, I crossed my arms over my chest and laid out my plans. "Okay. Here's what we're going to do."

Chapter Six

Aurora

My mother used to say we could make our own fate. Every choice we made could change that fate. It was ours to design.

And as I sat in another boring session, I thought about why I was there. To help make a change for those who could not. To help them change their fate. Kids of farmers usually never made it out of those picket fences. Most lived to carry on the family traditions, but with the downturn of local agriculture and most turning to massive manufacturing of grown goods, farms were being sold left and right, leaving nothing for those kids. They needed options, and I wanted to give them the best chance they could get. And not all kids were made to be farmers.

Aspen, was the only one with a true green thumb. She'd been my dad's shadow since she was little, but I worried she settled into her role because no one else stepped up. Andrew did what he could, but his knack was on the business side. Aspen was the one we all expected to take the helm when our father retired. Something I worried was going to happen sooner rather than later. And she was only in her early twenties.

As I sat listening to the pros and cons of Smart Board usage in the classroom, I should have been enraptured by the way we could utilize this newer technology. Instead of making notes and taking everything in, a stranger from the bar kept running through my mind. Why did he have to be so nice and so handsome? And he seemed to hang on to my every word. Something possessed me to stick around the bar far longer than I intended, and it took every ounce of my self-preservation to leave, when all I wanted to do was accept that fourth drink.

Though I was still miffed about my ruined packet. I asked the conference head if she could get me a copy, but that was going to take catching up with the speaker, who already caught a flight home. I tried to ask around for a copy I could make notes from, but no one had theirs on hand.

For whatever reason, I'd been the only one with an actual interest in the topic.

Plus, everyone had learned about my verbal scuffle with Gertrude, who seemed to be pretty popular amongst the teachers in attendance.

Of course she was. She and her horde of frizzy-haired mavens were the popular clique of the convention. It felt like high school all over again, and I worried if teaching at the local high school was going to feel the same way.

"That concludes our session for today. I'll hang around for the next five minutes if any of you have questions," the speaker said.

I glanced down as I gathered my things, harrumphing when I noticed all my blindly drawn doodles across the loose-leaf paper.

"Excuse me," a scratchy voice said from my aisle, and I looked up to find my supposed nemesis waiting to exit the row. I hadn't even noticed her there.

"Sorry," I replied as I twisted my body to the side for her and her friends to exit the row. I'd pack up afterward.

She glanced down at my paper and then giggled. "Aw, was all this talk of technology over your head? I can't imagine why you're even here for this session. Don't you use blocks and Play-Doh in preschool?"

I wanted to hold my tongue. I repeated in my head numerous times that she wasn't worth my time or anger. But as her friend purposefully knocked my papers to the floor, I'd had enough.

"I wouldn't know anything about preschool, since I'm qualified to teach both elementary and secondary school levels. I also know that preschoolers are better with most technologies than adults. I dare say probably better than you."

"Right." She huffed.

"I'm guessing you're embarrassed about what happened on the first day. That's okay. I mean, it's pretty common for bullies to underestimate me. But let me make a suggestion," I said once I stacked my papers, shoved them in my bag, and stood. "I'd be careful who you pick on. You may not know who they have standing in their corner."

With that, I shoved two business cards at her chest and walked off, not looking back to see if she struggled to catch them.

I knew the first thing that would happen was that she'd be riddled with confusion, then her friends would search the names of The Easterly Event Venue and Show-Stopping Sweets on their phones. It wouldn't take long for them to figure out the money and power I had to back me up. I didn't use my family often, but sometimes it was worth dropping our name.

Though I wished I could see her face when she figured out who I was related to.

But as I strolled down the long corridor, the guilt of using my sisters, and their famous other halves, Colton and Nate, to make me look more powerful started to get to me. The shame was… overwhelming.

I thought about finding Gertrude and explaining I shouldn't have done that, but the damage had been done, and once people knew who I had in my corner, they tended to treat me differently. I suspected that was why I'd been given a pay increase and what my superintendent called a "promotion." Even though it was just a move in grade levels.

As I entered the elevator car, the walls felt more constricting than before. And with every passing floor, my remorse grew until I felt as if I couldn't catch my breath. I tumbled out of the elevator and staggered over to a small seating area just outside the concierge area.

With shaking hands, I brought up the numbers for my sisters, Autumn and Alex. They both answered the group call quickly with a worried greeting. I was rarely the one to initiate conversations with my sisters.

"I did something."

"Oh! Did you finally get laid? Was it good?" Alex asked, and Autumn scolded her immediately.

"No, I didn't have a one-night stand."

Autumn calmly asked what was wrong, and I explained how I used their businesses to subliminally make it seem like they and their partners were powerful enough to bring down Gertrude and ruin her life.

"Well, they could," Alex said with a snicker. "I'm pretty sure Nate could do whatever you wanted."

"Colton too. Those guys would do anything for you, Rory. You're a sister to them too, you know."

"But I felt so dirty afterward."

"That's because you have a good heart. Better than any of us," Autumn tacked on.

"Did she deserve it?" Alex asked, and I felt myself smile for the first time since the encounter ten minutes ago.

"She and her friends were being complete bitches."

"Then, as Molly and Eloise would say, let it go."

I smiled, thinking of my soon-to-be nieces twirling around in their white-and-blue dresses.

"Okay. Thanks, you guys."

"So, you didn't get laid?" Alex grumbled, and I laughed.

"Have you met anyone?" Autumn added quickly, and I fell silent.

"Oh my gosh, you have!" one of them screamed. I couldn't determine which one, but I knew I needed to end the conversation quickly.

"Thanks for talking me through it. I'll see you guys when I get home in two days."

"Tell us everything!" one said, and the other shouted, "Rory, don't hang up!"

They knew me so well.

I disconnected the call, and messages immediately started pinging on my phone. I wasn't going to be able to keep them off my back for long. I had a feeling when I came home on Saturday that they'd be waiting with a bottle of wine, ready to learn all my secrets. I was lucky I didn't have many.

The guilt I'd been feeling melted away as I stood, and I felt like I was floating as I made my way to my room. With my phone in hand, I unlocked the door and tossed my bags onto the little end table nestled across from me in the hall. There was a mirror hanging above, and I peered at myself, noticing my eyes looked brighter and my cheeks were a subtle shade of pink. I wanted to think it was from the hour I spent out by the pool today after catching a drink during the concierge's happy hour between panels, but I knew it was from the conversation with my family. And maybe, just maybe, the daydreams about the guy from the bar helped.

Slipping off my shoes, I turned the corner, intending to rest before the closing dinner that evening. The convention hosted it, and I wanted to go, despite knowing I'd see Gertrude there. It would be worth it just to see how she'd treat me after learning about my family.

Before I could register what was happening, Talon greeted me from his perch on the small couch.

"Hello, Aurora."

"Wh-What are you doing here? How did you get in?" I asked, as clips from all the murder and crime shows I watched started filtering through my mind.

I left Talon no chance to answer as I spun around and darted out of the main room and toward the door, with every intention of leaving and calling the police. But just as I opened the door, I came face-to-face with the behemoth from the bar. I opened my mouth to scream, but he turned me around quickly and covered my mouth. His reflexes were crazy fast.

"Don't scream," he whispered in my ear, and I hated that his voice was velvety smooth. It was almost comforting, and wasn't that confusing? "Okay?" he asked after a moment, and I nodded. As he dropped his hand, I squirmed to get away, but he gripped my shoulders with his massive palms and carried my ramrod-straight body back into the main room.

"Sorry about this," Talon said. He was now standing at his full height, and instead of fear, I felt excitement at having him in my room. "I promise I'm not here to hurt you. I actually wanted to talk to you about something."

"You could have asked for my number like a normal person."

"I wouldn't need to ask. I have it already."

"What? How?" I squawked, my breath coming in pants.

"Because I own this hotel."

"You do?" He didn't look like any hotelier I'd ever seen. He reminded me more of a *GQ* model, straight off the cover of a magazine.

"Sort of."

"What does that even mean? And can you have your… beast… release me, please?"

As if Talon just realized his friend was holding onto my shoulders to keep me from leaving, he nodded in his direction and apologized once again. The man let go, and I rubbed my shoulders as if I were cold, but it was simply to get my blood flowing again.

"Sorry about that. This is my best friend, Dean."

Sarcastically, I said, "It's nice to meet you."

"Can we talk? I don't have a lot of time, unfortunately."

I was hesitant, but I had nowhere to go. And curiosity got the better of me. I wanted to hear what he had to say and how it involved me.

As I sat in one of the chairs, I noticed a stack of stapled papers resting on the coffee table. It looked freshly printed, the pages perfectly flat, no crease in the stapled corner, and when I inquired about it, a blush rose on his cheeks. My heart jumped inside my chest at seeing this vulnerable side of him.

"It's a copy of the packet that got ruined at the bar. I hunted down the speaker before they checked out, and I got you a copy."

Talon seemed anxious as he explained the gift, as if he wasn't used to doing something so thoughtful for someone else.

"Thank you," I said, my voice full of sincerity, as I reached for the packet and flipped through the pages. "I was really upset the speaker had already left and I couldn't ask for another copy. And no one else attending seemed to want to help me."

Gruffly, Talon responded, "I could have them all kicked out."

He looked so serious I almost expected him to growl.

"Um… that's okay. You came to my rescue. So, thank you."

"You're… welcome."

I could sense he was unfamiliar with someone thanking him for anything, which just left me feeling bereft and sad for him.

Dean coughed from over at his post in the kitchen and pointed to his very-expensive-looking watch. Talon got the hint and nodded.

"What's going on?"

"I don't have much time, but I wanted to ask you to do something for me."

"Is it illegal?" Was my first question, because gorgeous men like Talon and Dean didn't just show up in your room for nothing. I wondered if they were part of the mafia or the cartel. Of course, they would have charmed me first.

"Not technically."

"How is something not *technically* illegal? The law is pretty cut and dry. It either is or isn't, Talon."

The corner of his mouth quirked up as if he was amused. He stood from the couch and came to stand in front of me, then quickly dropped to his knees, grasping my hands in the process. I hoped they weren't sweaty.

The scent of his cologne washed over me, and the scent was familiar, but it wasn't just from the bar. There was something inside me that said we met before.

"I want you to marry me. To be my wife."

That was definitely *not* what I expected him to say. I wasn't even sure it would have fallen into the top hundred ideas of what he wanted my help with.

"Um… can you repeat that?"

"I want you to be my wife."

Why did that sound so good coming from him? But it seemed suspicious, and I found myself asking, "Want or need?"

"Told you she's smart," Dean chided from the kitchen, but my eyes were locked on Talon's.

"Need," he admitted. "My grandfather has a ridiculous rule that the heir has to be married to take over as CEO of the hotels. My uncle is running the chain down to the earth's core, but I can fix it. I just need to have a wife."

"I… I can't." I didn't need to tell him I'd made a mistake like that once before, and it had been the last time I'd done something without thinking of the ramifications.

"Can't or won't?"

"I…." I hesitated, and Talon swooped in.

"Please. It would be for six months, and then you'd be free to go. I'll pay you one-million dollars and take care of everything else that goes along with being my wife."

The money made saying no harder. Not that I could be bought, but there were so many people I could help with that much cash. Kids who came to school in dirty clothes after working the mornings in the fields. Kids who didn't think college was an option, because their family was already struggling to keep their farms or businesses afloat. And the town needed these farms and businesses to succeed.

Talon stared at me as he watched me cave with each passing second.

"What would everything entail?" I whispered.

"Anything. Clothing for events, designer handbags, shoes, cars—take your pick. We'll be photographed together at events, and tabloids are notorious for following me around when I travel."

"I've never seen you in a magazine before."

"Maybe you weren't looking at the right ones." That was true. I tended to read magazines other than celebrity gossip. When Colton came into our family, we all swore off the rags, because they notoriously published lies about him and Autumn. Nate always knew how to hide from photographers and lay low.

"That's fair. I don't pick those up too much."

"So, what do you say?"

I was torn. I knew I should say no. My past reminded me that I should decline. But the butterflies in my stomach fluttered wildly at the thought of saying yes. I was smarter than that though. I just needed to envision the disappointment of my family if I came home a married woman.

"I don't think I can," I whispered and watched the devastation consume Talon. Something about his reaction made it seem like he'd put all of his eggs in my basket. And I hated that I did that to him. Maybe there was a way we could compromise.

"What if I let you think about it? I'll leave the contract with you, and you can read it over. Please, Aurora. I promise I'll make it worth your while. I can answer any questions you have." He checked the expensive looking watch on his wrist and mumbled a curse. "I have to head to a meeting. Aurora, please give it a shot."

"Okay," I caved. If there was a contract, I could look at this entire thing as a business transaction. No hearts would be broken at the end. No family wreckage when the two of us went our separate ways. No picking up my pieces like before.

"Tomorrow?" he asked with childish hope in his eyes. His thumbs rubbed across my knuckles, and I never wanted him to stop.

"I'll let you know tomorrow," I croaked.

Talon stood with a flourish, and I fell back into the chair, more exhausted than I'd ever felt in my entire life. My eyes were drawn to his retreating back… and lower, and just as he turned the corner, he peered over his shoulder and winked at me.

Damn my stomach for flip-flopping in response.

Dean lingered in my kitchen, and I felt embarrassed that he witnessed my perusal of his friend. He smirked at me in that sneaky way, as if he knew my darkest secrets. And I feared maybe he did, and they had nothing to do with Talon.

"He'll do right by you," Dean assured as he turned to leave, and I watched him turn the corner. My eyes stayed glued to the wall far after I heard the door to my room slam shut.

Dean must have known the weight of his words, because they were carried with me through dinner and drinks, and then later in bed.

He said Talon would do right by me, but would I do the right thing for myself?

Chapter Seven

Talon

Leaving Aurora's room the night before had taken every bit of strength I had. She calmed me in a way that no one ever could. And even though I was throwing this outlandish suggestion her way, she stayed and listened. I could honestly say I wouldn't have done the same.

In the elevator, Dean assured me she would say yes to the contract. I wasn't so positive. But he was confident, and that left me wondering what about her past would steer her in that direction.

At my apartment, I spent the better part of the night thinking about how I could convince her to say yes. A hundred different reasons and scenarios came to mind, but I had a feeling all it would take was honesty. Aurora seemed like a woman who didn't care for being lied to, which was why she was hesitant in the first place. All of this would be one big lie.

My thoughts sprang back and forth—when I wasn't imagining all the ways she'd say no, I was making plans of how to make her say yes. She would be mine, and I wondered if she'd let me have her more than just on paper. I thought about running my hands through her thick hair and grasping it in my fist as I thrust my cock down her throat. I bet she made the most delicious sounds.

All of that was pushed to the wayside when my phone chimed with a message from Allison. She had the audacity to threaten me after I kicked her out the day I found her in my bed. I regretted ever sleeping with her in the first place, and I was certain we didn't have sex the night she snuck into my bed. Completely certain... except the small sliver of worry that crept down my spine like a spider.

Allison

> You're going to pay for what you did. I'm going to ruin you, Talon!!!

After taking a screenshot of the message, I sent it off to my lawyer with a note about what happened the night I called security on her. He said he would take care of it, and if she tried to claim a pregnancy as a way to trap me, I'd have evidence of her malicious intentions.

What was I doing, bringing someone good and sweet like Aurora into my life? All I knew and was surrounded by was deceit and greed. Everyone was looking out for themselves. Other than my grandmother, no one in my life—not even in my family—truly cared about anyone else.

I wouldn't put it past my uncle to partner with Allison to keep me from taking over the company. That man seemed to make it his life's work to make mine hell. It was why he refused to step down as CEO, instead spending his time wandering about with his girlfriends, not even caring about the trouble his kids were getting in.

My work out this morning had been brutal. I'd overstretched my muscles by extending my run three miles longer than normal and now I was paying for it. My legs felt like jelly as I sat behind my desk. I thought about using the hotel pool to cool them down, but fire after fire landed on my desk after a rough case of food poisoning hit a couple of guests. Luckily, I was able to narrow it down to a local restaurant across the street that had served all the parties involved. My keen eye kept us from a nasty lawsuit that I really didn't want on my plate while I tried to take over the hotel.

"Mr. Beckett, Mr. Wilder is on line two," Olive announced through our phone system. I always found it interesting that the men who married into the Wilder family took their wife's last name. For as traditional as they claimed to be, it was the most unconventional thing ever. Gigi said my uncle couldn't wait to change his last name to Wilder after he married my mom's sister. Which was yet another mark against my mother when she ran off with my dad. She wanted to take his last name, and her father scoffed that she had the audacity to drop the Wilder name. Whenever my aunt or grandmother told me the stories of why my mother distanced herself from her family, the Wilder name was always the first thing they mentioned.

I didn't want to speak with my grandfather. He was the reason I was in this entire mess to begin with, but I knew if I didn't, he'd continue to call until I answered. Better to get it over with and give myself more time to agonize over what answer Aurora would give me.

"Hello, Grandfather," I said as I picked up the phone.

"I hear you have a girlfriend," were the first words from his mouth. I had my grandmother to thank for that one. I hoped her excitement wouldn't be my downfall.

"Rumor mill swirling again?"

"Is it true?"

"I'm not discussing my relationship status with you."

I could almost sense his sneer on the other end of the line. My grandfather did not take kindly to those that talked back to him.

"You will if you want my company."

"You mean the company that should have gone to my mother?" I argued back. I was done playing these stupid games with the old man. He knew where I stood on the subject of the hotels and who should have inherited them.

"Watch your tone, boy," he growled and then body numbing coughs wracked his body. I wanted to feel sorry for him and his declining health, but a twisted part of me blamed him for my mother's death. He and his stupid rules were the reason she left and felt isolated. He could barely look at me growing up and I ended up losing the only connection I had to my mother. If it hadn't been for Gigi, I probably would have left the family when I turned eighteen and cut all ties.

"What is it you want? Some of us are working to keep these hotels afloat, you know?"

"Is there a girl?" he repeated.

"Have I attended any events with a woman in the last year?"

He hesitated and then replied, "Not that I can recall."

"Have I been photographed with anyone recently?"

"Nothing that I've witnessed," he said solemnly.

"So, what's your conclusion?"

"That you have a woman in your life."

He couldn't see my eyes gleam that he played right into my hand. Convincing him that I was happily married was going to be easier than I thought.

"Maybe you're right and it's serious. No need to feed the gossip rags. Or maybe you're wrong."

"Do we know her?" he questioned, assuming the answer was yes. Gigi must have sat him down with a checklist.

"Maybe."

"Does she come from a good family?" Just from what I knew about Aurora and her sister, I would mark that checkbox as yes.

"Maybe."

"Boy…." He snarled, and I wondered if his face turned as ruddy as a tomato. It probably wasn't good for his heart, not that I cared.

"Make sure to send my regards to Gigi."

I quickly ended the call and asked Olive to block all my calls from him for the rest of the day. I had a woman I hoped to see soon, and I didn't want to be interrupted.

Dean and I waited on the dock that jutted out into Biscayne Bay. I'd chartered a small boat in case Aurora agreed to a ride. I wasn't sure if she was a fan of the ocean. Most of the women I'd been with would only step foot on a boat that was larger than most people's homes.

I'd left a message with a concierge desk to request Aurora's presence tonight. She's eluded me all day, which left me… restless. I'd been hoping that she would have sought me out earlier, eager to agree to my arrangement, but as the evening grew closer, I feared she was truly going to turn me down. Dean didn't agree.

He hovered close by, waiting impatiently for this one woman to put me out of my misery. With a quick glance at my watch, something that I had purchased the first day I turned eighteen and had gained half of the access to my trust fund, I noticed Aurora was a minute late. Looking up, my eyes connected with Dean's, and he shook his head once.

She wasn't going to show up. With that premonition, my hopes dwindled.

I didn't need her to want to marry me. Hell, she didn't even have to like me. Most people didn't. I just needed her to help me get what should have been handed to my mother. She could have wiped her hands clean of me when we were done. She'd never have to see me again, as far as I was concerned. I ignored the ache in my chest at that thought.

I took a step toward Dean, wondering how we were going to start over. He had mentioned the bridal show happening next weekend. It wasn't ideal, but I could make it work. Someone there was likely to want one-million dollars to pretend to be my wife.

"Hey!" I heard a breathy voice shout from behind me.

Turning around, I watched with wide eyes as Aurora skipped down the steps, waving at a few smiling passersby as she made her toward me. An orange-colored sundress swirled around her ankles, and her hair hung loosely around her shoulders. She reminded me of the early dawn. Bright and alluring. Her name suited her perfectly.

"You're late," I said as she came closer. My default tone came out as I forced myself to keep my arms weighted at my sides. Her eyes dimmed just slightly, but her smile widened as she stopped a foot or two away from me.

"Sorry about that. I scheduled a massage, and I was enjoying it so much--" she rambled on, but I was focused on the fact that someone had their hands on her body, smoothing oils over her skin. I didn't want anyone touching what was mine.

"Are you okay?" she asked, reaching out to touch my arm, but I flinched in reaction.

"I'm fine." Usually, I could hold back my reaction to someone touching me, but hers had been unexpected.

"So," I prompted, hoping she'd end my misery and accept my proposal. "Did you make a decision?"

She took a deep, shaky breath, and my eyes darted down to the rise of her breasts behind the deep v-cut of her dress.

"At first, I was adamant at turning you down. What you wanted me to do was ridiculous." Hope flickered in my chest, blossoming into a full-blown fire as her words sunk in. "But then I thought about it, and I figured if I could help you, you could help me."

"What is it you want besides money?" I asked. I'd never met anyone like Aurora, and she continued to bewilder me.

"I have a proposition for you, Talon Beckett, if you'd like to hear it. Accept mine and I'll accept yours."

The little gleam in her sparkling brown eyes left me more than curious, in both a good and bad way. What is it she could possibly want from me? Was money not enough? I supposed I could up the amount for her, but one million seemed adequate. Did she want more luxury? I knew my cousin was materialistic, but I didn't imagine Aurora being that way. But what did I really know about her?

I didn't know how to respond and instead replied with my trademark grunt as the captain of the boat I chartered asked if we were ready to go. Dean stepped over to speak with him as I held out my hand for Aurora.

"Want to join me, Aurora?"

I watched in fascination as she licked her lips and glanced down at my outstretched hand. It took everything in me to keep it from shaking. I'd never been this nervous around a woman before.

"Um… okay. Though I really should get back to the hotel."

"We won't be out long."

Nodding, she placed her hand in mine, and I clasped her delicate fingers. Everything about her seemed small and fragile.

As we walked over to the boat, she glanced around the dock. Twinkling lights canopied the walkways, making it appear like we were walking in the stars.

"You know," she began quietly as we approached the boat, as if offering a piece of herself no one knew. Her breath fanned over my cheek as I leaned down to hear her. "You can call me Rory. Everyone else does."

"I think Aurora suits you," I said in return.

As the captain spoke up and assisted her into the boat, our moment was broken. I followed closely behind, though not taking Dean's assistance. The asshole even held out his hand with a cunning smile.

A table was placed out on the front deck with a light meal, and I ushered Aurora over to a seat, pulling it out for her to sit in. When our arms brushed, I tried to ignore the fact that her nipples pebbled beneath the slip of a dress she wore.

I was fucking awe-struck.

"Sir, are you ready for us to proceed?" a voice asked from behind me, and I nodded, then swiftly took my seat across from my guest.

The boat started off slowly, as I had instructed. I'd booked a casual cruise around the bay. Nothing too extreme. Just something to do while we ate dinner and discussed the contract, if she was interested in saying yes.

The breeze off the ocean rustled the tablecloth, and I watched as a shiver passed through Aurora. The skin on her arms erupted into little chill bumps, her nipples beneath her dress becoming even more visible. I tore my eyes away from them as I slipped off my suit jacket. Moving around the table, I draped it over her shoulders and relished the thankful smile she sent my way. As I settled back in my seat, I huffed a small chuckle when I noticed she slipped her arms fully into the jacket and was currently cuffing the sleeves to expose her hands.

It was fucking adorable.

"Are you hungry?" I asked, and the hair around her shoulders fanned out as she shook her head.

"Can we talk about… things first? My stomach is in knots."

"Of course."

"If—and that's a big if…," she began, then inhaled deeply. "If I say yes, I'd like to review the entire contract first, and I'd like you to agree to be my date at my ex's wedding," she said in one long breath.

I was astounded. That was it? All she wanted was for me to be her date at her—

"At your ex's wedding?"

"It's a long story. So, what do you say?"

"Dean!" I called out, and my friend immediately rushed out from the cabin and brought a stack of papers with him. The contract that would bind her to me for the next six months.

When I didn't offer my thanks to my friend, Aurora did, and I didn't miss the twinkling wink and smirk he sent to her in response.

"Please read it over. It's pretty straightforward—time frame, required functions, name change, stipend."

"Name change?" she questioned as she quickly flipped through the pages to find the section that required her to change her last name during our marriage. To make the ruse more believable to my family, it was one of the conditions. That's what I explained to her as we traveled along the coast of the bay.

"We'll handle all the paperwork for you and get all your new legal documentation like social security card and license."

"What?" Her eyebrows crawled up her forehead. "How?"

I shrugged. "Lawyers. People. It pays to have money."

The boat's motor rumbled, but I was fairly certain I heard her mutter, "Must be nice."

"The stipend… is that like a monthly allowance on top of the one-million, or part of it? Also, how will the payout occur?"

God, she was fucking smart. I could guarantee no one else Dean chose would have even thought of that. They would've been more excited to gain my name and be associated with my family.

"The stipend is part of the one million. You'll receive the first quarter of it the day we turn in the license. We will deposit the second quarter of these allotments each month for six months. And when we terminate the marriage, you'll receive the remaining half." This set-up was how I was to guarantee the woman I chose stayed married to me for the six months. Dangling that last half-million over their head was my ticket to keeping her close.

"Makes sense," she said, as if she were discussing nothing more than the daily news.

"Now, these functions may be an issue. Some of them fall on weeknights, and that doesn't work for me. Can we switch them out for something on the weekends?"

I respected she wanted to keep her teaching job and saw that as her priority, not being my wife, but I wanted to argue that she wouldn't have to work anymore. Or at least not while we were married. I was hoping she would take a year off to make it that more believable. But the longer I sat and thought about it, I realized her job was perfect. It was why I'd chosen to find someone at the teachers' convention, after all. No one would question her motives if she kept teaching, especially not the tabloids. They were going to make her life hard enough as it was.

"I'll have my assistant look over the calendar." I asked her to search my suit jacket for a red pen to make the amendment. Her handwriting was curvy and fun, just like she was. Dean liked to say my scrawl was akin to a doctor's. One he could barely read.

She flipped the contract to the front, then started reading over the second page of the document. I watched her at first, enchanted by the way she bit her bottom lip when she reached the halfway point on the paper. That was the section that discussed the vows and that we would keep up all marital appearances as needed. The "as needed" included housing, bedroom and public displays of affection. As much as I needed to keep my hands to myself with regards to Aurora, it wouldn't be a hardship to play house with her.

The setting sun's reflection shimmered on the water, and a fuzzy memory of sitting by a lake with my mom popped into my mind. The sun looked almost the same as it does now.

Shaking my head to rid myself of the vision, I lifted the silver tops off the large salad plates. The spinach and lettuce mix was a dark-green, contrasting with the sliced strawberries, pears, and mandarin oranges. The chef bottled his homemade salad dressing, and it sat in the middle of the table.

"Eat," I commanded as she flipped to the next page of the contract. In the short time it took for me to set up our meal, she had already read halfway through the document, which amazed me.

She lifted her head, eyes sparkling, as she smirked in my direction. "Is this part of the 'obey' section of the vows?"

Fuck, this woman was testing me in the best sort of way.

"Not even close," I replied as I offered her the dressing.

As we ate, she continued to read over the contract, asking a few questions here and there, but Aurora was brilliant enough to figure almost all of it out. Even the legal jargon.

With her final bite of food, she reached into the suit pocket and found the black ink pen.

"Before I sign this, are you sure this is what you want to do? Don't you want to marry someone for love?"

"This is the only way. Love isn't in the cards for me. All it ever did was destroy my family."

Aurora nodded; her lips turned downward as the pen hovered over the signature line.

"You barely know me," she whispered without looking up. And I knew what she was really saying. She had no idea who she was signing her life over to. Even if it was temporary.

"I know enough," I responded as genuinely as I could muster. "And we'll have time."

Aurora seemed to think for a minute as she trained her eyes on the contract, then surprisingly lifted her gaze to lock eyes with me, signing her name on the dotted line at the same time.

"So." My voice cracked, so I cleared my throat. "You agree?"

"Yes, Talon Beckett. I'll marry you."

Chapter Eight

Aurora

The boat ride with Talon had been romantic, which left me more confused when we docked than when we set off. It was unexpected. In the short time spent together, I'd grown accustomed to his snarky, one-word responses and stand-offish demeanor.

When I met him, I was already flustered. Running late was not something I made a habit of. Neither was lying. And I fibbed to Talon when I told him I was late because of a massage. That was only partially the truth, and if he cared to check, he would see I left the massage table three hours prior to our meeting.

Unfortunately, I used up my time on a call with Franny. She could tell I was out of sorts, even though I tried to play it off as being forlorn about leaving Miami and flying home. She didn't buy it for a second, but I had a suspicion Talon didn't want anyone knowing about his proposal. Franny kept prying for information about my mood, and I tried to be strong and fend her off. But I'm not sure I was that successful.

She let it slip that Jeremy and his family had begun infiltrating the town as they prepped for the wedding in a couple of months. His fiancée had been nowhere in sight though, which left everyone suspicious.

I'd been suspicious from the start. I didn't know what game Jeremy was playing, but I was going to be prepared. And now I'd have Talon by my side to fend off my grubby ex.

Talon. He was so handsome it hurt to look at him in those finely made suits. When our eyes locked, I felt like a giddy schoolgirl catching the attention of the most popular boy. And though Talon's smiles were few and far between, they were lethal. My heart stopped beating anytime he shot one in my direction. I was worried about taking another risk by agreeing to marry him, but then he looked at me and I feared I'd never feel those butterflies in my stomach again.

After six months with him, I was likely going to need an intervention to break the spell he's going to unknowingly put me under.

That was if we were together more than the few events he had listed in the contract. For all intents and purposes, it seemed like he'd stay in Miami for work, and I'd continue on with my life in Ashfield. I had no reason to get worked up about close contact with Talon, because it would be a rarity.

Or so I hoped.

Something about the way he was looking at me with a mixture of anticipation and worry left me with no choice but to sign the contract. Though, if I were being honest, I had very little reservations about signing to begin with. Something about Talon intrigued me. Maybe it was the mysterious air he had about him or that he looked like a man who desperately needed a hug.

And if anyone was going to give it to him, it was me.

Well, my tamped-down rebellious side. *She* really liked Talon.

I knew what I was signing up for—six months as Mrs. Talon Beckett. My identity was no longer my own. All of me was going to be wrapped up in him.

A quick internet search could have told me *everything* I was signing up for, but I felt like that would've somehow been a betrayal to him. He asked for help, and I was willing to give it, because what did I have to lose? Well, my last name for starters, but that could be easily rectified after the six months were up. My boss was either going to fawn over the development or horrified. I could only pray it was the former. The latter could very well cost me my job. And there weren't many alternatives for teachers in Ashfield. My heart was safe and secure in her pretty little lockbox deep inside my chest. I learned my lesson about falling for pretty words and a dashing smile. It happened more than once—a fool, I was.

But I was on guard around Talon, and as he escorted me back to my room that night, I tried to remember this was nothing more than a farce. He pressed a quick kiss to my cheek at my door and hurried away when his phone rang. It was strange, but I knew he was a busy man.

I was leaving Miami the next morning and hoped to have some sort of idea when Talon and I were going to be officially married. But I had to rely on the fact that he said he was going to handle it all. That knowledge left me feeling like a mail-order bride.

Those were some of my favorite romance books.

That night, I was afraid I wouldn't sleep a wink, but the minute my head hit the pillows, I drifted off into the best kind of dreamland.

My alarm shrieked in an obnoxious tone earlier than I cared for. My flight from Miami was scheduled to depart at 8:00 a.m., and I wanted to give myself plenty of time to get to the airport and head over to the terminal. There was likely a chai latte in my future as well. And possibly a mimosa in the first-class lounge.

I packed my suitcase the night before, so all I needed was a quick shower and to order a ride share to take me to the airport. The warm spray was something I'd definitely miss compared to the showerhead in my little house. The poor pressure and standard setup were something I hated since I moved in.

As I packed up my toiletry bag post-shower, I glanced in the mirror and was surprised at the flatness in my eyes. I looked… sad. Lost. Like I was leaving a piece of myself in Miami. And maybe I was. Talon was staying here, and he was going to be my husband, after all.

"That's all it is," I murmured as I carried the small, clear bag to my suitcase and zipped it in the front pouch.

I triple-checked the room to make sure I wasn't leaving anything behind. The fresh grant packet Talon procured for me was still sitting on the coffee table, and I hastily grabbed it and placed it in my bag.

After my final walkthrough, I grabbed my suitcase and checked the app for the ride share's distance. The vehicle was still around fifteen minutes from the hotel, since I'd chosen the option to get my ride cheaper if I waited a little longer, but I decided to go wait in the lobby instead of sitting in my room. The quicker I left this beautiful suite, the faster I could get back to my normal, boring life, which would hopefully equate to getting over this low feeling more swiftly.

Strangely deflated, I opened the door with my free hand, not expecting to come face-to-face with Dean. He reminded me of a hitman awaiting my arrival. If he hadn't smiled when I stepped over the threshold, I might have worried he was going to end my life.

That notion still simmered at the back of my mind as he gripped my elbow and directed me toward the elevators.

"Where are we going?" I asked, alarm rising with each step I took. I knew better than to try to wriggle my arm free. If he was anything like my college ex, he would only grip it tighter.

Dean remained silent as we loaded the elevator car and pressed the button for the lobby. I gazed up at him, my head tilting back in the process.

"Dean?"

My escort only grunted his response.

"Aw… couldn't let me leave without saying goodbye? You're too sweet."

He finally cracked a minute grin just as the elevator dinged our arrival on the lobby level.

"Well, Dean," I said, holding out my hand once we both exited the car. "It was a pleasure to meet you. I'm still not sure if you work for Talon, or if you're his bodyguard, or his lover, but please let him know to keep me in the loop about… everything. Okay?"

"Come with me," he demanded and turned on his heel to head down the corridor where I registered for the conference. I stood back, staring after him for a moment, then quickly grabbed my suitcase and hurried to catch up.

By the time I was in step beside him, Dean was mumbling about me saying he was Talon's lover, and I found myself giggling as he opened the door to what looked like a slew of offices. Following him down the hall, I noticed only the office at the very end had the lights on. It was still early in the morning, but I figured a manager or two would be on duty.

"Where are we?" I asked, suddenly nervous that we were in a space we shouldn't have been. "Dean!" I whispered more urgently. "We can't—"

My words stopped abruptly when Dean opened the door to the lit-up office, and I found Talon standing inside.

"Aurora."

I stepped over the threshold, leaving my suitcase in the hall, but Dean cut me off. "Talon, what am I—"

"She said I was your lover, asshole."

"What?" Talon asked, jerking his gaze from me to the beast standing beside me with his arms crossed against his massive chest.

"She thought we were fucking, dude."

Talon seemed to think on that for a moment. His eyebrows pinched, and that muscle along his jaw ticked. He didn't need to know I wanted to trace his jawline with my tongue. After a few seconds, he looked back at me with a tilted head. "Top or bottom?"

I sensed he was trying to rile up his friend, so I peered up at Dean and assessed him before I replied with a smirk. "He's a bottom."

"Ah, fuck you both," Dean growled as he stomped across the room, arms stiff at his sides and fists clenched.

Talon shrugged. "Guess his blip on the gaydar is reserved only for Bruce Willis. He's had a serious man-crush on him since we were young."

"Damn right," we heard Dean grump from his post by the door, and we finally laughed.

Tucking away that little tidbit about the guys knowing each other since they were kids, I asked, "So, what am I doing here? I need to head to the airport for my flight."

Talon spun around to grab something from the desk while Dean leaned against a large console table, looking way less annoyed than he had a minute earlier.

"Talon, my ride will be here in a couple of minutes," I said urgently. "Is there something you needed?"

"Yes, we're getting married."

"I know. Just let me know when to show up in a white dress," I joked.

"No. Now," Talon corrected as he held out a piece of paper for me. I took it reluctantly and read the header. It was a marriage certificate.

"Now?"

"Yes. My lawyer will be here shortly to serve as a witness."

Heat started crawling over my skin, as all of this was supposed to happen within the next few minutes. "What…?" I licked my lips. "What about Dean?"

"He's going to perform the ceremony."

My mouth hung open as I looked at Dean again. His smile was wide and showcased a set of perfectly straight teeth. He must have had braces, because I'd never seen a natural smile so flawless.

"Ah, Mr. Daniels. Did you bring it?" Talon went to greet a newcomer at the door, who held a small black bag in his hand.

"Yes, sir."

"Good."

"Uh, hello," I said in greeting as the man briskly walked by me and placed two velvet boxes in Talon's waiting hands. The marriage license shook like a leaf in a strong breeze within my hold as I witnessed the exchange.

The man paid me no mind as he moved to the back corner of the office, as Talon placed one box on his desk. In one step, he came closer to me, slipped the paper from my hand, and placed it back on the desk behind him. Then he faced me. His lips were downturned, and his eyes looked… sad.

My breath caught in my throat as he held the box between us and lifted the top. I glanced down quickly, afraid of what I might find, only to breathe a sigh of relief when it was two simple wedding bands. One in classic gold, the other in a dark metal I wasn't familiar with.

"Ready?" Talon asked, and I glanced up to find his stare on me, waiting for my reaction.

"Um… yes, I am." I wasn't at all, but he didn't need to know that. I didn't wake up this morning thinking I'd be Mrs. Beckett before I even hopped on the plane to go home.

Talon called Dean's name, and as the man approached—in far better spirits than when we entered the room—he took the rings out of the box, placing them in his pocket. Dean then reached into the inside pocket of his suit jacket and pulled free a slip of folded paper.

"Please turn to face each other. I assume you want the quick version?"

Talon nodded, and I replied with a brisk, "Sure."

Dean bobbed his head once and then began speaking, but I couldn't recall a single word he said. I felt like I was in an alternate universe, and it was all happening far too quickly for me to catch up. Talon must have sensed my incoming panic, because I suddenly felt his fingers on mine before he clasped my hand within his firm grip. His touch immediately soothed me, and I thought maybe he needed my touch to anchor him as well.

I turned my head to look at Dean, who winked in my direction as he continued to read the passage.

"Do you, Talon Beckett, take Aurora Easterly to be your lawfully wedded wife, to live together in matrimony, to love her, to honor her, to comfort her, and to keep her in sickness and in health, forsaking all others, for as long as you both shall live?"

"I do," my almost-husband said with a genuine smile I could get used to.

Dean repeated the section for me.

"I do," I replied, excitement building in my stomach as my heart pounded like a bass drum in my chest.

Soon, we were reciting the second part. I thought it was interesting that we were repeating the very old, traditional vows, when there were modern and less… oath-like versions these days. Either way, Talon smirked when he heard me promise to obey, even though he had made the same commitment just moments before. That was a line most of the ceremonies at our event venue left out.

Reaching deep within his pocket, Dean captured the rings in his fist. He lifted his hand, opened it with his palm facing up, and exposed the two gleaming bands.

"Talon, please place this ring on Aurora's finger and repeat the following: 'I give you this ring as a token and pledge of our constant faith and abiding love.'"

Talon lifted the ring from Dean's palm, and I swore I saw just the slighted shiver in his hand before he slipped the ring onto my finger, reciting the words.

I did the same when it was my turn, and Dean concluded the swift ceremony with the pronouncement of us being husband and wife.

"Talon, you may kiss your bride."

I heard Dean chuckle as I quickly exclaimed, "Oh, you don't have to—!" But the rest of my words were left unspoken, as Talon sealed his lips over mine after sliding his hands on either side of my face, his fingers delving into my hair.

I stood there motionless as our mouths connected, and when his tongue begged for entrance, there was nothing I could do but grant him access. My internal rebel wanted this kiss more than my next breath. She didn't care what happened to average-Joe Rory; she wanted her taste of Talon.

Off in the distance, someone coughed. Then I vaguely heard Dean say, "Knock it off," before Talon pulled away. He looked as dazed as I felt.

The kiss had been a surprise, but so was my reaction. I'd never been kissed like that before.

"You're going to miss your flight."

As if pulled out of a swamp, I came alert instantly and spun around the office, searching for the time. A clock on the wall showed an entire hour passed since I left my room.

I didn't even feel like we'd been here for that long. Something about being in Talon's presence made all my surroundings fall to the wayside.

"Shit," I murmured as I pulled out my phone to find a negative review from my ride share driver and a bill for the missed fare. "I missed my ride share too."

"I'll take care of it," Talon insisted, and I wasn't going to argue. It *was* his fault, after all.

"That's great and all, but how am I going to get home? My family is relying on me." I made it seem far more urgent than it was, but I knew I needed to get back to my life.

Talon grabbed his cell phone, pressed a button, and put his phone to his ear. "Charlie, I need a flight to Tennessee within the next three hours." He listened to the person on the other end before finishing the call abruptly. "Your flight now leaves in two hours."

"That's when my old flight was going to leave. I won't get through security in time," I tried to explain, but he was busy grabbing a few things and sending a message on his phone.

"Talon," I said more urgently.

"I chartered you a private plane to get you home. You won't have to go through security when you're with me."

"You're coming?"

Talon walked up to me and pressed his lips to my forehead. I bit my cheek to keep from smiling. He didn't need to see how deeply I enjoyed that show of affection.

"No."

True to his word, Talon escorted me all the way up the stairwell of the plane on the hot tarmac. Dean didn't travel with us, and even though the car was empty sans the driver, it felt like another presence was in the vehicle.

Probably my wild child's guilt filling the space. She enjoyed that kiss with Talon a little too much.

The flight attendant grabbed my suitcase from his grasp and stored it inside the plane, leaving me and Talon standing alone just outside the plane.

"So, you'll just call or message me the details for the first event?" I asked, twisting my hands in front of my body.

"Something like that," he grunted as he scrolled through something on his phone that appeared to be far more interesting than my leaving.

"Classes will begin soon, so hopefully you'll be able to rearrange a few of them."

Silence grew, and I was ready to bid him farewell and head into the plane. I was quite curious about the interior.

Suddenly, a wicked grin slithered across Talon's lips, and I felt like there was a secret I was not made privy to.

"Something going on?" I inquired as he finally slipped his phone into his suit pocket and gave me his full attention.

"Nothing for you to worry about."

That ominous reply didn't leave me feeling any better.

"I have something else for you," he added as he reached into his pants pocket and brought out something clasped tightly in his fist. "Hold out your left hand."

My eyebrow cocked immediately at his demand.

"Please?"

I lifted my hand, the gold band shining under the Florida sun, and held it between our bodies. Instead of glimpsing at Talon's hands, I focused on his face as he slid something heavy onto my finger.

"Better," he declared, taking a step back.

With a shuddering breath, I peered down at my hand and gasped. The largest diamond I'd ever seen was resting on my ring finger, just above the wedding band I gained that morning.

"Talon… it's too much."

"It's not."

It looked like a golf ball perched on my slim fingers. A little too flashy for my taste, but I didn't want to disappoint Talon, especially since I'd be giving it back to him in six months.

"It's… beautiful," I told him, not wanting to lie.

The flight attendant peeked out from the plane's entrance, alerting us that the pilot was ready to take off.

"Okay, I guess I should head inside. I'll see you in a few weeks?"

"Sure."

"Take care of yourself, Talon. I think what you're doing to save the hotels is admirable."

He nodded. It felt awkward leaving him, as I watched him descend the stairs, waving down at him when he turned to look back up at me, but all that unease fell away as I took in the lavish chartered jet.

At least I was going to arrive back in Ashfield in style. Because once we landed, my life was going to return to normal.

Chapter Nine

Aurora

Miraculously, the plane landed in Nashville with time to spare before Franny was scheduled to pick me up. She had put her foot down with my brother, demanding that she be the one to give me a ride home—no doubt so she could pry more details out of me about my trip. It was hard to disembark the opulent aircraft filled with supple tan leather and shiny fixtures. The facilities were nicer than my bathroom at home. The entire experience left me feeling a little jealous of the nicer things Talon was able to surround himself with.

And a bit worried I made the wrong decision. Maybe he only wanted to save the hotel chain from his uncle because he was afraid of being *normal*. But I suspected there was more beneath the surface, like an iceberg in the ocean. There was always something larger than what the naked eye could see.

As the attendant helped guide me down the stairs, I wasn't sure what would wait for me once I landed. The fear of the paparazzi catching wind of the abrupt nuptials crawled over my skin. I didn't want to be front and center of a magazine. That was never an ambition of mine.

Thankfully, the coast was clear, and all that greeted me was a standard security guard to check through my bag as I entered the airport. I'd messaged Franny when I landed to let her know I arrived safely. She was still twenty minutes away.

Inside the small airport, I busied myself with some freshening up in the bathroom and grabbing a drink from the small coffee shop. I sat in a corner seat, watching people gather their bags off the conveyor and sipping my beverage, when the enormous rock on my hand caught my attention. Anxiously, I looked around the airport to see if anyone had noticed it. Noticed *me*.

I was now a married woman with a ring that probably cost more than most people's homes.

"Shit," I swore, panic crashing over me as I worked to slip the ring off my finger.

My now very swollen finger.

A symptom of flying that I really didn't need right now.

"Come on," I mumbled as I twisted the band back and forth. A trickle of blood formed around the edge of gold as my skin caught between metal and bone.

Tears pooled along my lower lids as I worked at removing the oversized jewelry. With a mighty tug, the ring pulled free, and I sat back in the chair, gasping for air as if I just ran a marathon. My chest heaved with each deep inhale as I closed my eyes, trying to calm down my anxiety. The edges of the ring bit into my palm, where I fisted it tightly. The wedding band slipped off much easier.

A chime sounded on my phone, and I glanced down to find a notification that Franny arrived. Shoving the rings into my purse, I hurried out of the airport with my luggage trailing behind me. My best friend jumped from her car and wrapped her thin arms around my shoulders. Franny was both tall and lean, reminding me a bit of Olive Oil from the *Popeye* cartoons. But Franny's frame was all attributed to her athletic skills. She could, and did, play every sport I could name. She was just naturally thin. Girls in school used to tease her for it, but my mom always liked to say it was because they were jealous of Franny. I didn't believe it as a young teen, but as an adult, I could understand the possibility.

"Hey, how was the trip?" she asked after we were settled, and she pulled out of the airport terminal area.

"It was… good. Eventful."

It killed me not to say anything to my best friend about Talon and our agreement. I wasn't sure she would understand my motivation for saying yes. I barely understood it myself.

"Any cute guys there?"

I coughed uncontrollably as an image of Talon kissing me popped into my head.

"You okay?" she asked as she merged onto the highway and headed toward Ashfield.

"Yeah, sorry. And um… there were a couple."

That wasn't a lie. Both Talon and Dean were incredibly attractive, just not actual attendees of the convention.

With a devious grin, she asked, "Hook up with any of them?"

"Franny!" I exclaimed as she laughed.

"Did you do *anything* fun?"

"Um… I told off a lady yelling at the front desk worker for something he had no control over."

Franny sighed. "Of course you did."

"Sorry. The conference was pretty uneventful otherwise—though I did get some great information on grants we may be able to apply for."

Franny asked about the grants and some of the other sessions, then went on to tell me about Draco's antics while I was gone. She said she never saw my cat any time she went over to feed him and clean the litter box, but every morning, the food was gone. So, she knew he was still alive and likely hiding somewhere in the house.

That meant Draco was either going to be super affectionate when I arrived, or he was going to be a little shit and tear up a piece of furniture.

"Want to come with me to dinner tonight?" My parents hosted a family dinner every weekend, and since my siblings and I had gotten older, it tended to fall on Sunday evenings. If the farm was busy like during the harvest, or if a storm was covering the land, my parents would host some of our farmhands as well. None of them lived on our property any longer, as they all had families, but every once in a while, we had newer employees who would stay in one of the field houses. My parents always made it a point to treat them like family, just like my grandparents and early ancestors had before them. It was one of the reasons I thought Sunny Brook Farms was always so successful. Not all the farmhands thought of their work as a job, because they were always so well taken care of.

Maybe I can help with that too when this arrangement with Talon is all said and done.

"Not tonight, though I wish I could. Grandma has an appointment early in the morning, so I need to help her get settled. You know how she gets herself all worked up."

Her grandmother was suffering from the early stages of dementia. Franny moved into her home along with her mother to help keep her grandmother comfortable. Every day, I could see it was weighing on my best friend.

"Okay. Well, let's get together this week for dinner. I want to get over to the school and find my classroom." The principal was waiting on the previous instructor to grab her things, since she was removed from the property so quickly.

"That sounds good."

Franny dropped me off at my house, and I carried my luggage inside, calling out Draco's name as I closed the front door behind me. I waited patiently by the door to see if he'd show himself, but after a minute, he still hadn't made an appearance.

"Fine."

As I started throwing my clothes into the washing machine, Draco slithered between my legs, nuzzling his face against my shins as he passed. I turned on the machine and then lifted the black cat into my arms, asking him if Franny took good care of him. He replied with a purr, and I grinned, knowing he was satisfied with my friend's care, despite what Franny thought.

Checking the clock on my nightstand, I noted I had about four hours before dinner at my parents' house. For the first time in years, I wasn't looking forward to it. There were going to be questions about the trip and likely more gossip about Jeremy's upcoming wedding. Something I very much enjoyed not having to hear about for the past several days.

Normally, I would have snuck in a quick shower to rid myself of the smell and germs of the plane and airport, but there was nothing grotesque about Talon's jet. It had been immaculate.

Through my entire stay in Miami, I had longed for my camera. It was nothing fancy. Just a digital I got on sale in high school. My love for photography wasn't a well-kept secret, but it was something everyone saw as a hobby, not a passion of mine. That love had been extinguished almost a year ago, and it only recently started igniting again.

I looked around my barren walls, walls that once held some of my favorite images. My living space didn't seem nearly as lived-in as it once had, but until I found a replacement camera, I was going to have to settle. Sure, I could buy something from a big box store in the next town over, but none of that would've expressed who I was as a person.

But who is Rory?

In the last four years, I spent so much time letting people dictate who and what I should be, and now I was married to someone who was going to do the same for the next six months. When was the last time I did something for myself?

Scrolling through my phone, I brought up a shopping app and pulled up the digital camera I had been coveting for the last year. One of my favorite photographers used a similar model. The price was high, and I couldn't hold back my startled gasp as I saw all the digits.

But I'd been saving, and this was something I wanted for myself. Something I'd given up a year ago for the sake of someone else.

Quickly, I brought up my banking app and transferred the money from my regular savings account to my checking. Luckily, whatever money Talon planned on sending me hadn't been updated yet. So, I didn't have to worry about that shock.

I clicked the order button for the camera and sat through three minutes of utter panic at making the risky decision, contemplating canceling the order every thirty seconds. But then Draco slid onto my lap and curled into a little ball, immediately calming me. As I stroked his soft fur, I peered up at my walls again. The vacant spaces reminded me of the hollowness I felt inside when Jeremy upended my life.

"I think it's time we did some decorating," I said to Draco as an idea began forming. I'd always been a fan of the dark academia aesthetics I found on the web. I'd been living here for the past three years, since I graduated college. Because of the scholarships I received for tuition and boarding, I was able to save all the money from my job as a tutor to put toward the down payment.

My parents had also helped, which I was incredibly grateful for.

It was a modest one-bedroom, one-bathroom home, with an extra room that held no closet, which I turned into my office. The fenced-in yard was my favorite part. Toward the back, there was a nature preserve that gave me a glimpse at the wildlife of Tennessee and a view of the majestic mountains I couldn't get enough of. But the house itself was as boring as I felt.

With an idea in mind, I set Draco back on the ground, fed him dinner, and dashed out of the house in the hopes of reaching the hardware store before it closed. I was about to spend as much on tools and supplies as I did on my recent camera purchase.

I thought about calling or messaging Talon as I perused the aisles in the store, but he left me no way to contact him.

What kind of mess did I just get myself into? Legally marrying a man and not even asking for his phone number? I'm a freaking moron.

I was busy berating myself as I added a few paintbrushes to my cart and didn't notice the tall man standing at the end cap. My cart caught his hip as I headed toward the cash register at the front.

"Sorry," I apologized, my face squishing into a grimace that probably resembled a pug.

"No harm," he replied, turning to look at me directly. He held a set of tape measurers in his hands and was dressed nicely, in a blue button-down shirt and khakis. He had neatly trimmed blonde hair, longer on top and shorter on the sides and back, and he was wearing wire-rimmed glasses that made him appear older than I believed he was. "Do I know you?" he asked.

I didn't recognize him, but with the way the town was growing, there was a good chance I'd never ran into him. A sudden notion dawned on me that he could be a friend of Jeremy's, and that left a sour taste in my mouth, making me smack my tongue loudly.

"No. I don't think so." I excused myself quickly, telling him I had a prior engagement, which was the truth.

Just as I placed an order with the cashier to have some planks of wood delivered to my house, the man came up behind me to stand in line. I watched nervously, using the reflection in the mirror behind the cashier.

"Thanks," I mumbled as I grabbed my bags and the receipt. I signed the confirmation for the delivery in two days and headed toward the exit.

"I remember! You work for the school."

"What?" I asked fearfully. Something about this guy was giving me the heebie-jeebies.

"Sorry. I'm Liam Franklin. I teach Biology at the high school. Your classroom is right next to mine."

"Oh!" I replied, my creep meter still running on all cylinders.

"Have you been by there yet? If you need help setting up your classroom, let me know. I'll be there all week."

Lovely.

"Thanks for the offer. I'm not sure when I'll get a chance to head over that way," I lied. "I have somewhere to be, but it was nice meeting you. Glad not everyone will be a stranger at the first teachers' meeting."

"Uh. Sure. See you."

I didn't allow my thoughts to linger on the teacher next door. I was excited to get started on my new project. I was one of those people who, the moment I had a goal in mind, I wouldn't stop at anything until I achieved it. Talon and I seemed to have that in common. It was one of two things I knew about him. We were goal-oriented, and we were husband and wife.

On the drive to my parents' house, I kept thinking this arrangement might have been the easiest thing I'd ever signed up for. For all I knew, Talon and I would see each other just a handful of times, and after six months, we'd call it quits. Maybe my family didn't need to know anything.

Pulling up to the farm, the interaction with the guy in the hardware store long forgotten, I braced myself for whatever was going to come. As I shut off my car, it was clear that whatever was headed my way had camouflaged itself as my three sisters. The trio leaned on the front porch railing with matching impatient looks.

I couldn't help reverting back to my early-teen years and wondering what I'd done wrong.

Apprehensively, I exited my car, leaving my new purchases stored in the trunk. I assumed the paint would be fine for a couple of hours.

"Well, look who finally came back from the Sunshine State," Alex called out obnoxiously.

"Did you have a nice vacation?" Autumn added with a flip of her long, wavy locks.

Aspen remained quiet. She was the one I worried about the most, rarely showing much emotion anymore. She had been the liveliest toddler, always giggling, but since middle school, she'd slowly hid into herself.

When I didn't respond to Alex and Autumn, they left the porch with a huff, grabbing their matching glasses of white wine from the bench on their way.

"Hi, Aspen," I said, reaching an arm around my sister to hug her. I noticed she clung a little tighter than usual, and it made me smile. Maybe she missed me just a tad.

"I was afraid you weren't going to come back. Not that I would've blamed you. I bet there are a ton of hot guys in Miami."

Ignoring her quip, I asked, "Everything okay?"

"Yep, everything is exactly the same. I'm glad you're home."

With a smile, I told her that I was too. It wasn't a complete lie, since I loved being surrounded by my family.

Aspen crossed the porch to enter the house, and I trailed behind her, immediately making my way toward the fridge to get a glass of wine for myself. I held the bottle up for Aspen, but she declined.

The rest of the people gathered in the house had yet to notice my arrival. Surprisingly, Mom wasn't in the kitchen, which was where I could usually find her. With my glass filled with a sweet Moscato, I snuck a peek in the large pot and groaned. Mom was making her seafood scampi. It was legendary in this house, and she only made it for special occasions.

"What do you think you're doing?" Mom shouted as she caught me red-handed trying to sneak a spoonful of the sauce.

"Nothing," I explained, tucking the arm of the empty spoon into the back pocket of my denim shorts. She knew better though. Mom marched around the large kitchen island and tried to grab what she suspected. I twisted out of her grasp twice, but she caught me by the underside of my arm when I wasn't looking.

My yelp alerted the rest of the house of my arrival, and a gathering quickly formed in the room. Mom confiscated the spoon and promptly smacked my backside with it like she had when I was younger.

"What's going on here?"

"Hi, Dad," I said as I slunk away from my mother in the hopes of avoiding another reprimand and tucked myself under my dad's waiting arm.

"Rory thought it was a good idea to try to have a taste of my sauce before it was ready."

"Ah, Rory. You know better," Dad scolded with his signature grin.

"I know, but it smelled so good. I couldn't help it. Sorry, Mom."

After my half-hearted apology, everyone, including the twins, welcomed me home, then left the kitchen and took their seats at the dining table. Mom prepared a large garden salad as an appetizer, and the starter was always so much better when it was all locally grown.

I tried to keep my head down and only participate in the conversations when called upon, but I could sense everyone's eyes on me. It was… nerve-wracking. All I wanted was to eat a delicious meal. Mom's cooking could rival the Wilder Hotel's.

Finally, I had enough and released my fork, letting it fall onto my plate with a clank. "What?"

My eyes met Alex's, who was seated directly across from me.

"It's nothing."

"Then stop staring at me," I demanded, picking up my fork and stabbing a piece of lettuce.

"Alex," Mom began. "Leave your sister alone."

"Doesn't she look different to y'all? There's something…. She's like, glowing. I can't put my finger on it." Alex tilted her head as if to get a better look at me.

Autumn quickly joined in, slanting her head in the same direction as Alex's. "Yeah. It's like she just had—"

My mouth dropped open to cut her off, but Dad beat me to the punch.

"I do not want to hear about my daughters... and... that. If you please."

"Thanks, Dad."

He nodded, but his eyes moved over my face, like he was examining me for something. "There *is* something different about you. Did you spend some time at the beach?"

Knowing I needed to end this discussion, I dipped my head and lied. "I liked to eat my meals out on the patio, then take a walk on the beach. It was beautiful."

Ending the conversation, Mom chimed in, "Well, that sounds lovely. Maybe your father and I can go on vacation there when he finally decides to retire next year."

My dad retiring was less likely than pigs flying over an exploding Yellowstone.

"Now, let me go grab the meal," she added.

As she started setting dinner on the table with both Molly and Eloise's help, my nosiness grew by the second.

Until I finally pointed out, "We usually only have this meal for special occasions."

"That's true," she replied.

I looked around the table to find all my siblings carrying similar perplexed expressions. All except Alex.

Collectively, we all turned our attention to her and Nate.

"Alex?"

"Um… well… you see…," she rambled, until Nate finally put her out of her misery.

"We eloped yesterday. Your mom and dad stood as our witnesses."

It seemed I wasn't the only impulsive one in the family.

Congratulations rang out, and I wondered if my quickie wedding to Talon would have received the same outpouring.

Alex, Nate, and their little ones left right after dinner, and I left not long after them, explaining to my family that I wanted to spend some time with Draco. The reality was that I felt out of sorts in the house I'd grown up in. Everyone seemed happy with where their paths in life were headed, and I felt… stuck.

"I love you, Mom," I mumbled as she wrapped me in a warm embrace.

"I love you, Sunshine. You know you can talk to me anytime, even as an adult."

"I know. That's why you're the best." I smiled as I leaned back.

"I know when you're hiding something. As long as it's not something that puts you in danger, I won't pressure you to tell me. Just know I'm here."

There was no doubt my mom could pick up on the out-of-sorts temperament I was giving off. Growing up, she had the ability to know what we were up to even before we did.

"I love you," I repeated and then settled into my car.

I tried not to look back at the house as I crested the hill on the rubble path leading to the exit of the farm. I couldn't bear to see my mother's concerned face. I knew the skin between her eyebrows was wrinkled into a V and her lips pursed just a tad. Even from this distance, I'd be able to make out that expression she wore often.

And I knew, without a doubt, she'd be hurt when she found out what I did in Miami. I'd only done something worse once before, and I almost paid dearly for it.

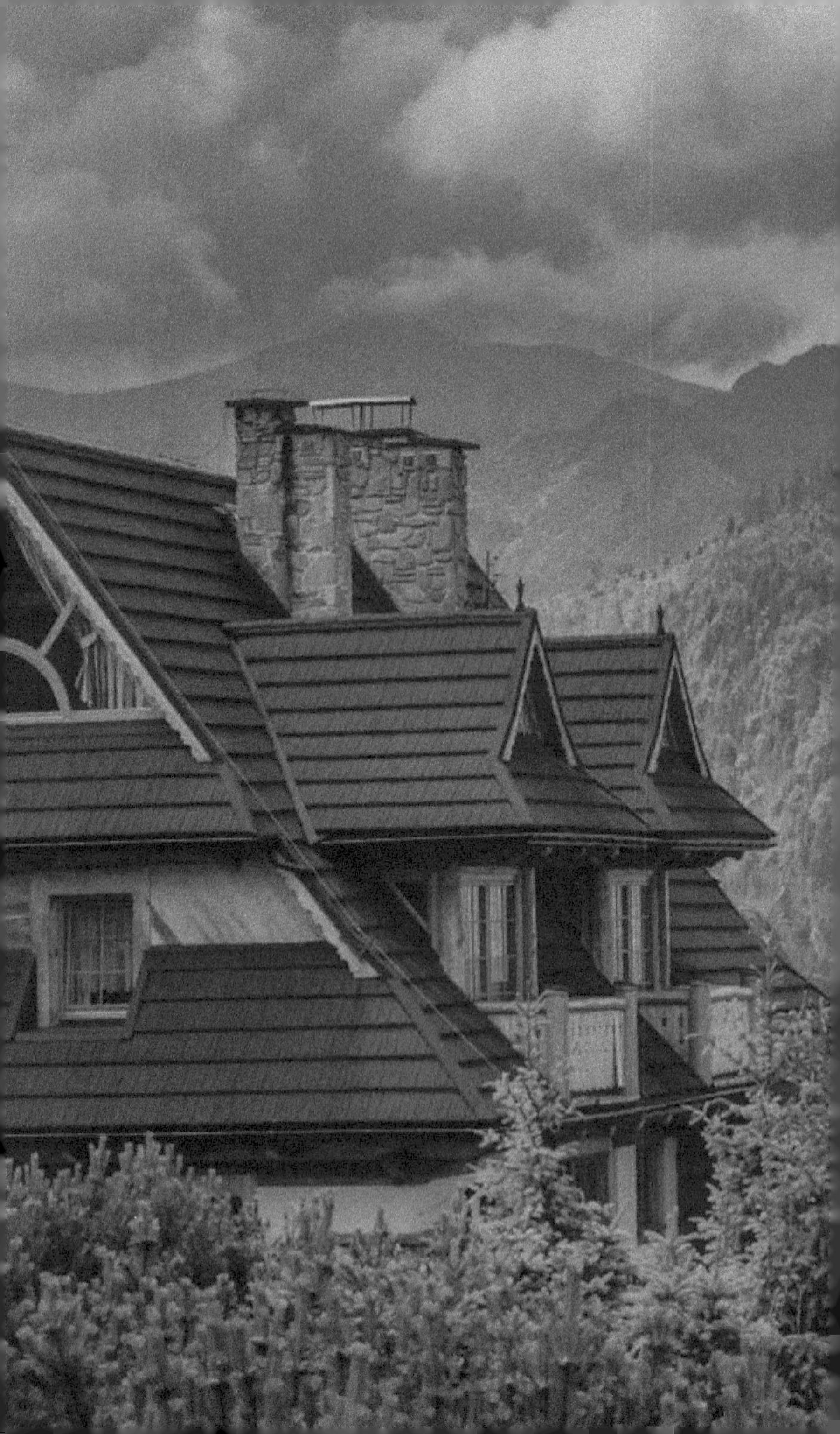

Chapter Ten

Talon

It had been three days since Aurora boarded that private jet to head back to her small town, and I hadn't stopped thinking about her since. Which was fucking annoying. I couldn't sleep, so I ended up working out into the late hours of the night. Every muscle in my body ached from the overuse. I had bags under my eyes like I did when I rode out a hurricane in my houseboat. Something I ten out of ten *don't* recommend. And I was far more irritable than normal. Which was saying something, because most of the employees, and probably people on the street as well, thought I was an asshole on a good day. Now, they were turning and walking in the opposite direction if they saw me coming.

Dean was the only holdout though. He knew I was more bark than bite.

The sunrise started illuminating my office in a myriad of oranges and pinks. I had been working hard for the last two hours, trying to keep myself busy, so the clock on my laptop reading 6:00 a.m. didn't surprise me.

Leaning back in my chair, I tilted my head toward the sun, its warmth radiating through my suit and over my body. It was instantaneous, those thoughts of Aurora. Her name meant the dawn, and that's exactly what she felt like when I stole that kiss from her after we recited our vows. Bright, warm, promising. I could have simply pecked her lips. Something innocent, like a first kiss, but I wanted more. The greedy part of me didn't care it wasn't necessary. I wanted her mouth, her lips, her tongue. I wanted every fucking piece of her in that moment.

And after a split-second decision, I claimed it.

I hadn't expected her reaction. That soft mewing noise she made when my tongue slipped past her lips. I wasn't 100-percent sure she even knew she made it. But I remember that harmless sound like I'd just lived it. I could close my eyes and witness the entire exchange all over again. It plagued my thoughts.

"Fuck," I mumbled as my mind drifted off to thoughts of Aurora again. She'd been front and center lately, and it was disrupting my work.

Leaning forward on my desk, I grabbed my cell phone. I hadn't given her a way to contact me, not that I had any doubts she'd be able to track me down if she wanted. It was more I'd simply forgotten. But I had her number and her address. I had all her personal information down to the classroom number she was assigned at the high school. It was easy to find without having to call Dean to track it down. A simple internet search gave me most of what I needed to know. Which was something I was going to have to recruit Dean and my lawyers to take down. Once word got out about our nuptials, the press was going to swarm her like angry bees.

I really lucked out having a friend who dabbled in practically everything. He had his hands in so many different fields that I think even he confused himself sometimes with all the investments he made over time. I tried my best to help him keep track. The man refused to have an assistant.

"Good morning, Mr. Beckett," Olive's overly chipper voice called out. She hovered right behind the threshold of my office.

I didn't offer a reply. My eyes darted upward to meet hers while my body continued to hover over the desk.

She immediately swallowed. "Would you… uh… like some coffee? You… um… look tired."

Again, I gave her no response, my gaze dropping to my phone resting in my palm.

Olive turned and left her area—I assumed to get me a cup of coffee. I lived on caffeine for the past three days, so I wasn't sure the stimulant was really going to do anything.

The screen on my phone went black from lack of use, and I touched the home button to bring it back to life.

I made a mental note to investigate why Olive was arriving at the office well before her scheduled time. But right now, that was going to have to wait. I had something else I needed to do. I pulled up my contacts, added the number I found, and typed out a message.

> Good morning, wife.

My thumb hovered over the Send button. I ignored how it shook.

"Here you go, Mr. Beckett. One black coffee." Olive startled me as she placed the cup on top of the coaster on my desk. In doing so, my thumb hit the button and sent my message to Aurora. Panic immediately set in, and I fumbled with my phone, dropping it on the desk twice.

My vision blurred as a growl sounded throughout the office. I glanced up once I captured my phone to find Olive scurried back to her desk like she was running from a fire. Or a dragon, going by the throaty sound that echoed in the room.

Finally pulling up the messaging app, I hurried to try to unsend the text. Fear prickled up my spine as I noticed Aurora had already read the text.

"Dammit," I cursed, tossing my cell back onto the desk. It promptly knocked into my files, scattering a few of the papers onto the floor.

Pushing my chair back, the wheels carrying it away from the desk, I stomped over to the papers and began picking them up.

"What a fucking mess," I mumbled just as one sheet left a paper cut.

"Are you kidding me right now?" I yelled at the stack of papers as I stood like they actively attempted to maim me.

"No, but I do have a good joke for you." My back had been facing the door, and I peered over my shoulder to find Dean entering my office as if he owned the place. My employees thought he was in management, since he was in the office complex as much as I was.

"Do tell," I said sarcastically, placing the pile of papers back into their respective folders.

"Ok. Why did the golfer wear two pairs of pants?"

I gawked at my friend, who wore a childish grin as he waited for my reply.

"In case he gets a hole in one," I deadpanned, wheeling my chair back behind the desk. Except I was too antsy to sit. I was paranoid about the message and what Aurora would think. Excitement and fear filled my body as I anticipated her reply.

"Dude, how did you know?" Dean stated as his shoulders slumped in defeat.

"Sorry," I uttered as I walked over to the wall of windows looking out toward the ocean. In the last couple of days, I caught myself staring at the water more often than not.

"You're out of sorts today. More so than normal," he pointed out.

I crossed my arms against my chest and leaned my shoulder against the glass, turning my body halfway toward Dean, who was now standing in the middle of my office.

"I've got a lot on my mind."

"Like a certain blonde who now officially carries your last name?"

I may have perked up a little at that knowledge. Usually, the process took a few weeks and required a ton of legwork, which I thought was ridiculous, but somehow Dean was able to square everything away in seventy-two hours. The man could work miracles.

"Good. When will she receive the paperwork and updated social security card?"

"It's headed to her house now by overnight courier."

I replied with a single nod.

"What's wrong, dude? You're acting even grumpier than normal."

"Nothing. Just not sleeping."

"You do carry quite a resemblance to a vampire. I'm not sure if it's the pale skin, the dark circles, or the insatiable need for blood."

"I don't have an insa—" Olive opened the door and stuck her head inside the office.

"Get out!" I barked, and she immediately jerked back and slammed the door closed.

"See? Insatiable need for blood."

"God, you're a real asshole, you know that?" I told him as I pushed off from the window, shooing him away as I went back to my desk. My paranoia over the message was growing by the second.

"I do. Now, what's got your panties in a twist, my friend?"

"Nothing," I mumbled just as my phone chimed with a message from Aurora.

Wife

I wondered if I'd hear from you.

She wasn't even in the same room, and I felt like my entire body lit up from the inside out. My palms grew sweaty, and my pulse quickened.

"Well, now. Please do share with the class what suddenly has you smiling like that."

Was I smiling? I reached up to touch my face, and fuck if there wasn't a toothy grin on my lips.

"Nothing," I repeated as I closed the screen and placed the phone back on my desk.

"Oh. Okay." He approached the desk, and before I could react, he swiped the phone right off the corner.

"Dean," I snarled, but he ignored me completely. "How the fuck do you know my password?"

"Oh, come on. It's your mother's birthday. And you've had the same password since you were twelve and made it your locker combination."

Sometimes, I really hated that we'd been friends for so long.

"Dean," I warned again, but he didn't listen. Not that I expected him to. Despite being my best friend, Dean looked and listened to himself and no one else.

Wordlessly, he stared at my phone, then placed it back on the desk. "You like her."

"What's not to like? She's smart, pretty, and agreed to my ridiculous proposal."

"True," he said as he sat his large frame on my desk's corner closest to me. The wheels of my chair squeaked as I rolled backward and away from the chance of the desk collapsing on top of me. "But I mean… you *like*-like her."

Denying it, I rolled my eyes. "*Psh*. You're being ludicrous."

"Maybe, but I'm not the one who has a thing for my fake wife."

"Dean."

"Talon. Get it together. It's one thing to entertain the thought of fucking her, but man, you need to rein it in. Our world will destroy her. You know this."

I did. I knew how destructive our circle could be. It wasn't just the absenteeism, or the daily recreational use of anything that could be snorted, injected, or smoked. It was the lies, the deceit, and the blackmail.

"I...." My words hung in the air. I never lied to Dean about anything. He was the one friend who knew every nasty truth. It was why he was so gung-ho about helping me gain control of the hotels and my trust fund left to me by my mother.

"It's okay to like her. Hell, I'm pretty sure it's almost impossible *not* to like her. But you just have to remember it's all temporary. After six months, you're going to have to let her go."

I hated when he was right. And I had a feeling that losing Aurora was going to be right up there in devastation level with losing my mom. That was something I never wanted to experience again.

"*I* know!" Dean exclaimed as he finally moved his large body off my desk and positioned himself in the leather chair on the opposite side of it. "Sleep with her and get her out of your system."

I cocked my head to the side and glared at him, my fists clenching in my lap.

"Hasn't the past shown us that sleeping with someone to get them out of your system *never* works?"

Dean tried that with a girl in college who cheered for his football team. He was only interested in sex… only to end up falling for her. They dated all four years until she moved back home to Wisconsin after graduation. "True, but this time, you know *without a doubt* you can't catch feelings for her. One and done, man. Isn't that your motto?"

Usually, except when Allison was involved, and it was clear as day how awful that turned out.

"Maybe you're right. Or I could just stay in Miami and only see her when it's required."

"Fuck that. You're an angry asshole on a good day. Now, you're a miserable one who leaves employees crying any time you open that mug of yours. Do us all a favor and go visit your wife."

I had to bite back my smile at hearing him refer to Aurora as my wife. The sound of it was growing on me every day.

"There's one problem though. How the fuck am I going to explain my sudden absence here to my grandfather and Gigi?"

The room fell quiet for a beat, then Dean smiled in that slimy kind of way that usually landed one of us in jail. It happened more than once. The corners of his mouth continued to curl upward. He looked like a modern-day Grinch.

"Well, that's where I come into play."

My friend and I stared at each other like a lazy game of chicken, only for me to break first, because—let's face it—I was damn curious about what he meant.

"Explain," I rumbled.

Dean indicated the door of my office with a quick jerk of his head, and I knew that meant I needed to make sure there was no one in earshot.

"Olive," I said through the intercom on my desk phone. "Please go retrieve a sugared-up coffee for Dean."

"Yes, sir." Through the glass, I watched her scamper off, then I flipped the switch that turned the windows opaque.

"You have about five minutes. So, shoot."

"You know how I like to dabble in various business ventures? Biotech, security, agriculture, clubs. So, why not hotels?"

"I'm not selling you shares of Wilder Hotels."

"Will you shut your trap and listen?" Dean barked, his tone serious. And I knew immediately that what he was going to suggest wasn't just some one-off. It was something he'd been thinking about for some time.

"Apologies. Continue."

Dean began asking about our first hotel in Knoxville, Tennessee. A little retreat-type hotel that brought the outdoors in. It was rustic and homey, and it felt like you were walking into a massive lodge. The lobby itself was three stories high. I always hated that we stopped taking reservations on the property decades ago. The only expense was the minimal utilities and round-the-clock security. We did send management onsite randomly to make sure the place hadn't been ransacked. I only stepped foot in there once in my lifetime.

"That was your mom's favorite place, wasn't it?

He wasn't seeking an answer, but I nodded anyway.

"I want to invest in it. This gives me another asset in my portfolio and gives you an excuse to travel to Tennessee."

"My grandfather isn't going to buy that."

"You don't give him a choice. Tell him you have a vested interest in the property—i.e. me—and that you've been provided the financials of similar ventures and their successes. Even if there wasn't an ulterior motive, it would still be a good gamble. Mountainside retreats that cater to families and the outdoors are sought after right now."

"Okay. When can you provide all that to me?"

"You already have it. I scheduled the email to hit your inbox around five minutes ago."

Quickly, I flipped open my laptop and brought up my email. Lo and behold, there was an email from Dean outlining all the details. The investment, the proposed budget for renovations, the comparisons. Everything my team would have spent weeks compiling, Dean provided.

"You've been thinking about this for a while," I said.

"I need a change, and this partnership would be direct between me and you. There wouldn't need to be a shareholder vote, since it's already a Wilder Hotel."

"Okay, well, there is only one other thing to do, since you would be investing over fifty percent. We have to contact my grandfather."

"Aren't you interim CEO?" he asked with that Grinch-like grin again.

"I… am," I replied hesitantly. Then I stated more confidently, "I am."

"Then it's your decision, correct? He doesn't need to sign off on anything."

Dean was correct. My grandfather had no say in any Wilder Hotels business. All he had was the matching last name. My grin matched Dean's.

"There is one call we should definitely make though," Dean added.

I was puzzled for a moment, then it dawned on me. The one person who loved that first hotel even more than my mother had—Gigi.

"Call her now."

"Why?" I asked as I began dialing her number I had memorized from my time at boarding school. She'd never changed it.

"Who do you think gave me the idea?"

"You two have the weirdest friendship."

The phone's ringing clicked over to a breathless greeting. "Hello?"

I was instantly worried. "Gigi, are you okay?"

"Of course. I'm running on the treadmill right now."

"Why?" My worry dialed back to curious concern.

"For the marathon, of course," Dean chimed in as if it were common knowledge.

"Marathon? What marathon?" The worry had returned, and I spoke quickly. "Is there someone there to spot you, Gigi?"

"Oh, calm yourself, Talon. It's a marathon for senior citizens, and Wilder Hotels is sponsoring it. I'm running in support of the charity. You should know this."

Though I wasn't always aware of the ins and outs of the public-relations side of Wilder Hotels, my grandmother risking her life to join the marathon was something I should have been alerted to.

"Sorry, Gigi." I hated apologizing. Almost as much as I hated everything my grandfather was forcing me to do.

"Why are you calling me? You never call me out of the blue."

"I call you!" Dean shouted just as Olive ducked inside my office and handed him his sugary brew.

"You treat me better than my own grandson."

"Gigi!" I knew she was pulling my leg, but it hurt just the same. I spent what little free time I had with her. I'd even taken her to a few of those hot yoga classes she loved so much.

"I'm teasing. Now, what did you boys want to talk to me about?"

I paused and looked out at the ocean one last time. Sailing through the waves was where I was meant to be. Instead, I was here, digging out of the trenches my family created, all for the sake of my mother—the child they cast aside because she was a woman and loved someone they didn't approve of.

"The Knoxville hotel. Dean and I are going to partner up and make it what it should have always been."

Silence fell on the other end, and I immediately wished I video-called her instead.

"Gigi, are you okay?"

"I'm…. Really? You mean it? You're not just messing around with your old grandma?"

"Why would I do that? Of course I'm being serious. Dean has a good plan, and with his large investment, I won't need grandfather's approval."

"I was certain you'd turn it down. I even told Dean so. You know how much your moth— I love that place," she said with a shaky breath. "What convinced you?"

Dean spoke up again, "A girl."

I glared in his direction, the expression deepening when I saw Olive stiffen in her chair. I'd been so distracted by Gigi's teasing that I didn't notice my assistant hadn't closed my door after bringing Dean his drink. I nodded to my friend and he quickly made work of shutting the door and locking it.

"It's getting serious then. I can't wait to meet her. How did you meet? Where is she from?"

Not getting the hint that he needed to shut his trap, Dean answered, "Ironically, she lives just an hour outside of Knoxville."

My grandmother squealed in delight. I imagined her delicate cheeks turning a pinkish hue like her favorite carnations.

"Gigi, I'll call you later. Right now, I need to kill Dean."

"Okay." And then after a pause, "Don't hurt him too badly, Dean. He's my favorite grandson."

Throwing my hands in the air, I looked over at my cackling friend as Gigi ended the call.

"What the fuck was that about? When were you going to tell me that Aurora lives only an hour away from the hotel?"

"Because you're a genius who has access to a map and her address. I didn't think I needed to hold your hand when it came to locating your wife."

"Well, is there anything else I need to know?"

"Maybe, but I don't think you're ready to hear it."

"Dude, you're pussyfooting around me like I'm a fucking child."

"What does pussyfooting even mean? It's a terrible term."

"It's like… being cautious," I said without thinking. "Seriously, Dean. Are there any other surprises you should share?"

He shook his head without breaking eye contact. The fact that he was picking at the fabric of his pants while doing so told me he was lying. But I was too worked up to push him on it.

Breaking the tension in the room, I began sifting through the email Dean sent. His budget was large but timeframe slim. As in, he wanted to get started as soon as possible. I wasn't even sure where I was going to find a construction crew on such short notice.

"Dean, this timeline isn't reasonable."

"Yes, it is. I already have everything lined up, waiting for your go-ahead. The money is being transferred over as we speak."

"Were you planning on me saying yes?"

"No, just hopeful. And I knew you'd see it was a good business decision. Wilder Hotels needs to continue to branch out from the beachside oasis."

"Based on your timeline, I need to have a crew ready to go next week. I'd need to be onsite for most of this."

"Look, Talon. All of these hotels run like a well-oiled machine. That's thanks to you and your ability to hire the best managers. You turned the entire chain around in less than a year. *You* did that.

"You don't need to be in this office every day to do your job. All you need is a computer and a phone."

"What will you do?"

"I'll be a silent partner, mostly. But I may come visit every once in a while to see the progress. I like to know how my money is being spent."

"Fuck, I guess I should figure out some temporary living arrangements."

Dean's smirk morphed his features, and I was wary once more about what he was thinking.

"No need to do that. Your girl lives close enough. Better go pack those bags. You've got a wife to visit."

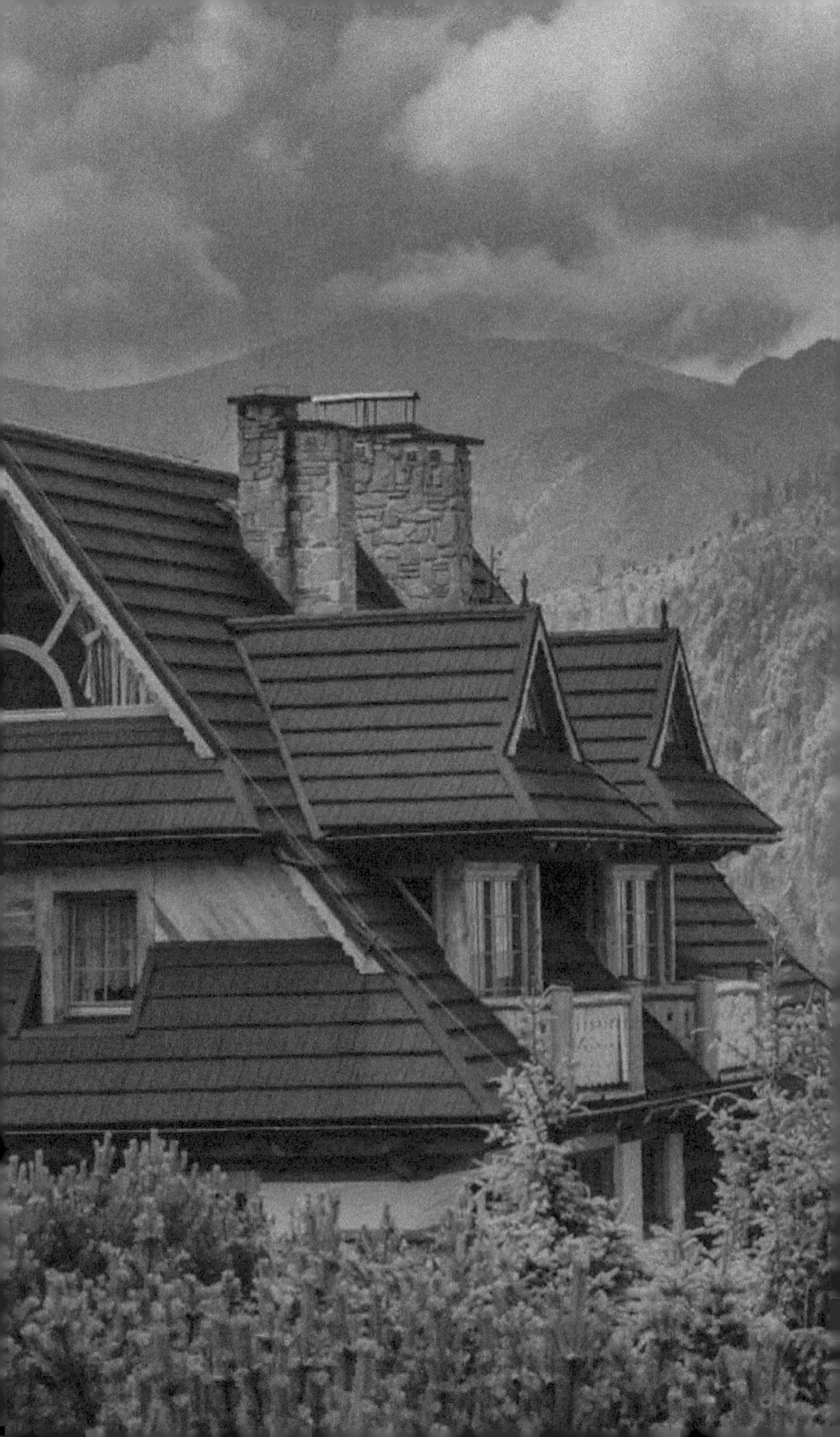

Chapter Eleven

Talon

Twenty-four hours later, I was resting in the cushioned leather seat of my chartered plane. I used Charlie again, because he was one of my favorite pilots. He didn't put up with my bullshit either. He felt like more of a grandfather to me than my own. He and his family had been flying the Wilders around as long as I could remember. My uncle had a private plane he used our company money for, but none of us were allowed to use it.

I mentioned once before that it seemed as if he was using business finances for personal use, and I received a black eye for it. I was fifteen at the time and much smaller than my uncle. I doubted he would try to lay a hand on me now, since I towered over the man.

"Mr. Beckett, can I offer you a beverage?" Leon, Charlie's grandson and my flight attendant, asked just as the plane reached altitude.

"Gin and tonic," I told him brusquely as I booted up my computer. Even though Dean said I could work from anywhere, I always found it the most difficult to work away from a standard office. I knew others could. I just preferred the confined space to focus on my tasks. I'd already started scoping out the layout of the lodge to determine the space where I'd like to construct my office.

I was apprehensive at first when thinking about setting foot in the old hotel. But it was a place my mother loved, and it would offer me a glimpse of the woman I barely knew. That was the only reason I agreed. The longer I let the idea fester during the night, the angrier I became at the fact that my family let the property go to waste. They could have spent all this time making it the go-to rustic haven, in memory of my mother.

Well, *they* didn't do it, so I would. I even started throwing around ideas for the name. The Hilltop by

Wilder Hotels. The Escape by Wilder Hotels. The Mallory by Wilder Hotels—an homage to my mom. The third idea was my number-one choice. It would be a big "fuck you" to my grandfather and the rift he caused.

"Here you are, Mr. Beckett." Leon set the drink on top of a napkin he placed on the table in front of me. I peered around the screen of my laptop and noticed he also set a key beside it.

"What's this?"

"A… um… gift from Mr. Rossi."

Dean. What was that bastard up to now?

I lifted the shiny piece of metal, studying the ridges.

"What is it?" I rumbled. Luckily, my gruffness didn't put Leon off.

"A key, sir."

"Yes, but to what?"

"Apologies, Mr. Beckett. He said you'd know. Is that all?"

I had no idea what it was for, but I slipped it inside my pocket regardless as I nodded to dismiss Leon. Then something crossed my mind, and I found myself calling out to him. "You… uh…. Were you on board when Ms. Easterly traveled?"

"Oh, yes, sir. She was the loveliest passenger. She had the entire crew, except my grandfather, singing karaoke."

That sounded like her.

"Huh. Was she any good?" I wondered out loud.

"Is anyone really good at karaoke? I wouldn't say she's Adele, but it wasn't unpleasant."

Slipping the key free from my pocket, I twirled it between my fingers as I thought about watching Aurora sing along to some cheesy song with the crew I'd known for years.

"Is that all, sir?" Leon asked again. He was still standing in the same place, except his hand was braced on the doorframe of the main opening near the front. It was then I noticed we were experiencing a bit of turbulence.

"Yes. Thank you."

"And, sir?" Leon called out just as I turned my attention back to the key in hand. "I believe that is a key to a house."

Grinning, I brought it up to eye-level and examined it closer. Dean was a fucking miracle worker. It was a key to Aurora's house. I just knew it. The man had connections everywhere, so it wasn't unheard of for him to secure something like this. But it did leave me wondering who might also have a key to her home. That was something I was going to have to rectify once I moved in temporarily.

The flight was a quick two hours, and even through the turbulence, it was relaxing. I reviewed and revised the budget Dean set up along with the projections for reservations over the next five years.

As I departed the plane, I thanked Charlie for the safe landing and shook hands with Leon.

"Good luck," Leon added as I took the first step out of the plane, and I nodded in thanks. I wasn't used to asking for luck, but I was glad to have it on my side.

I'd spoken to Gigi before I left Miami. She seemed less lively at my departure, almost as if she was worried. And I didn't think it was business related. I was trying to get some information about the resort and how it flourished in its heyday, but she seemed reluctant to give me anything. Not even what she liked most about the area. After our conversation, I was left feeling like she was holding back on something.

A large, blacked-out SUV was waiting for me at the rental car kiosk. It was one set aside for politicians and celebrities and decked out with more gadgets than anyone could name. Olive set up the vehicle for me, and as I handed over my license to the team member, I asked if I could exchange it for a different vehicle.

As I zipped down the highway in a bright-red Ferrari, I smiled. My luggage barely fit in the small trunk and the passenger seat, but I made it work. I was surprised the rental agency had a car like this available, but it seemed my luck was growing with every mile I put between me and Miami.

The area was beautiful, with cascading mountains on either side of the highway. Not much existed along this road like it did in Miami. Here, it was field after field. Farmlands and an occasional gas station or a small town would pop up every twenty or so miles.

I could see why my grandmother thought the area was beautiful. If the hotel overlooked all this, it would be a huge draw if we marketed it correctly.

My phone chimed from its spot on the cell-charging center console, and I glanced down to see a message from Dean. I'd have to read it later, but I did send him a thank-you earlier when I landed.

The car maneuvered into the far left lane as I passed a tractor trailer climbing an incline. Just as I moved back into the right lane, I noted the sign for Ashfield approaching a mile ahead.

After taking the exit, the road heading into the town was desolate except for an occasional tractor I saw moving through fields or a vehicle moving in the opposite direction. There was a fork in the road about ten minutes later, and the sign showed which different towns were in each direction.

Am I in Mayberry? I asked myself, remembering a black-and-white show Gigi loved.

I continued on, being mindful of the turns, since I wasn't familiar with the road. There were a few times I was worried the sports car was going to bottom out on steep slopes.

The GPS in the car alerted me of a change in speed limit ahead. As I slowed at the crest of a hill, I noticed a picturesque town below. It was everything one would imagine a small town to be. No high-rises. No oversized shopping centers. Just two- or three-story buildings and on-street parking. Flags waved in the breeze from their holders on lamp posts. People walked down the sidewalks, waving and chatting with friends.

An ache formed in my chest as I approached the area. As the car growled its presence, the people on the paths narrowed their eyes, trying to get a look at who was inside the car. I was thankful for the tinted windows. A few waved in my direction, and I was left wondering who they thought was inside. A billionaire sports star and world-renowned chef lived in town, so there was a good chance everyone thought I was one of them. That worked in my favor as I made my way to the other side of the downtown area.

The GPS instructed me to take a right, and I followed, noting a sign for the schools in the same direction. I thought it was smart Aurora lived close to her workplace.

I turned down another road and slowed the car to meet the twenty-five mile-per-hour speed limit. I'd memorized her address and watched as the numbers on the mailboxes grew.

There—512.

Before I pulled the car into her driveway, I took in the house with a small sedan parked outside it. It was a tiny bungalow with pale-yellow siding and white shutters and door. With a quick glance up and down the street, I noticed it was the only house with a pop of color. It instantly reminded me of Aurora. Light and bright.

I pulled my car behind hers and turned off the ignition. Leaving everything in the car except my phone, I strutted up the single porch step and knocked on the door. I assumed she was home with the car in the driveway, but when no one answered, I took a step back.

The desire to see her space superseded her privacy. I was her husband, after all. And I had a feeling Aurora had nothing to hide.

Reaching into my pocket, I pulled out the key Dean had copied for me and slipped it into the lock. Surprise registered—even though I had the feeling all along this was what it was for—when it fit and didn't jam as I turned it in the deadbolt. I did the same with the knob and opened the door a crack before removing the key completely.

"Aurora?" I called out as I stepped inside and closed the door behind me, looking around at the small space that appeared to be in the middle of a renovation. There were boards lying in the center of the living room floor and paint cans scattered in the hallway. A few streaks of color were up on a wall in the corner of the living room.

I noticed those were the only bits of color in the space. It was dull in comparison to the outside of the house. And not at all a setting I would have imagined Aurora living in.

From down the hall, I heard what I thought were people talking.

Maybe Aurora is on the phone?

"Hello," I said, with no response.

A door was cracked, and I pushed it open, not expecting what I found. Aurora was lying on her bed, legs bent, knees pointing to the ceiling, and her laptop next to her was playing a video. She held something between her legs while her head was tossed back, pressing into her pillow. Sounds were coming from the movie, and I quickly realized it was an erotic scene playing out.

"Yes," Aurora moaned as the sound of buzzing increased.

My fake wife was watching porn and pleasuring herself. This was the best fucking day ever. I wanted to give her more time to reach her climax, but then something came over me.

I wanted to be the one to bring her to her peak.
That orgasm should be mine.

Or she should at least know I was enjoying watching her.

Without much thought, I greeted, "Hello, wife," my voice coming out in an unintentional growl.

Chaos ensued as she jerked upright. The laptop clattered to the floor as Aurora tried her damnedest to cover her lower half with the blanket she was lying on top of. And that pesky vibrator landed only about a foot away from me. It was almost laughable how it continued to vibrate, dancing enthusiastically along the floor.

I picked it up and located the button on the bottom, silencing her little friend.

"We'll have to play with this later," I said as I walked casually into the room, setting the toy on her nightstand.

"What are you doing here, Talon? How the hell did you get inside?"

"Why, visiting my wife, of course. And I had a key made." I wasn't about to throw Dean under the bus.

"Yes, I see that, but why?" She yanked at the bedding, trying to cover up more as I sat on the edge, which trapped the end of her blanket. Her legs were now twisted in the soft material.

"Because I missed you?" I made it sound like a question, disguising the truth of the words. I was met with her angry, orgasm-stolen glare. "If you must know, I have work in Knoxville. It was easiest just to come stay with you."

"You weren't invited."

"What's yours is ours… remember?" I reminded her of our recent vows. Which prompted me to look at her fingers, which were bare.

"Where are your rings?"

"Where is yours?" she bit back, noticing I wasn't wearing my wedding band either. Until the marriage was officially announced by my team, which was something I was still working on, I thought it best not to be seen wearing it.

"Touché. I'll wear mine if you wear yours."

"No," she countered. "Can you please leave so I can get dressed?"

"I was enjoying the show."

"Oh, I bet you were." She stared at me, waiting for me to buckle, but she didn't know me well enough. I wasn't going to back down. "Fine."

She tossed aside the blanket with a flourish, the soft, pink material floating down in a heap beside me as she stomped over to her dresser. She moved so quickly I only got a quick glimpse of her before she tugged on cotton panties and then a pair of denim shorts. But from what I saw, she had a great—

"Are you done gawking?" she asked with narrowed eyes, continuing her clomps over to the nightstand, snatching up the toy I set on top and tossing it inside the drawer. Her shorts hugged that glorious ass with frays that must've tickled the backs of her thighs.

Ignoring me completely, Aurora left the bedroom, and I watched a black mass dart down the hall behind her. I was intrigued, so I went after them both, finding Aurora perched on a barstool, drinking from a bottle of water.

I moved to the opposite side and leaned against the counter, facing her.

"Why are you really here, Talon?"

"Does it matter?"

She snarled at me, and I felt something brush against my ankle through my suit pants.

"Who is this?" I asked as I scooped up the black cat. Its eyes were a startling shade of green. When I didn't get a response, I looked up from petting the cat to catch Aurora's confused gaze.

"What?"

"That's Draco. He hates everyone but me."

"Draco?"

"I'm a fan of *Harry Potter* fanfic. Draco and Hermione."

I had no idea what she was talking about, and I told her so.

"Never mind. He usually only likes to come out when someone feeds him; otherwise, he hides. He's notorious for nipping at people. My sisters call him a grump."

"Well, then the two of us have something in common." With one last stroke of his soft fur, I placed the cat back on the floor.

"So, roomie, where can I put my things?"

"You're not staying here, Talon."

"I am. I'll put my things in your room."

I moved around the island and headed for the front door, with Aurora hot on my heels.

"Talon, you're not staying here!" she shouted as she reached the porch.

I spun on my heels and encroached in her space. Aurora tried to take a step back, but I cupped her jaw with my hands. With my fingers brushing the back of her neck, I leaned forward and pressed my lips against hers. This wasn't an exploratory kiss, but it lasted longer than a peck.

I pulled away when I felt her body relax against mine.

Turning around, I made my way back to my car and began grabbing my things. I spotted Aurora leaning against the jamb of the front door, watching me closely. I wheeled both suitcases, carried the garment bag, and wore my laptop bag up to the house.

"You know, you can't just kiss me every time you want your way."

"I know. There are a lot of things I can do with my tongue to get my way," I said as I passed her and lugged my items into her bedroom.

It was spacious but just as dull as her living room. While I was unpacking my things, she moved onto the bed with her laptop in hand, slamming a button repeatedly after she opened it.

"Your house is boring."

Ignoring me, she said, "You broke my laptop."

"I didn't break anything. I didn't realize I was going to walk in on you watching porn."

"It's my house!" she shouted.

"I'll buy you a new one."

"I don't want a new one. I want *this* one."

I finished hanging my last suit in her surprisingly large closet and then went over to the bed. Crawling up the mattress, I moved her laptop out of the way, then hovered over her seated body. She tilted her head back to look up at me.

"I'm sorry I broke your laptop. I will buy you a new one, because I *should*, not because I *can*. Also, if you didn't hear me earlier, your house is boring as hell, and you aren't. What's that about?"

"I… um…," she stuttered, and I reached out and stroked a piece of her long, blonde hair. "I can't think when you're this close."

Releasing her hair, I put my hand on the bed and brought myself even closer to her. Aurora leaned back more and more until she was fully lying on the bed. I rested my lower half between her legs and stifled a groan when I felt the warmth radiating from her center.

I rubbed the side of my nose against hers and watched as she closed her eyes. We barely knew each other, but our chemistry was off the charts. It was still early in the day, which left me plenty of time to help her reach that orgasm I denied her earlier with my unexpected arrival.

Moving one hand toward her hip, I let it trail upward, skimming the barely visible skin of her waist. It was soft and smooth, and I wanted to taste it. Aurora shivered at the contact.

Maybe she would be more interested in a physical relationship than I first presumed.

Her eyes opened slowly, and she gave me a coy grin.

"What do you think if we—," I began, but a sudden screeching noise sounded from her dresser.

"Shit," she cursed as she shoved me out of the way to grab her phone. "I have to leave for my parents' house in a few minutes."

"Okay," I said as I rolled off the bed and walked over to my suitcase, where I left it open in the corner.

"What are you doing?"

"Changing. I figured your family would prefer a more casual meeting, not me in the suit I wore to work this morning and on the airplane."

"You're not meeting my family."

"Oh, I am. Meeting my in-laws is top priority."

I turned back to the luggage to bend and grab a T-shirt and a pair of navy shorts. As I stood up again, I felt Aurora touch my arm. I held back my flinch.

"Talon, you're taking this whole thing too seriously."

"It *is* serious. I'm assuming you got your new social security card and the copy of our marriage certificate. Our wedding may have been for an arrangement that suits both of us, but make no mistake; you're my wife in every shape and form."

"But—"

"And that includes meeting my in-laws."

Aurora looked defeated. "Will you at least be… nice? I don't want you growling at everyone."

"I don't growl at everyone."

Aurora's brows arched, and she tilted her head to the side.

"Well, I'm nice to *you*."

"That's true, I guess. Your employees are terrified of you though."

"And that's a bad thing?"

Tired of arguing, Aurora huffed as she left the bedroom, but I didn't miss her quick glance over her shoulder as I slipped my dress shirt down my arms.

I wished I had a chance to take a quick shower, but I spritzed a bit of cologne over my T-shirt and shorts, knowing it was the best I could do. I didn't have a lot of time, but I snooped a little by examining the pictures propped up in frames on her dresser. Her family looked happy. She had numerous images of all of them.

Grabbing a pair of casual sneakers, I slid them on my feet, then dipped inside the bathroom to untie my hair that had been twisted at the base of my neck since this morning. The elastic slipped free, and it was a relief to have the strands loose around my shoulders. With a quick splash of water in my hands, I ran my fingers through it.

"Talon!" Aurora shouted from somewhere in the house, and I watched my face transform in the mirror. It was a side of me I'd never seen before. I was… happy.

I left the bathroom and met Aurora just inside the front door of her house, seeing her breath catch when she caught a glimpse of me.

"We're taking your car," Aurora said breathlessly as she bent to pet Draco.

I smiled inside. "Yes, dear."

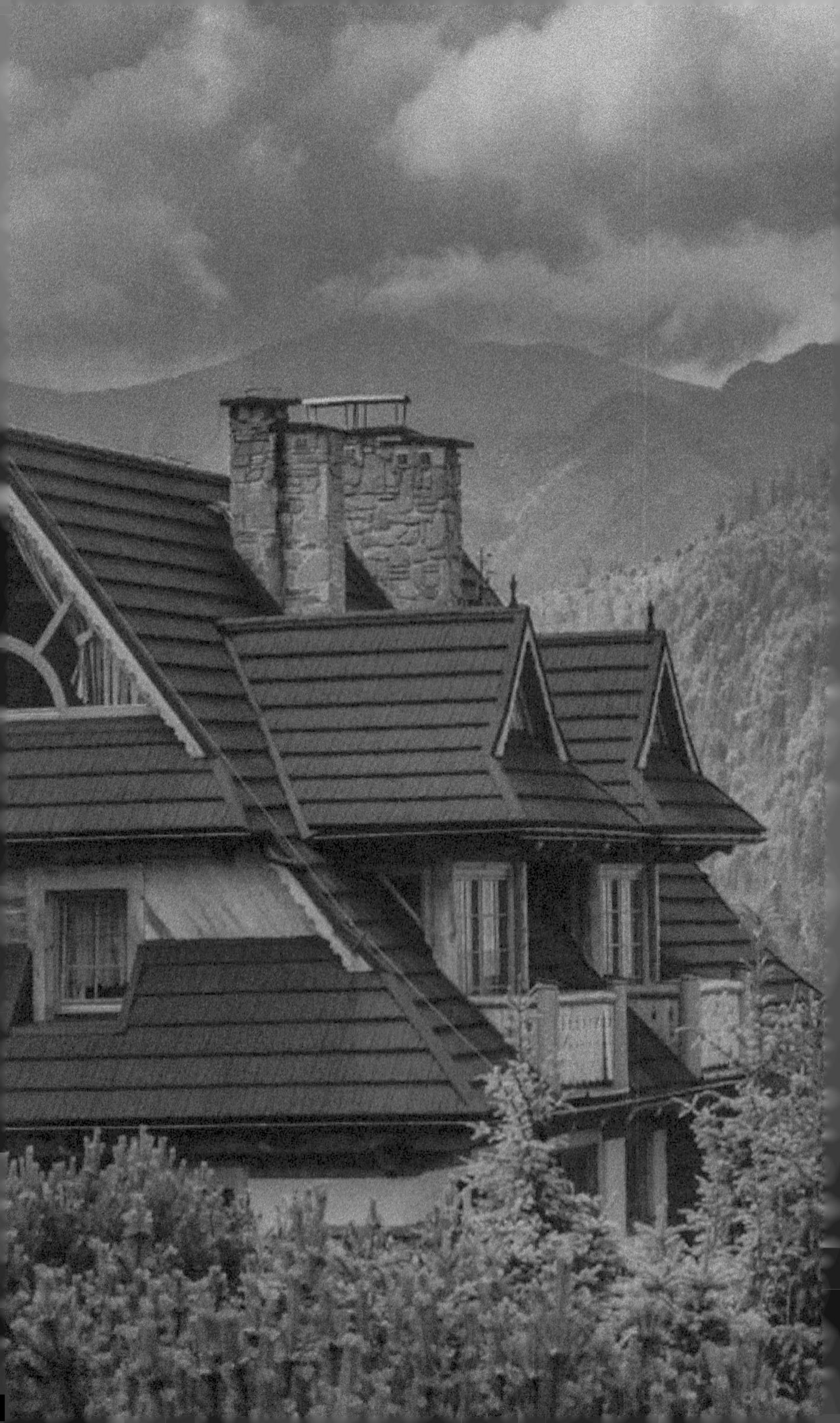

Chapter Twelve

Aurora

How did the man have the most beautiful hair I'd ever seen? Not only was he incredibly gorgeous in his fitted suits, but even in his casual wear, he looked like he hopped right out of a magazine.

As he stepped past me onto my front porch, I had to grip the back pockets of my shorts to keep from reaching out and stroking my fingers through his dark strands. Every time I was around him, I had this staggering urge to touch him—though he tended to flinch, even when he was expecting it.

"See something you like?" he hollered. Talon was already standing next to the expensive car, which I barely took notice of. I had no idea how long I'd been standing there looking out into oblivion.

Ignoring him, I quickly shut the front door, locked up, and made my way to the car. A light summer breeze picked up just as I reached the driveway. It swirled around me like a playful child. Something strong and masculine-scented floated in the air, and I knew it was Talon's cologne straightaway. I wasn't good with fragrances, but it reminded me of sandalwood and vetiver, a smell I was only familiar with because I had a candle with that name on the label. The combination of the two scents was potent in the best way.

Which meant the coupling of the cologne with Talon's innate sex appeal was going to make this twenty-minute car ride torturous. I must have done something bad in a past life.

I went to grab the handle of the car, but Talon was there before I could even reach the door. He opened passenger side and waited patiently for me to slip inside.

His gesture surprised me. Not only because it was him being chivalrous, but because no man besides my father had ever opened a door for me. Not Jeremy. Not any of the boyfriends before him. No one.

"Thanks," I mumbled as I slid into the low bucket seat, admiring the stitching and leather as I settled in.

I was already a nervous wreck by the time Talon pulled out of the driveway. The car was loud, almost annoyingly so, and my neighbors made their existence known as they loitered in their yards to check out the vehicle. I sank low in my seat, even though I knew they couldn't see inside. Talon glanced over at me once and winked before he revved the engine and darted down the street. The car rumbled as we came to a stop, and I caught myself smiling.

We sat at the stop sign for a minute, and I wondered why we were waiting, until Talon asked, "Directions?"

"Oh! Sorry. Take a right. I can plug it into the GPS if you'd like, but it's a pretty straight shot once we get onto the main road."

"I'll follow your lead," he replied, and I clamped my legs together. I had a sinking suspicion he wasn't just referring to the directions to my childhood home. There was something sexual in the way he said it.

"Take another right, then straight for about twenty minutes. There will be a sloped ninety-degree turn halfway, so be ready for that."

"I'll be fine."

In the car, there was no music, no talking… just the sweet purr of the engine as we zipped down the road. Talon drove the car flawlessly, but I supposed when you had endless amounts of money, you had access to driving luxurious, exotic cars whenever you wanted.

The fields on either side of the road were tall, with wheat and grass rippling in the breeze. I tied my hair back so I could ride with the window down without creating a knotted mess of my locks. Leaning my head back against the headrest, I took it all in. It was rare that I was ever driven around so that I could enjoy my surroundings. Ashfield was beautiful, and I often forgot how much so. It was an idealistic place to grow up, and usually it took me visiting a big city to see that. As much as my sisters wanted to spread their wings and leave the small town, they both found their way back here.

Thinking about my sisters left me wondering what their reaction would be when they met Talon. I hadn't even said anything to Franny, and she was my best friend. It was going to be a shock when she carpooled with me to school tomorrow.

The reaction I was most worried about was Andrew's. He was overly protective of me, and for good reason. He was there to help pick up my mess when it all blew up in my face.

Suddenly, I felt a hand land on top of my own, halting their twisting motion.

"You okay?" Talon asked, and I nodded.

"Just nervous."

"Why? They still pining for your ex?"

I was surprised he remembered that part of our deal. Since our kiss after the wedding vows, I hadn't thought about Jeremy for a second.

"No."

"Then what is it?" He moved his hand back to the steering wheel, and I immediately missed its warmth.

"It's nothing. Don't worry about it."

Smoothly, Talon maneuvered the car off to the side of the road. Well, as far as it could go. There wasn't much of a shoulder on these winding paths.

"What are you doing?" I asked frantically as I checked all the mirrors to make sure there was no one coming up behind us. "Talon, someone could hit the car."

"I don't care," he explained as he slipped off his seatbelt and turned to face me. "We're going to sit here until you talk to me. I can tell something is up."

"We're going to be late, and you don't want to be late for my family dinner."

"I don't give a flying fuck about being late. I give a fuck about what's bothering you. You were over there, nearly pulling your nails away from your skin. So, we're going to sit here until you get everything off your chest."

"Talon...," I warned, but he lifted his arm to rest on top of the steering wheel and continued to stare at me. "Ugh. Do you always get what you want?"

"Mostly."

I contemplated lying to him, or giving the barest of details, but I had a feeling Talon didn't get to where he was in life by believing someone's bullshit.

"Fine. I'm just nervous, okay? I can't just introduce you as a boyfriend. You're living at my freaking house, for God's sake."

"I'm not your boyfriend."

"I know. We're married, and my parents are going to flip when I tell them."

"Why? It's better to tell them now before we leak it to the press."

The press? I hadn't really even considered the fact that the tabloids would find out sooner or later.

"What do you mean?"

"There's always the chance that someone at the registry office leaked it when my name came across their desk. My plan was for us to make an appearance at that charity event in Nashville in two weeks."

"Oh."

"Now, please continue."

Slouching in my seat, I turned away from Talon and stared through the windshield. A large dual-wheel truck turned the corner and started coming in our direction. He slowed down as he got closer and asked if we needed any help, and Talon let him know we were fine. As the truck moved down the road, I realized I missed my opportunity to hitch a ride.

Talon faced me again and waited patiently as I picked at the threads on my shorts.

"I made this mistake before," I mumbled quietly when his stare became too much and I felt like a circus act.

"What mistake?" Of course he would have wolf-like hearing.

"Do we have to do this right now?"

"Mm hm."

"Ugh," I groaned, then went on to tell him that my high-school boyfriend and I went to Pigeon Forge, Tennessee right after graduation. I'd just turned eighteen, and we thought since we were adults and in love, we should get married. We got a marriage license in the morning and were married that evening at a little drive-thru chapel. And that night, instead of enjoying our honeymoon, I found him screwing the neighbor of the little log cabin we rented for the week. I was so angry and called him every name in the book. I didn't understand how he could treat me that way, especially after we had *just* exchanged vows.

We argued for hours, and then he just hopped into his Jeep and left me there. He had even taken the key to the cabin, so I couldn't go inside to get any of my things. For whatever reason, the woman he was having sex with took pity on me and let me use her phone. Andrew was the first person I called, because I was so embarrassed.

He came to my rescue, with my dad in the passenger seat. They kept saying how disappointed they were in me. That I should have known better.

"You have to understand that I was the wild child. I snuck out, went to bonfire parties, drank. All the things you wish and pray your children will never do.

Thankfully, I stayed away from drugs, because I have no idea where I'd be in life if I'd fallen down that path.

"When we got back to Ashfield, Dad took me to the courthouse right away and had the marriage annulled based on refusal of marital rights. Something about him consummating our marriage with someone else fell under that line."

"What happened to him… the guy?"

"I don't know. He never came back to town. Probably a good thing. My brother is waiting for retaliation. So, you can see why me coming home suddenly announcing our marriage is going to rock my family. Not even my sisters know I've been married before. I'm sure my dad told my mom, but I'm not even positive about that."

"If they don't know, then it shouldn't rock them *too* much, right? I think your family might surprise you."

I was skeptical that they would believe the lie. An actress, I was not, and this was the show of my life I was about to put on.

"Do you feel better now?" he asked me, and I shrugged as I unclenched my hands and slipped them under my thighs.

"Marginally."

Talon put the car back into drive, and we were back on our way to my parents' farm. He maneuvered the sports car around the sharp turn with the ease of someone who had completed it a dozen times before. When we crested a small hill, I pointed out the Crawford Bed & Breakfast that Autumn and Colton ran. They lived on the third floor but had been discussing building their own home farther up the property so they could open up the third floor living space to more guests. As someone who loved her nieces, I was hoping that meant the two of them were trying for a baby.

"Farther down that dirt road is my sister Alex's house. In fact, all of this land and some on the other side of the town belongs to my family. The Easterlys were one of the founding families of Ashfield. My parents set aside parcels of land for each of us if we ever decided to build on it."

Talon didn't speak up, but I watched his fingers tighten around the steering wheel and the muscle in his jaw pulse.

"Sorry," I whispered. I hadn't considered how hard it might be for him to hear about my family, which to any outsider would seem perfect. I was aware of that fact. His messed-up family was the reason he and I found ourselves married in the first place. "Up ahead, you'll see a sign for Sunny Brook Farms on the left. You can turn there. It's a few miles down the drive."

Dirt kicked up around the car as he turned toward the farm. Just like last week, a few of the tractors and UTVs were out assessing the land as we approached the harvest. Nate was probably somewhere on the property, testing the soils with one of his robotic gadgets. The man was an engineering genius.

"There it is."

"Wow," I heard Talon breathe. Cocking my head, I tried to see the farm from an outsider's perspective. It was a large, classic farmhouse with white siding and a wrap-around porch my sisters and I loved to play on when we were younger. My parents recently installed a green metal roof, and I really loved how it blended in with the mountainous background of the farm.

"It's not the original farmhouse that was on the property. That's farther back. But my parents did a nice job renovating this one decades ago. It's timeless."

"I bet you had a great childhood here."

"I did."

Talon put the car in park in front of the garage as I unhooked my belt.

"Don't get out."

"What?" I asked as he slipped out of the car and walked around the back. He opened the door on my side and held his hand out to help me.

"Thanks," I replied, and then I froze as something we hadn't discussed crossed my mind. "Talon—" I jerked his arm back to get him to face me. "—we don't have any backstory. What are we going to do?"

"Everything will be fine, Aurora. Just follow my lead."

"Will you please call me Rory? They're going to be suspicious if you use my full name."

"No. Now, please lead the way."

Mumbling to myself about how this was going to be a nightmare, I trudged across the driveway to the porch, Talon following closely behind as if we were an actual couple, and opened the door to let us inside the house.

"Mom! Dad! We're here," I called out as I set my small bag on the bench by the door.

"We're in the den, sweetie!" I heard my dad reply, and I gestured for Talon to follow me.

The house smelled delicious, and I was hopeful that Mom was making her Greek chicken with feta and hummus.

"Smells good," Talon said as we moved toward the back of the house. It wasn't a full open concept, but most of the rooms now had large openings connecting them together. Except the kitchen. It opened completely to the large den, where we all usually congregated.

"Deep breath," I whispered to myself as I stepped into the living room, with Talon hot on my heels. "Hey."

Dad's back was facing me from his recliner as he watched a baseball game on the television. Mom, Alex, and the twins were seated on the extra-long couch against the wall.

"Hi, sweetheart," Mom said to me, quickly glancing over before returning her attention to the game. It took just a second for her head to spin back in my direction. "Oh! You brought a guest. My word." She jumped up from the couch and gestured for us to join the group. "Well, now. Rory, please introduce your guest." She held out her hand. "Hi, I'm Rory's mom, Marisol."

"Mom, this is Talon. He's…."

Talon reached out his hand and greeted my mother. "I'm her husband."

Silence fell across the room. Even the twins. And the game playing on the television was muted.

"I'm sorry. Did you say *husband*?" my dad asked as he stood from his chair and moved behind my mother.

"Yes, sir. I'm Talon—"

"Beckett. Talon Beckett, heir to the Wilder Hotels," Colton called out, drawing attention away from me. "I've been to a few of your charity events."

A buzzer sounded in the kitchen, and my mother quickly slid her hand free from Talon's and fussed with the apron tied over her clothes. "Oh dear. Dinners ready, everyone. Um... Rory, please go grab another chair from the dining room for your... uh... husband."

For lack of a better word, dinner was... awkward. Talon had reverted to his grumpy self once I situated a chair for him at the dinner table. Whenever someone asked him a question, he responded with a one-word answer. It wasn't until Molly and Eloise took control of the conversation that I saw him crack the smallest of smirks. It was hard not to smile with those two little girls around.

"Auntie Rory, why don't you have a ring like Mommy?" Molly asked as my mom brought out the cookies and crème pie. It was the first question anyone asked about the marriage. Before then, the questions were about Talon's job and upbringing. Something I knew he absolutely was not going to give an inch on.

"Oh, well…." I hesitated as I tried to come up with the most believable answer.

Talon looked over at Molly and said, "I had to get them sized correctly, and sometimes that can take a couple of days. It's why I wasn't here with Aurora right away."

It was the most I heard him speak since we walked through the door. And this time, instead of being annoyed that he used my full first name, I found it kind of… sweet.

"Huh. What does it look like?" Molly added.

"Would you like to see?"

She and her sister nodded enthusiastically, and Talon reached into his pocket and pulled out the trio of rings. Two wedding bands and the obnoxiously large diamond ring. The twins' eyes widened as they took it all in.

"You brought them?" I asked, surprised.

Talon leaned closer to me, his lips brushing against my ear as he whispered, "Figured no one would believe you would marry me without the evidence."

I felt the rush of blood to my cheeks as I blushed. All eyes were on us as he pulled back and held the rings up between the two of us.

His eyebrows lifted in question, as if asking if he could slip the rings back onto my finger. My smile was his answer, and he gently placed the wedding band, then the diamond ring, onto my third finger.

"Wow, that's some ring, son," my dad said, and I suddenly remembered there were other people in the room with us. Anytime Talon touched me, I tended to forget we weren't alone.

"It's very big," Eloise chimed in as she shoveled a forkful of the pie into her mouth.

Across from me, Autumn tilted her head to the side as she and Alex examined the ring perched on my finger. "Princess cut. About three or four carats?" she prompted, and Talon nodded. "It's pretty, but not really Rory's style. She's more into antiques and classic cuts. But I guess you need something flashy."

"She can always pick out something more suited for her."

"Don't you think you should have known what was more suited for her when you went ring shopping?" Alex was gripping my hand as she tried picking a fight with Talon. From the corner of my eye, I watched his fist clench under the table and his jaw tick in that way I loved.

I darted my gaze over to my mother, eyes wide as I silently begged her to steer the conversation in a different direction.

"That's enough, Alex. Rory getting married in Miami is no different than you and Nate eloping without notice."

"Sure it is. Nate and I have known each other for a year and met a year before that. I mean, Rory, did you even go to Miami for a teachers' conference, or was it to traipse around on a quicky honeymoon?"

"Alexandra," Dad scolded.

"That's not what happened," I defended.

The desserts I plated for myself and Talon remained untouched on the table, and as one of my favorite desserts, it left me miserable. I whispered to Talon to try some, and he reluctantly lifted his fork to gather a small bite. At the same time, I reached under the table after Alex finally relinquished her grasp on my fingers and clasped his hand with my own, securing it with my other hand around his wrist. I could feel his heart was racing.

I looked him over. His hair covered half of his face on either side, and I wondered if he was using it as a way to mask some of his emotions. He had it tucked behind his ears until Alex started her accusations.

Letting go of his wrist, I reached up and tucked the strands closest to me behind his ear again. When he turned to smile at me, I felt myself melt just a little more. A smiling Talon was lethal.

"Mom, do you want to hear how we met?"

"Oh, yes. How rude of me. I was so interested in learning about you, Talon, and your family that it completely slipped my mind to learn how y'all met. I'm sorry. You just remind me of someone. Please, dear, I want to hear all about your meet cute."

"What's a meet cute?" Eloise asked Mom just as I was about to speak. Instead, I answered her. "It's when two people meet in a funny or unlikely way that sort of forces them together."

"Oooh," she said in a long exhale, absorbing the response.

"Now, Talon and I met in a *very* interesting way," I said to my niece but addressed the entire table. When he stepped out of my bedroom earlier with his hair loose around his shoulders, it didn't take me long to figure out we had indeed met before, and not under the best circumstances. "A year ago, when I was attending the same conference, everything that could've gone wrong chose to do just that. Everything was delayed from my flight, right down to my ride to the hotel, since traffic was insane. On top of all that, I was going to miss registration, so I got out of the car and decided to hurry to the hotel on foot. Well, Miami is hot and humid, so by the time I got through the door, I was a sweaty, frizzy mess.

"After rushing to check in to the conference, it was time to check in to the hotel itself, and this guy bumped into me so hard that I fell on the floor. I was so shocked that I just laid there on the cold marble for a second, thankful I hadn't hit my head."

"What did you do?" Eloise asked, enraptured by the story.

"Well, I asked this person why they weren't helping me up. And when they didn't respond, I saw they were on the phone. I swear, he looked like he had been sleeping on the streets. He had a scraggly beard, torn clothes, and hair down past his shoulders. If he hadn't smelled so good, I would have thought he lived under a bridge like those trolls you love to read about."

Both of the twins giggled, and I straightened in the chair to find Talon looking at me curiously. I wondered if he was reliving the moment as I described it. Did he remember it differently, or at all?

"What happened next?" one of the twins prompted.

"Well, I noticed this man seemed really distraught, so I got up on my own and grabbed my suitcase. But you know what happened? The handle broke. It was the worst."

"Oh no! What did you do?"

"Nothing. The guy handed me a piece of paper with his number on it," I fibbed. "He offered to replace my suitcase, and then he was gone."

"Wow."

Alex was mumbling something from across the table as she scrolled on her phone. I finally caught a few of her words. "It's true. He took over the week she was there. Damn."

"That's not the entire story," Talon stated as he released my hand. "Eat your dessert, Aurora. I'll finish this up."

With a chortle, I agreed and took a hearty bite of my favorite pie.

"Now, everything your aunt said is true, but the part she left out was that I tripped over her suitcase she was pulling behind her, and that's what made me bump into her so hard. And not because I was in a rush, but because I was too busy staring at *her* to look down at where my feet were going."

Using my hand to cover my mouth around the large bite of dessert I'd just taken, I spoke up to add to his made-up story, "Yeah, because I looked like a wet, frizzy rat."

The twins chuckled.

"No, because she was beautiful, even as a sweaty mess. When I ran off, it was to meet with my grandfather. I had been living on my houseboat. I wasn't planning on taking over the family business, but my uncle was nowhere in sight. Someone had to run the company. That's why I seemed 'distraught.' When I gave your aunt my number, I didn't expect her to call. But she was adamant I replace her suitcase. And… here we are."

"That's so romantic," my mother cooed. I could practically see cartoon hearts in her eyes as she looked at Talon.

The story had been an embellished version of the truth—except for the phone number portion and everything after. Had we truly been in a relationship, I could see how someone would find it dreamy.

"So, you two have been… talking for a year? Andrew is going to flip when he hears this," Autumn asked as she scooched her chair closer to Colton's. She leaned into his side as he draped his arm around her shoulders. Andrew had been overprotective of all of us when it came to dating. Even more so with me, after my quicky marriage left me stranded in the middle of the mountains with no way to get home.

"For the most part."

"Well, I'm happy for your, Rory and Talon. Maybe you'll let us host you a reception this fall for all your friends and family. I'm sure we can find a date that fits into both of your schedules," Mom said as she began to collect the plates. My father quickly got up and took her place, urging her to sit back down.

There was one problem with this entire idea though. Not only was this entire charade going to be over in six months, but Talon was likely going to be leaving soon. There was no way he planned on staying in Ashfield for longer than a week or two. He'd never survive the small-town life. Talon Beckett was born to shine, and I refused to be the one to dim his light.

Chapter Thirteen

Talon

Aurora's family was exactly as I expected them to be—minus the retired hockey star and the dirt-covered billionaire. Though I was aware they were a part of the family, it was still surprising. Alex's husband, Nate, didn't join us right away, but he came into the house just as dessert was finishing up. He had been working on new soil robotics software and wanted to test it before the harvest.

Aurora's father was gung-ho about describing the harvesting process to me when I asked. It was fascinating. I'd always been envious of people who used their hands for work. Those were the people who made our world what it was. Not greedy people like my grandfather and uncle, or even Dean's relatives. Though, at one point, his family was deep into the rum business. Now they spent their time on extravagant yachts.

Nash, Aurora's father, even offered to let me help with the harvest. I agreed despite Aurora's wide eyes and gasp. She had no idea that back in boarding school, I'd been on the rowing team. I still had calluses on my palms from that time in my life. I was sure that harvesting corn couldn't be much more difficult than that.

Plus, living on a houseboat, I had to learn all sorts of handy skills, especially when I rode out that hurricane.

The longer we were in the house, which truly felt like a home, I felt those intrusive thoughts crawl over me like little black widows ready to strike at any moment. It seemed like every second her family accepted my presence, the deeper into my dark reflections I fell.

And I knew exactly what it was when I caught Aurora and her father laughing as they played a board game together. I was jealous. And I hated it. I'd never been jealous of anyone before, not even in boarding school. Every kid there had come from some sort of dysfunctional family. It's why I fit right in.

By the time the family was chittering about the event venue and I heard Aurora's ex's name brought up more than once, I'd had enough. I was suffocating in their space. Not only were the walls closing in, my vision growing gray around the edges, but I couldn't catch my breath.

Aurora caught my eye with her infectious grin I couldn't get enough of, and I felt bad for being the reason the grin slipped further and further into a frown.

"I... uh... think we better go. Talon's been traveling all day," she said as she pulled herself up off the floor. She leaned over her dad and hugged him tight, then did the same with her siblings and her mother. She looked so at ease with her family, and I couldn't understand why she had been so nervous before we arrived. That only made my whirlpool of emotions that much more unsteady.

I didn't say goodbye—couldn't have even if I tried. I lifted my hand in the air as if I had somewhere else to be, and I did. A world of self-pity.

We made it outside, and as I inhaled deeply, Aurora wordlessly slid into the car, not allowing me to even open the door for her. She was angry at me, and probably had every right to be, but I wasn't in the right headspace to deal with her emotional drama.

As I slid into my own seat, I started the engine. Up on the porch, I was amazed to find her family waiting patiently for us to depart. Aurora plastered an overzealous fake smile on her face to appease her family as she waved goodbye.

We darted down their driveway, and I only glanced into the rearview mirror as I crested the hill that kept their home hidden from the road.

The tension in the car was too much, and I didn't know how to ease it, especially since it was my own doing. Pulling out onto the main road, I told Aurora I thought her family was nice and that their home was beautiful. She immediately told me to can it.

After a moment, I tried again. "Sorry we had to leave early. I was… uh… having a hard time."

"Is this your typical M.O., Talon? Push away anyone who could care about you? Not just me, but my family? Despite this being a fake marriage, they don't know that. During dinner, we had them thinking we're in the midst of wedded bliss, and they probably would've assumed we're rushing home to jump in bed together had you not been such a dick. Hell, Alex most likely thinks I'm knocked up already. But the way you acted *after* dinner is going to leave them questioning all sorts of things. If you would have spoken to maybe… anyone, you would've seen they immediately accepted you. Now, they're going to wonder what is going on. We may live in a rural part of the South, but we're not stupid."

"I'm sorry."

"Why do you push people away, Talon? It seems like you use your grumpy exterior to keep everyone at a football field's distance from you. Everyone except Dean, because he's too hardheaded to do what you want."

I maneuvered the car around a sharp turn that felt similar to my emotions today. "I don't want to talk about it."

"Well, I do."

"Aurora," I growled, my hands rotating back and forth on the steering wheel as I clenched it in my fists.

"Don't you *Aurora* me, Talon Beckett. You stop this car and tell me what has you so fucking pissed off that you practically rushed out of my family's house like your ass was on fire."

"No."

"Why are you being such an asshole?" she shouted at me, and my fury was bubbling at the surface, ready to detonate. All it needed was the flicker of a flame to set it off. From the corner of my eye, I noticed her yanking off her rings again. She was struggling with the large diamond. When both were free from her finger, she shoved them into her bag.

Something about her removing the jewelry I'd given her was the last straw.

"I'm fucking *jealous*, okay? You have this family who loves you unconditionally. Even after everything you told me about your annulment and the sleazeball exes, they still love you."

"They don't know about the annulment, remember? Only my dad and Andrew do."

"I can guarantee your dad did not keep that information from your mother. God, you're so jaded that you don't even truly *see* how in love your parents are. And from what I've heard, people that in love don't keep secrets from each other. Do you have any idea how lucky you are, Aurora? How I would have *killed* for that growing up?

"Instead, I was stuck having to marry you to convince my grandfather that I should have the position that is *rightfully* mine and full access to the trust fund my mother left me."

We'd been arguing and stewing for so much of the trip that I was surprised we were already pulling into her driveway.

"So, you did it for money?" she asked quietly, but I knew she was on the verge of an outburst.

"No, that wasn't the only reason."

Before I could blink, she was out of the car and marching up to the porch.

"Aurora!" I hollered as I followed her inside the house. I couldn't even remember if I turned the car off.

I found her in the bedroom, the door locked. My fist collided with the wood as I knocked repeatedly. "Aurora, we need to talk."

The door swung open, and I nearly collided with the small sprite as she dashed from the bedroom. In the span of a minute or two, she changed her clothes and now wore a body-hugging blue dress that reminded me of the Caribbean.

"Where the fuck are you going?"

"Somewhere else. I expect you to be gone when I get back."

My hands clenched the openings of my pockets as I stared at her in bewilderment. "And where would I go?"

"Use some of that money you like to throw around. I'm sure you can be resourceful."

Her hips swayed with each step as she approached the front door, and I panicked. I'd never had someone who I wanted to stay leave me so abruptly. Usually, people were too busy trying to appease me and apologize for whatever they did to piss me off, because they were afraid I would destroy them, whether personally or in their business.

"Aurora!" I called out again as I dashed after her. She was already climbing into the passenger seat of a car idling on the street.

Geez, how quick did she set this up?

I stood there on the porch in awe, watching the retreating taillights. She'd left me here. Not just on her porch, or at her home, but alone in a town where I knew no one.

Slinking back inside with my shoulders hunched, I stalked over to her kitchen and opened the fridge. I was surprised to find a few beers inside. Popping the top off a Stella, I took a hearty sip. I hadn't had the fizzy beverage in a while, usually opting for something stronger so I could relax more quickly.

I stepped over all the random items in her living room and sat on the couch, surprised to find a piece of paper with a picture from a magazine sitting on her coffee table. I examined it closely and realized she was trying to recreate the image in her own space. It was a little busy for the smaller wall, but I could see where she was going with it. Redesigning spaces was one of my favorite parts of the hotel renovations. We had a team who worked on the specifics, but I made sure they followed my vision.

Tossing the paper back on the table, I looked at the wall again. As the setting sun began to disappear behind the mountains, the shadows showed a slight discoloration in the ivory paint. At one point, she must've had large picture frames hanging in the room.

During a quick tour her mother gave me after dinner, she caught me admiring a few images on a wall in the dark office. The Easterly matriarch seemed sad when she mentioned they were photographs Aurora had taken when she was in school. To the untrained eye, they were simply just pictures, but to someone who examined art and photographs as part of my job when picking what to showcase in the hotel, I could see the skill Aurora possessed.

The longer I sat, the longer I pondered if these frame outlines were from images she had taken.

Grabbing my phone from my pocket, I quickly typed a message out to Olive and asked her to send a package overnight to Aurora's address. My assistant still wasn't in the know about the quicky wedding, but she had grown suspicious at my disappearance and undisclosed return date.

Finishing the beer, I looked around the room for a television but found none. Not that I watched TV often, but I was surprised Aurora didn't have one. What she did have were three floor-to-ceiling bookshelves in a small room across from her bedroom. The bookshelves were completely filled with books, and as I looked closer at the spines, they were all romance novels. Some of them seemed tame, but then others left me wondering what kind of porn Aurora had been watching several hours ago when I arrived.

An hour passed, and despite my better judgement, I'd fallen victim to a small-town romance I struggled to put down. I was rooting for the underdog in the story—the lifelong friend—and not the billionaire who swooped in and caught the main female character's eye. Just the thought of Aurora catching someone else's eye made mine twitch.

With an idea in mind, I quickly sent Dean a message, and he immediately responded.

Dean

> No

> Fuck you!

As I waited for his follow-up, I changed out of my casual clothes and put on the suit I wore the night I met Aurora at the bar. She may not have said the words, but after years of having women sexually pine over me with their eyes, I knew she liked what she'd seen.

When I was fitted for it in London, the tailor referred to the suit as "bespoke." It fit my body like a glove. I guessed it was worth the ten grand it cost to have it custom-made.

Dean still hadn't replied by the time I slid my feet into my dress shoes. I looked myself over in the mirror Aurora had propped in the corner of her bedroom. The suit was my armor, and I was ready for battle. No one was going to look at what was mine while I had her, even if it *was* all just a ploy.

> Still waiting.

I left the house, locking up with the key Dean made, but not before I gave some love to Draco, who had come out of hiding for a second when I clicked off the bedroom light.

Dean
Asshole. She's at a place called Ole Days.

Thanks

You owe me.

Nope

Message bubbles kept popping up and then disappearing as I started the car. I plugged the name of the location into the GPS. Was it an invasion of privacy to keep track of Aurora? Probably, but I also didn't care. With our marriage, her safety was going to be my top priority.

> How did you lose your wife already?

> We had a fight. She left.

> She won't answer your call?

> I know better than to try.

> Better get her before someone else does.

Leave it to Dean to know exactly what I feared. I had no idea how Aurora hadn't been snatched up already. I supposed she had been for a while. At least twice. And both of those idiots had broken it off with *her*. I couldn't understand it.

As the car purred to life and I pulled the Ferrari onto the street, my screen flashed with a call from Dean. I pressed the button that would allow his voice to play through the speakers.

"Have you looked into the hotel yet?" was his first question. Dean didn't mess around with pleasantries when his money was involved. It probably wasn't the best idea to have the two of us working together. We were both the kind of people who always think we're right. But our friendship had lasted thus far, so as long as he dealt with the company for any financial decisions, then our friendship should stay intact.

"Not yet. I'm going by this week. Though, if the view from the lodge is anything like the view during the drive, then we won't have any trouble selling that part."

"What did your grandfather say when he found out?" he asked.

Gigi was thrilled I was taking on the project, but Grandfather had been less than, as expected.

"He was livid. It was a property they'd been trying to ignore for years. But if he didn't want it, then he should have sold it."

"You think he kept it in memory of your mother? The picture you have of her is from that location, right?"

It was. The image had been blown up for her funeral, something my grandmother thought I was too young to attend. But my grandfather insisted I should go. I was an inconsolable three-year-old, and Gigi said the nanny sat in the hall with me after the first five minutes of the funeral, because my grandfather had been angry I wouldn't stop crying.

"I don't care why he kept it. I'm going to make it the place she would have wanted."

As the car approached the downtown area, I saw the blinking sign for the bar.

"Hey, before I go save Aurora from herself, I wanted to… you know… thank you for this. All of it." I wasn't about to go down a checklist, but I hoped Dean knew me well enough that he would understand I was thanking him for everything.

"You're my best friend. No thanks needed. Now. Tell Aurora I said hello and not to hurt your pretty face too badly."

She really was likely to slap me when she saw I followed her to the bar. And again when she figured out I tracked her here. Chuckling, I exited the car after I found a place to park on the street. I couldn't wait to feel her wrath.

Because she was fucking hot as hell when she was all worked up.

Chapter Fourteen

Aurora

Typically, I didn't head to the bar on a Sunday night, but when Talon and I started fighting on the way home from dinner, I immediately messaged Franny that I needed a night out. When she asked why, I told her I would explain everything when she picked me up.

The Ferrari resting in my driveway hadn't even crossed my mind. So, when I flung myself into her aging sedan, I thought I had more time to come up with my excuse. Then, of course, my GQ model of a husband himself had to appear on my porch, calling out my name, and Franny wasted no time asking who he was and why he was in my house.

She almost ran the stop sign at the end of my street when I told her he was my husband. I fed her the same story I gave my parents, and I could tell she was hurt by the end of my explanation. Franny couldn't understand why I kept the relationship hidden from her; we'd been friends since we were little.

Now, I was sitting at the bar next to my best friend, who wouldn't even look in my direction. We had only been seated for ten minutes, and Franny was already on her third piña colada. I was going to have to call us a ride home. I gestured to the bartender, someone I didn't recognize, and asked her if she could make sure Franny and I found a safe way home tonight in case we both had too many. The bartender nodded in understanding.

"Franny, talk to me."

"No." She turned her back to me. Now, she was facing the dartboards and pool tables. Not a minute later, she spun back in my direction, her hand gripping my forearm.

"What, Franny? You look like you've seen a ghost."

"I forgive you. I think we should go. Maybe we can go get a margarita at Rodeo Chico's."

"But I just got a new drink," I said as she tried to pry me off the stool. "Woman! What's going on?" But any more words died on my lips as my eyes fell on Jeremy and his friends at the farthest pool table in the room. I didn't have the kind of luck that would allow me to sneak out of the bar scot-free. No, I had the worst kind. Jeremy and I locked eyes, and that asshole had the audacity to smile in my direction. Like he hadn't upended my life and told me my hopes and dreams were foolish little hobbies.

"Oh, God. He's coming over." Franny was perched back up on the stool she'd vacated, but I was struggling to get situated back on mine.

"Fuck," I mumbled as my heel slipped off the metal footrest again.

"Rory Easterly, aren't you looking mighty fine." The sound of Jeremy's practiced politician's voice made my skin crawl. My eyes caught the bartender's, and we both sneered. Thankfully, she was cleaning glasses right in front of where Franny and I sat.

"Jeremy. I'm surprised to see you here." I wasn't only surprised to find him in Ashfield, but also in the bar. In the years we dated, he never stepped foot in Ole Days. He called it dirty.

"I'm full of surprises," he said, sleazy vibes pouring out of him in waves. I had to choke back the vomit at his unspoken meaning.

"Another old fashioned," Jeremy demanded from the bartender.

"You can leave," Franny said, her lip snarling as he positioned himself between the two of us, his arm snaking around my waist possessively. I tried to twist my body out of his hold, but he held on tighter.

"Don't you want to hang out with your friends?" I asked.

"Naw, I want to be here with you, baby," he replied, leaning so close to me I could smell the whisky on his breath.

"I am *not* your baby. You dumped me, remember? Your family's political aspirations didn't involve a girlfriend whose dad is a farmer. I'm pretty sure those were the exact words you used."

"You know I didn't mean that. It was all a thing to please my mom. Marry the broad she picked out, and I can have a mistress on the side. That's how it works."

I was disgusted. It wasn't that he and Talon weren't doing something similar with the fake wife situation, but I knew Talon wasn't the kind of guy who would keep someone else on the side. He'd been honest with me from the beginning. And there was no denying I wanted something more than a kiss with him.

They were both guaranteed to inherit their full trust funds with marriage, and they each were doing it for their mother. But with Jeremy? He made his entire arrangement seem dirty. Talon did not.

"Franny," I said as I leaned around Jeremy, trying to ignore him, "I think I made a mistake." I'd given her the basic reason why Talon and I had been fighting. She was still in the dark about our marriage being a sham, but I'd convinced her that the argument was over Talon's inheritance. She just didn't know the specifics.

Thinking I was talking about him, Jeremy leaned closer to me, his hand on my waist slipping up to touch the bare skin of my upper back. "Of course you did, baby. But I forgive you."

"Jeremy, no—"

"Oh my gosh," I thought I heard Franny whisper.

"If you want to guarantee you still have a hand to jerk off your tiny little pecker later, you better get your hands off my wife." Talon's voice behind me, though menacing, was like a life vest pulling me out of an ocean during a storm.

But instead of dropping his grip, Jeremy reached around and drew me closer to him. My face was nearly pressed to his neck, and the pungent cologne he wore assaulted my nostrils.

"Your wife? I don't see a ring on her finger," Jeremy pointed out.

Even with my back turned, I could feel the fury emitting from Talon in waves, but not toward me. Jeremy was the sole recipient.

"So, you just assume any woman not wearing a piece of metal around her finger is up for grabs?"

"Well, yeah. That's how it works."

"You're a fucking moron." Stepping closer to the two of us, I could feel Talon's chest press against my back as he pried Jeremy's reluctant fingers off my bare shoulder. The moment I was free of him, I tried to lean closer to Talon, but he had moved right into Jeremy's space.

Talon towered over my ex by a solid five or six inches. Jeremy was always on the shorter side, but that never bothered me, since I was barely five feet myself. But watching their heated exchange, knowing Talon had both height and weight on Jeremy, it was almost funny.

I couldn't hear what Talon was saying, but the threats turned Jeremy's fake tan into an ashen hue. In a flash, Jeremy slipped from between Talon and Franny, nearly tripping over her stool in the process, and stomped back to his friends. I didn't try to make out what their group was saying, but the longer they were in town, the longer I was going to have to watch my back. Talon didn't know Jeremy was known for getting revenge in the sneakiest ways possible. It was why all the walls in my house were barren.

"You have five minutes to get your things and say goodbye to your friend." Talon's nostrils flared as he gripped the edge of the bar, his knuckles turning white in the process. But he didn't look in my direction.

"Talon." I rested my hand on his forearm, surprised he didn't jerk like he had so often before. Instead, his body deflated beneath my touch. He turned his head to peer at me over his shoulder, his eyes heavy in a way I hadn't seen before.

"That was so hot," Franny said beside us, but we completely ignored her as our gazes locked. My throat and lips were growing drier with each passing second, and my skin was so hot I felt like I'd been sunbathing in the desert. My tongue darted out unconsciously to wet my lips. Talon groaned, closing his eyes as if the movement caused him pure agony.

In a flash, he dropped a hundred-dollar bill on the counter of the bar.

"Say goodbye to your friend," he rumbled, as he finally fully turned in my direction.

"Oh, let me introduce you. Franny, this is Talon—"

"Her husband. We'll make pleasantries later. Let's go, Aurora."

"But my dri—" Wordlessly, he pushed the drink toward Franny and then placed another bill on the counter. "Make sure you call someone to take you home. Do not drive, and stay away from the assholes in the back," Talon commanded my best friend, and I was certain Franny was going to listen.

Hell, I was pretty sure the entire bar was going to listen.

"Yes, sir," she replied with a full salute.

"Ready?" He held out his hand to help me off the stool I finally managed to climb back up on.

"For what?" I asked, feeling him twine his fingers with mine when I expected him to drop my hand once I landed with both feet on the floor.

"For me."

It was said as both a threat and a promise. And with how turned on I was after his exchange with Jeremy, I absolutely couldn't wait.

I bobbed and weaved as we exited the bar. If it weren't for Talon's strong grip on my hand, I probably would have tripped and fallen. He likely thought I drank too much, but I barely had a few sips of my single drink. No, I was drunk off him, and I was too damn tired to fight my attraction to him anymore.

As we crossed to the exit of the bar, Talon seemed fed up with my slower pace. In an instant, I found myself lifted in the air and cradled in his arms. I might've been small in stature, but he carried me like I weighed no more than a flower.

"Talon."

"Yes?" he urged as we approached the car. He gently set me on my feet, then opened the car door. He was probably expecting me to slip inside, but I took a step closer to him, sliding my hands up from his waist to his chest, feeling the hard planes beneath my fingertips.

"I want to apologize for earlier. I shouldn't have gotten so worked up."

Talon wrapped his arms around my waist, the opening of his suit jacket covering my arms.

"I'm sorry too, for shouting at you and making accusations."

"Look at us, making up after our first fight." I smiled up at him, and my body immediately warmed as he grinned. "You know what this means, right?"

Chuckling, he shook his head.

"It means we get to have makeup sex."

Talon reached up and pushed aside a section of hair that had fallen over part of my face. His fingers lingered on my shoulder. "Does it now?"

"That's the rule. I don't make them."

He leaned closer to me, and I had to take a step back. My body now touched the edge of the car frame where the door was open. Night was falling over Ashfield, and it was dark enough that no one driving or walking by would see how close we were, but anyone paying attention would've seen that not even a sheet of paper could slip between us.

Talon's face was even closer. His nose traced my jaw and then trailed up next to my lips, then my nose.

"Are you saying you want to have sex with me, Aurora Beckett?"

"No, not sex." Sex involved feelings, emotions, actual relationships. Not whatever it was we were doing. Even though hearing my new last name on his lips did something deep inside of me. And also soaked my panties. "I want you to fuck me, Talon Beckett."

"Whatever my wife wants, my wife gets." He chastely smacked his lips against mine and then drew back, leaving me more confused than ever. "I can't fuck you properly on the side of the road where anyone could see you. I don't share, ever. Get in the car, peaches."

Unable to hold back, I gripped either side of his face and yanked him down. I pressed my mouth against his again, only this time I slipped my tongue between his lips. I audibly groaned as he shifted his hips against my stomach. Talon's cock was growing harder by the second. If I didn't pull back, he likely wouldn't be able to drive us home. His large hands gripped my ass, his fingers digging into the material covering my flesh, as I continued to explore his mouth. He rocked against me twice, then used more strength than I could ever muster to pull himself back.

"Car, peaches. Car. Please." Talon's voice was hoarse and filled with something close to pain as he demanded I get inside the sports car. Reluctantly, I dropped into the bucket seat and strapped myself in, all while watching Talon hobble around the car to his own seat.

The moment he turned the car on, I knew this ride was going to be torturous, not just because I was so incredibly turned on, but because the car's seat was vibrating in the best kind of way.

"Fuck," I moaned as he turned the car around on the street, almost cutting off someone driving in the opposite direction.

"Spread your legs, Aurora."

"What?" I whispered, even as I followed his order. There was just enough light left in the sky that it cast everything in shades of navy and black. Talon's hand slid over the console and onto my thigh, where his deft fingers bunched the bottom of my dress higher on my legs until my panties were exposed. The tip of his finger brushed across the damp material at my center, and my entire body jerked.

"Fuck, you're soaked, peaches."

Breathlessly, I asked him why he kept calling me that, as he moved the digit up and down the wet gusset of my panties.

"Your name means the dawn. And it reminds me of the colors of a sunrise. At dawn. Peaches."

"Oh," I moaned, eyes closed, as he slipped a finger past the elastic barrier and touched the skin beneath.

"I bet your pussy is the color of a peach's center. All dark-pinks and reds. I bet it'll be tight around my cock the way a peach squeezes its pit too."

I had no idea how Talon was capable of driving and flicking my clit. Before him, I never had a man be able to talk dirty and rub my clit at the same time, yet here was Talon, doing all three—something previously incomprehensible.

My legs started to shake as I felt my releases inching closer. I was already so worked up from the interaction in the bar that it wasn't going to take me long to go over the crest.

"You going to come, wife?"

"Yes," I moaned, gripping his forearm to hold myself steady against his hand. My body exploded the moment he smoothly turned the car onto my street without braking, and by the time I came back into myself, Talon had parked the car in my driveway and was making his way around to me.

He yanked open the door before I could even finish unlatching the seatbelt, and I found myself upside down, being carried fireman-style over his shoulders. My bag dangled from his arm as he shut the door, then he carried me to the front door. He shoved his key in the lock and cursed impatiently when the knob didn't budge. I squirmed on his shoulder, trying to force some friction between my legs, because just him carrying me like this had restarted my engine.

Finally, after what felt like a decade, the door unlocked, and Talon carried me inside, kicking the door shut with his foot. The dim lamp I kept on in the corner of the living room cast shadows that cascaded through the area. It barely illuminated the opening of the kitchen.

Suddenly, I was flipped around, and my ass collided with the counter of my island. Talon's palms rested on my knees, slowly snaking up the center of my thighs until his body pressed against my legs. His lips brushed against mine in the softest of sweeps.

"Spread these legs, peaches. Show your husband how well you can obey."

A moan reverberated from my throat as I submitted, opening my legs as wide as the counter would allow. I rested each foot on one of the bar stools jutting out from the island.

"Good girl, listening to your husband like a good little wife." Talon's fingers slid toward the outside of my thighs, then up to my waist, clasping the cotton of my panties along the way. "Do you like these?"

I shook my head, then said, "No."

The tearing of material echoed through my kitchen, and Talon tossed the panties somewhere behind him.

He pressed his lips against mine, his tongue exploring the inside of my mouth quickly, then he moved in light pecks along my cheek, jaw, then neck. His hands came up to cup my breasts as he licked and nipped the sensitive skin at the spot where my shoulder met my neck. I resisted the urge to close my legs, wanting to use my heels to pull his body against mine. I wanted to feel his stiff erection against my center.

"Talon," I whimpered as his fingers slipped beneath the slinky fabric of my dress and caressed my nipples. My breasts had always been extremely sensitive. None of my previous boyfriends or lovers had ever picked up on that, but Talon did almost immediately. He urged the neckline down and stroked the hardened tips before setting his lips around one nipple. He licked the peak in swirls and flicks. My body was still so highly alert from the finger-fucking in the car that I could barely stand the ministration he was giving each breast. Just when I thought I'd had enough, Talon pulled his mouth and hands free, then squatted before me.

"Do you want my mouth here, wife? Would you like that?" His fingers had pushed my dress up to my waist, leaving me exposed on the island. His hands rested on the insides of my thighs, his thumbs stroking my soaked folds, teasing me but not slipping in where I really wanted to feel him.

Moaning, I replied, "Yes."

Talon leaned forward, his nose brushing against the pulsing area. "Yes, what?"

I had no idea what he wanted me to say, so I replied with the first thing that came to mind, praying it would put me out of my misery. "Yes, husband."

"Fuck, yes you do, peaches."

Immediately, Talon's mouth sucked on my clit while a single finger rubbed up and down my slit before slipping inside. I squirmed on the counter, letting out a whimper, and Talon wrapped his free arm around my waist to settle me in place.

His strokes were slow, in and out of my channel, but his tongue moved in ways I'd never experienced.

Talon's name tumbled from my lips in a soft cry as his finger rubbed against a certain spot inside my body that a man rarely ever found.

"That's it, wife. Come on my tongue. Let me taste all of you."

His mouth and finger worked in tandem as he brought me closer to the edge faster than I ever reached it on my own.

"Oh, God!" I cried out when I came, my voice rattling as I clenched his hair, riding out the waves against his face. Talon's fingers gripped my body, pulling me closer as I writhed on his tongue.

When my shakes finally subsided, he leaned back, his face glistening with my juices but smiling as if I just gifted him the sweetest of treasures.

"Wow." My voice was rough and breathy as I tried to calm my racing heart.

Talon finally stood, wiping his face on his sleeve, but not before he licked his lips clean. I noticed the protruding rod behind his suit pants, and desire filled me to return the favor.

On shaky legs, I hopped down from the counter and kneeled in front of him, reaching up to unbutton his pants. His hands landed on top of mine, halting my movements.

"Aurora, you don't have to do that."

I cocked my head to the side. I wasn't the best at blowjobs, but I'd never had a guy turn one down. Yet, here I was, with the man who just feasted on me like I was his favorite dessert, being told I didn't need to pleasure him with my mouth.

The wild child in me immediately perked up and swatted his hand aside. I was going to give him a blowjob he'd never forget.

The zipper came down with ease, and I tugged the pants to his ankles. Talon wore black boxer briefs that I was sure cost more than my car. Those quickly followed the path of the pants.

Once free of its confines, Talon's cock stood proudly… with a silver ball at each end of a barbell winking at me from the top and bottom of his crown. His dick was the largest I'd ever encountered, and I had never experienced one with a piercing. At that moment, I could just stare at it in all its glory.

Tentatively, I reached out, my finger barely grazing the soft skin of the underside.

"Ah, fuck," Talon groaned as his cock jerked.

I smiled. It was my turn to have my husband obey.

Chapter Fifteen

Talon

Seeing Aurora, my wife, down on her knees and begging me for my cock was an image I was never going to forget. It was imprinting itself in my mind with every tentative touch of her fingers along my shaft. She had done nothing more than gently caress the soft skin, and I was nearly ready to explode.

"Aurora." I called her name to get her attention, but she was so focused on the piercing at the head of my cock that she didn't listen. Or simply didn't care. The apadravya was a piercing I got as a dare when I turned eighteen. I lost a bet to Dean about him fucking one of our boarding school teachers the day of graduation. I'd caught them in her classroom right after the ceremony. He got nailed, and so did I. Just in two different ways.

But as Aurora ran her fingers around the balls of the barbell, I was really happy with my loss at that moment.

Coyly, Aurora gazed up at me. Open. Submissive. Innocent. She blinked twice, then a salacious grin grew on her lips.

"Lean back against the counter." Her words were forceful and not up for debate. I followed her demand, ignoring how the precum dripped from my dick's opening as she stroked my cock while I adjusted my feet.

"Such a good husband, giving your wife two orgasms before he even thought of pleasuring himself."

"Yeah. Yeah, selfless." My head tilted back until I was staring at her ceiling as her tongue licked the delicate underside of my shaft.

"Where do you want it, husband?" Her strokes were more forceful as she kissed the head.

My confusion was growing by the minute as all my blood rushed to the area getting all the attention. "What?"

"Where do you want to put your cock?"

Everywhere was the first answer that popped into my head.

"Squeezed between my breasts? Using my mouth? My hands. Or do you want my pussy? Maybe my a—"

I jerked my head down to look at her. My sweet Aurora from the teachers' conference had been replaced by this vixen on her knees, asking me where I wanted to put my cock on or in her.

I placed a hand against her hair, and then I dug my fingers in deep, gripping it with my fist. "Stop playing around and let me fuck your mouth."

Beneath her lashes, Aurora gazed up at me while she smirked. "Yes, husband."

Before opening her mouth, Aurora leaned forward and spit on the base of my cock. Her hand stroked the shaft, spreading the lubrication across my erection.

Then she parted those beautiful lips and placed them just around the mushroom head, my piercing disappearing into her mouth. She didn't bend forward. She waited while watching me. My cock was barely going to fit, her teeth likely to scrape, but I didn't fucking care. I wanted to claim her mouth.

"Open wider, peaches."

Not only did her mouth widen just a tad, but her thighs parted enough for her to slip her hand between her thighs.

"That's it; touch yourself. I want to hear you."

The sound of my moan as my cock reached the back of her throat harmonized with her whimpers of pleasure. Her hand moved in swift circles as she rubbed her clit, bringing herself pleasure.

I swapped the hand that was holding her hair and placed the other on the edge of the counter, using it to hold myself in place as I thrust my cock into her mouth repeatedly. She would gag occasionally but never asked me to stop.

When I could feel my balls tightening up, that little minx used her free hand to reach under my balls and just behind them, massaging the sensitive skin there.

"Coming!" I shouted before I could release myself into her mouth. I let go of her hair, not wanting to hold her in place if she didn't want to taste me. But Aurora surprised me when she swallowed every bit that landed on her tongue. There was a small trickle out the corner of her mouth, and she swiped it with her tongue, moaning as she did.

Aurora sat back on her heels, the hand that had been rubbing her clit now resting on her thigh. Small bits of black makeup streaked beneath her eyes, and I leaned down to wipe it away. Her lips were red and well used, and as she smiled, she looked pleased.

Bending farther, I gripped her ass and lifted her into the air and against me. God, she was fucking tiny. Her legs instantly wrapped around my waist, bringing her exposed pussy up against my cock. Even though it'd just spent its entire load, it jumped to life as if it never happened.

I ignored it for a second, kissing my wife instead. I was addicted to her mouth. I was addicted to her tongue and the way it swirled against mine. I was addicted to how she fit up against me. I was certain when I slid my cock into her sheath I was going to be addicted to her pussy. It didn't take a scientist to figure out I was quickly growing addicted to *her*. To Aurora. To my wife. At least I had six months to figure out how to get over it.

"Mm…," she moaned against my lips as I toed off my shoes and then stomped in place until my pants and briefs were no longer around my ankles. I had a suspicion she enjoyed my hardening cock rubbing against her swollen pussy lips with each shake.

Once I was free of the confines, I carried her to the bedroom wearing my shirt, jacket, and my dress socks that were pulled up to my calves. Despite my better judgment, I slowly set her on her feet, regretting my decision immediately, because I missed the feel of her wrapped around me.

Swiftly, I slid the jacket off my arms and began unbuttoning my shirt. My fingers worked deftly to shove each button through its hole, and I grew agitated as the last few refused to come free.

Aurora's hand rested on mine, and she asked if she could finish it for me. I nodded, and soon the shirt joined the jacket, and I tugged my undershirt over my head, tossing it onto the pile.

"Take off your dress," I snarled as I bent to remove my socks, which seemed to have grown Velcro and stuck to my legs.

"Dammit." I continued to pull them down until finally they released and fell to the floor.

Aurora had just finished unzipping her dress. I watched as it pooled in a mass of blue at her feet. My own Venus standing before me as a siren in the ocean.

"You're beautiful," I told her, and she glanced away, her chin tucking into her shoulder.

On the dresser stood a small lamp. Reaching over, I flicked it on, the room illuminating in a soft glow. It made Aurora's skin mimic the peach nickname I'd given her earlier. The mirror in the corner of the room held her reflection, and I stepped behind her, my body a towering presence over her. I looked almost menacing in comparison.

"Look at you, wife," I began as my hands spanned her waist. I cupped her breasts, letting the weight of them fill my palms. "Look how perfect you fit in my hands, like your body was made for me." Even in the warm glow, I noticed her skin pinken the longer I held her breasts and caressed the sensitive nipples.

Continuing to hold one breast, I slid my other hand down between her legs at an agonizingly slow pace. I felt her breath quicken and her heart race. My middle finger stroked the slickness of her sex. Back and forth. Back and forth. Until I heard her breath hitch. Our eyes never left the mirror.

I watched, enraptured.

She stared, entranced.

"You like the way I touch you, wife?" I slipped the finger into her slit, the walls closing around the digit. I pulled it back out, then repeated the motion again. "You like when I fuck you with my finger? You like watching me get you off?" When she didn't respond, I prompted, "Wife?"

"Yes. Yes, I like everything, Talon."

In a flash, I spun her around, cupping her jaw with the hand that had been bringing her pleasure between her legs. My thumb rested on one side of her face and my fingers on the other. I wanted her attention as I brought my face closer to hers. "Husband. I'm your *husband*."

Her panicked expression melted before me.

"You see that bed right there, Aurora? I expect you in it every night. We don't have to fuck, but you can damn well be sure I'll be pleasuring my wife in it. Understand?"

Her body was like putty in my hands as she said, "Yes, husband."

"Good girl. Now, get on the bed. I need to *finally* fuck my wife."

The moment I released her jaw, Aurora spun around and put both her knees on the bed before crawling toward the headboard. I didn't know if it was necessary or solely for my benefit, but her moves were achingly slow, and she swayed her hips. Her pussy and ass were within reach, but I held myself back. I wanted to enjoy the show.

When she reached the headboard, Aurora turned around and settled her backside on top of her heels. Then she wickedly spread her knees apart, giving me the perfect glimpse of her pussy I became so well acquainted with thirty minutes before.

"Fuck, you're gorgeous. I'm a lucky bastard."

She gathered her hair in her hand and draped it over one shoulder. "You're just lucky."

As much as I wanted to ignore that she was saying I wasn't a bastard, I couldn't. And it shattered the block of concrete around my heart. I was standing there, arms hanging loosely at my sides, staring at this stunning woman offering herself to me.

"Are you going to join me? Or am I going to have to do the work myself?"

I sprung onto the bed, practically tackling her onto the mattress with my enthusiasm. Her bent legs wedged between us, and somewhere in the back of my mind, I knew she couldn't be comfortable. Wrapping an arm around her waist, I flipped us over so that my back was on the bed, and she was seated above me, rubbing her body back and forth along the ridge of my dick.

"Fucking magnificent," I breathed, and her hips quickened with each pass. "That's it, peaches. Take what you want. Ride my dick."

Twice, the tip of my cock almost slid inside her, and I knew she'd regret it in the morning if I let us keep going without a—

"Condom?" I asked through gritted teeth. I couldn't help imagining what it would be like to feel her without anything between us. But that was something I was reserving for… my wife.

"What?" Aurora questioned as if lost in a haze of her own pleasure.

"Condom? Do we need one?" Now that the idea had been planted, it rooted and was growing at an unwavering speed.

"I… um…." She licked her lips, lids heavy with lust.

I placed my hands on her hips to slow her pace, then I reached over to the nightstand beside her bed. Blindly, I searched the drawer until I felt the signs of an aluminum wrapper.

"Let me put this on, peaches."

She groaned as I lifted her off my lap and set her next to me. I glanced at the expiration, just a week shy of the date, and then tore the foil with my teeth. My cock was overly sensitive as I slid the latex down my shaft. As much as I wanted to watch Aurora bounce up and down on my dick, I wasn't sure I could withstand it at the moment. I was likely to blow too soon as it was.

"Lie back, beautiful," I told her as I moved onto my side. Everything before had been hot and heavy, but

I wanted to remember this moment with her. We were about to consummate our marriage, whether it was real or fake. It was something Aurora hadn't done with anyone before, and she was giving that honor to me.

I reached out and stroked her hair, tucking the wild wisps away from her face. She was relaxed, and her eyes blinked slowly as she turned her face toward me.

"Talon?"

"Yeah?"

"I'd really like you to fuck me now."

Smirking, I moved my body between her legs, keeping my cock just an inch from her sex. My hands were on either side of her head as I held my body above hers.

"Are you sure?" I asked her, rocking my hips forward, sliding my erection against her pussy.

"One-hundred *thousand* percent."

"How does my wife want it?" I asked her as I shifted my weight onto one arm. My eager hand needed to feel the heat pulsating between her legs, or I might die. She squirmed under my touch, and I knew she was still sensitive from her previous orgasms.

"I just want to feel you," she groaned, her legs trying to jackknife and pull me tight against her body. "I *need* to feel you."

Removing my hand from her center, I grabbed my throbbing cock and guided it toward her entrance, slapping the top of her mound covered in trimmed dark-blonde hair before gliding downward through the folds. Even with the condom, I could feel her heat radiating around my tip.

Aligning the head at her entrance, I slowly guided my erection deeper inside her pussy. The walls tightened around me like a fist, and it took everything in me to keep from thrusting to the hilt to feel her grip me completely.

Sweat began beading along my hairline as I paused, waiting for her tightness to adjust to my size. Aurora's eyes pinched closed, and for a moment, I worried I had hurt her. I began to pull back, but I suddenly felt her hand on my ass, her fingers gripping the muscle.

"Don't stop. Please."

"Are you sure?" I asked her through clenched teeth.

"I'll kill you if you do," she practically growled, her eyes popping open in rage.

"As you wish, wife," I replied as if I was Westley in *The Princess Bride*.

I rocked into her as deep as she could take me. I was only able to fit a little more than half of my shaft inside her before I was stopped by her body. Aurora was so tiny I was afraid to hurt her by going any farther.

Pulling back out completely, I then slid my cock inside her sheath once again, blissfully aware of how her walls squeezed me. Grabbing the back of her left leg, I hitched her knee closer to her chest, thrusting into her again.

"Yes," she purred, her back arching at the same time.

Beneath my hand, I felt her leg start to shake after a few more thrusts.

"You want more, peaches? Tell me what you want," I asked, my breath coming in quick pants.

"Faster. Touch my clit," she panted as her other leg wrapped around my waist, her heel digging into my ass.

Reaching up, I grabbed the pillow next to Aurora's head and shoved it under her hips. With her change in leg position and the lift of her ass, my cock slipped deeper into her sex.

"Yes! Oh, God!"

Leaning forward as I continued to piston my throbbing erection in and out of her pussy, I brushed my lips against her mouth. "Husband. Not God. And you'll call out your husband's name when I make you come." I slipped my hand between our bodies, my fingers flicking her tight bundle of nerves as I rested my forehead against hers. "Fuck, I'm close."

"Me too," she whimpered, her hips rocking against my hand as she soared toward her release.

I felt her walls quaking as my dick and piercing rubbed that special spot inside her sex. When she came screaming my name, Aurora's nails clenched my back, digging into my skin as she held on while riding out her orgasm. The moment I felt her sweet walls squeeze my cock like a clenched fist, I poured myself into the latex.

My body jerked from the exertion, and I tried my best to move my body off Aurora's, but she surprised me as she wrapped her arms around my neck and held me close while dropping her legs on either side of my hips.

We didn't speak, just laid there silently, our breaths slowing by the minute. Our bodies were covered in a sheen of sweat, the saltiness lingering in the air, mixing with the scent of our fucking.

There was a noise somewhere off in the distance, but I ignored it, running my nose along Aurora's chin instead as I maneuvered my hands under her back to hold her closer.

"Talon," she whispered, her lips brushing against the bridge of my nose. I moaned in response. "Talon. I think your phone is ringing."

My voice was dark and gravelly as I said, "They'll call back."

"They've called back three times already."

With a huff, I pushed up and off Aurora, but not before kissing her one last time. My cock slid free of her body, and I instantly missed her warmth. My phone continued to ring as I tugged off the condom, knotted the end, and tossed it in the trashcan beside her dresser. I searched around the floor for my jacket and found the culprit that disturbed my post-coital bliss with my wife.

"Dean was calling. The fucking cockblock," I told her as I stood with the phone in my hand. She rolled onto her side, resting her head in her hand on top of her bent arm. I was half tempted to take a picture of her lying just like that, so I'd have it forever.

The phone started ringing in my hand, and I snarled as I pressed the green button, accepting the call. "What the fuck do you want? I was in the middle of something very important."

"It leaked" was all he said.

Standing straighter as I paced the bedroom, I asked Dean, "What?"

"Your marriage to Aurora. It's been leaked to the press. The tabloids and blogs will probably start running articles on it tomorrow. Some have already posted."

Trying to calm my racing heart, I replied, "Leaked what exactly? Just that I'm married?"

"Yes. Nothing else."

I blew out all the air in my lungs. I wanted to control the news of my marriage on my own, using this weekend's charity event as the perfect way, but it seemed someone beat me to it. But it could have been far worse if the actual details had been disclosed as well.

"Okay. Thank you for the heads-up. Sorry about the way I answered."

"Talon Beckett just apologized? Who are you? What did you do with my best friend?"

"Things change," I said as I glanced back to Aurora, who was now lying back with her head resting on a pillow and a blanket draped over her body. Her eyes were heavy with exhaustion.

"They sure do. I'll keep you in the loop if I hear anything more. It may be a good idea to employ some security for you and Aurora. Once the press figures out where you're at, it won't take long for them to swarm like locusts."

My eyes were trained on the woman that was my wife, and my first thought was that I needed to protect her at all costs, especially since I was getting the better end of our deal. She didn't need to worry about her safety just because I wanted control of the Wilder Hotels and the money that should've been mine.

"Thanks." I ended the call and crawled up the bed toward Aurora, who sleepily smiled at me as she cuddled closer.

"Could you hear him on the other end?"

"Mm… bits and pieces."

"I'd planned for our marriage announcement to happen at the charity event in Nashville this weekend, but it seems it will be our confirmation announcement instead."

"Okay," Aurora mumbled as she tucked her head against my shoulder.

"I'll keep you safe," I told her as her breath began to even out.

"I know," she mumbled, quickly falling into her dreamland.

I was going to honor my promise. I'd keep her safe.

Even if that meant safe from me.

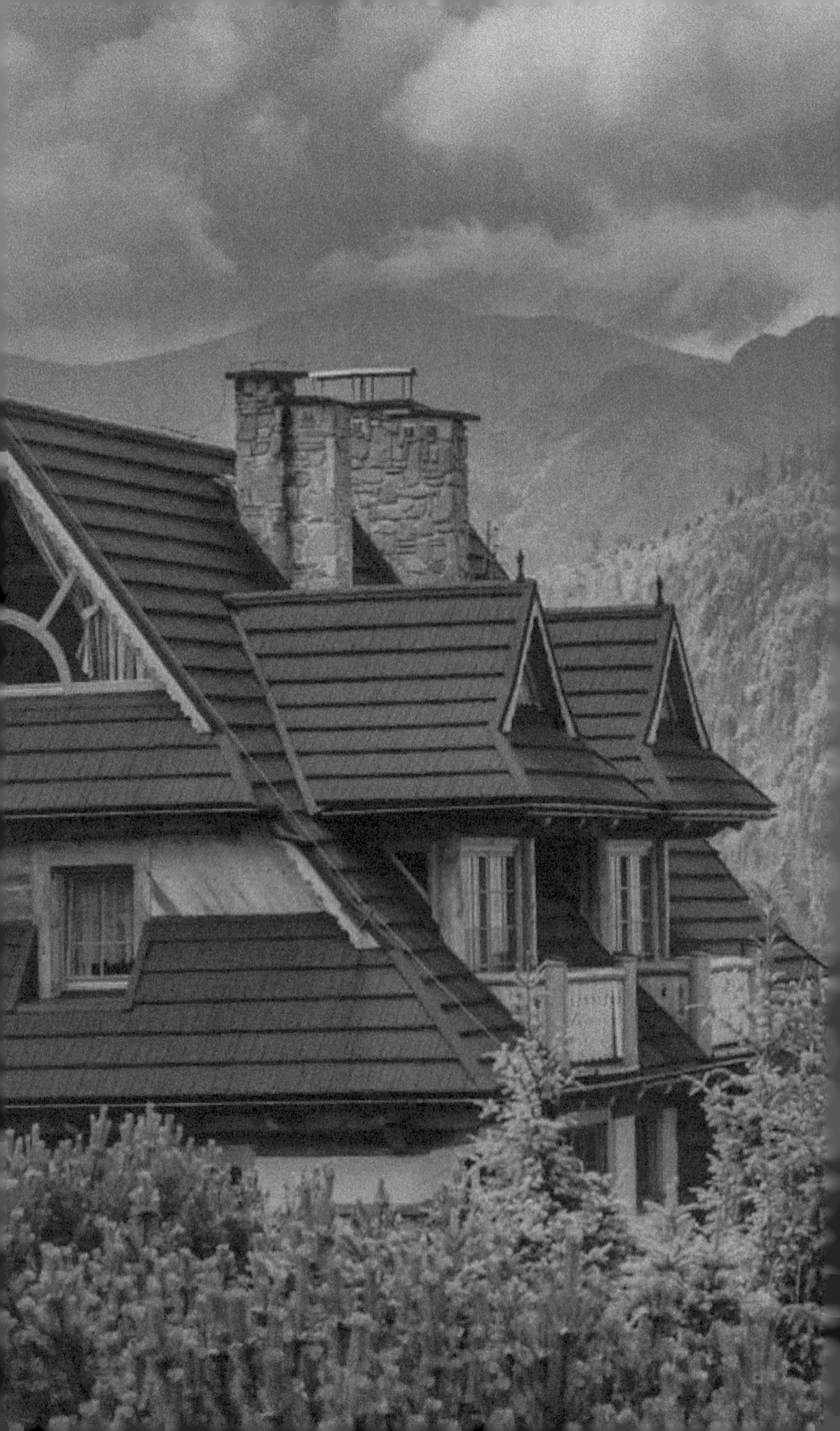

Chapter Sixteen

Aurora

I woke to Talon shifting around my bedroom before the sun even began to make her way over the mountains. After our enthusiastic lovemaking, I fell asleep quickly. Three orgasms would do that to a girl. We'd fallen asleep with the lamp on after Dean's call.

"Sorry, I didn't mean to wake you."

I sat up in bed, stretching my arms above my head. The blanket draped around my body fluttered down to my waist, exposing my breasts. Glancing down,

I noticed little purplish marks there along my flesh. Marks Talon fervently left on me with a smile on his face.

"You didn't. I'm usually up early."

Talon stopped tying the drawstring on a pair of basketball shorts, and his eyes widened while he stared at me. "Really?"

"When you live on a farm, you have to be ready before the sun."

He nodded and moved onto the end of the bed. "What do you typically do in the morning, now that you live here and not on a farm?"

"Some yoga or, if I'm feeling adventurous, go for a run. But honestly? I hate running. It's the worst."

"I agree, but it's a necessary evil." He chuckled as he ran his hand down his exposed abdomen.

"Well, I approve of your devilish ways."

Talon turned completely to kneel on the bed, then crawled toward me. It was one of the sexiest fucking things I'd ever seen.

"Do you now?" he asked as he moved between my legs. They eagerly parted despite the soreness at their apex.

I laid back as he hovered his much larger body over mine, then replied, "Definitely."

He glanced at my clock on the nightstand, one passed down to me by my parents. Pretty sure it was from the '80s. "What are you doing today?" he questioned, leaning down and running his nose over the column of my neck. I never knew such a subtle movement could turn me on so much.

"I'm… I'm going to set up my classroom today. Franny is helping me."

"Mm hmm…." He moved to the other side of my neck, and my body shivered at the contact. "What time do you need to leave?"

Sitting back on his heels, Talon reached for my hands, grabbing my wrists. He locked both in one of his fists, keeping a gentle hold, and pressed them against the bed above my head. He shifted his weight and rested his hips against me.

I was too lost in the feel of his hardening dick to answer his question, but Talon leaned down and nipped my lip to prompt a response. "Nine. We're meeting at nine," I replied as my tongue dipped out to lick his bottom lip, but the bastard moved away too quickly.

"Good. That leaves plenty of time. Leave your hands there," he demanded as he launched himself off the bed, yanking his shorts and boxers down the moment his bare feet touched the floor.

"Plenty of time for what?"

Talon ignored me. Standing beside the bed, he trailed a single finger from the inside of my ankle up to the inside of my thigh until he reached my pussy. His eyes widened in delight when he stroked the wetness between my legs.

"What's got you so wet this morning, peaches?"

"You, Talon." I reached over with a hand, trying to hold on to his forearm as his finger glided across my slick folds.

"Hands," he barked, and I immediately placed mine back where he'd left it.

"So, you're wet for your husband?"

"Mm hm," I mumbled as he dipped a finger inside my channel, then brought it back out, only to swirl the wettened finger around my clit.

"I can't knowingly leave you in this state," Talon said as he leaned closer to my center, focusing his eyes on his fingers slipping in and out of my slit.

Licking my lips, I replied, "That wouldn't be the husbandly thing to do."

Talon's head dove between my legs, and I felt the smoothness of his tongue lick at my entrance. Then, in a flash, he flipped me over and hitched my hips into the air, my ass and pussy now completely exposed to him.

Ravenously, Talon pressed his face against my pussy again, licking and nibbling the sensitive area as his fingers swirled my feminine liquid around my clit.

"Fuuuck," I moaned as his tongue flicked my clit at an astonishing rate. I felt something warm and thick against my anus. Talon's thumb massaged the erogenous area as he consumed my pussy. My fists clenched the comforter beneath me until I wobbled on my legs from the arising orgasm.

"Talon!" I cried out as the waves crashed over me.

"That's it, peaches. Fuck my tongue," he told me as it darted in and out of my entrance while I rode out the orgasm from him rubbing my clit.

My body started to relax, and I felt Talon run his hands along my back, massaging the muscles. By reflex, I rocked my hips against Talon's, the head of his cock nudging at my entrance but slipping away.

I felt his lips press between my shoulder blades as his hands moved onto my hips. "I'm going to fuck you, wife. Nothing between us."

Should we have had a discussion about birth control, which I was on? Yes. Should we have talked about whether we were clean? Also, yes. But I was so fucking lost in him I barely knew what my own name was.

He left no time for me to respond. His cock prodded at my slit and edged inside. Inch by fucking glorious inch until I felt completely full.

"Yes. Take all of me, peaches. That's my girl. My good wife obeying her husband," he growled as I felt his balls hit the back of my thighs.

"So full," I whimpered when I could barely take any more. Talon's hand skimmed up my back and around my neck until he cupped my jaw. He twisted my head to the side as he leaned forward to capture my mouth with his.

"You're fucking perfect, Aurora," he rumbled as he pulled his hips back and then thrust his cock back into my tight channel.

When my body loosened, Talon started moving behind me, holding my hips as he rocked against me. One of his hands reached under my body to grasp my breast, rolling the nipple between two fingers.

That magnificent piercing of his was rubbing me in all the right places, and soon I felt the waves of my release growing unstoppable.

"Talon!" I shouted when my body was close to breaking apart. I rocked my ass against his body, increasing our pace as I chased my orgasm. Finally, the precipice was within reach, and I jumped over the edge.

"Shit! You're squeezing me so fucking good. Gonna make me come."

With my head resting on the bed, I felt Talon lose control as he fucked me at a back-breaking speed.

"Aurora!" he growled as I felt the warmth of his cum shoot inside my body.

His cock slid out of my sex as I fell forward onto the bed. Hot drips seeped out of my pussy and onto my thighs, but I didn't care. I was so well-sated I didn't want to move.

I was surprised to feel a warm cloth between my legs, Talon telling me he was just cleaning me up, and I fell right to sleep while Talon went for a run. When I awoke, he was in my office, using my desk for his laptop, and I got busy getting ready to meet up with Franny.

Wanting to remain professional, I pulled on a pair of bright-pink pants, a white sleeveless shirt, and a pair of casual sneakers. I twisted my hair into a messy knot at the back of my head and slid two small gold hoops through the tiny holes in my earlobes.

"You look nice," Talon said as he walked into the bedroom holding a package as I was spritzing on a perfume Autumn sent me when she lived in New York.

"Thanks. Even though I'm just setting up my room, I figured I'd see a few other teachers and administrators around the school."

He nodded as he set the box on the bed.

"Is that for me?" I asked. "I didn't hear the doorbell ring." The delivery of my big purchase was still a few weeks off, since the camera was on back order.

"Sure is," he said as he walked over to my closet and pulled a suit jacket off a hanger. He was already wearing suit pants and a pale-blue button-down shirt. He must've changed after his run while I'd been asleep.

Clapping my hands joyfully, I sat on the bed and hauled the medium-sized box onto my lap. The box was the palest of pinks, almost white, and the ribbon was jet-black. I pulled the ribbon free, then lifted the top of the box and peeked inside, then immediately set the box on the bed and stood. "Talon."

He turned around from where he was adjusting his tie in front of my mirror and faced me with eyes the size of saucers.

"I can't accept this."

He instantly relaxed and turned back to the mirror, flipping one end of the tie through a loop. "Of course, you can."

"No, I can't." I wasn't sure how he knew about my love of photography unless someone in my family snitched. It wasn't something I liked to talk about. I didn't even have any more of my favorite images in the house. Jeremy had been sure of that.

Once Talon was satisfied with his tie, he walked over to me and rested his hands on my shoulders. "You can accept it, because it's a gift from me to you. Nothing more."

"But how did you…?" I began to ask, as he lifted the Leica M6 from the box. It was a dream film-camera and highly sought after. Talon held it out to me, waiting for me to take it, but I was terrified to touch it. The relic from 1984 should've been in a museum.

"I assumed, based on the photos scattered around your parents' home, that you enjoy photography. I wasn't sure if you preferred film or digital, so I took a chance and went with the best I could find." He was still holding the camera out to me, ready for me to take it. "If you don't like it, I can send it back."

"Don't you dare!" I cried out as I finally took the silver-and-black gem into my hands. God, it was perfect. My photography teacher in high school always talked about this camera and how it was highly coveted by traditionalists.

Tears welled up in my eyes at the thoughtful gift from the man who only *pretended* to be in a relationship with me. Gently, I set the camera on my bed, then I launched myself at Talon. Thankfully, he caught me in his arms.

"Thank you."

"You're welcome," he said as he embraced me tightly. "There is one small catch though," he added as he smiled. I could hear the taunt in his voice.

I slid down his body and sat back down on the bed, admiring my new toy.

"I had film already installed. I am giving you one week to fill up the reel with any pictures you'd like to take. Then I'm going to develop them."

"Okay, what's the catch? I'm pretty sure I can go through the film in a day."

"I have a second surprise attached to that task, so be mindful of what you're capturing on film."

It was both ominous and exhilarating. I was never one to back down from a dare, which was why I was in this arrangement to begin with.

"Deal. So, where are you headed?"

"I'm going to check out the Wilder Lodge in Knoxville."

"Okay. I hope it's not too damaged." I learned through a quick internet search that the original Wilder Hotel was in Knoxville, so that was Talon's excuse to his family for coming up this way from Miami. "If you give me a heads-up, I can have something ready for dinner."

Talon smiled, and I couldn't help but do the same as he leaned down to press his lips against mine. "Not kicking me out yet?"

"If you can repeat last night, I'm pretty sure I'll let you stay as long as you want."

"Greedy wife," he whispered against my mouth, then nipped my lip.

I watched his retreating back as he left the house, but not before he made sure to pay extra attention to Draco on his way out. I was pretty sure my cat was switching teams and was 100 percent batting for Talon. I couldn't really blame him.

In the living room, I looked over my swatches of paint again and finally decided on a dark-olive color for my office and a tad lighter shade for my living room. Green was one of my favorite colors when I needed to relax.

On the kitchen island, my phone buzzed with a message. Assuming it was Franny, I opened the message, only to find a screenshot of an article online about the marriage of Talon and me.

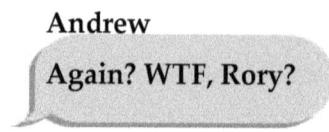

Andrew
> Again? WTF, Rory?

    I wasn't in the mood to deal with my brother, so I closed the message, heading out the front door when Franny sent a text that she was leaving her house.

    At the school, Franny helped me rearrange the desks in the way I wanted, then we hung a few items on the bulletin boards. I knew that in high school I wouldn't have a set number of students, so decorating my room was more or less just adding objects related to the subject I was teaching. I was certified to teach secondary school in both English and Mathematics—"overachiever," my best friend called me. But the principal needed me to fill in the English spot when the previous teacher left. I was excited, since books and I went together like peanut butter and marshmallow fluff. It was far better than peanut butter and jelly.

    Franny spent the better part of the morning learning everything she could about me and Talon and what we did the night before. Whatever anger she had toward me the night before had melted away, and now she was being the nosy best friend.

"Ms. Easterly, I was hoping I'd run into you today," Liam Franklin said from the door that adjoined our two rooms.

"It's Mrs. Beckett," I said to him, loving the way the name sounded from my lips. "I got married recently. I'm waiting for the school to update my information."

"Oh, apologies." Liam adjusted his wire frames on his nose as he looked around my room covered in huge posters that looked like bookshelves I found online. I wanted the kids to feel like they were walking into an ancient library when they stepped foot into my class. When his eyes landed on Franny, I watched as he readjusted the glasses again and shoved his fingers through his blonde mane.

Stepping in, I said, "Franny, this is Liam Franklin. He teaches biology next door."

"Nice to meet you," she said. Franny was tall, but Liam was taller—something that was rare around Ashfield. "Are you new here?" It was an innocent question, since Franny and I both grew up in the area. It was rare we didn't already know someone if they lived in town.

"I started working here three years ago, but I commuted from a town called Ainsley a couple of counties over until I found an apartment in town. I'm living above the ice cream shop."

The two of them were still holding hands but no longer shaking. They were entranced as I stepped away, and I bet they barely even noticed.

"I love ice cream," I heard Franny say as I stepped over to my desk and gathered my laptop. I'd spent the last month compiling my lesson plans, and I already submitted them to administration. Now, I just had to wait another three weeks for school to begin.

"Franny, I'm about done here."

"Oh," she said, her mouth downturned. Liam quickly suggested that maybe the two of them could go grab something for dinner.

I watched them proverbially ride off into the sunset as they followed each other out of the school and then out of the parking lot.

With the entire afternoon at my disposal, I decided to head to one of my favorite trails to use the camera Talon gifted me. Thankfully, I stowed a change of clothes in my car just in case I had the time today.

An hour later, I was standing at one of the peaks overlooking the town. It wasn't the tallest or the most difficult, but it had a beautiful ledge that jutted out over the valley, showcasing the farms and the town in all its splendor.

I set up the camera in the same way I'd done in high school when I won my first scholarship with the image I captured. The only difference this time was there wasn't a storm rolling in.

With a steady hand, I snapped one image over my head, to make it seem as if I was looking down on the valley from high above the tree line. Second, I settled on the ground and set up the view from the camera so that my running shoes framed the mountains and town off in the distance.

While I enjoyed the instant gratification of a digital camera, I loved the surprise of using film. You never knew what the outcome was going to be. You had to rely on your skill, your expertise.

I stored everything in my backpack and made the trek back down the hill. I was going through a mental checklist of items to pick up from the grocery store for dinner, when another call from Andrew came through. I'd ignored him long enough and took the call.

"Hello, Andrew."

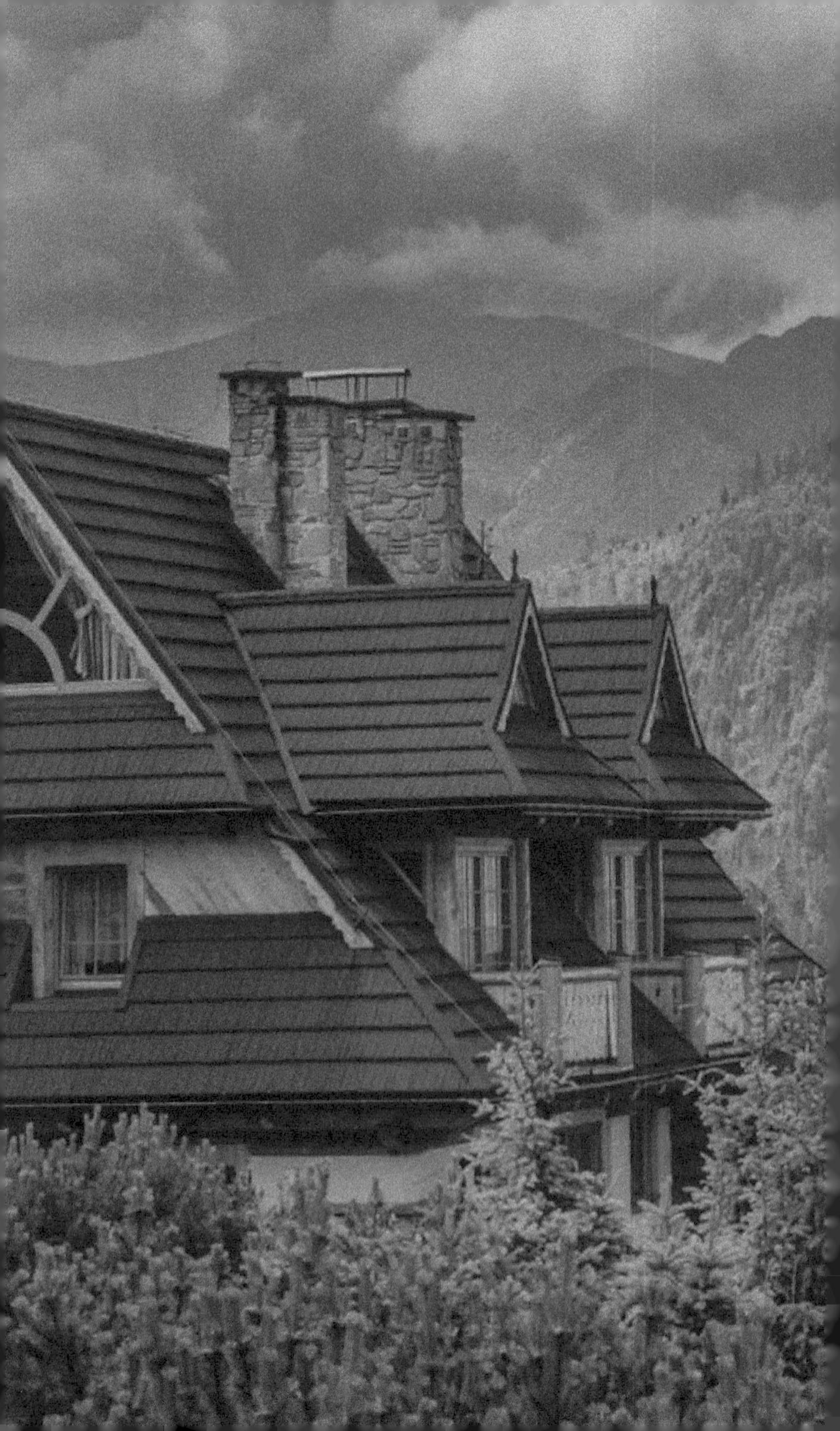

Chapter Seventeen

Talon

Despite the numerous arguments from family members over the week, Aurora and I had been able to push it all aside. She showed me pictures on her phone of her classroom. Something I could tell immediately she was proud of. She even showed me a picture of the teacher in the neighboring room who went out with Franny. Apparently, the two hit it off.

Kind of like Aurora and me.

Despite my better judgement, and the numerous times Dean told me to hold myself back, I was falling for my wife every day. It was hard not to.

Tonight was the charity event in Nashville, and Aurora and I drove up Friday evening to stay in the Penthouse Suite at the Central Wilder Hotel. We were hosting the event, which was a combination ball and charity auction. In years past, I never walked the red carpet, leaving my family members to do that part. This year, no one—except Gigi—knew I was even going to be in attendance.

As her favorite event of the season, she managed all the planning with our Wilder Hotels Team. She made sure to leave two place cards at her table that read **WC1** and **WC2**—Wedded Couple 1 and Wedded Couple 2. When I spoke to her this morning, she had been over the moon to meet Aurora. Luckily, none of the press had been able to dig up much on *her* except that her family were corn farmers in Tennessee. The only connections they reported on were with Colton and Nate, and then the two thriving businesses of The Easterly Event Venue and Show-Stopping Sweets.

Once those were mentioned, they became the focus of the articles. Aurora had told me she was thankful they spent more time on her family than on her.

She liked to say it was because she was boring, but she was anything but.

And as she stepped out of the bedroom in her dress for the event, I knew without a doubt the rest of the world would agree with me. The shimmery silver number fell down her body in a column, the bottom just barely touching the floor. Aurora stood a few inches taller than before. She usually came up to my chest, but she now stood at my neck.

"What do you think?" she asked as she gripped the material of the dress, exposing a long slit that showcased her tanned legs up to her thighs.

"Wow," I mumbled, damn near drunk on her beauty.

I was flabbergasted at the image she made, but even more so as she turned around. Her entire back was naked. The flimsy material scooped to just above her ass, showcasing my two favorite dimples. The modesty in the front did nothing to distract from the back.

Digging the heels of my hands into my eyes as I tilted my head back, I moaned, "Fuck."

"Oh no. I told the stylist this was too flashy. Let me change. She had a black dress that may be more suitable."

Immediately, I reached out and gripped her arm to keep her from leaving. "No. You look stunning."

"Really?" she asked, and her eyes glistened. I could have told her that she'd be beautiful even wearing a potato sack, which would have been the truth. Or that she was going to be the most beautiful woman in the room tonight. Also, another truth. Instead, I said, "No one else could ever come close to you, Aurora. Thank you for letting me be your date tonight."

She paused and then coughed as if she was holding back tears. "You know. You're getting better at this whole talking thing."

"I did tell you that I'd try."

We stared at each other, her bright-red lips calling to me, and I desperately wanted to smear the stain, but I held myself back.

"I'm just going to spray my hair one more time. It's a little windy out." It wasn't, but I let her escape into the bedroom to spray the curls draped over her shoulder once again. The hair and makeup team didn't need to do a lot to accentuate her beauty. Aurora was gorgeous even when she rolled out of bed.

"Ready, Mrs. Beckett?" I asked as she joined me again.

"As I'll ever be."

We didn't *need* a limo, since we were staying in the hotel, but to keep up pretenses, Aurora and I slipped out the employee exit of the hotel and into the waiting car. Only for it to zip around the corner and drop us off so the photographers could capture the moment.

I stepped out of the limo first, and a frenzy occurred, seeing as I never walked the red carpet. But when Aurora reached out and took my hand to exit the car, the crowd and photographers went absolutely wild. I leaned down to remind her to look away from the flashes. Gigi always told me to stare at their stomachs.

"I wish I brought *my* camera," she said as we stepped onto the red carpet behind a celebrity with a blockbuster movie currently playing in theaters. I laughed at her joke, and the cameras went berserk.

She'd handed me the film canister yesterday, and I already sent it out to get developed. I had no doubt Aurora caught the best parts of small-town and mountain living.

She gripped my hand as we traveled down the red carpet. The only press in attendance were those invited. That meant no paparazzi were mingled in the crowd. The Wilder Hotels had strict security for events like this.

We stopped for a reporter from a magazine who wrote a yearly report on the event. As expected, their first round of questions focused on the woman I was with. Aurora answered her questions like a seasoned pro. I suspected having Colton and Nate in the family helped. Through it all, she never released my hand, and I never budged when the diamond cut into my palm from her hidden nerves. She was worth the pain.

When the end of the carpet came into view, I felt Aurora's body relax.

"Hello, dear," a familiar voice called out from behind me, and I felt my wife stiffen once again. This was the moment she'd been dreading, even though I spent the entire week trying to convince her that she had nothing to worry about.

I turned us around and smiled at my grandma, who was wearing a dress that resembled a Picasso painting, a multitude of colors splashed over the material. It was quintessentially Gigi.

"Gigi, I'd like you to meet Aurora Beckett. Aurora, this is my grandmoth—" I was cut off as Gigi pulled Aurora into one of her tight embraces. The two women were practically the same height, but it was comical to see the elderly woman cinch her arms around Aurora.

Not wanting to draw the attention of the photographers, who would surely pick up on the fact that Aurora had yet to meet the Wilder matriarch, I whispered that the three of us should probably head inside. The only press allowed beyond the doors was the reporter writing about the speeches and auction.

The moment we slipped into the darkened ballroom, Gigi tried to pull Aurora aside, but my wife held on firmly to my hand.

"Well, now," Gigi scoffed.

"Sorry, I'm just not very comfortable," Aurora spoke, revealing a bit of her insecurities.

"I understand. I remember my first big event. I was petrified. And that was before all this social media stuff. But you have nothing to worry about, dear." Gigi reached for Aurora's other hand and clasped it within her gloved one. "I may not know much, or anything about you, but you made my Talon smile, and there is nothing more I could ask for in the world."

Aurora nodded as Gigi turned her attention to me. "Of course, it would have been nice to be invited to the wedding. I'm assuming this wasn't a shotgun ceremony?"

With wide eyes and eyebrows lifted toward the sky, Aurora shook her head and answered for me when I ignored my grandmother. "No, ma'am."

The dinner portion of the ball was called over the intercom, and we marched across the ballroom floor to our seats. Aurora drew the attention of every man in the room, just as I expected she would. She whispered in my ear that everyone was staring at her, and I simply pressed my lips to the top of her head. My sweet, naïve wife had no idea the appeal she projected to others.

Because not only were the men interested, but the women were too. I'd seen numerous cat fights at these events over the years, but most of the women here seemed to only look at Aurora with respect. Only a few sneered as she passed, and anyone could've seen it was only from jealousy.

"Thank you," I leaned down and whispered in her ear.

"For what?" she asked as we reached our table.

"Being here with me. Agreeing to marry me. Take your pick."

Surprising me and our tablemates, Aurora leaned in to place a chaste kiss on my lips. As she pulled away, I caught the thoughtful smile and watery gaze of my grandmother.

"Well, now. Please don't hog our beautiful guest," a familiar voice bellowed as he stood behind my vacant seat.

Aurora's eyes lit up when she noticed our interrupter. "Dean! I didn't think we'd see you again until we were in Miami." She wrapped him in a tight hug I thought lasted a bit too long.

"Plans change. I need to steal your husband for a bit. I'll have him back before the dinner starts."

"Oh."

I looked at my friend, and I could see something was brewing. He never attended these events, so for him to be here, there was something serious on the line.

Gigi quickly took the reins with Aurora, and the two of them sat and called over a server for a bubbly beverage.

I followed Dean to a darkened corner close to the auction table.

"What's going on?" I asked him as he pulled out a slip of paper from his suit pocket. "Look this over. I know you didn't read it in her background check, but I missed it too. And this is common knowledge, so there is a good chance the press could catch wind of it."

I read over the notarized script on the first page. It detailed Aurora's annulment to her high-school boyfriend. The second page listed her times spent completing community service as a minor when she was caught spray-painting the water tower and super-gluing the doors to the school shut. The third page detailed how she was the mistress of Jeremy Mitchell, the son of a politician. Apparently, Jeremy had an entire second life Aurora knew nothing about.

"I know about the annulment, and the stuff when she was a teen is admissible to anyone. I mean, look at the trouble we caused in school."

"Yeah, but we had money to save our asses. She didn't."

I thought to myself, *She does now.*

"Okay."

"The mistress piece could really ruin her reputation if it got out, and Talon, it wasn't hard to find. An article was posted about Jeremy and his fiancée just the other day. It said they'd been college sweethearts."

I didn't believe a word of the orchestrated article. He was doing it to hurt Aurora, probably after our incident at the bar. I told Dean what happened, and he agreed, but the damage was there in the writing.

"Talk to your lawyer, for her sake," Dean surmised as I folded the sheets of paper and shoved them in my tuxedo pocket. I'd show them to Aurora later. She had every right to see what was coming to light, even if it wasn't true.

We walked back to the table just as the salads were set in front of us.

"Everything okay?" Aurora whispered next to me.

Gently, I slid my hand over the exposed skin of her thigh, relishing the touch of her soft skin. "Everything is fine. We'll talk about it later."

She nodded, but I could sense she knew something was amiss.

At the table, Gigi held up the conversation, going on about past events and some of her travels in the upcoming year. At one point, I asked her how Grandfather was taking the news of my nuptials. It was the only time she frowned throughout dinner.

"Everything is being adjusted," she said with a heavy sigh. After that, the group quieted.

After Aurora reapplied her lipstick, we returned to the ballroom where the auction was finishing up. Music began to play, and I guided her out onto the floor despite her yanking on my hand and her saying she couldn't dance. She may not have been able to dance, but I could.

By the end of the night, Aurora had captivated Gigi, just as I knew she would. She even promised to come visit the small town where Aurora lived when my wife talked up the restaurant by Roland McEntire and the cake shop her sister ran.

Honestly, the deal was sealed when Gigi learned Colton Crawford was Aurora's brother-in-law. She'd always been a big hockey fan.

Beside me, Aurora leaned her head on my shoulder as I spoke with Dean about the auction prize he won. A trip for two to Edinburgh, Scotland. When she yawned for the third time, I knew it was time to end our night.

We'd done what we came to do. Eat, dance, and show the world we were married. Even in her sleepy state, Aurora was spinning the large diamond around her finger. Though it was big and what I imagined anyone marrying a billionaire so he could gain control of his family's hotel would wear, her sister was right. It wasn't Aurora's style at all.

We said goodnight to Dean, who was taking a flight back home tonight. I thanked him for what he did. Not just tracking me down but keeping me calm while making sure Aurora smiled and had a good time during the evening. He was growing just as protective of her as I was.

Gigi left an hour after the dancing started and went up to her room.

As Aurora and I made our way over to the elevators, I could tell she was dead on her feet. Just as I pressed the button to call the cart down, a hand came down heavily on my shoulder, knocking me off balance. Aurora nearly fell to the ground, as her weight had been resting against me.

I turned to find my uncle standing behind me, looking disheveled and drunk. His tie was askew, his shirt half untucked from his pants, and his jacket had a tear along the shoulder seam. His face was red and glossy. Sweat poured down it like rain. He looked… terrible.

"Uncle. I didn't expect to see you here."

He tried to reach out to me again but missed his mark by a foot.

"This is still my hotel, boy, and you're damn sure not taking it from me," he slurred.

"Yet I've been running your hotel for the last year. Before that you relied on your VP who retired. I'm pretty sure grandfather will have something to say about that."

"Pssh, you think your little slut here is something special? I know what you're doing, and I'm going to make sure everyone else knows too."

"Security is coming," Aurora whispered beside me as the uniformed men stomped down the hall toward us.

Then my uncle made the biggest mistake ever. He leaned over and cupped Aurora's face. Not gently, but gripped it in his meaty fingers.

"You are a pretty little thing," he said, leaning into her.

Without a second thought, I wrapped an arm around his neck and tugged him backward until he released his grip. "You will never, *ever* lay your hand on another woman. Especially not my wife," I said as I locked my arm at his throat. He struggled to breathe. "Do you understand, old man?"

He couldn't speak but smartly nodded as the security guards approached with the police in tow. They cuffed him for assault after they witnessed him putting his hand on Aurora, while I still held him in place. The second they yanked him away, I rushed over to my wife, whose face was growing red where his fingers clenched.

"I'm so sorry, baby," I said as I held my arms open for her. She quickly fell against me, her silent sobs shattering me.

I ignored the crowd that had grown around us. There was a good chance pictures of the incident would be on social media within minutes. Rumors would swirl, likely painting all of us in some sort of bad light.

We were the world's favorite form of entertainment.

"Let's get you upstairs," I told her as her whimpers began to subside.

Back in the room, she stood in front of the bed while I stripped her out of the dress. Earlier, I asked her if she wanted to keep it. Then, she'd said yes, but now, I wasn't so sure. I draped it over the chair in the corner in case she changed her mind.

Kneeling at her feet, I unhooked the strap that wrapped around her ankle and helped her step out of the silver shoe, then repeated the process with the other. She'd worn no bra with the backless dress, and it surprised me when she covered her breasts with her crossed arms.

It wasn't hard to tell she was upset about what happened tonight with my uncle, but the fact that she was feeling vulnerable with me was poignant.

I stood before her, leaving her skin-toned lace panties in place. I stripped out of my tuxedo, all while Aurora watched with tired, red-rimmed eyes. Wearing only my black boxer briefs, I bent and lifted her into my arms. I was worried she'd ask me to set her down, but instead, she curled against me, resting her head on my shoulder as I carried her over to the side of the bed she slept on last night. Not wanting to be separated by the massive mattress, I slipped under the blankets right behind her. My ass hung off the side, but I didn't care. All I cared about was that she let me wrap my arm around her waist and hold her close.

"I'm sorry about tonight," I whispered. I knew it wasn't a good time to talk to her about everything Dean found. That was something we could deal with in the morning. "It looks like my uncle has returned from whatever bender he's been on."

Her body shook against mine, and my heart broke. On the tip of my finger, I could feel the drip of her tears as they fell across the bridge of her nose.

I pressed my lips against her exposed shoulder and apologized again for my uncle's behavior. Really, for *most* of my family's behavior. All I kept thinking was that Aurora was too good for all of us, too good for me. All because of my family and their misconstrued views, this beautiful, innocent woman was about to have her world flipped upside down.

"I'm so sorry, Aurora. What can I do to make it up to you?"

With a speed that surprised me and a glare that spoke volumes, Aurora turned around to face me, and I instantly quieted.

"Stop apologizing for your family. If anything, *I'm* sorry you had to grow up with that man. I'm sorry if he ever laid a hand on you, Talon. You didn't deserve that. No child does. I'm sorry your mother was taken away from this world before her time, leaving you with that beast of a man. And I'm sorry you can't see you're so much more than a name." Her voice quaked on the last word, and she shoved her face into my shoulder as another round of tears fell from her eyes.

As she cried for the child I once was, I held her, wishing I could take away her sadness. Take away anything that caused her pain.

As she fell asleep against me, I made a promise to myself that when our time was up, I was going to make sure whoever captured Aurora's heart was worthy of it. Because this angel mourning my childhood at the hand of my cruel uncle deserved the absolute best man. Even if that wasn't going to be me.

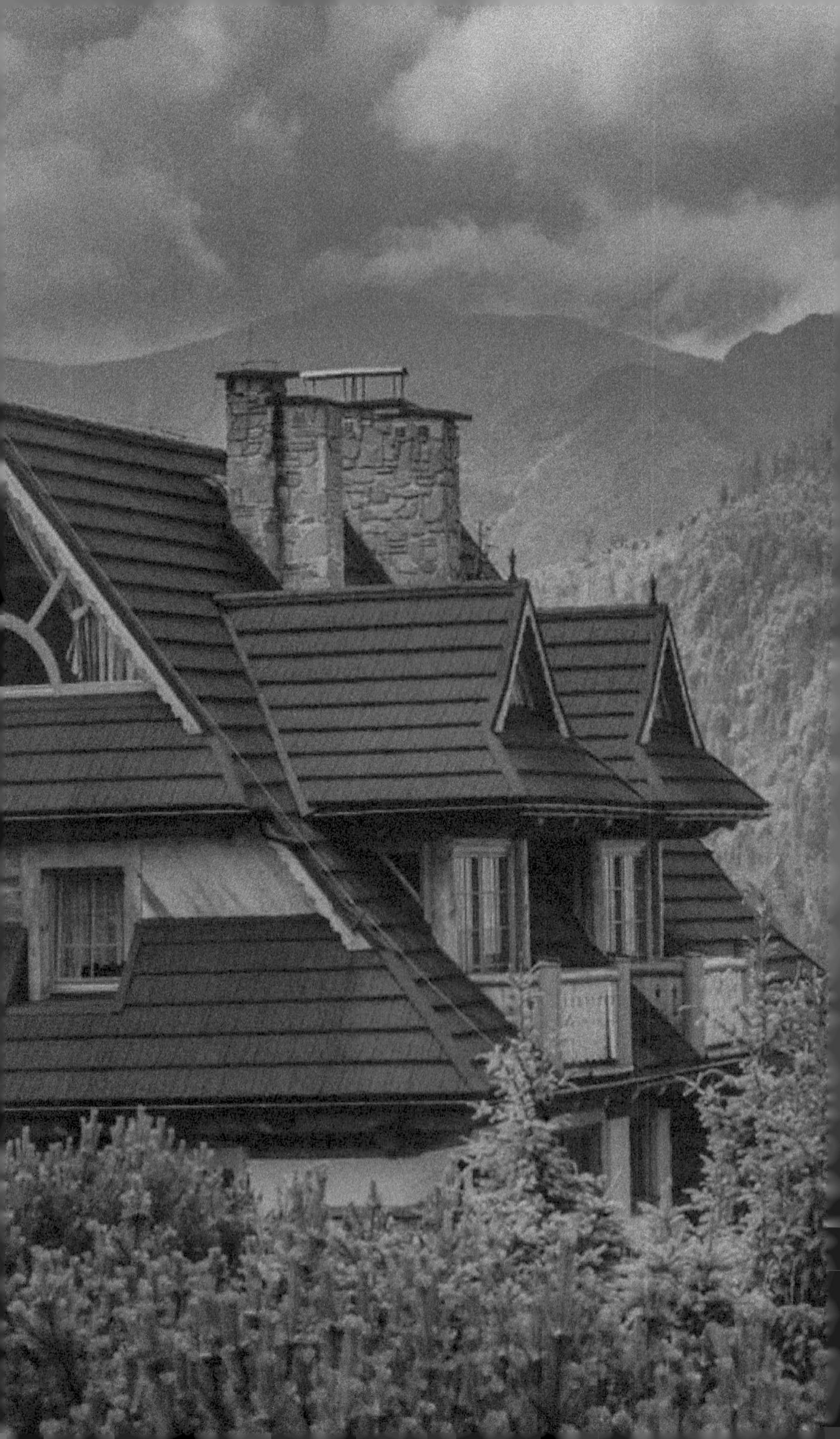

Chapter Eighteen

Aurora

Weeks passed as Talon and I fell into a routine. I figured after a month or two, he would have grown bored with the town and all its nosy neighbors, but that hadn't been the case. Betsy, who worked in the bakery at the grocery store, was Talon's best friend in town. I suspected it was because she reminded him of his grandmother.

The first time I took him shopping, she asked him why he was walking around looking like he stepped in a heaping pile of dog shit. In his grumpy state, Talon tended to scrunch his nose a bit when he was listening to someone talk. Her assessment had been right on.

Other than Dean and me, Talon never had anyone call him out like that before. Since then, he and Betsy had a weekly lunch date. I thought it was the cutest thing ever. He was excited to have his grandmother come visit so the two women could meet. I had a feeling, despite her enthusiasm during the charity event, Gigi wasn't going to be as enthralled with the town as Talon was.

Every day, I'd been on guard for an article calling me a politician's mistress. Ever since Dean crashed the charity event and handed Talon a stack of articles about me, I'd been waiting for the other shoe to drop. So far, there had only been rumblings, but that could change any day. I didn't expect Talon to throw money around to cover it up, especially since the story about being Jeremy's mistress didn't add up. The article dated vacations and his years at school that didn't coincide with the truth, which I had evidence to verify. Both Dean and Talon said it was easier to ignore than to make the press think we cared.

Well, I cared. Especially since Jeremy's wedding was coming up this weekend. My sisters and their newly hired planner were working overtime to get the venue ready for who my sister called a "groomzilla." Autumn said Jeremy and his mother had taken the reins of the wedding, not allowing his fiancée a say in anything. I wondered if she'd been able to pick out her own dress. I almost felt bad for her.

Almost.

With the article, our fears about the press finding out what we'd done grew. But whenever either of us brought up the topic of what we'd do or what we'd say, the other person would change the subject. I wasn't sure if it was fear of the past or dread of the future. But it became a scenario where I hoped the longer I ignored it, then maybe it would go away.

I was in the middle of my planning period at school, talking with Franny on the phone while her preschoolers were taking their naps.

"How are things with Liam?" I asked her. Over the past few weeks, she and my neighbor had been on multiple dates. And Franny said they were taking things slow. Which in Franny's world meant they had yet to have sex.

"Good. He's taking me away for the weekend. He didn't say where. I'm hoping maybe it will happen then."

I knew from Franny's overly informative messages that the two of them had done everything but seal the deal. She went into more detail, telling me about the wild places they were hooking up. I had a hard time looking my room neighbor in the eye.

"I'll keep my fingers crossed for you."

"Thanks. What are you and Talon doing this weekend?"

"It's the wedding."

"*The* wedding?"

"Yep."

I'd been dreading this weekend. Even with Talon by my side, it was going to be awkward. I even asked my mom if Jeremy or Mrs. Mitchell rescinded the invite after the fiasco at the bar. But nothing. We were still on the guest list and had been added to the seating chart.

"I kind of wish I could be a fly on the wall for that."

"It's going to be something; that's for sure."

A quick glance at the clock told me my planning period was almost over, and thirty teenagers would soon greet me.

The first few days of class, it took a while for the students to take me seriously. It wasn't until Talon made an unexpected visit that my students started paying better attention. I wasn't sure if they were all under Talon's spell like Indiana Jones in *Raiders of the Lost Ark*, or if they were afraid of him. Either way, the weeks since his spontaneous visit, students had been acing exams and showing up to class on time. I wasn't convinced it was purely due to my teaching capabilities. Though I enjoyed lying to myself and saying it was.

"I have to go, Franny."

"All right, want me to come over later to help you pick out something for the wedding?"

"I think Talon is going to have some dresses delivered for me to choose from."

"Oh, to be rich." I hated when she said that. *Talon* was rich. I was just his wife. Though it did help that he had a team of people review my grant proposals before I submitted them last week. I didn't expect to win it the first year, but it gave me an idea of how to put together the proposal in the future.

So far, the money Talon deposited in my account was sitting there collecting dust. The little I did spend was to have some scholarships set up for the students. The criteria required them to work so many hours on a farm during the week. And when I say little, it was tens of thousands of dollars, but overall, they barely made a dent in my million. Especially since the scholarships wouldn't be issued until the end of the school year.

"Bye, Franny," I said before I hung up the phone.

There was a commotion out in the hallway, and as I stood from my desk, Jeremy traipsed inside, nearly colliding with a desk as the school principal followed behind him.

"Baby," he slurred. "I knew I'd find you here. Why'd you leave me like that?"

I had no idea what he was talking about. With my cell phone still in hand, I clicked on the record button and placed it on my desk.

"Do you know this man, Mrs. Beckett?" the principal asked, but before I could reply, Jeremy shouted.

"Her name is not Mrs. Beckett!"

"Jeremy, I think it's best that you go. My class is about to start."

"No! I'm not leaving until you and I make up."

The bell rang overhead, and the principal shook his head.

"I'll get him out of here. Give me just a second," I assured him.

"Get him out, then come to my office. I'll have the secretary watch your class."

Shit. I was going to get in trouble for this, and I hadn't even done anything. The principal never had teachers in his office unless they were being reprimanded for something. I watched him stomp out of my classroom, then I focused on my ex.

"Jeremy, listen to me right now. We aren't a thing, and we never will be a thing again. You're getting married tomorrow, remember?"

"But you're supposed to still be with me. You weren't supposed to go find someone else. I'm the best you are ever going to find."

God, I'd forgotten *just* how self-centered the man was.

From my desk, I saw Liam as he passed my doorway, and I quickly caught his eye.

"Need any help, Mrs. Beckett?"

"Yes, please," I replied as Jeremy continued to mumble to himself, sitting down at one of the student desks.

Thankfully, Liam was able to lift Jeremy out of the chair and maneuver my ex's arm around his shoulders. I grabbed my phone and bag while setting the pop quizzes on the end of my desk for the secretary. As I turned around, Liam had only made it as far as the door. Jeremy was dragging his feet, literally.

"Aren't you coming—" He hiccupped. "—baby?"

I rolled my eyes and walked over to them, doing my best to help Liam drag Jeremy to the front office. The students looked at us with both shock and curiosity. Jeremy's family was well-known in Ashfield and in Tennessee, with his father's gubernatorial billboards plastered along the highway.

"You'll still be my mistress, right, baby? The sex isn't good with that woman… Tal… Tail—"

"Talia? And no. I have no desire to be in your presence ever again."

Finally, we reached the office, where the resource officer was waiting with the town sheriff. The principal wasn't going to stand for someone drunk in his hallways, disrupting the students.

When he handed my ex off, I thanked Liam, then followed Mr. Donahue to his office. The day was definitely not going to get any better.

"I'm on probation. Can you believe that?" I asked Alex as she hugged Molly and Eloise. She asked if I could watch the girls last-minute, as she and Nate had an appointment that evening she'd forgotten about.

I wasn't sure what kind of appointments happened after 5:00 p.m. except the recreational kind that required no children around.

"It's ridiculous. You should have Dad talk to him. Aren't they old friends?"

"Yeah, but I guess I get it."

"Don't let them push you around. This place looks great, by the way. I'm sorry I didn't come by sooner."

When Talon and I finished all the little projects around the house, we had a housewarming, post-wedding shower type of party. It was for my family, but only my parents and Aspen showed up. I tried not to let my disappointment show that night, but I knew everyone could read me like a book. Talon paid extra-close attention to me after they left, in the best kind of way.

"That's okay. You've been busy." As she headed for the front door, I asked, "What time will you be picking them up?"

"Nine?"

"Okay. I'll text Talon to grab us something to eat on his way home. He was picking up the new plans for the lodge."

She paused by the door, her hand resting on the knob. "Things still going well?"

"Yep," I replied with a smile. It was going better than I could have ever imagined, and it made it harder with each passing day to remember it was all fake. This was all going to end soon. Gigi had let it slip the other night on hers and my weekly call that Talon's grandfather's health was declining rapidly, but she hadn't had the heart to tell him yet. That meant our timeline could be over sooner than planned.

Talon's overtaking of the CEO position was being pushed through the legal department, which was something he hadn't anticipated when he set the six-month timeline for our marriage. It seemed Gigi had pulled some strings and was having it fast-tracked. But three weeks ago, they signed over access to his trust fund left by his mother. I knew he didn't need a penny of it, but he wanted what his mom had set aside for him, just because it was from his mom.

"Good, I'm glad. You look happy, Rory."

"Thanks." I smirked, wondering if I looked miserable *before*.

"Girls, be good for Aunt Rory!" she shouted before heading out the door.

I turned to find the twins sitting around my coffee table with a bag emptied out. There were palettes of eye shadows, blushes, and bottles of nail polish. Looked like it was going to be a fun evening of makeovers.

With Talon's insistence, I turned on the television that hung on my wall in a gold frame that matched the pictures hanging. I didn't know how he'd done it, but Talon reprinted all the images that had once belonged there. They had been some of my favorites, but when Jeremy and I started dating, he called them "amateur." Then one night when I'd been on vacation with my parents, he'd thrown them all away. I'd been devastated, but I was too cautious then to say anything. Jeremy was the kind of guy everyone wanted to be with, The good-looking politician's son.

In the time since our breakup, I could have replaced them with something new or found the old images, but something held me back. I feared that my hobby was something silly. Jeremy's lack of support made me question my deepest passion.

Even with Talon's history and expertise, he'd only ever been supportive of my photography. When my mother learned what he'd done with both the camera and the images, she hugged him for a solid five minutes. My dad had been the one to help Talon search the attic in their house for the original film. The two were nothing alike, but my dad filled a void for Talon that he missed out on at a young age.

When Gigi told me that Talon's father passed away in a car accident, then his mother died a few months later from what Gigi thought was a broken heart, I cried the entire evening. Talon had come home to find me curled up in the middle of the mattress, hugging the pillow from his side of the bed.

I wasn't sure if Gigi told him that I knew, but I suspected she had when he asked me the next morning if I wanted to see a picture of his mom and dad he found in a photo album stored at the lodge in Knoxville. I wondered what other secrets Talon could learn about himself from that place.

"Where's Talon?" Eloise asked as she brushed a blue eye shadow across my lids.

"He's on his way home from work. He'll be here in a little bit with some pizza." I'd texted him about the last-minute change of plans before I subjected myself to the six-year-old version of a makeover.

The corners of Eloise's mouth tilted upward, revealing her wide smile that was missing a front tooth. The two of them had a special little bond. One night after we met up with Alex, Nate, and the twins downtown for some ice cream, Talon had given her his full ice cream cone when hers toppled out of her hand and onto the sidewalk. Since then, she thought he hung the moon.

Headlights passed across the wall, and I looked through the window to see Talon's Ferrari in the driveway.

The girls cheered when he came inside carrying the two boxes of greasy goodness.

"Hi, peaches," he said as he leaned down to kiss me. "Loving the blue."

"Thanks. It's Eloise's specialty. Do you mind sitting with them while I grade some papers? I'll be busy for like an hour, tops."

"Sure, take some pizza with you. Sorry about the probation. I could have the guy fired if you'd like."

I giggled. "Maybe just get rid of Jeremy. That would do us all a favor."

"It's like you don't think I know powerful men who could do just that," he said as he chuckled, then hollered at the girls to wash their hands as he pulled plates down from the cabinet.

I grabbed two slices and a bottle of water before heading to my office to grade the pop quizzes from today and get a head start on the essays that had been turned in. They weren't due until next week, but I had a few students who liked to get them out of the way.

An hour and a half later, I rubbed my eyes and pushed back from my desk. The words on the paper were all starting to blend together.

I carried my dish out to the kitchen and checked up on the girls. Hopefully, they hadn't tied Talon to a chair or anything. I'd heard horror stories from Franny about her preschoolers.

The moment I stepped into the living room, I gasped in horror. Talon sat on the floor, eyes closed, with a green shadow on his eyelids, hot pink on his cheeks, and bright-red fingernails. But the catastrophic part was that both Eloise and Molly held scissors in their hands.

"Um... girls...," I said calmly, trying not to frighten Talon. Chunks of his gorgeous hair laid haphazardly on the floor behind him. "Where did you get the scissors?"

Talon's eyes opened and doubled in size as he began to turn and take notice of the hair lying around him.

"From our school bags," Molly answered gleefully, but Eloise wore the kind of down-turned expression that said she knew she'd done something wrong.

"You know you're not supposed to ever use real scissors on someone's hair."

"Yeah… but I wanted to play hair salon, and you don't have the pretend scissors."

"Did you *ask* if I had pretend scissors?"

Molly tucked her chin to her chest as she shook her head. I suspected tears were going to quickly follow.

"Girls, please apologize to Talon while I call your mom."

There was still an hour remaining before Alex was scheduled to come pick up the girls, so I was afraid I wouldn't be able to get a hold of her. And I was right. Her phone rang six times before it clicked over to voicemail.

"Come on," I mumbled in the kitchen as I tried Nate's number. His did the same as Alex's.

In my head, all I could think was, *Glad this isn't an emergency.* I supposed they assumed I'd know what to do if it were.

Pulling up the messaging app, I typed out a text to Alex.

> You should come get the girls.

I hesitated to go back into the living room. The television was loudly playing a princess movie, so I couldn't hear what was going on, but knowing Talon's temperament, I was afraid he was ready to verbally explode at the girls. But when I walked into the room, I found the complete opposite. He'd tied what was left of his long strands at the top of his head and was helping them clean up the mess they made. There were splotches of nail polish on my rug and minute strands of Talon's hair all over my floor, but I didn't care.

Talon was there with my nieces, acting as if they hadn't just destroyed his gorgeous locks.

I moved closer and crouched beside Talon who, by all accounts, looked freaking great with the green eyeshadow smeared up to his brows.

"Are you okay?"

"Yeah. It's just hair."

"Talon—"

"It's okay, peaches," he said, and then he leaned over to smack a chaste kiss on my lips. "Come on, girls. Let's finish cleaning up." Molly and Eloise kept their faces toward the floor, neither girl wanting to make eye contact with Talon or me. It killed me to see them so sad, but something worse could have happened with the sharp instruments than clipping hair.

I went back to the kitchen to pack up the few extra slices of pizza and put them in my fridge. It was too late in the evening to call the one salon in town to fix

Talon's hair, and I knew tomorrow was going to be a bust with the wedding. Thank goodness I didn't need to be there for the rehearsal tonight.

When I returned to the living room, both twins were curled up against Talon's side. He draped an arm around each of them as they watched the movie they selected. Seeing him with the twins, even after the chaos they just created, made something in my stomach knot. Something about him, in such a vulnerable state, made me realize he was turning into more than just my fake husband. He was quickly turning into my everything.

"Aurora? Are you okay?" he asked, and I quickly shook my head to clear my thoughts.

"Of course. What are we watching?"

"*Tangled*. It's my favorite," Molly said as she jumped up and down on the couch, nearly knocking her head into Talon's chin.

I sat with the crew as the movie played. The clock was approaching 9:00 p.m. when I saw the headlights shine across the living room wall. Neither Alex nor Nate returned my messages or voicemail from earlier, and I was fighting between not caring and being angry. To me, it felt thoughtless for them to saddle me with the kids last-minute, expecting I didn't have anything going on. I realized this was the same thing my sisters always did to me when I was younger. I'd just never spoken up about it.

I felt… used.

"Hi, girls," Nate said as he stepped into my house behind Alex, who hadn't even knocked. She just barged right in.

I stood from the couch, eyeing Talon for a moment, then made my way over to them. The girls didn't move from their spots. They only snuggled in closer to him.

"Did either of you get my messages?"

"Um…," Nate mumbled as Alex looked around the kitchen. It was clear from the way they refused to make eye contact with me that they hadn't.

"Thank goodness there wasn't an emergency," I said in a snarky tone. "Or, you know, that I didn't already have plans."

I was working myself up, thinking about all the times Alex and Autumn had thrown things my way without a care. They'd been doing it since we were little. I was well past my breaking point.

"Rory," Alex said in her melodic voice.

Just as I was about to explode on my sister, I felt a warm weight rest around my waist, holding me steady. Talon.

"Everything all right in here, Aurora?" he asked, and I loved how he addressed me first and not my sister or her husband.

"I was just expressing to Alex that if she is going to drop the girls off with me last-minute, without even considering I may have plans, then she should make sure she's available to answer her phone if there's an emergency."

"You're right," Nate added, and my sister looked shocked that he responded. "Rory isn't a paid babysitter. She's their aunt, and her time should be respected. I'm sorry we dropped them off without asking in advance. Did something happen?"

Alex was still standing in my kitchen, gawking at her husband.

"Yes," I replied, crossing my arms over my chest. "Would you mind showing them, Talon?"

"I don't think that's necessary."

"Girls!" I shouted. If Talon wasn't going to spill the beans, then the twins were. They needed to learn to own their mistakes. I lived most of my life hiding from mine. I didn't want that for them.

Eloise and Molly slowly made their way to the kitchen area. By the drooping shoulders and shuffling feet, they knew they were going to have to confess what they'd done.

"Yes, Aunt Rory?"

"Want to tell your dad and mom what you did tonight?"

Both girls sniffled. I wasn't sure if it was because they wanted to gain some sympathy or if they were truly regretful of their decision. I worked with kids their age enough to know it could have been for either reason.

"Not really," Molly said, and I felt Talon chuckle behind me.

"I think you should," I implored.

Eloise spoke this time. "We brought our scissors from school to play hair salon instead of using pretend scissors."

Alex's eyes widened as she looked at the twins. Nate crouched down to their level. "And what happened?"

Thankfully, the scissors had rounded tips, so they couldn't stab anything.

"We played salon with Uncle Talon."

"No." Alex's gasp rang in my ears, and my eyes narrowed at her.

Nate's head hung between his shoulders in defeat.

"We're sorry. We didn't ask Aunt Rory for the pretend ones."

When Nate stood, he met Talon's eyes. "How bad is it?"

"Honestly, I haven't looked yet."

I chimed in, "It isn't good."

"Frick, man. I'll pay whatever it costs to fix it," Nate said apologetically.

Talon shrugged in that way that said not to worry about it. He unfurled his arm from around me and directed the girls back to the living room at Alex's insistence.

Nate chimed in again as I offered them a piece of pizza. "I'm sorry that we… uh… sprung the twins on you tonight."

"Actually, I'm not," Alex said coldly, her arms crossed over her chest. Her tone took me by surprise.

"What?" I asked in shock.

"Let me clarify something. I know we rely on you too much. I do. Autumn does. Mom does. We all do, Rory. But you let us, so it becomes a habit. But tonight, it wasn't because we were being selfish. We did it to protect you."

I was knocked into a catatonic state and had no idea what to say. Talon spoke up instead. "What do you mean?"

"The rehearsal dinner was tonight. None of us planned to be in attendance, but Autumn called me frantic, because Jeremy was causing a scene with his fiancée. And his mother was… something else entirely. It was a shit show. They weren't happy with the dessert cake I delivered, even though it was what Mrs. Mitchell ordered. I had to rush and make a champagne cake instead. And then reporters showed up. They were asking Jeremy questions about you, and we wanted to shield you from all of it. Watching the twins was the first thing we could all think of.

"But you're right. We should have been more respectful of you. I should have considered you might've had plans tonight *because* of the wedding tomorrow. I still can't believe that asshole invited all of us."

Like me, Alex had always been a horrible liar. She tended to twirl her hair between her fingers whenever she was being untruthful. Right now, her fingers never budged from her arms.

"Were any of you going to tell me? About tonight, I mean."

Her shoulders rose and then dropped. They weren't. I wasn't sure how I felt about that. It left me thinking about other things they may have kept secret.

"Don't keep secrets from me anymore, please. I'm twenty-four. I can handle it."

"You're right. I'm sorry again," she stated, dropping her arms, her hands dangling against her thighs. "Nate and I never considered an actual emergency could have happened. You're the best with kids. If anything, we would have called *you* to ask what to do."

I laughed and added that they were probably right.

"Um… thanks for taking one for the team, Talon."

"It's no sweat. Those are good little girls."

Nate and Alex smiled as they looked across the room to watch their twins on the couch snuggle together, watching the movie. They called them over, and the family left my house as we watched them from the porch.

Talon tried to ask me how I felt about their stunt tonight, but I shook the question away. I didn't want to talk about Jeremy, the wedding, or the twins. I reached over and tugged the locks free from the tie at the top of his head.

"Come on. Let's see if I can fix this."

I found it surprising that Talon didn't argue. He dutifully followed me toward my bathroom, where I kept a pair of sheers for the times when I needed a quick trim and didn't have time to make an appointment with the local salon.

He probably could call a world-renowned hair stylist to fly in and fix the mess, but he was trusting me. And that meant far more than he would ever know.

Chapter Nineteen

Talon

Last night, I lived out a fantasy I never knew I had. When I trusted Aurora to trim my hair, she seemed shocked. She didn't know I'd trust her with just about anything—my fortune, my hotels, my life. She held the wheel.

As I waited patiently on one of the barstools from her kitchen that she directed me to move into her bathroom, she went to change out of her school attire, opting for a pair of loose-fitting shorts that skimmed her upper thighs and a cropped oversized T-shirt that showed just the barest hint of her midriff.

With the sheers in hand, she snipped at sections as if she did this professionally. I tried to ignore the chunks of hair as they fell to the floor. When she moved to stand in front of me, I reached out and grabbed her hips. I couldn't help but touch her. My hands moved upward to her waist, then I cupped her breasts. When her arms dropped as she reprimanded me for getting handsy while she was wielding a sharp object, I commanded her to put the scissors aside.

Within five minutes, I had Aurora balanced on her bathroom counter as I fucked her.

We didn't get around to finishing my haircut until after midnight. Even with a pair of dull clippers she said belonged to her brother—who she hadn't talked to her since he confronted her about our marriage—Aurora had done a decent job. Better than I ever could've on my own.

When we woke in the morning, I did my best to keep her distracted. She was adamant about not going to the wedding, especially after the chaos her ex's family caused yesterday. But I sided with her parents and agreed that any waves Aurora might cause today by not showing up would affect her family.

We already learned the kind of revenge Jeremy was capable of—not that I couldn't throw money at it and make it go away. But I knew that wasn't what Aurora wanted. It was a tricky situation from whichever angle you looked at it. If she didn't go, Jeremy was going to continue to spew lies about her to a *very* interested press. There was also a good chance his family could use their political background to hurt the Easterlys, even though they'd been friends in the past. If I paid Jeremy and his family to leave Aurora alone, she'd be angry with me. There was always the chance she'd never know, and that was something I considered for after our contract was up, but I wasn't willing to risk it. If we went to the wedding, it would be over and done with. We'd get cake. We'd get to dance. And then we'd get to come back to our home.

It seemed like the easiest thing to do.

But really, I never understood why someone would invite their ex to their wedding.

We were headed downtown for lunch at my favorite place, The Purple Goat. Harold made a killer jalapeno-and-pimento cheeseburger. I had it at least once a week during my lunches with Betsy. That woman knew everyone and everything that was going on in town. She was better than any entertainment channel on television. She also kept me aware whenever she saw someone new snooping in town, trying to pick up a story on me and Aurora. It wasn't often, but every couple of days, someone inquired about us. The press was meddlesome at best, sneaky and intrusive at worst.

And Aurora and I had gone long enough in peace that I was now waiting for the worst.

We'd been able to brush aside the stories that sprouted about our quicky wedding. Gigi played her part by saying how much she adored Aurora. And even the PR team from the hotel was able to back up the story that we met the year prior.

So far, it was smooth sailing, and I was one step closer to signing the contract to establish myself as the official CEO of Wilder Hotels. I was ready to move into my rightful place. I wondered what my mother would think of all I'd done to get back into the business. Would she be proud of me? Or would she be disappointed in the lengths I went to cement myself in the role?

"I'm so hungry," Aurora said as she gazed out the window. She was rubbing her stomach lightly, and I had the craziest vision of her being pregnant with my child. It wasn't a future I ever envisioned for myself, but every day that passed with Aurora as my wife, it became more and more clear.

I was so fucking in love with her.

When I presented her the contract almost three months ago, I never thought this was where we'd end up. Where *I* would end up. Miami had been my home since I was three, but here I was, considering a permanent move to Ashfield, because I'd fallen in love with not only my temporary wife, but the mountainous area. But I knew when things ended, I wouldn't be able to stay here. It would kill me to see her move on.

"Are you okay? Your face is more pinched than usual," Aurora said as I slid the car into a parking spot on the street. I relaxed my features as I met her gaze. She lifted her hand, the oversized diamond sparkling on her finger, and brushed a few strands of hair back from my forehead. The cut Aurora gave me was neat and trimmed along the sides and longer on top. I wasn't used to hair tickling my face, since I always kept my long hair tucked behind my ears when it wasn't pulled into a man-bun, and I kept pushing it back.

"Is it still growing on you?"

"Yeah, but I like it."

"I bet Dean won't even recognize you."

I laughed as she giggled. "Maybe that's a good thing."

"Whatever," she said. "I still think y'all are secret lovers and not just a bromance."

I shook my head and exited the car, moving swiftly to her side. Opening the door, I held out my hand to help her step out. The sun shone behind her like a halo, and I had the strangest urge to tell her how I felt. About how deeply I cared for her, but that wasn't even something I did with Gigi. I had no idea how to express myself.

"You're scowling again. Are you sure everything is okay?"

Ushering her into the restaurant, I assured her everything was fine. We ate our lunch as she relayed the text Franny sent her that morning. Aurora's best friend and her coworker had grown serious over the last couple of weeks. My wife disclosed how, when she first met Liam, he'd given off major creep vibes, but she learned quickly the man was just awkward. Franny and Liam were away on their first overnight trip together, and Aurora was hopeful this was "the one." I liked Franny, and if Liam made her happy, I hoped it would all work out.

After lunch, Aurora seemed distant. Even when I offered to walk with her to the ice cream shop, she declined. I was worried about how tonight would go, and I feared she was too.

Thankfully, we didn't have to be at the wedding in any sort of professional aspect. The asshole had the nerve to request Aurora as the photographer. Autumn nipped that in the bud quickly. I was still in shock that the dick who had thrown out all her beautiful images and chucked her camera thought she would take him up on the offer. There was no amount of money on the planet that would've made Aurora agree to his proposal.

We'd had a few conversations about their relationship and why she was ever with him. She said when they met, he'd been charming and swept her off her feet, but after the puppy love period subsided, she began to see his true colors. Aurora had been so deep into her work life that she let their relationship go on longer than she should have, even though the warning signs had been there all along. She even confessed that right before the two of them parted ways, she'd been expecting a proposal. Instead, what she received was him dumping her on stage at one of the town's popular festivals. It had been the talk of their small town for weeks afterward.

"Are you sure you don't want something else while we're out? We can grab some more film for your camera." Even though her new digital camera she ordered for herself arrived a couple of weeks ago, she'd been using the Leica regularly. We'd already developed seven rolls of film since the day I surprised her with it. There was only one roll she had yet to see processed. *That* was something I was still working on.

"I'm okay. I think I still have some at our house."

Over the last month, Aurora had gone from calling the place where we lived *her* home to *ours*. I thought of it that way as well, and even when things ended between us, I'd still look at that little bungalow as my first real home.

"All right."

On the drive back to the house, I noticed she ignored a call from her brother—something she'd been doing more and more of. The two of them were on rocky terms after he confronted her about our marriage. Somehow, I was going to fix things between the siblings, but I wasn't sure how. I tried to speak with him when I was at Sunny Brook Farms with Aurora during the harvest, but he ignored me the entire time.

Thank goodness I had Nate and Colton there. The three of us stayed busy with whatever task Nash needed us to work on—mostly things that didn't require the heavy machinery or tools, because other than Colton's minor construction skills, we were all pretty worthless when it came to the heavy-duty parts. I learned very quickly that farming wasn't for those who grew up fed with a silver spoon; that's for sure. And seeing firsthand a harvest worked by people who made it look so *easy* for them made my respect for the farmers skyrocket.

And mere minutes after that educational moment, when I humbly relinquished my man card, I watched my tiny wife jump right up into one of the huge green tractors and begin working alongside her dad.

I'd never been more turned on in my life.

Both Colton and Nate agreed Andrew would come around with time, but I wasn't so sure. Especially after learning Aurora's history. He was likely afraid she made the same mistake again. It was unfortunate we couldn't tell him all the details to help clear the air, but the fewer people who knew why we were married, the better. HR and the legal team were taking their sweet time establishing me as CEO of Wilder Hotels, but I was afraid if I pushed them harder, someone would get suspicious.

When she sent her brother's call to voicemail, I asked Aurora gently if she was ever going to speak to him, but she replied only with a shrug. I really hoped we weren't going to run into him at the wedding. I hadn't heard if he would be there or not.

I exited the car, surprised Aurora got out at the same time—something she hadn't done before, since I always insisted on getting her door. Dashing around the front of the car, I stopped in front of her, placing my hands on her shoulders. I tried not to notice how her nipples puckered beneath her tight blue-and-white baseball T-shirt at my touch. But I was human, after all.

"Aurora, talk to me," I pleaded.

She smiled, but her eyes didn't crinkle in the corners the way I loved. "I'm fine, Talon." She hitched onto her tiptoes and pressed a kiss to my lips, then slipped under my arm as she moved toward the front porch.

I followed her inside and wasn't surprised to find Draco waiting for her on the counter, since it had become his routine whenever we returned from an errand.

"She's having a rough day, buddy," I said as I ran my hand down his back, curling my fingers around his tail.

Draco purred as if he understood. He walked in a circle around the countertop, flicking his tail in the air until he leapt to the floor. Looking at me over his shoulder, Draco practically beckoned me forward as he pranced toward the bathroom.

"You're right, buddy. Thank you."

Aurora's bathroom was small, but I knew she loved taking baths to relax. While I heard her moving around the bedroom, I ran the hot water and tossed in a scoop of the bath salts she enjoyed. As the tub filled, I walked out to find Aurora sitting in the middle of our bed with her legs crossed, her hair draped around her like a veil. I walked over to the bed, leaned on the mattress next to her, then scooped her up into my arms. As I carried her, Draco followed us. He was probably just as concerned about his human as I was.

In the bathroom, I set Aurora on the counter and used my thumb and forefinger to tip her chin up so that she met my eyes.

"Tell me what's on your mind. Is it about the wedding? If you don't want to go, then we won't go. I'm on your side on this one. It's a slimy trick that man is pulling."

"It's stupid."

"What's stupid?"

"The reason I'm upset," she admitted, her cheeks a little pink.

"That's doubtful. You'll feel better once you get it off your chest."

"I'm just jealous, I guess."

I was shocked at her confession. Jealousy was not one of the reasons I tossed around in my mind as the reason for her change in mood. Draco was weaving himself between my feet, so I lifted him and placed him on Aurora's lap. The cat immediately nuzzled her hand, wanting to be petted.

Eyeing the water in the tub, I turned off the faucet, then leaned on the wall across from Aurora. "What are you jealous of?"

"The fact that Jeremy is getting my dream wedding. Autumn said he's pretty much planned it with every idea I ever mentioned to him when we dated. But like… why does he get this perfect day? I've technically been married twice, and neither time had anything to show for it but a piece of paper. Even though ours is only contractual, I can't stop thinking about how we'll never get to have an actual wedding."

The typical lung-crushing fear I had when thinking about marriage and wedding ceremonies didn't come. Instead, I had a flash of Aurora walking down the aisle of a church toward me while wearing a long, white gown, and I suddenly felt that same longing she must be experiencing.

"Do you think you'll want to get married again?" I asked her.

Chuckling, Aurora replied, "Third times the charm, right?"

My nails dug into my palms as I thought about her marrying someone else one day. It was bound to happen. Aurora was both beautiful and smart. And young. She was the perfect package.

"Am I being silly?"

"No, I don't think so. You're entitled to your feelings. And your ex is a complete douchebag. He doesn't deserve any of the good things that seem to come his way."

"I almost feel bad for his fiancée. Autumn said whenever Jeremy allows her to speak, she's really nice."

Now that she disclosed everything, Aurora's face softened.

"Is that for me?" she asked, her eyes flicking over to the bath.

"It is."

She hopped down from the counter and started lifting her shirt. I stepped backward toward the door.

"Don't you want to join me?"

"Do I? Yes. Will I? No. This is for you. I want you to relax."

Aurora let her shirt fall back into place as she sauntered up to me. She lifted onto her toes and pressed the softest of kisses to my cheek. "Thank you for listening and not letting me clam up when I was upset. I'm not used to having a significant other who actually listens."

"You're welcome." I returned her kiss with one of my own, then left Aurora, my chest ready to explode at her inferring that I'm her significant other.

Draco and I made our way over to the living room, where we laid back on the couch until Aurora stepped out wearing only a towel an hour later.

"Did you enjoy it?"

She nodded. "Maybe I can repay the favor?" she purred as she let the towel fall to her feet, revealing her gorgeous, naked body. I was on my feet in a flash, following her into the bedroom.

We were almost late for the wedding.

The organizers had set up the renovated barn for the actual ceremony, and most of the chairs were occupied except for a few in the back row. Aurora and I snagged two there, in the corner. Luckily, no one caught our late arrival except her family sitting in the middle of the row in front of us, and her sisters visibly sighed with relief.

Jeremy stood at the altar, looking like the giant asshole he was. He even had the audacity to grin at Aurora when he noticed her in the crowd. The motherfucker was already on thin ice and was about to get a beat-down on his wedding day. Luckily for his sake, the wedding march began, and his bride made her way down the aisle.

Despite my hatred for Aurora's ex, his fiancée looked beautiful, making her way toward him. She couldn't hold a candle to my wife, of course, but no one could.

The ceremony was short, and we mingled with her family during the cocktail hour while others started searching for their tables in the reception space. The entire event venue was stunning and was far larger than it looked on the outside. I made a mental note to add the venue as an option for the lodge—a partnership for a wedding and honeymoon package. I'd have to talk to Autumn about that after the opening. If she'd even speak to me when Aurora and I parted ways. Something I'd been thinking about more and more.

Through the dinner, Marisol and Nash kept up the conversation, doing their best to make up for the fact that there was a vacant chair, left open by Andrew. When the dancing started, Eloise dragged me out onto the dance floor, while Molly did the same with her dad.

"I like your hair," she said when I finally convinced her I wasn't angry about what happened the night before.

"Thanks. Your aunt did a great job. If she ever stops teaching, so could probably open her own salon."

"Oh! Do you think she'd let me and Molly help? We're getting much better with painting nails."

Their skills still needed work. This morning, Aurora spent more time getting the polish off my skin than my nails. The girls' choice of purple had tinted my nails the same shade, even after soaking in acetone. Thankfully, it was only noticeable when you looked really closely.

My phone vibrated in my pocket, and I released one of Eloise's hands to check it. There was a message from Olive saying **It's done**. I assumed that meant the paperwork naming me as the CEO had been signed and finalized.

"Mind if I cut in?" a sultry voice asked from behind me, and Eloise twirled away toward her mom.

Wrapping one arm around Aurora's waist, I held her close as our joined hands rested on my chest.

"Have I told you how beautiful you look?" She wore a dark yellow, almost mustard-colored dress that reminded me of leaves in the fall. It had sleeves that ended at her elbows, and the skirt stopped just above her ankles.

"Not in the last hour."

"Well, it deserves repeating," I added as I spun her outward, then tugged her back to me.

She adjusted her arm around my shoulder, and I brought our joined hands to my chest. Whatever I could do to keep her body pressed against mine. Together we swayed to the music, ignoring the couples surrounding us.

"Oh, it looks like they're going to cut the cake."

We left the floor during the cake tradition. I found it strange there were no speeches made. Even more so that Jeremy didn't dance with his mother, nor the bride with her father. I knew Aurora and I had a contractual marriage, but this coupling felt even more so. I asked Autumn, who was seated on my other side, if they planned it that way, and she said they hadn't. And to make matters even stranger, a few minutes later, when the event planner who worked for Autumn scurried over to our table in distress, the two of them darted away.

Servers stopped by our table and divvied out pieces of the cake. Alex had done a remarkable job. The first bite of the Earl Grey cake was both sweet and savory. Mixed with the vanilla and lavender, it melted in my mouth. She beamed when I told her so.

I felt Aurora's hand press on my thigh as she leaned in to whisper in my ear. Her fingers were dangerously close to a part of my anatomy that was begging for her to slide an inch higher.

"Want to see my favorite spot in this place?"

"Sure." My voice croaked like a teenager's as I agreed.

She grabbed her dessert plate with her barely touched piece of cake and stood to walk toward a hallway in the back. I glanced back to see her parents were watching us with mirth in their eyes. I tried not to think about them knowing we were sneaking off.

"Come on," Aurora called out as she vanished into the darkened area.

"I'm trying not to make it suspicious, wife." I used both hands to try to feel around for the walls and nearly yelped when Aurora grabbed my wrist.

"This way."

Suddenly, some light from the reception—probably the dance floor being lit up brighter, since the

MC called for everyone, including kids, to join him there, because it was time for the "Cha-Cha Slide"—shone in the hall, illuminating a stairwell. Upon climbing the steps, we were greeted with a storage area and a large paned window at the end. The sun was just beginning to set over the Smoky Mountains, casting the sky in oranges and reds. The mountains beyond the range were shaded in navy.

"Wow," I said, leaning an elbow on the window frame as I took it all in, then looked at her.

"It's beautiful, isn't it?" she asked as she stood with her toes against the floor-to-ceiling window.

"It's the most beautiful thing I've ever seen," I replied, not pulling my stare from her. As if she could sense my gaze, she glanced up at me, then quickly tucked her chin to her chest. The rosiness of her cheeks nearly matched one of the vivid colors in the sky.

I moved to stand behind her, wrapping my arms around her shoulders. She leaned her head back against my chest as we watched the sun dip behind the mountains until disappearing completely. After another minute, she turned in my arms, her chin resting on my chest as she gazed up at me.

"So, do you want to go back to the reception... or maybe... entertain ourselves in other ways?" Her grin was wicked, and her eyes sparkled. I was up for whatever direction Aurora's thoughts were going.

"What did you have in mind?" I asked.

"Well, I have this delicious piece of cake, and I'd really like to taste it on your cock." Her voice was so innocent, even as Aurora's empty hand roamed down to my waistband and unhooked the button, the zipper her next conquest.

"What my wife wants, my wife gets." Before my pants could drop to the floor, I shuffled us over to the corner of the room, where we could duck behind some crates in case anyone walked in.

The music from the reception echoed up into the space, and the floors nearly vibrated from the volume of the country song now playing through the speakers.

Grabbing my phone from my pocket, I turned on the flashlight and turned it toward the ceiling, brightening the dim corner as I placed it on a crate. Aurora's mouth around my cock was not something I wanted to miss seeing.

She made quick work of yanking down my pants and boxer briefs, the duo resting at my ankles as she stroked my cock with her talented fingers. Her tongue teased around my barbell, sending jolts of pleasure to my balls. And when she collected a dollop off the top of the cake with her finger and trailed the icing down my shaft, only to lick it away seconds later, I nearly died from the erotic show as much as the feel of it all.

Aurora smiled proudly at each of my moans. I nearly came in her mouth twice. Too bad for her, she forgot two could play this game.

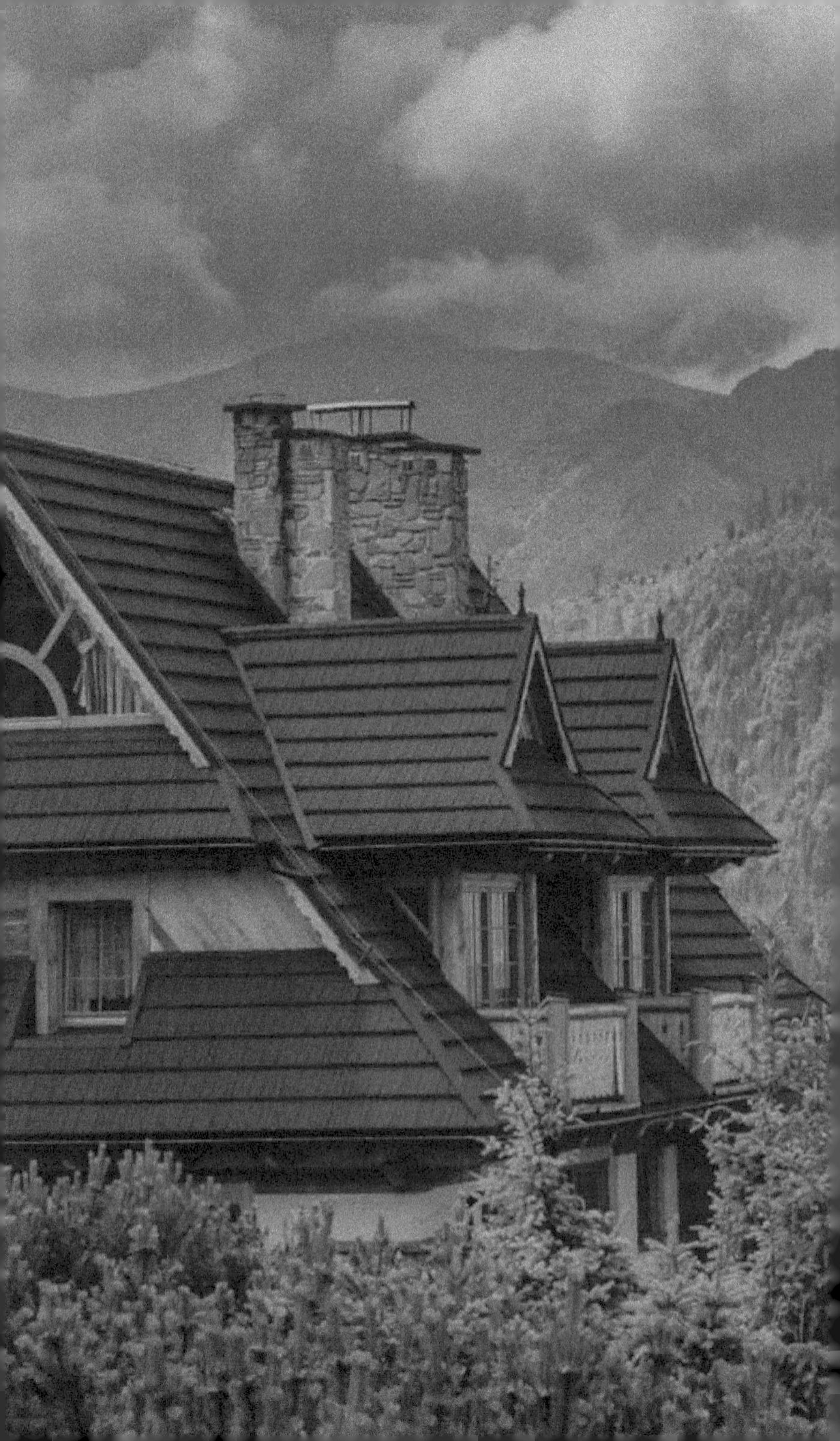

Chapter Twenty

Aurora

It wasn't that I would've called Talon's cock perfect, but he had what all my romance books described the fictional boyfriends as having. So, I took that as a win for me.

I was having fun teasing him. Bringing him so close to the edge and then letting off, only to repeat it all over again. I knew he was figuring out a way to exact revenge, but in the long run, even if I didn't get an orgasm later, I would at least get to feel that ache between my legs that only Talon could provide. It was the best kind of pain.

"Peaches," he groaned as I tugged gently on his balls. "Fuck, I can't take any more. I need to feel your pussy."

"Hm... I'm not ready for that yet," I whispered, the tip of his cock resting against my lips.

Unexpectedly, I felt his hands dive beneath my arms and lift me into the air until I was standing.

"Turn around and lean over that box," Talon demanded, and he was using that voice that sent both a surge of fear and lust through me. The combination was exhilarating.

When I followed the order, I felt the back of my dress flip over my body until the material covered my head. I couldn't see anything around me but the smallest shimmer of light through the material. My lace panties were tugged down my legs before Talon lifted each of my feet to slide them free.

Just when I thought he was going to put me out of my misery, his hand landed on my ass with a smack, and then he dropped that hand between my legs to swirl within the pool of moisture.

"You're lucky I'm not in a teasing mood. You've been a naughty wife tonight. Normally, I'd punish you, but I want to fuck you too badly to play games."

His fingers worked at my clit, rubbing and circling the bundle until my legs shook.

"Fuuuck," I groaned, my knuckles turning white as I clenched the edge of the box.

"Lift your leg," Talon commanded before he shifted my knee onto the box, exposing more of my pussy to him.

"That's it. My wife is so wet for me. Aren't you?"

"Yes, husband."

"I wonder if this cake is as good on your pussy as you said it was on my cock."

His hand left my body momentarily, then I felt him spread something soft and cool onto my heated folds. His tongue hurriedly replaced his fingers.

"Delicious," he moaned, the vibrations causing my body to quiver against his mouth as he continued to feast on me.

"Talon!" I cried out wantonly.

"My tongue not good enough for you?" he asked, pulling the dress back from around my face. I turned my head to the side, and he sealed his lips to mine. The flavor mixture of myself and the cake was as delicious as he said.

With his mouth still on mine as I grew drunk on his kisses, the head of his erection probed at my entrance. I tried to rock back, but Talon placed his hand firmly on my lower back to hold me still.

"Steady, peaches. Let your husband make you feel good." He nipped at my bottom lip before pulling away and standing up behind me, his hand still planted above my tailbone. I felt his cock slip up and down my sex, being coated in my warmth. Then he fed the tip inside my slit. He went excruciatingly slow until I felt like I was going to faint from desire.

"*Please*," I begged.

Finally, Talon plunged his cock into me so ferociously that the box I was resting on scraped against the floor. Lust overpowered all my reasoning as I met each thrust of his hips with my own.

"That's it, wife. Fuck me. Take what you want. My cock is yours."

My orgasm came on swiftly as he called upon his masterful skills to pleasure me. He used his thumb to massage my clit while his piercing rubbed that spot inside my pussy that only he was able to discover.

Clenching the box, my back arched as the orgasm crested. I heard Talon curse in the background as he filled me with his cum. We stayed connected, both of us panting as our bodies calmed.

"Fuck, how is it better every single time?" Talon questioned as he gasped for air.

My voice was breathy as I replied, "I don't know."

He pulled out of me gently, and my body shivered at the loss. I felt his warm cum drip down my thigh as I looked around for a napkin or something, but then Talon's hand was between my legs, making me jump.

"It's just my handkerchief," he assured, kissing my shoulder. I didn't realize men still carried those around, but I was thankful. Returning to the party with his cum sliding down my legs was not the entrance I wanted to make.

Together, we got dressed and tried to look as if we hadn't been naughty in the storage room for the last hour. Talon looked perfect. I looked like I'd been riding in a convertible. There was no way I was going to fool anyone.

As he was shoving one of the buttons on his suit jacket through the hole, I asked, "Do you want to try to sneak out of here? I'm pretty sure I've paid my dues."

"Sure. I go where you go."

How true I wished those words were. I feared the day he was established as CEO, which would mean our speedy marriage would end in a speedy divorce. Because I wasn't ready to let him go yet. Of course, I didn't have the courage to tell him that. There were days I thought maybe we were on the same page, like this morning, but then there were others in which we barely spoke. We'd end up in bed together but seemed like we were miles apart.

As we made our way downstairs, it seemed we weren't the only ones with the idea to dip out early. We found my parents saying goodbye to Mr. and Mrs. Mitchell, and Alex, Nate, and the twins were headed toward the exit.

Just as we collected my purse, I felt a hand latch onto my arm before spinning me around.

"Where have you been, Aurora?"

Before my eyes could even focus after the sudden movement, I heard a much deeper voice growl, "What did I tell you about putting your hands on my wife?"

Jeremy immediately dropped his hand, but his eyes narrowed on Talon. "Don't think I don't know what you're up to."

"I have no idea what you're talking about," Talon replied coolly as his arms looped possessively around my waist. Normally, I didn't like a pissing match between men, but in this instance, I would be grateful to Talon for the rest of my days. "I know it must be hard seeing Aurora has moved on with me, or with anyone for that matter. But you need to get over yourself." Talon looked over Jeremy's shoulder, then met his gaze again. "Also, I believe your *wife* is looking for you. Congratulations on the nuptials."

The arms around my waist slipped away almost sensually until he was holding my hand, and together, we walked away from my rose-colored ex.

Except for when we were getting inside the car, Talon and I kept our hands joined, even during the entire ride home. As he turned onto my street, I noticed an unfamiliar car parked in front of my house. Talon approached it slowly and tried to peer inside as we passed, but the windows were tinted. He steered the car into the driveway, and then we both looked over our shoulders to see Dean stepping out of the back of the SUV, wearing a glum expression. Not even seeing me or his best friend as we exited the car changed his demeanor.

"Hey, man. What's up?" Talon asked as Dean walked across my lawn.

"We need to talk," he replied ominously, shoving his hands into his pockets.

Whatever he had to say obviously wasn't good, and dread grew around me like a storm cloud.

The SUV continued to idle on the street, which meant Dean wasn't staying long. As we approached the porch, I asked him if his visit had anything to do with my contract. He smiled down at me and shook his head, and I felt a moment of relief.

Talon unlocked the door, and Draco immediately scurried away when he saw Dean enter.

"He doesn't really like people. Just me and Talon, and whoever feeds him," I explained as I excused myself to head to the bedroom to change.

As I closed the bedroom door, I leaned my shoulder against the wood attempting to eavesdrop, but I heard nothing more than Draco purring under my bed. Quickly, I slipped out of my dress, laying it across the chair in the corner to send out for dry cleaning on Monday. I pulled out an oversized T-shirt and a pair of leggings and yanked them on.

I snuck out of the bedroom, carrying my ink-furred best friend, and was surprised to find Dean and Talon hunched over something on the kitchen counter.

"What's going on?" I asked, hoping they'd fill me in, but both men ignored me. Talking to Draco, I asked if he wanted to go sit outside on the deck with me for a little bit. The air was turning colder, so I grabbed a blanket from a basket I kept by the couch and draped it around my shoulders before letting myself out through one of the French doors.

The fireflies of summer were long gone and were replaced by the scattering of leaves in the air, flipping around as they fell from trees. Fall in Ashfield was something to behold. Watching the forest-glazed mountains change into autumnal shades was breathtaking. Sometimes, I took it for granted, knowing I could witness the colors every year.

It wasn't long before I heard the hinges of the back door creak.

"Hey, everything okay?" I asked Talon as he took the seat next to me. The plastic chair's legs bowed a little under his weight.

"Yeah, I think so."

"You don't sound positive about that."

"That's because I'm not." Talon was quiet for a few minutes. I watched him stroke his fingers through his hair, tugging at the shorter strands. The soft skin between his eyebrows formed a V. "My grandfather died today, just after my uncle visited him to protest the CEO position being changed over to me."

I gasped and turned to face him. "You don't think…?"

"We're not sure. There will be an investigation. The thing is, I need to be there for Gigi." The light from the kitchen shone through the glass door pane, illuminating Talon. The muscles in his face ticked as if he was grinding his teeth.

"Of course you do. I wish I could go with you," I said, reaching out to grasp his hand.

"I know."

"How long do you think you'll be gone?" I asked, wondering if this was the last time we'd be together. With his grandfather out of the picture and his new role secure, there was no reason for us to remain married.

"Maybe a week or two?" he replied, sounding unsure of himself. "Dean said Gigi is distraught. Even though she never loved the man as her husband, he was still a part of her life since she was young and the father of her children. Dean flew to come get me the minute he heard about the passing from her."

"It's okay, Talon. Take your time." I was trying to be supportive, even though I was silently breaking inside. I'd grown attached to the man I called my husband. We'd fallen into a routine, and I wasn't sure if I was ready to go back to the way things were before I signed that contract.

"I'm sorry, Aurora."

The chair slid backward as I stood. "It's okay. Do you want me to help you pack?"

"I have everything I need in Miami."

Everything but me, I thought to myself.

Dean called his name from somewhere in the house, and I followed him back inside, Draco jumping off my chair and doing the same. Talon spent a few minutes grabbing the items he'd need for work, then he joined us back in the living room. He still wore the tuxedo from the wedding.

Dean must have noticed that neither of us was ready for a goodbye, so he quietly exited through the front door, leaving us alone. The moment the door shut, Talon's hands were cupping my jaw as he smashed his lips down on mine. This kiss was urgent. It was one of need and necessity. It was desperate. When he pulled back, we were both gasping for air.

"I…" His words hung in the air. I hoped he'd say two more that would complete the phrase I felt down to my bones, but instead, he said, "I'll miss you."

Smiling, I told him that I'd miss him too.

"Take more pictures for me."

"I will," I promised, and when a knock sounded on the front door, I knew Talon needed to be on his way.

"I'll call you when I land."

"Sounds good. Please tell Gigi that I'm sorry."

He didn't say another word. Instead, he leaned down and left me with a kiss that promised his return. And as I watched the two of them hop into the back of the waiting SUV, I couldn't help thinking it was the last time I'd ever see him.

Chapter Twenty-One

Talon

After spending the last few months in Ashfield curled up around Aurora every night, Miami held none of the appeal it once had. Other than Gigi and Dean, there was nothing here I cared about. The bustling city couldn't compare to the small downtown area and its people I'd grown attached to in Aurora's hometown. They looked out for each other in ways the people I passed on the busy streets around the hotel did not. My apartment didn't hold the same appeal as Aurora's tiny home. It wasn't the size, the furnishings or the location. It was all *her*. She made that place feel like a home in a way the apartment never could.

The police had been investigating my grandfather's death for the last two weeks and were getting nowhere. My uncle swore he was still alive when he left the Wilder mansion, but the police, and Gigi, feared the elderly man had been poisoned. We were supposed to get the toxicology reports back this morning, and then I could finally make my way back to my wife.

"Gigi!" I called out as I waited in the massive foyer. This house always reminded me of a prison, despite its lavish fixtures.

"Coming!" she shouted back from somewhere down the hall. I was taking her to the lawyer's office for the reading, and hopefully the arrest of my uncle. My grandfather had been sick but stable, and the doctor said his death was unexpected. We'd know soon.

While I waited, I sent a message to Aurora. I knew she was in the middle of class but figured she'd see it when she checked later.

> How's BOB holding up this morning?

Last night, during a voracious round of phone sex, I made Aurora use her vibrator while I watched on the video call. She came three times with the toy and had to replace the batteries before we were finished.

Aurora
<eye roll emoji> Any news?
How's Gigi?

Aren't you in class?

They're taking a test.
Update me.

Gigi is holding up—probably better than your battery-operated boyfriend. I'm taking her to the lawyer's office.

Give her a hug from me. And one *for you* too. Good luck.

"Who has you smiling? That beautiful wife of yours?" Gigi asked, as she finally graced me with her presence. Most women mourned their dead husband by wearing all black. Not Gigi. Today, she was wearing a bright-orange business suit.

"Aurora sent you a long-distance hug," I replied, my chest a little looser than it was when I left Tennessee. With our messages and video calls a constant since we parted, the closeness I felt to Aurora that I worried would wane was just as strong.

Tucking Gigi's arm through mine, she said, "Such a sweet girl."

"Yes, she is."

As I helped settle my grandmother into the seat of the town car, my cell buzzed in my pocket. It was a forwarded email from Dean. I'd normally wait to read the message, but he tagged it as urgent, so I opened the email immediately and read through the information.

It seemed my assistant, Olive, was the cousin of Allison, the woman I'd scorned months ago. At first, I didn't think anything of the message, until I noticed there was a zip file of images attached. Extracting the contents of the folder, I found about a hundred pictures of Olive and Allison together, and then quite a few more of each of them with my uncle in *very* compromising positions. There were even some of the three of them hooking up at a popular sex club.

I wasn't sure what the information meant, other than I was going to fire my assistant, but I sent a thanks to Dean.

Once I buckled myself into the town car, I shot human resources an email with some of the less lewd images of Olive with my uncle and requested her termination due to the fraternization policy we had in place. Despite me being the interim CEO until recently, Olive was still *his* assistant whenever he decided to show up for work. The timestamps showed their relationship had been going on for a while. Allison seemed to have joined in within the last few months. I sighed with relief, knowing that she wasn't fucking me and my uncle at the same time.

"Everything all right?" Gigi asked as the car left the gated exit.

"Just fine. A little issue with work, but that will be solved soon."

As we continued toward the lawyer's office, she asked me for updates on the Wilder lodge. I knew Dean had most likely shown her the pictures of the renovations I'd been sending his way. I even video-called them when we finalized the new designs for the bedrooms. But it was nice to talk about something unrelated to my grandfather.

As the car approached the office, reporters were scattered along the sidewalk. News of my grandfather's death had been rampant, especially after the coroner stated it might not have been from natural causes.

I helped my grandmother out of the car and kept the photographers at bay as they tried to encroach on our space. We nixed the security detail, and I was second-guessing that choice. Thankfully, the security guard at the office assisted when he noticed we were swarmed and quickly got us inside.

The large conference room was filled with doctors, lawyers, and officers. There were only a few vacant chairs remaining and Gigi took the one closest to the door. My uncle paced by the window, mumbling about having to be there. On the couch sat his estranged wife, Kate, who was my aunt and mother's sister. She stared at the wall in a trance. Their children Delilah and Charles Jr. were busy on their phones. I was surprised to see them in attendance. I hadn't seen them in person in years. I wondered if Gigi requested they all attend the meeting or if my uncle demanded it.

He continued to walk back and forth, his hands fisting and unclenching at his side. If ever there was a man that looked suspicious, it was my uncle. "Let's get this over with," Gigi said as she placed her fist on the table, her bracelets jangling loudly in the process.

"Yes, Mrs. Wilder," the doctor sitting at the head of the table said. His white jacket was crisp and clean, and I wondered if he wore it just for show. "The toxicology reports came back with lethal levels of arsenic in your husband's system."

The room fell silent, and I pulled my attention from the doctor to glance over at Gigi, who was looking closely at the investigators in the room.

"Ma'am?" one of them asked when they noticed she was watching them.

"Is there anything to add regarding these findings? Perhaps an anonymous tip you received this morning? One similar to what I received?"

What? This was all news to me, and I was curious about the information Gigi held on to.

"Yes, ma'am. Something more substantial than a tip, in reality," he replied before standing to address the group. "This morning, our department received a package, with the list of items as follows. Photos from a private investigator showing Charles Wilder Sr. entering a hardware store the day before his father-in-law James Wilder's death. A receipt obtained from the manager of the store, showing a purchase of weed killer containing arsenic made with Charles's credit card. A thumb drive with the store's security footage of Charles making said purchase. And finally, a long-range but high-definition image of Charles in his car, pouring the weed killer into a flask while still parked outside the hardware store.

"With this information in conjunction with the toxicology report, Charles Wilder Sr. will be placed under arrest for the murder of James Wilder."

My uncle stood in the corner, his self-assured, smug smile fading away with each piece of incriminating evidence that was read off. The moment an officer stepped forward with the cuffs open, my uncle dashed toward the door. Unfortunately for him, he was stopped by more policemen in his attempt to escape. While the group scuffled with my uncle, I maneuvered Gigi out of the way so she wouldn't be caught in the middle. In the corner, my cousins were still captivated by their phones. I wasn't sure if they were even aware of what was going on, or that their dad was being arrested.

"Are you okay, Gigi?" I whispered as I crouched beside my grandmother's chair. I couldn't imagine being in her position. She just lost her husband, and her son-in-law was being arrested for his homicide.

"I've had better days."

"What can I do to make it better?" My grandmother lifted her shoulders, looking frailer than I'd ever seen her. It was rare she was ever speechless. Trying to get her to open up, I asked if she knew who might have left the anonymous tip she received. A little bit of color came back to her features as a small, knowing smile lifted her lips for the first time since we left her house, but those lips stayed zipped.

I was ninety-nine percent sure Dean was the culprit. He had the means to hire a private investigator to keep an eye on anyone and everyone, especially if it meant it would help Gigi or me. And the more I thought about it, the more it made sense Dean would've put constant eyes on my uncle after the threats he made in Nashville—which Dean would've done with or without his investment in the lodge. He was just that good of a friend.

As the room started emptying out, I realized I wasn't needed in Miami any longer, and an idea occurred to me.

"Hey, Gigi. How would you like to come back with me to Ashfield?" When I voiced the idea, it sounded even better. I knew Gigi and Betsy would hit it off. And Aurora's family would accept Gigi as if she was part of their family. In a way, she was, even if only temporarily.

"Oh, sweetheart," she said as we made our way out of the room and toward the front of the office building. "My home is here."

"Well, what if it's just for a visit? I'm sure I can get you a room at the bed-and-breakfast Aurora's sister, Autumn, and her husband run."

Gigi paused with her hand on my arm. "She's the one married to Colton Crawford?" Her eyes shimmered in excitement.

Smirking, I said, "That's the one."

"Well, now, I may have to take you up on the offer."

I loved that she wanted to go for the hockey star and not her grandson. I told her as much, and she brushed it aside as a joke the way only Gigi could.

"It's perfect timing. The lodge is close to being finished," I added to sweeten the deal.

"And I *do* want to spend more time with that sweet wife of yours," Gigi stated.

"Okay then, so let's get you home, and we can get the housekeeper to help you pack some bags."

After dropping Gigi off and promising to pick her up in a few hours so we could catch a flight to

Tennessee, I grew more and more excited, anticipating getting to see Aurora by the day's end. Quickly making a list of things I needed to bring home with me, I stopped by the office to grab my computer.

Only to find security fighting with Olive in the lobby of the hotel. She was causing a scene that drew several guests out from their rooms. Many had their phones held up, recording the incident.

I tried to calm the situation, explaining to her but loud enough for everyone to hear that fraternizing with her superior wasn't allowed by company policy. I feared many would assume that her relationship mentioned was with me—which would look extra bad since I was already linked to Allison—but hopefully they had sense enough to know she would've been able to sue me if that were the case, so I obviously wouldn't be firing her under that policy.

I had no desire to release the images of the two women with my uncle—as proof that I wasn't the superior Olive was fraternizing with—but that didn't mean someone else wouldn't leak them to the press. I might have had Dean work his magic to make the footage he showed me disappear from its origin, but there was no guarantee some random patron of the sex club hadn't recognized my uncle and snapped photos themselves.

"Fuck you, Talon Beckett!" she shouted, as security worked to move her toward the front door of the building. She kicked and screamed with each step. "Your biggest mistake ever!" was the last thing I heard her screech before the police arrived to escort her out of the hotel.

In my office, I wondered about her threat, in addition to Allison's threat this past summer. I messaged my lawyer and brought him up to speed with Olive's firing and her parting words. He was well-versed in the drama my uncle currently found himself in. So, when I disclosed to him the evidence showing my previous assistant, my uncle, and my ex-fling were together, he started putting restraining order documents in place, since we agreed the probability of retaliation was high.

After the call, I thought about messaging Aurora and letting her know I was heading back to Ashfield, but I hesitated. Something about surprising her was thrilling. I wanted to see her face when she realized I was back. Through her messages, she made it seem like she was convinced I wouldn't return. Even though we talked and joked every day, and had phone sex nearly every night, she would still randomly ask about my clothes and toiletries I left there. Or where she should send her rings when our time was up—something I didn't want returned, even when it was time for us to part ways. She could pawn them if she desired.

But I had something else in mind.

"Gigi," I said when she answered my call. "I have to make a quick stop, then I'll be headed your way to pick you up."

Her response was to question why I was bothering her while she was trying to pack her favorite outfits that might "woo a hot former hockey player away from his young, talented, and gorgeous wife to give your eighty-five-year-old Gigi a second chance at love."

Her joking and uplifted mood combined with my excitement to get back to Aurora was all I needed to hurry up with my new plan.

Thankfully, the lobby was empty of disgruntled employees when I made my way out of the office. I stopped by the front desk and asked them to issue anyone currently staying at the hotel a voucher for a free night stay at any Wilder Hotel for the disturbance. I probably should have run it by various departments, but I didn't turn the hotel around by ignoring our guest services.

The pit-stop went smoothly, and my gift to Aurora was nestled in my computer bag as Gigi and I flew high above and away from Florida. My grandmother wasn't saying much about everything she'd been through today, but I hoped she felt a bit of closure where my grandfather's death was concerned.

Next week, I was going to have to hit the ground running to fix all my uncle's mishaps and mistakes he made with the business. I'd done what I could over the last year, but there were many files and financials he kept hidden.

"You okay, Gigi? Have you talked to Aunt Kate?" She was my grandfather and Gigi's daughter, after all. My mom's younger sister. And my uncle-by-marriage's estranged wife.

"I tried calling her, but she's not answering. I'm not sure she cares, if you want my honest opinion. You saw how *removed* Delilah and Charlie were from the entire situation."

I nodded, because Gigi's relationships with Aunt Kate and her family were strained at best. The revelation that her daughter's husband—separated or not—murdered my grandfather on his deathbed would likely push them even farther apart.

Halfway through the flight, I decided to work on some of the small task lists for the lodge, when a notification sounded from my phone. It was Dean.

Dean
> It's out. Man, I'm sorry.

At first, I thought he was referring to Charles's arrest, but then he sent a link to an article. The headline was all I needed to read.

HOTEL HEIR FAKED MARRIAGE TO GAIN CONTROL

It was as if our good luck had run out. The wind was strong as the plane descended on Tennessee. So much so that we had to circle an extra hour before we could land safely. Then, to top it off, the rental car vendor had nothing available that was suitable for Gigi and me. I was growing impatient, and the grumpy man I thought I left back in Miami apparently followed me here like a stowaway.

Since the plane landed, I'd been checking the news and gossip feeds like a madman. So far, it seemed only one tabloid reported on the marriage between me and Aurora, detailing the contract and all the finite specifics. There was only one person who came to mind—Olive—even though I had no clue how she could've gotten a copy of the contract. There had been only one, the very one Aurora signed at dinner on the boat. And according to the article, their "highly credible source" tipped them off well before Olive had been let go.

I'd been firing off messages to my lawyer and Dean to see what we could do. The hotel PR team was about to make their money's worth, what with my scandal *and* my uncle's arrest. I was hoping we'd be able to keep at least the gossip about me tampered.

I'd finally decided to contact Aurora instead of keeping my arrival a surprise, believing a warning about the current situation that came from me instead of being hit with it out of nowhere would be more appreciated, but she wasn't answering. There was a chance she was still at the school, so I was hoping she just wasn't able to get the call.

"Talon, dear. They have a car ready now," Gigi said as she placed her hand on my arm to get my attention. I looked over at my grandmother, with her stern yet loving eyes.

Will she be disappointed in me? Will she sneer at the lengths I went to, even if it was to restore my mother's birthright, to run the hotels that belonged to her family?

"You're drifting away again."

"I'm sorry, Gigi. I can't seem to get a hold of Aurora."

She nodded in understanding as I went over to the desk and signed for the rental car. I hated that the Ferrari wasn't available again, but I doubted Gigi would've been able to ride in it comfortably. Worse, she probably would've tried to drive it.

"Well, she'll be in for a surprise when she sees us, won't she?"

I rubbed my hand against the back of my bare neck. I still hadn't gotten used to my much shorter hair, though Gigi said she loved it when she first saw me walking through her door. "I suppose so."

After securing all of Gigi's luggage into the SUV, I pulled out onto the highway. I was desperate to see Aurora. I *had* to come up with a plan to shield her from any backfire from all of this.

The longer I sat in the car while Gigi napped in the passenger seat, the more I was able to convince myself this entire thing was going to blow over like it was nothing. Because really, weren't all marriages a contract of sorts? Love only came into play if you were one of the lucky ones. People married for money, insurance, and children all the time. What made what I did any different?

And on Aurora's side, there was nothing wrong with her agreeing. She didn't hurt anyone in the process. As for my job, I kept thinking back to the monarchies and kingdoms of the past. Royals were married as a contract between two lands, uniting them. Or to marry into a "higher level" family to increase their status. In the long run, what we did was no different.

What's more—I did it for a noble reason. My mother. The woman whose father shunned her, all because she fell in love and had me, instead of marrying someone out of duty, for the sole purpose of that man taking over the hotels. Gigi's always said my mother was smarter than any of the men in our family and would've been better at running Wilder Hotels than anyone before her. Stupid, antiquated rules kept her from taking over what should have been hers. So, since she couldn't be CEO of the company, and instead of living a loveless life like her own mother had, my mom decided she'd live the life *she* chose, one that would make her happy and fulfilled and out from beneath the thumb of her last name.

"What's that, dear?" Gigi asked as she yawned and clicked the button to sit her seat back up. "You were mumbling something."

"It's nothing."

"Are you sure? Maybe I could just listen while you talk through it."

As much as I wanted to talk it over with Gigi, I was worried it would be too much for her after the day she had.

"It's okay. I'll get it all sorted."

For the remainder of the trip to Ashfield, I answered her questions about the town. What restaurant was my favorite? The Purple Goat. What shop did I frequent the most? The local distillery's tasting room, Sip and Sit. What did Aurora and I do in our spare time?

I refused to answer that question, and it earned me a surprisingly strong slap on my bicep.

Gigi gazed out the window like a child at Disney World when we drove into town. It was just about 5:00 p.m., so people were bustling around the sidewalks. They waved at the vehicle blindly, but Gigi ate it up, waving back as if she knew every single person.

"We're about twenty minutes from the bed-and-breakfast," I told her as we passed through the far end of Ashfield.

"It's so pretty here. I can see why no one wants to leave." Gigi's voice was solemn, not filled with the excitement I expected.

As we passed Aurora's street, I debated turning around and seeing her, but I wouldn't want to leave. Though she might very well kick me out when I explained what was happening. I clenched the steering wheel in frustration as I continued down the main road, maneuvering the truck around the sharp corner with ease, as if I lived here my entire life. Up on the hill, I pointed out the bed-and-breakfast to Gigi. Not only was she excited to meet Colton, but she was also a huge history buff. I knew she was going to keep Autumn busy with all the ancestral details she'd want to know about the house.

When I called Autumn to make the reservation for Gigi, I explained the situation with my uncle, and she made sure there would be space available to her for as long as she needed. She hired a chef, and dinner preparations were underway for all the guests, so it was no sweat to add one more.

"I can come back later tonight," I offered Gigi, standing inside her room, and she looked at me over her shoulder as she started unpacking her suitcase.

"You need to take care of your wife. I'm sure if I need anything, Colton will come to my rescue," she said devilishly.

"All right. I'll head out then." I walked over and kissed her on the top of her gray head of hair. "I love you, Gigi," I told her, something I didn't say nearly enough.

"Oh, dear boy. I love you too. This is a special place. I'm glad you've found it."

I left Gigi as her melancholy words lingered. This little blip on the map had more of an impact on me in the last couple of months than all my years away at boarding school and in Miami combined. The only other time I'd been as affected was the short three years with my mother, though I couldn't remember that time anymore.

I spoke with Autumn and Colton momentarily as I thanked them for the last-minute reservation. The duo offered their condolences over my grandfather's death. Gigi and he had already begun compiling his funeral arrangements when his health took a nosedive. So, after the autopsy was complete, he'd been cremated. Gigi didn't want any fanfare, not even holding a wake or funeral. He made more enemies than friends during his lifetime. The reading of the will was scheduled to happen next month. That gave her time to grieve and be out of the public eye.

The trek to Aurora's house seemed infinitely longer than I remembered. By the time I pulled the SUV into her driveway, I was antsy as hell to get inside. Thankfully, her car was parked, and I hoped that meant she was home.

I slid my trusty key into the knob, only to find the door already unlocked.

"Aurora! I'm home!" I called out, anticipating her running into my arms. Until I walked into the house, I hadn't truly realized *how much* I missed her.

Draco greeted me as he swirled around my legs.

"Hey, bud. Where's your momma?" I asked the cat as I lifted him and nuzzled his face. I'd never been a pet person. I spent too much time travelling and at work to take care of an animal properly. But I loved this little dude.

The toilet flushed down the hall, so I made my way toward the bathroom. I stood just outside the door, excited to hold Aurora in my arms. But when she opened the door, I was surprised to find her wiping tears from beneath her eyes. At her shocked expression, I could tell she hadn't heard me calling her name.

"Talon?" she asked as I set Draco on the floor.

"Aurora, what's wrong?"

"I…," she began, and then she sniffled. "I lost my job today."

"What?" I shouted. Her losing her position at the school had never crossed my mind as an outcome of our contract. I grabbed her hand and guided her over to the couch, silently begging her to divulge everything. Her grip tightened as we sat down.

"Yeah… um… I guess the administrator found out about your uncle and grandfather. Then today, it was all the kids were talking about it. He called my personal life a distraction and let me go."

"That's wrongful termination."

"It's the truth though, and the students *were* distracted."

"We can sue them."

Aurora nodded but didn't respond. She was already overwhelmed and upset. I hated having to add more to her plate, but I didn't want to hide the tsunami headed our way.

Draco jumped onto her lap, and I was thankful for his comforting presence while I pulled up the messages from Dean. He'd added two more article links. Thank goodness for my friend. I owed that man my life right now.

"Oh," she said, with a bit more pep. "I *am* happy you're *here*." She smiled at me, and my entire world stopped its too-fast spinning. The way she looked at me left me feeling like everything would be all right. We could figure it all out.

I halted my scrolling and returned her smile.

"I'm happy to be here too." I leaned forward and softly pressed my lips against hers. They were sweet, like the cherry ChapStick she wore, and a little salty from her tears. "Unfortunately, it's not under the best circumstances. My trip here started out as this great, happy surprise. But… something happened midflight, and we need to talk."

Chapter Twenty-Two

Aurora

I knew from experience that it was never good when someone said you needed to talk. In the past, it usually involved a breakup, or more recently, my brother. More specifically, the background check he ran on Talon that he decided to present me with while Talon was gone. I wasn't sure what Andrew hoped would be his end game, but I hated that he went behind my back. Talon and I may not have started as a real couple, but we felt like one now.

I'd kicked Andrew out of my house and ignored his phone calls once again. I didn't want to know what dirt he dug up on Talon. None of it mattered. I knew enough about him. And though he wasn't the most open person, the people he let in and kept close showed the kind of man he was. And both Dean and Gigi were the best.

"What... What do you want to talk about?"

Was it that our contract was going to expire early, now that he'd been named the official CEO of Wilder Hotels? Was it something to do with the mess of his grandfather's death and the arrest of his uncle?

Maybe he didn't need the added stress of a wife, on top of all the chaos and changes happening in his life.

Or maybe he just didn't want me anymore, now that he'd gotten everything he set out to get.

He leaned forward on the couch, running his hands through his short locks, then rested them on his cheeks before turning to look at me. "Someone, I think Olive, told the press about us. She gave them everything. A copy of the contract. The marriage certificate. The bank transfer statements. All of it."

Shock hit me like a tidal wave. I knew there was always the possibility we could get caught, but the longer the marriage went on, the less likely I thought it would happen.

"How?" I whispered. "Why?"

"She was in cahoots with my uncle, and it appears her cousin was a woman I fu— had sex with occasionally. Apparently, the two women were already trying to find a way to destroy me when I met you. Then, when I started gunning for the official CEO role, my uncle got involved. They were in some weird love triangle, and he was helping them gather information on me. At least, that's what Dean thinks. It was the only explanation we could come up with."

I stared at him, dumbstruck. Talon continued talking about blackmail and exploitation, but I was stuck thinking about the woman he had been screwing. I'd never felt this level of jealousy before. It was so strong and severe that I wanted to hunt her down and show her how scrappy us small Southern girls could be.

"Aurora?"

"Oh, sorry. What... What did you say?"

"I just asked if you were okay. Right now, Dean has found information running on three news sites. There will probably be more soon."

"Oh. Okay. What do you want to do?"

"Honestly?" he asked, and I nodded. Talon's features dropped like he just fought a battle and lost. "I just want to make love to you and go to sleep."

My stomach did a crazy flip, like I was out on a boat rocking in the waves, when he said he wanted to "make love."

"That sounds like the perfect way to end the day."

Talon brought me to orgasm three times before he finished inside me. We'd made a mess in my bed with some chocolate syrup he found in the refrigerator. After changing the sheets and taking a shower, where he fucked me against the shower wall, we laid in bed silently. I rested my head on his chest, listening to the strong thumping of his heart. On his left hand, he wore his wedding band, and I ran my finger across the metal. Once news of our contract spread, things were going to change. And as I laid there with my husband, I was too afraid to fall asleep. I wasn't ready for our bubble to burst yet.

I woke before Talon, something that never happened. I was sure with the stress of the last two weeks that he had to be exhausted. He had wrapped his arm around my waist and held me close, as if he was scared I'd run off during the night. As I slowly slipped out of his hold, Draco lifted his head from the foot of the bed.

"It's okay," I whispered. "You stay there." The menace never listened to me, and so he stretched, then jumped down from the bed to follow me out to the kitchen.

I didn't suspect Talon would sleep much longer, so I raided the fridge and pulled out some fixings for omelets. I added some peppers and sausage to the egg mixture—peppers that were grown in my family garden and left over from the farm stand.

"Shit," I mumbled as I looked at the calendar. Today was my day to work the market. I didn't need to be there for three more hours, but it put a damper on spending the morning with Talon. And I wasn't ready for the questions everyone would have. Not just about his grandfather but with my job. News traveled fast in a small town.

Quickly, I plated the omelets, left them on the counter, and went to open the bedroom door, only to find Talon standing in the doorway, wearing only his boxer briefs. His eyes were rimmed in red, and there were almost purplish smudges underneath them.

"You okay?" I asked him.

"Yeah. I kept waking up last night."

"Oh, what from?" I stepped forward and wrapped my arms around his waist. He did the same around my shoulders as he kissed my forehead.

"Everything. Regretting I brought you into all this, but not regretting that I got to have you."

"I'm sorry." I wasn't sure what my apology was for, but it seemed to please him just the same.

At the counter, we ate breakfast, and I told him about the market. The last few times it was my weekend, he stayed at home or was busy in Knoxville. Franny was usually on board to help me, but for some reason, I wanted Talon there. Surprisingly, he agreed.

The morning passed by quickly as we went to my parents' farm to load the crates into Alex's vintage truck—something Talon was thrilled to drive. But Mom must've set out the produce the night before, because everything was packed in the truck for me by the time we got there. The workers were already making headway out on the farm, aerating the soil for the next planting season, and my parents weren't in the house when I popped my head in to tell them I was leaving with the goods, so they must've been out in the fields too.

We made our way to the stand before most of the other vendors. The Sunny Brook Farm booth was one of the more popular spots, so we usually tried to have it stocked long before others arrived. It gave us time to barter with some of the other local farmers in town.

While I worked on setting up the crates, Talon called his grandmother, inviting her to come to the market today. He offered to pick her up, but she stubbornly refused and said she'd find a way there herself. I wouldn't be surprised if Gigi walked the entire way.

As I pulled out one of the canopies from the back of the truck, my phone rang. I answered when I saw it was my mom.

"Hey, Mom."

"Hi, sweetie. Are you already set up at the market?"

"Um… yes, for the most part."

"Autumn mentioned Talon's grandmother is staying at the B&B. Is he with you?"

I was confused by her question, but answered, "Yes."

"Okay. I have something for him. Oh, and your brother is looking for you. So, don't be surprised if he stops by."

Great.

"Okay. Love you."

"Love you. We'll see you in a bit."

I ended the call and set my phone on the rustic wooden tabletop. It wasn't uncommon for my mom to find her way to the market on the weekends if the harvesting season was over. She loved to stock up on some of the local jellies and soups for the winter. But I was concerned about her having something for Talon.

Out of nowhere, a hand wrapped around my neck from behind, and I yelped with surprise. The pressure of the fingers twisted my head to the side, where Talon's lips crashed down on mine, and I instantly melted.

I moaned against his mouth as his tongue swiped across my upper lip, and I opened for him. We kissed like two teenagers until a catcall rang out from somewhere off in the distance, reminding us we were in public.

"Where did that come from?" I panted when he broke our kiss.

"Fucking missed this," Talon whispered as he rested his forehead against mine.

"Me, too."

We pulled apart, but only slightly. Talon stood behind me with his arms wrapped around my waist as a chilly breeze whipped around us. I'd worn a light jacket but shivered from the cold.

An unfamiliar alert chimed on my phone, and I looked down to find a browser notification. Last night, Talon suggested I ignore everything I found on the web, but I thought it was best to know what was being said about our marriage. I set up a browser search notification that alerted me whenever there was a news article released containing my name. Last night, it was just the few Talon had already shown me. When we were getting ready this morning, there had only been one more.

The notification I was staring at showed seven *thousand*.

"Oh no," I whined as I closed my eyes and leaned against Talon's strong body. Maybe if we stayed right here, he could protect us from whatever was about to come our way.

When he asked what I was groaning about, I lifted my phone to show him the notification.

"Shit. Okay. I'm going to call my PR team and see what they think."

"You have a PR team?" I asked.

"Well, we already had a team for the hotel, but I hired a personal team when I took over as interim CEO as well."

"Oh. Okay." I had no idea what they could do to deflate this rapidly growing news story. I just hoped something more interesting would catch their attention soon.

Talon's hands slipped away, and I instantly missed his touch, his shelter, his quiet strength.

People started arriving at the market, and I felt like a circus act on display. The customers were probably minding their *own* business, but every time I looked up, it seemed like someone was staring at me. I was going nuts.

Finally, after thirty minutes, Talon reappeared, looking much more relaxed than I felt.

"What did they say?" I asked him immediately, hoping they offered some sort of immediate resolution.

He reached for my hand and intertwined our fingers. "Well, they said the best thing to do was to wait it out. We could make a statement, but that would just keep it in the news longer. They hinted at a huge scandal between government officials that will most likely take over the news coverage next week."

"But for now, we're the talk of the town."

He nodded solemnly, his gaze drawn to our hands. His thumb circled my knuckles, and normally that would've had a calming effect, but not this time.

"Literally," he said as his eyes trained on the group of customers standing around and watching us.

"Okay... um... maybe it would be best if we went ahead and packed up," I suggested, as it was clear no one was going to buy anything from our stand, even though it wasn't like the fruit and vegetables were tainted or anything.

"This is all my fault, Aurora."

I lifted one of the crates. "We're equals, remember? I said the vows too."

Silently, we started replacing the crates into the back of the truck, still full of all the produce from our small garden. From the corner of my eye, I watched the crowd grow, but it was only Mrs. Henson who stepped forward and inspected a few of the items at our booth.

I'd told Talon all about her crazy antics, and I prayed she would deliver today, because I was afraid if I didn't laugh soon, I was going to cry.

"The squash look nice and plump," she said as she held one of the larger butternut squashes.

"Mom made some soup with some the other night, and it was delicious."

"Hm... I'll take three please."

"Of course, Mrs. Henson." I rang her up and sniffled as I fought off the tears. Not even the crazy lady of Ashfield was acting like herself.

Once I bagged up her picks, I returned her sympathetic smile and went back to packing up our things. Talon seemed to pick up on my worsening mood, because I soon found myself tucked behind the other side of the truck, out of sight of the customers. He wrapped me in his arms, swaying back and forth in a soothing motion.

"I'm so sorry, Aurora."

I couldn't speak, too distraught and not even sure why. Not until this moment did I ever truly care what people thought of me.

"Rory!" I heard a familiar voice call out. I looked up at Talon, and he wiped away the tears on my cheeks with his thumbs.

"It will be okay. I promise you, Aurora."

"You know… you've never called me by my nickname, even after all this time."

"Because I like that I get to call you something different than everyone else," he replied as he tucked my hair behind my ear. I mimicked his smile, and that was how Franny found me as she moved around the front of the truck.

"Aurora Grace Easterly, you better tell me that you haven't been lying to me and that the article I just read was a bunch of made-up crap," she hollered as she stomped toward me. Talon's protective instincts were on high alert, as he wrapped his arm around my shoulders and pulled me back against him.

Before I could answer, Talon spoke up. "Aurora Grace *Beckett*, actually."

Even though he was correct, Franny's head damn near swiveled around like the young girl in *The Exorcist*. "Excuse me?" she asked, her fists sitting on her hips, itching for a fight.

"Her legal name is Aurora Grace Beckett."

"So, you're saying you two are legitimately married? None of what they're saying is true."

"Well… that's not entirely the case," I said, preparing to explain the situation, when I heard a loud *thunk* on the other side of the truck. I jumped out of Talon's arms and sprinted over to find my entire family and Gigi huddled around our market booth. Andrew was standing front and center, with his hand pressed on top of a stack of papers resting in the middle of the now bare table.

"What's everyone doing here?" I asked enthusiastically, pretending everything was fine. I could tell by their expressions that it wasn't.

Andrew's face was close to the same color as the tomatoes I just stacked back into the truck, and his eyes kept darting between me and Talon, who was resting against the side of the bed, looking far more casual than I felt with both his feet and arms crossed.

Behind Andrew, my family stood shoulder to shoulder as if in solidarity with him. Everyone except Gigi, who stood to the side, watching us with amusement as if we were her favorite soap opera.

In a menacingly low voice, Andrew asked, "How could you do this again, Rory?"

I noticed my sisters mouthing the word "again" to each other, while my parents' gazes never wavered from me. It seemed Mom wasn't left out of the loop after all.

"It's not the same thing, Andrew. Nor is it any of your business. I'm an adult."

"Of course, it's my business. You're my sister!" he shouted.

"Andrew," I urged, trying to get him to calm down. The crowd had grown double in size.

"And it's not the same thing at all, because we can't just get this one annulled like last time. This time, you really screwed yourself, Rory. Do you have any idea how hard it was to get these divorce papers drawn up this morning?"

"I never asked you to do that," I said defiantly.

"That's because you keep making the same childish mistakes over and over. You say you're an adult, but you married this… this stranger. For what? Money? Status? Free hotel stays? And what has he done for you except drag your name, *our* name, through the mud?"

"He's taken care of me, Andrew."

"Has he though? His family just cost you your job, Aurora. This is a small town. You'll never be hired as a teacher again."

"Then I'll move."

"And then he'll have cost you your house. Don't you see it, Rory? The man used you to get what he wanted, but all he did was take from you and gave you nothing in return."

"That's not true," I replied, crossing my arms over my chest but sneaking a peek at Talon, whose smile had flipped. His eyes looked sad.

"Are you going to say anything?" I asked him, praying he would try to defend himself, but true to Talon's form, he remained silent.

"Sign the papers, Rory. We can argue it was under fraud and maybe get your job back. Let us fix this for you." It's the same thing he said last time, when I was eighteen and hysterical over my then husband leaving me abandoned with no way home.

I looked over the expressions of my family members. A combination of pity and sympathy marred their faces. Thankfully, Eloise and Molly weren't anywhere in sight. It made me feel like I'd committed a grievous crime and was being offered life in prison.

"I…." I approached the table and looked at the legal papers. Little stickered arrows pointed to the places I needed to sign.

Talon didn't budge as I flipped through the stack. He didn't say anything as I reached for the pen Andrew placed on the tabletop. He didn't object when Franny came to stand beside me and offered to hold my hand, even though she'd been livid at me only moments before.

If it had been any other day, I would have ignored the papers completely, but I let those nuggets of doubt creep in and fester with every point Andrew made. The entire contract had been selfish on Talon's end. He got what he wanted, but I was left with money I'd never use and guilt that I lied to my family.

I took a moment to take Talon in, to memorize him, then I turned back to the papers before me. My mother gasped as I took the top off the pen. My hand hovered over the first signature line. Memories of my months with Talon flooded my mind. Not only had he shown me a sexual side of myself I had no idea existed, but he gave me back a part of myself that Jeremy destroyed. A part of me that I'd lost hope in ever returning.

With my other hand, I wiped away the tear that seeped from my eye before I pressed the pen to the paper. I never on my worst day imagined I'd be signing divorce papers with my family and a crowd of people watching me.

"Aurora, don't."

I turned my head to look at Talon, who was frantically tugging at his shorter locks as he stepped closer to me.

"Aurora, think of us. Think of how good it felt to be together yesterday. Think of how far we've come. How can you look at me and pretend you even *want* to sign those papers? You have to know there is no life for me to go back to without you as my wife. And I don't want there to be. You're it for me, Aurora. And even if you sign those stupid papers, I'm not going anywhere. You can't get rid of me."

Somewhere in the distance, I heard someone mutter that *they* could get rid of him.

I set the pen down and turned to look at my husband. He wore an expression I'd never witnessed on him before. Fear.

"Do you love me, Talon?"

Talon scoffed in a prideful way. "Aurora, that's a ridiculous question to ask me."

"No, it's not. It should be easy enough to answer."

He stepped forward and grabbed my hand, though I was reluctant. "Nothing to do with you, with us, is ever easy. It hasn't been since the moment I knocked into you over a year ago. You asked me if I love you. Every molecule in my body comes to life when I'm near you. I can't take a single breath without the thought of you crossing my mind. I physically ache in my chest when I'm not around you. And I have felt that way from the second you let me sit next to you at the bar. Does that answer your question?"

I paused, his words wrapping around me like a warm hug, but it still wasn't enough.

"Talon, do you love me?"

He stepped closer, his other hand resting on my cheek, his thumb stroking my tear-stained skin. "Mrs. Beckett, I love and adore you with every single part of me."

"Good," I replied, playing it cool and smiling up at him, even though my heart was about to explode. I wiggled my hand free from his grasp and moved it to rest on his chest. His heart pounded like a bass drum under my palm. "I didn't want to sign those papers anyway. Because I love you too, Talon Beckett, and I can't imagine not being your wife."

I expected him to kiss me wildly, but he only wrapped me in his arms tightly, as if he was afraid I'd change my mind and walk away.

"What do we do now?" I asked as I nuzzled my face against his neck.

"We stop playing pretend."

"And tell everyone it's not fake anymore. Think if we stay like this, they'll just eventually leave?"

Talon chuckled and loosened his grip, then turned us to face the crowd. My sisters smiled. They were always suckers for a good romance. My parents were whispering to each other, while Andrew stared at us, his eyes wide, deep wrinkles crossing his forehead.

No one said a word, and I looked up at Talon awkwardly. "I kind of wish Dean was here to break the ice."

"Oh, he is, dear," Gigi called out from her spot on the right side of the stand. She was standing in the sun, holding a cell phone at her waist. "I called him when I arrived, thinking something like this may happen."

"I'm sorry we lied to you, Gigi," I said, stepping away from Talon and making my way toward her.

"Well, it wasn't a complete lie. You did meet in the hotel the way you claimed. I've seen the footage."

"That's true."

"And the marriage was real, legally speaking."

"Seems that way," I heard my brother mumble.

"So, the way I look at it, you're just two people who eloped and fell in love along the way."

"I guess you're right, Gigi," Talon agreed as he came to stand beside me.

"Of course, I am. I'm always right. Your friend may have also given me a heads-up when things started to get serious."

"What do you mean?"

"I mean that my *bestie* knew you were falling for this precious lady long before you did. As in a week after the marriage was official. Dean told me everything to protect you, Talon. He didn't want you screwing up what you found, all for the sake of the hotels."

"I'm a little lost, Gigi."

"I just mean, we knew what you two had was real. So, in case anything ever turned sour, like things getting out to the press, your position was secure, as was your trust fund. I am sorry it had to come to all this, but I think in the long run you got the best end of the deal," she added as she winked in my direction.

"That's why you and Dean came up with the Wilder Lodge renovation. It was a way to keep me closer to Aurora."

"You always were a smart boy."

"Can someone tell me what the hell is going on?" Andrew shouted with his hands in the air.

Alex turned and smacked her hand across the back of her brother's head. "They're in love, you idiot."

"What?" he asked, as if that was never a possibility.

I walked over to my stunned brother and hugged him. It was a full-body, all-encompassing hug like I used to give him when I was little. Those days when I was in kindergarten, and he was in high school.

When I pulled away, he gazed down at me in the same way, as if he remembered how much I looked up to him when I was that age. He used to read me fairytale stories before bed at my insistence. I wondered what made him so jaded toward love. I hoped he would find his other half one day.

"What may have started off as a contract with a stranger turned into the love of a lifetime, Andrew. It's real, and I love him. I hope, one day, you can forgive me and maybe get to know my husband."

"Rory…." He sighed.

"It doesn't have to be today, but someday. I love you, Andrew. You're the best big brother."

Once everyone was convinced Talon and I were indeed in love and not getting divorced, chatter started carrying through the crowd about another local wedding. I looked to Talon to gauge his reaction. He whispered something about wanting to see me walk toward him in a white dress.

Long after the farmers market hours were over, my family finally started to disperse. The twins had been busy at the library booth reading books, so Alex and Nate took them home with a new stack of paperbacks.

Talon and I loaded everything else into the truck and headed toward the town church to drop off all the produce and vegetables we didn't sell. We were driving back to the farm to exchange the truck for Talon's SUV, when I remembered my mom had something for Talon.

His excitement and curiosity were palpable in the cab as we traveled down the winding road. The sun was warming the fall air, and I held my arm out the truck window, letting the breeze flow through my fingers. It was freeing, sharing my feelings with Talon. I wasn't sure why either of us waited so long. Fear of rejection. Fear of the unknown. Fear of being unloved. It weighed on me for weeks. But now? Now, I felt like the leaves that were floating in the air, spinning and twirling without a care.

Across the bench seat, Talon squeezed my thigh before he shifted gears. I stared at this complex man who I once saw as domineering and intimidating but quickly realized he was putting on an act to gain respect. Alone, he was one of the most caring men I'd ever met.

"What has you smiling like that?" he asked, and I tucked my chin to my chest, my cheeks heating after being caught staring at him.

"You, Talon Beckett. I'm smiling because of you."

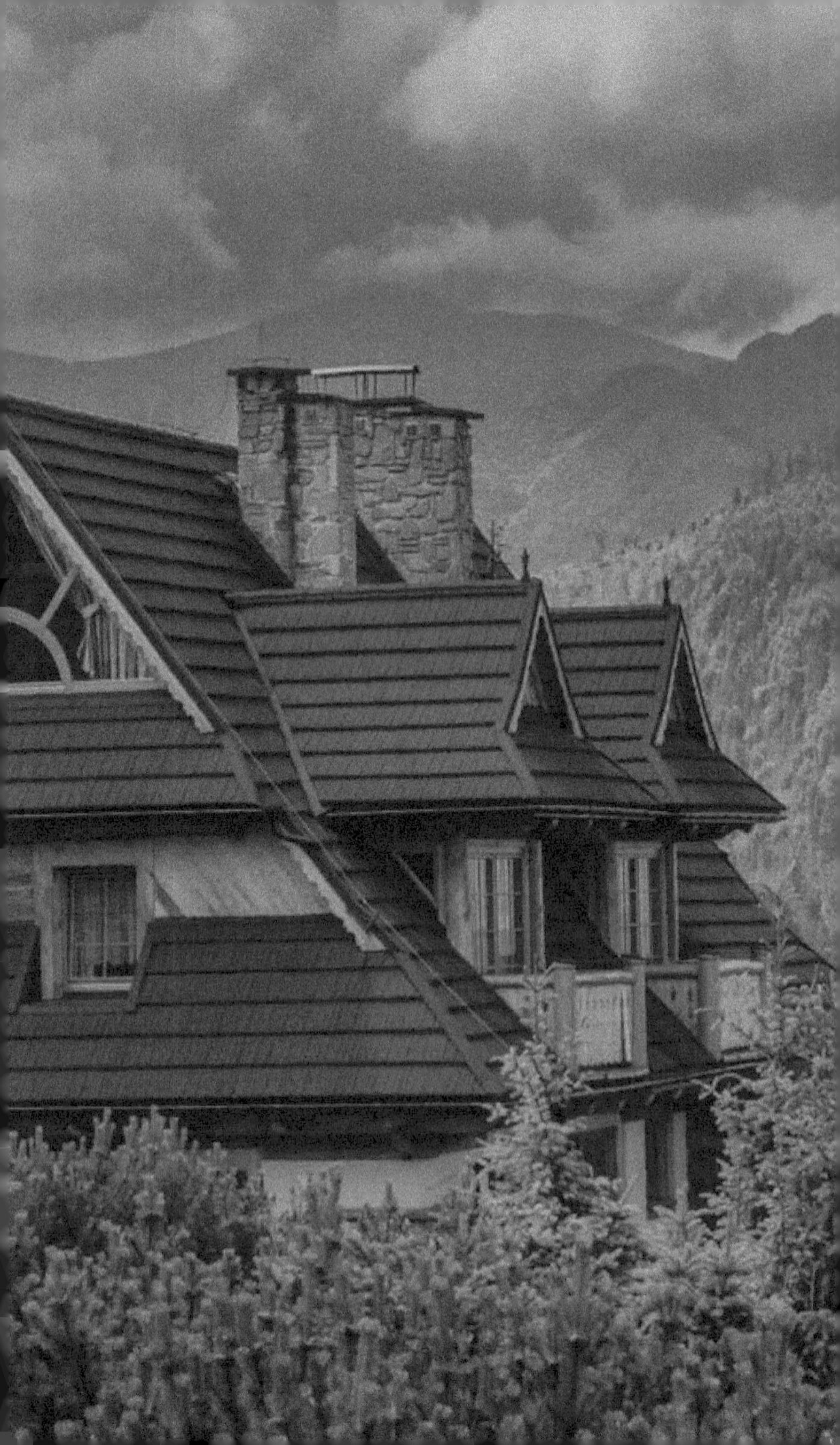

Chapter Twenty-Three

Talon

The truck ambled down the path that led to Sunny Brook Farms. The massive farmhouse felt more and more like a home to me over the last couple of months, between the Sunday family dinners and the time spent helping during the harvest. It was a home that made you feel like you belonged.

At the Miami mansion I'd grown up in under my uncle's watchful eye, I felt like an outsider looking in. Holidays, for me, were only *celebrated* with Gigi. My uncle and aunt were usually out gallivanting separately while on some remote island. Their children were off with a nanny, and I was left to fend for myself. Sometimes, I think about what would have happened to me if Gigi hadn't been around. I also wondered why she hadn't been granted custody of me instead of my aunt. Of course, there was a good chance my grandfather nixed the idea.

"What do you think about living out here?" Aurora asked me as I pulled the truck around the backside of the garage, where it was typically parked. I put it in park and shut off the engine, then turned to look at my gorgeous wife.

"What do you mean?"

"Well, I love my little house, but maybe we can rent that out and build something… for us."

I thought back to some of our earlier conversations. She'd mentioned that her family had set aside plots of land for each of their children, if they wanted it.

"We don't have to," she continued. "Nate and Alex only used a small portion of their lot, and I believe Autumn and Colton will do the same. I mean… I understand if you want to move closer to Knoxville or build somewhere else. Oh, or do you want to go back to Miami? I hadn't even consider—"

I stopped her rambling with a kiss as I leaned across the bench seat of the truck. The leather squeaked beneath my hand under my weight. The scenario felt similar to when I first came to Ashfield.

"I want to be wherever you are, Aurora. We can build any sort of home, anywhere you want."

"What about your job? What about *my* job?"

I ran my hand over her hair, twisting the ends in my fingers. "I can work at the hotel in Knoxville. There are spaces for offices. Or I can work from home. I may have to travel every once in a while, but we can figure it out. And *you* don't need to work at all. You married a billionaire, remember?"

I laughed as her face pinched, as if she smelled old, crusty milk and a rotten egg. It was obvious she hated the idea.

"I like to work."

"I know, but you're not in a rush. Maybe you can do something with photography. You have all the time in the world to figure that out. But until then… I want to show you the lodge today, if you're up for it. I know Gigi wants to see it too."

"I think my entire family wants to see it. You've been so hush-hush about it."

She was right. I didn't want to give too much away while we were developing the lodge, because it felt so much more personal this time around. It wasn't just another hotel renovation; it was a way to remember my mom. I also had a few surprises up my sleeve for Aurora.

"Okay, maybe we make it a group thing. See if they want to try the new restaurant. The chef is there experimenting with new recipes before we open after the new year. I'm sure he'd like some feedback."

Aurora agreed to ask her family. She seemed excited about visiting the lodge again. She'd only been once before, when we started the renovations, and had wanted to wait until it was finished to see it again. Overall, the lodge was complete. We were just in the process of some final touches and training the staff. There was going to be a grand reopening in January, and I hoped that people would fall in love with the serenity of the lodge and the splendor of the surroundings the same way I had.

With one last kiss, Aurora and I exited the truck. She was still learning to allow me to open the door for her, and I fussed at her whenever she forgot. Gigi would be horrified if she witnessed me not opening a lady's door.

Inside the house, we found all Aurora's siblings crowded around the living room, looking at various photo albums spread across the floor. Nate and Colton were laughing at something on the television, and Nash, Marisol, and Gigi were seated at the oversized kitchen table with a photo album between them.

"Hi," Aurora greeted shyly. "We dropped the leftovers off at the church and brought back the empty crates."

"Thanks, sweetie," Marisol said as she looked up from the photo album. "There are fixings for sandwiches on the counter for lunch if you want to help yourself."

Aurora smiled and shuffled beside me. "Thanks, Mom. You... uh... said you had something for Talon?"

"Oh!" Her mom practically bolted out of her chair and dashed toward the living room. She scooped up something off an end table and brought it over. It was a stack of pictures. They were bent on the edges in some places, curled in others, and anyone could tell they'd been stored away haphazardly. "Here they are. I thought you might like to have them." She held out the stack, and I took them suspiciously.

Turning them over, I didn't recognize the group at first, then my eyes recognized a face in the crowd. It was my mother. She stood in front of a tall man with jet-black hair, and a tiny boy stood between her legs.

"That one was at a church cookout."

"How?" I asked, my fingers shaking as I moved on to the next image.

"When we first met you, I thought you looked familiar, but I didn't think much of it. But each time I saw you, I'd think the same thing, and it started bothering me. Then, the other night when I was watching Molly and Eloise, they pulled out all the old photo albums. These were tucked in the back of one of Autumn's albums. I suppose you're only a couple of years older than her. She was a tiny baby then."

"So, you're saying my mom lived here? In Ashfield?"

"She did. For a year or so anyway. Then she moved to Knoxville one day, and we never heard anything else about her until Betsy saw her name in the obituaries."

"Wow," I had so many questions. So many thoughts. Did they know her well? Was she a good person? Was she strong and resilient? Did she regret leaving? Marisol must have noticed how my entire body trembled at the revelation. I'd waited my entire life to learn more about my mom, and here it all was, ready for me.

"Talon. I know it doesn't make up for her loss, and I don't remember *much* about her or your dad. He didn't live here with her. But I do remember clear as day how much she loved you. She kept to herself mostly. I think she was battling her own demons. But whenever we ran into her, you were all she would talk about. You were her pride and joy. And I think the name she gave you fits you perfectly."

"Mom, are you saying Talon lived here in Ashfield?"

From the table, Gigi spoke up, and I looked over to find her wiping tears from her cheeks. "They did."

"You knew, Gigi?" I asked her, even more flabbergasted than before.

"I knew she moved closer to the Knoxville hotel she loved. I didn't know her exact location, but she once sent us a postcard with the return address of Ashfield. Honestly, I didn't even know the town existed. You couldn't find it on a map back then. But when I learned of Aurora being from the same town, I knew your mom must've been playing matchmaker up in heaven. She was always a romantic girl like that."

I let the older women's words sink in. Their stories filled me in a way that left me reeling but made me feel like the impossible was attainable after all.

"You really do look just like your mom," Aurora pointed out as I flipped to a closeup of the young woman. My features were more masculine, but I had similar-shaped eyes and her smile. I got my height and hair from my dad. I knew nothing about him except that once he and my mom got married, he wasn't around much. But I believed it was because he worked a lot, trying to give my mom the life he felt she deserved, even though all she really wanted was *us*.

I sifted through a few more pictures until I came to the last one and did a double-take.

"Where is this?" I asked, holding up the image for the room to see.

Alex answered first, her eyes squinting. "Oh, that's the local watering hole. That's way before the town took it on and revamped the area around it."

"Is something wrong?" my wife asked, and I turned to glance at her. Her concerned gaze melted away as she took in my smile.

"I remember this. I mean, sort of. I've been having dreams for weeks about this place. And here it is. This was one of my mom's favorite places."

I was overwhelmed by the entire thing. The moment I stepped foot in Ashfield, I felt like I had come home. But now? Knowing it was a place my mom once loved made it all the more special.

We sat together, looking over a few more pictures. I asked Aurora questions when something funny or confusing was in an image. Marisol generously offered to let me keep the photos. They were all I had with me of my mother. And I offered to make Gigi copies, since all her images of my mom were mostly professional, like portraits. My grandfather treated his family like a business. No running around. No playing outside and getting dirty. And certainly no candid photos taken by family and friends, even though there would've been no fun to document. It was like living in a jail. It was no wonder my mom was ready to break free.

Sitting at their kitchen table with my newly acquired treasure, I felt antsy. I hadn't gone running this morning, after not sleeping well, and this revelation now had me filled with energy I needed to expend.

I was dying to show Aurora my surprise. Could it wait a few days? Sure. But with everything that happened this morning, our confessions of love, and the gift her mom had just given me, I was bursting with gratefulness, and I wanted to show my wife how much I worshipped her.

Suddenly, my voice rang out above all the chatter as I invited everyone to the lodge for the afternoon. If they agreed, I'd still have time to set up some course and wine tastings with the chef. At first, they were reluctant, but when Aurora went to the restroom, I explained quietly to them that I had a surprise for her, and their answers changed.

Even Andrew, who had been silently stewing in the corner, looked interested.

I understood he was looking out for his sister and thought he was protecting her, and I couldn't fault him for that. I didn't have siblings, so I had no idea how I would've reacted in his shoes.

But I had Dean, the closest I had to a brother of my own, and he'd proven time and time again he would have done the same as Andrew, so that was validation enough to convince me Andrew was a good guy. I made a note to text Dean to invite him to Ashfield for an extended stay.

In my rental SUV, Gigi, Marisol, Nash, and Aspen rode with us. Andrew, Colton, and Autumn climbed into Nate's SUV with Alex and the twins. It was a tighter fit for them, for sure, but Nate's had more seats than this one did.

It was a pain that the lodge was an hour away from Ashfield, but I'd grown accustomed to the trip at this point. During the drive, Marisol mentioned how she used to drive the kids to Knoxville multiple times a week for dance classes or games.

We chatted about what renovations we took on at the lodge and the things they would see. I glanced over at Aurora halfway through the trip and noticed she was leaning against the door, asleep. The stress of the day must have caught up to her, on top of the fact that we stayed up late last night, even though both of us were early risers.

Thirty minutes later, I pulled the SUV up in front of the log-style lodge. The main entrance had a large triangle-framed window on either side, which looked out onto the valley of Knoxville on one side and the mountains on the other.

"Aurora, baby. We're here," I said softly as I gently ran my hand across her face to wake her up. She stirred and stretched out her arms as she roused.

"Hi." She smiled sweetly, still half asleep.

"Hi. I want to show you something."

"Okay." I jumped out of the SUV and jogged around to her side of the vehicle while her family exited through the back doors. Once she was on her feet, Aurora began to move in the direction of the automatic front doors, but I grabbed her hand and tugged her toward the courtyard in the middle of the circular driveway. The temperature was at least ten degrees colder up here, and the wind picked up as we walked to the opposite side of the courtyard. I wanted to make sure she got the full view of the signage.

"What am I looking at?" she asked as she turned around.

"Do you see it?" I wrapped my arms around her body, and she instantly leaned her back against my chest.

"No? I…. Oh my—! The Dawn by Wilder Hotels."

I'd gone back and forth on what to name the lodge, wanting it to reflect my mother, but when I realized I fell in love with Aurora, my thoughts on the name changed. The Dawn was the perfect name for the lodge that watched the sun rise over the adjacent mountain range, while also paying tribute to my wife.

"You named your hotel after the dawn?"

"I named it after *you*."

She turned around, wrapped her arms around my neck, and she squeezed tightly. "Oh, Talon. I don't know what to say."

"Do you like it? I mean… you're okay with it?" I was nervous, waiting for her response.

She pressed her lips against mine, and that was all the answer I needed.

"Thank you," she said as she pulled back.

"You're welcome. But that's not all." I reached up for her hands and guided her to the lodge's entrance, passing her family on the way. I swore I heard Andrew mumble, "Nice touch," as we walked by, and I knew then he realized I wouldn't have named a place that meant so much to me after his sister if what she and I had weren't real.

Inside the lodge, I knew she wouldn't notice the items I added for her right away, but I had no doubt she would eventually.

I left the group in the large multi-story foyer, knowing what they'd see when they wandered around. Two stone fireplaces roared on either side, with leather couches scattered throughout. Above each fireplace were four of the pictures Aurora had taken using that first roll of film I'd given her along with the camera of her dreams. I'd blown them up, framed them, and leaned them against the stone along the mantle. Centered on the tables and hanging on the walls were more of the images I commissioned Aurora to take. They were all breathtaking views of Ashfield.

When I returned with the chef, I silently joined the group as if I'd been there the whole time. They were eyeing one of the images. A bird's-eye view of their town.

Aurora must have sensed my presence. She turned around with pools of saltwater holding on for dear life along her bottom lashes.

"These are my pictures. You used my pictures. I wondered what happened to the film," she said in awe. Her breathy voice did things to me that weren't appropriate around her family. At some point, I was going to have her sneak her away to the spa, where I'd snuck in a few images of my own. They were of her naked back, a sheet covering her backside, and her hair draped across her shoulder. No one working at the hotel knew it was Aurora, but I did. My wife was gorgeous in the photographs.

She was probably going to kill me. Not just for the image, but for using her camera. But it was a risk I had been willing to take.

"You took these, Rory?" her dad asked, and I could hear the pride in his voice.

"She did," I replied on her behalf. The group all congratulated and praised her, and Aurora tucked herself against my side as she took in their compliments.

The chef directed our group to the dining room, where he set up the tasting. I was glad he answered my call earlier before we left Ashfield; otherwise, we'd be having hot dogs and s'mores over a campfire. That was about all I could cook.

As Gigi passed, she patted me softly on the cheek. "You did good, my sweet boy." I wasn't sure if she was referring to the lodge, the surprise, or snagging Aurora. There was a good chance she meant all three. I was going to believe that anyway.

Aurora and I held back from the crowd, and she turned a full circle in the middle of the oversized room.

"This place is unreal, Talon. You did *all* of this. You must be so proud."

"I am. Dean and Gigi may have tricked me, but I'm glad I agreed to their offer. It's one of the best things I've ever done."

"Oh yeah?" she questioned, stepping up to me. Her fingers hooked the loops of my dark-denim jeans as she pulled me closer to her. Our hips collided, and my cock immediately rose to attention.

"Yeah."

"What's the other best thing on your list?"

Leaning down, I slanted my lips over hers in a soft kiss. "Forget the hotels and the money. Asking you to be my wife was the best damn decision I ever made. It might have started off as a fake marriage, but you're stuck with me for life now, Mrs. Beckett. I'm never letting you go."

"Well, that's good. Because I'm exactly where I'm supposed to be. With you."

Epilogue

Aurora

My husband made eyes at me across the room as if we hadn't just snuck away to our favorite spot in the event venue. Since we started trying for a baby a month ago, he had been chasing after me like I was a dog in heat.

"I think your husband is about to pounce," Franny said in her ivory satin gown. We were standing together on the edge of the dance floor, while her new husband, Liam, went to get her a new glass of champagne. The two of them had a whirlwind romance.

They dated for three months, got engaged at Christmas, and tied the knot in spring. It was fast, but I'd never seen Franny happier.

"He already pounced since we've been here," I joked. Franny knew we snuck away—I wasn't about to relinquish my matron-of-honor duties without her knowing. Even if it was for a quicky.

"Any luck on the baby front?"

I'd gone off birth control pills two months ago. My doctor said it could take a year for my body to adjust to the hormonal change, but I was trying to be positive. My period was also a week late.

"The test was negative. I called my doctor this morning. She said it was normal with the removal of birth control for your periods to be out of whack."

Franny apologized as Liam joined us and handed her a glass of bubbly. I had a sip earlier but was being cautious.

The two lovebirds started making their rounds through their guests. Once they left our spot by the dance floor, I went to join Talon. He was seated with most of my family and Dean. I wasn't sure how the man secured an invitation to the wedding, but from the way he was flirting with Aspen, I had a feeling he added himself as her plus-one.

On my way I was intercepted by Andrew. Our relationship had been strained over the last few months since the day at the market.

"Rory," he said my name like a plea. It was the forlorn expression he wore that convinced me to take his hand and follow him out onto the dance floor.

"Are you… doing okay? Any baby news?" My entire family knew that Talon and I were trying for a baby.

We swayed to the music as I told him that the same thing I'd told Franny, minus the period comment. I was certain my brother didn't care to know that information. The dance was awkward in a way. For the first time in twenty-four years, things between me and Andrew were strained, and I was unsure if we could ever fix it.

I felt him take a heavy breath before he said, "You're really happy, aren't you?"

Glancing up at my brother, I noticed how tired he looked. I wondered if the change in our relationship affected him as much as it had affected me. The only difference was that I had Talon in my life.

"I'm the happiest I've ever been."

"That's good."

"I think you'd like Talon if you really gave him a chance." Andrew nodded and looked across the room where Talon was watching us with a contented smile.

"I'll try harder."

"Thank you."

"I know I've said it a hundred times already, but I *am* sorry… for everything. What I did was wrong. Sometimes I forget that you girls are all adults. You're still those little girls that begged me to play dolls with you when I would have rather rode my bike outside."

I smiled remembering all the times he helped us play house and take care of our babydolls. "You played with us every time."

"Because I love you."

"I love you too, Andrew." We were already close from dancing, but I released his hand and wrapped both arms around his shoulders, hugging him tightly.

He leaned down and whispered, "I only ever wanted to protect you and make sure you were happy."

"I know, big brother."

We finished dancing to the song, and I felt Andrew and I had a turning point in our relationship. Maybe we were on the right path to the friendship we once had. He made his way toward the bar in the corner, and I set my sights on my husband.

Instead of taking the vacant seat, I casually sat on Talon's lap. His strong arm wrapped around my waist, tugging me closer to him.

"Hey, peaches."

"Hi."

"Aurora!" Dean shouted over the music from across the table. "Did Talon tell you about Jeremy? It's all over the papers." I'd been so consumed with making sure Franny had the perfect wedding that I'd been out of the loop for weeks. The last news article I read was about Talon's uncle being sentenced to life in prison. That was the same day Gigi officially moved to Ashfield, over a month ago. Between the wedding and the baby-making, I was already stretched thin.

"No, what about him?"

"He was caught embezzling political funds from investors for his father's campaign."

"What?" I knew he was a sleaze, but that was a new low, even for Jeremy. I still couldn't believe we'd dated for so long.

Dean was cackling as he scrolled through his phone. "That's not even the best part." He turned his screen around to show me the picture beneath the headline. It was Jeremy's mug shot showing a *very* receded, sparse hairline. It seemed like the last time we all saw him, he had been wearing a toupée. "His wife was the one who turned him in."

I was glad she found a way out of that farce of a marriage. I knew a contractual wedding wasn't going to work out for everyone, but I was sure glad it worked out for me.

"Where'd Aspen run off to?" I asked Dean noticing my sister was no longer in sight. Neither was my dad.

"She and your dad went to talk to someone. Well, in reality your sister freaked out when she saw some guy walk in while you were out on the dance floor. I assume she went to ask why he was there and your dad followed." Most of the people in attendance were from Ashfield, except a few out-of-towners on Liam's side.

"Hm... Mom any idea who it was?" I asked her, interrupting a conversation she was having with Alex. When she asked who I was referring to, I repeated what Dean had just said.

"Oh, I'm not sure, but Betsy was telling me that Owen Ramsey was back in town." He had been Aspen's nemesis growing up. The two had some sick pleasure in tormenting each other.

Talon's fingers ran along the exposed skin of my back as I leaned my head against his shoulder, nearly curling up in his lap. He twisted his head, his lips brushing along my forehead, as he asked, "Think Franny would notice if I took you home?"

"And miss all the dancing and fun?"

A puff of air escaped his nose as he chuckled. "We danced and drank and entertained all these same people three months ago at our own reception."

"That's true."

At the insistence of my mother and Gigi, we hosted a very quaint renewal of vows ceremony, so Talon could live out his dream of seeing me walk down the aisle to him in a white dress, and a reception to celebrate our marriage. It was mostly locals from Ashfield and a few of Talon and Gigi's family, including his aunt, Kate, and his cousin, Delilah. No one had heard from Charles Jr. since his father was arrested.

On my ring finger, Talon replaced the oversized princess-cut diamond with an antique-looking setting that held a marque. It was perfectly my style. We donated the previous ring to an auction where the proceeds went to supporting children of farmers and their education. Something that was near and dear to me, since, after losing my job, my grant proposal had been denied. When I refused to spend more of the money Talon sent after I signed the contract, nor accept the rest of the million after six months came and went, he surprised me with a scholarship fund named in my honor, using the same stipulations I put into place for the much smaller one I created when I first got home from Miami.

With a wicked grin, I told him that was an acceptable way to spend my hard-earned money.

"So, what do you say, wife? Think we can sneak back to our house, where I can spend the rest of the night showing you how much I love you?"

Even though I was still sore from our earlier escapade, my pussy clenched in yearning at his sweet words. I twirled myself off his lap and stood beside the chair. I grabbed my jacket and purse, then held my hand out for Talon.

"Goodnight, everyone," I said without a second thought as Talon placed his hand in mine. Talon laughed as I pulled him through the crowd toward the exit, and the cool, spring air smacked me in the face as we stepped outside.

"Eager much?" Talon asked as I reached our SUV—owned, not rented. My car was parked at Franny's house, where we spent the morning getting ready.

"For you? Always," I replied honestly.

The drive home to our little house was unbearable. We were still a month away from our custom build being finished, so we weren't nearly as close to the venue as we would've been if our new house were complete. Draco was waiting by the door when we arrived, and we both bent down to stroke his soft fur.

"So, wife," Talon began as he unbuttoned his suit jacket. God, I loved that man in a suit. "How do you want it?"

The lamp in the corner barely illuminated the room, but it made my soft periwinkle dress glow. I slowly stepped toward Talon, slipping each thin strap down my arms as I approached.

"Do you remember the day you came to Ashfield and broke into my house?"

"I didn't break in," he added as he began unbuttoning his shirt while toeing off his shoes. "I had a key."

"Do you remember what you caught me doing?"

His eyes lit up like a kid in a candy store as he nodded.

"Well, what I'd really like…," I purred as my dress slipped down my body into a pool of material on the floor. I stood before him, wearing only a pair of lace panties. "…is for you to obey your wife tonight."

In a flash, I was flipped over Talon's shoulders as he sprinted on socked feet toward my bedroom. I landed with a plop on the bed, and his body instantly covered mine.

"Are you ready to play, husband?"

"Show me what've you got, wife."

Stay in Touch

Newsletter: http://bit.ly/2WokAjS

Author Page: www.facebook.com/authorreneeharless

Reader Group: http://bit.ly/31AGa3B

Instagram: www.instagram.com/renee_harless

Bookbub: www.bookbub.com/authors/renee-harless

Goodreads: http://bit.ly/2TDagOn

Amazon: http://bit.ly/2WsHhPq

Website: www.reneeharless.com

Acknowledgements

I loved writing this book. Bringing Rory and Talon to life was a complete honor.

Fran Stanley, for your bid in the LIFT Auction that allowed me to give a side character your name. I hope you loved reading about Franny.

Patricia Rohrs, for alpha reading this book and holding my hand whenever I questioned where the story was headed and wondering if this book should even see the light of day.

Crystal Burnette, for believing in me and loving this story as much as I did (after convincing me over and over that it did, indeed, *not* suck).

Kayla Robichaux, for your keen eye and working on a ridiculous timeline. Your work was invaluable.

Lisa Hemming, Sally Sutherland, Kelli Harper, for being some of the sweetest and brightest beta team I've ever had.

Carolina Leon, for being the absolute best PA and for all your advice.

And to all the readers that read this book and loved it. Thank you for taking a chance on Aurora and Talon.

About the Author

Renee Harless is a *USA TODAY* bestselling romance writer with an affinity for wine and a passion for telling a good story.

Renee Harless, her husband, and children live in Blue Ridge Mountains of Virginia. She studied Communication, specifically Public Relations, at Radford University.

Growing up, Renee always found a way to pursue her creativity. It began by watching endless runs of White Christmas- yes even in the summer – and learning every word and dance from the movie. She could still sing "Sister Sister" if requested. In high school, she joined the show choir and a community theatre group, The Troubadours. After marrying the man of her dreams and moving from her hometown she sought out a different artistic outlet – writing.

To say that Renee is a romance addict would be an understatement. When she isn't chasing her kids around the house, working her day job, or writing, she jumps head first into a romance novel.

Milton Keynes UK
Ingram Content Group UK Ltd.
UKHW041819140224
437823UK00001B/19